The
CHAOS CRYSTAL

Tor Books by Jennifer Fallon

THE HYTHRUN CHRONICLES

THE DEMON CHILD TRILOGY
Medalon (Book One)
Treason Keep (Book Two)
Harshini (Book Three)

THE WOLFBLADE TRILOGY
Wolfblade (Book One)
Warrior (Book Two)
Warlord (Book Three)

THE TIDE LORDS

The Immortal Prince (Book One)
The Gods of Amyrantha (Book Two)
The Palace of Impossible Dreams (Book Three)
The Chaos Crystal (Book Four)

The
CHAOS CRYSTAL

The Tide Lords:
Book Four

JENNIFER FALLON

A Tom Doherty Associates Book
New York

THE CHAOS CRYSTAL

Copyright © 2008 by Jennifer Fallon

Originally published in Australia by HarperCollins Publishers

A Tor Book
Published by Tom Doherty Associates, LLC
175 Fifth Avenue
New York, NY 10010

www.tor-forge.com

Tor® is a registered trademark of Tom Doherty Associates, LLC.

ISBN 978-0-7653-1685-1

First Tor Edition: May 2011

Printed in the United States of America

0   9   8   7   6   5   4   3   2   1

For Princess Lee—
finally

OCEAN
STERILA.

Fyr Alamsest.
Fyr Firdha.
Fyr Doykhoben.
Fyr Gunda.
Fyr Elutind.
Fyr Cananor.
Hepatic Pt.

FYRENNE

Byrmeze.

ANDELIA

Byrm Ice
Desert.

Vyn.

PALINOVIA.

Rhodkyl.

Abyzinan.

Maynx.

Perzyn.

Cape Cloan.
Mogy.

Deathmask I.

Cycadia Coast.

Symeze.

Koryt.

Entrade.

Eyertue.
Planse.
Hanford.
Gambona.
Lascelle.
Oran.
Tirene.

Valley of the
Tides.
Lebes.
Herino.
Fiorna.
Darra.

Baleen Bay.

Port
Whalebone.

CAELUM

Cabo Bord.

Desert of
Caelum.

Ryne.

Pandella.

Byrene.
Rigantha.

Whitewater.

Balkon.

Northway.

SHEVRON MTS.

Solmah.

THE FERL
Dry Country

Sorbay.
Galan Tesue.

Pas Enhedra.

Sanorna
Sea.

GLAEBA.

Armada
Gulf.

Great
Ramana.

Cabo Forlorn.

WESTLANDS.

Cabo Fairweather.

Denrah.

Ramanabela.
Eastmost
Head.

Dewdrop Is.

Petra.

Northwaite.

Relefe.

Barambutol.

Sallarn.

CHELAE
ISLANDS.

Southwaite.

Bryenze.

Butla.

Tosca.

Tenseris.

The Dark Shore.

Irigiray.
Bell Hook.

TORLENIA.

Kyrlah.

Shileff.

Gilass.

Torlene Highlands.

Elvere.

Banuba
Bight.

Abbey of the Way of the Tide.

Ramahn.

GREAT INLAND
DESERT.

Stormway Head.

Junction.

The Burning Waste.

Demon's Breath.

Iamscan
Oasis.

Bhukree.

Photdaar.

Isp.

Essandaar.

COMMONWEALTH OF
ELENOVIA.

Lanfall.

Y' Brare
Espm. Musch.

OCEAN

DOCILAE.

Fumtuk.

Contanya.

Kanovahn.

Meli Sqax.

Panopoly.

VETORIA.

Anfari.

Behtn.

CYLENIA.

Narmen.

Kelgyn.

Dome.

Rees.

Empty
Bay.

Pypsis.

Cape Narmen.

Ramusha.

Meyshire.

ERICANIA.

Irite.

OCEAN

FOMENIA.

Snowscape.

Elishass.
(abandoned)

Shiptrap
Peninsula.

Bitter
Sea.

Kentrarion's Prison.
Bitter Peaks.

Ice Fields of Jelidia.

JELIDIA.

OCEAN
TEMPURA.

OCEAN
TEMPURA.

The supreme irony of life is that hardly anyone gets out of it alive.

—Robert A. Heinlein (1907–1988)

The CHAOS CRYSTAL

Prologue

Seven years ago . . .

The thick stone walls of Lebec Prison seeped misery as a rule, which made this day quite unusual. For the first time in months, Bary Morel had hope. He hurried after the guard escorting him to the Warden's office, filled with an emotion he thought he'd never feel again. Despite everything that had befallen him since they'd raided his house a few months ago and found him treating a runaway feline in his basement, finally, out of nowhere, there was a glimmer of hope.

The Duke of Lebec had come to visit him.

Morel had no idea why such an important man would take the time to visit a convicted felon. Admittedly, he'd once enjoyed a tenuous connection with the ducal family. He'd visited the palace a number of times when the current duke was a boy if the old duke's regular physician was out of the city. But he hadn't seen Stellan Desean for a number of years. Not since he'd been called to treat a young man at the palace—a friend of the new duke's who'd almost died from food poisoning—a few years back.

Bary couldn't think of any reason why Stellan Desean would visit him now. Only that he had—and it must mean good news. Dukes didn't bother delivering bad news personally; they left that sort of thing to their underlings.

Maybe Arkady had managed to gain an audience with him. She promised she'd try on her last visit, despite his attempts to discourage her from doing anything so brazen. In reality, Arkady had nothing else left she *could* do. They were out of money. They couldn't even afford the most basic representation to lodge an appeal through legal channels. And even if they could, there would be no chance of overturning the conviction—not with the calibre of witness the court had been able to bring against him.

Bary stopped for a moment, gripping the wall as his lungs spasmed painfully. The guard heard him coughing and stopped, turning to look at him.

"You all right?"

"I'll be fine . . . just give me a minute to catch . . . my breath, would you?"

The man waited until Bary had recovered sufficiently to continue. When the doctor pushed off the wall, he resumed his walk toward the Warden's office, albeit at a less enthusiastic pace.

The Warden wasn't in his office when they arrived. He had already vacated it for the duke. Stellan Desean was standing by the window, staring out into the rain that trickled down the glass and pattered softly against the stonework. He was wearing a fur-trimmed cloak against the cold. He turned as Bary entered, indicating with a wave of his hand that the guard should wait outside.

"Dr. Morel."

"Your grace."

Stellan smiled. "Please, take a seat. You look like you could use it."

Bary did as the duke suggested, gratefully taking the chair opposite the desk. He coughed again into his bloodstained kerchief and then focused his attention on his visitor, who frowned at the sound of his rattling chest.

"I see your daughter was not exaggerating the seriousness of your condition," Stellan remarked, studying him closely.

"She was able to gain an audience with you then?" Bary said. "I'm assuming that's why you're here?"

Stellan nodded and took a seat in the Warden's big worn leather chair. "To call it an audience would be a kindness. If you must know, she pushed her way past all the people I have in place to prevent precisely that eventuality, burst in on me in high dudgeon and began berating me soundly for allowing you to spend a single minute longer than you had to, here in prison, all for the crime of being nothing more than a great humanitarian."

Bary wished Stellan's neutral tone gave away some sort of hint about what he was feeling. Arkady's interference might have doomed him, rather than helped him.

"I'm sorry, your grace. She wouldn't have intended to offend you . . ."

Stellan was smiling. He held up his hand to stop Bary's apology. "It's all right, Dr. Morel. I was happy to hear her petition on your behalf. Once I realised who she was, of course. I didn't recognise your daughter at first. She's grown into a stunning young woman. You must be very proud of her."

Bary nodded, his eyes misting at the thought of what she'd done to protect him. Bursting in on the Duke of Lebec and demanding his release was the least of it. "She is a very good daughter," he agreed, wiping his eyes. "You have no idea."

"She demanded I pardon you."

Bary smiled wanly. "She's optimistic, too."

"And very eloquent. She tells me she's studying to be a historian."

Bary nodded. "She wanted to be a physician but they wouldn't consider her application at the university because she's female."

"I'm sure the powers that be have a good reason for their stance."

Not one that will ever convince Arkady they're nothing more than misogynist fools. He shrugged, not sure what his daughter's academic aspirations had to do with anything. "Well, unless you know the reason and can defend it soundly, your grace, I suggest you don't bring up the subject with my daughter."

Stellan smiled even wider. "Yes, I learned that the hard way."

"It was kind of you to spare the time to hear her out, your grace. And to take the time to visit me."

Stellan's smile faded. "I have to admit, Dr. Morel, I'm not here just to pass the time of day, or look up an old family servant, if your infrequent trips to the palace even qualify you as that."

Bary's heart skipped a beat. That didn't sound very encouraging. *Tides, what did she say to the man?* "Then why have you come here, your grace?"

"Because I believe we can do each other a favour, Dr. Morel," the duke announced. "We both have something the other wants."

Bary couldn't help but smile at that remark. "Well, you certainly have it in your power to grant *me* what I want, your grace," he said. "But I cannot, for the life of me, imagine what I can offer you."

"I could give you a pardon," Stellan agreed, leaning back in the Warden's chair. "But not without causing considerable comment. You were caught red-handed, my friend, helping an escaped slave evade capture. Even worse, the main witness who testified against you is a very prominent member of Lebec University's faculty. I can't just dismiss Fillion Rybank's testimony out of hand because I happen to like you more than him."

At the mention of Rybank's name, Bary could feel his ire rising. What that man had done to his daughter was beyond unconscionable and it made him sick just thinking about it. Arkady didn't know her father knew about what went on, of course. As far as she was concerned, he was still ignorant of the whole affair. It was with bitter irony that he recalled worrying about her a few years ago, when he came to the realisation that his daughter probably wasn't as innocent as he would have liked. He'd thought she was sleeping with the Hawkes boy at the time. He was a decent enough lad, it turned out, for all that he was a bit of a rabble-rouser. They'd been inseparable, after all, for most of her formative years.

Bary wished now that his daughter *had* been sleeping with young Hawkes. That, at least, he could have dealt with like any father. But the truth—the bitter knowledge that his daughter had given herself to a man like Fillion Rybank for years to buy his silence, believing she was saving her father from being arrested—was almost more than he could bear to think about.

Arkady worried about him now because she thought he was sick with consumption. She had no idea that his physical illness was nothing compared to how nauseous with guilt her sacrifice had made him.

"That man is the criminal," Bary said, clenching his fists. "He blackmailed an innocent child for sexual favours and yet he walks free, while I am in prison for the crime of helping a wounded Crasii."

"Your wounded Crasii was an escaped slave, doctor," Stellan reminded him. "And while I'd love to do something about Fillion Rybank for what he did, neither you—and certainly not your daughter—is willing to testify in an open court to what he did. That does rather tie my hands in the matter, don't you think?"

"Then you've come here today for what reason? To tell me you're sorry you can't help?"

Stellan shook his head. "On the contrary. I can help you. A great deal. I'm prepared to give you a pardon. You could be out of here by the end of next week."

"But there is a condition," Bary said warily, not fool enough to think there were no strings attached to such a generous offer.

"Just a small one," Stellan said. "I want to marry your daughter."

Bary stared at the duke. "You *what*?"

"I need a wife, doctor. More to the point, I need a wife who'll not . . . make certain demands on me—demands I'm not in a position to fulfil.

Arkady fits the bill perfectly. She is astute, intelligent, articulate, glorious to look at, and has a very good reason to broker a deal with me that suits us both. So everybody will be happy. You'll get your freedom, I'll get my heir—and, incidentally, get the king off my back about me getting married, which is an added bonus."

Bary looked at him, dumbfounded. For a moment, the offer made no sense.

"Why?" This was a wealthy, handsome duke, who was third in line for the throne. What possible reason could he have for turning down every eligible highborn woman in Glaeba, to take the penniless daughter of a convicted felon as his wife? "You can't possibly be in love with my daughter."

"No, of course not," the duke said. "Nor is she in love with me. But she has agreed to this."

Tides, what is that girl thinking?

And then it came to him. His late-night visit to the palace several years ago, to attend a young man suffering the effects of eating a meal of bad oysters. He'd not thought much about it at the time, but his patient hadn't just been visiting the Lebec Palace. He'd been in the duke's bed.

"You need more than a wife, I think, your grace. You need an alibi."

Stellan didn't answer immediately, but when he did, he didn't try to deny the accusation. "She will have wealth. Position in society. Tides, I'll even endow the university so they have to keep her on there, if I must. I will make no demands of her other than she is discreet and conducts herself in a manner befitting a duchess. And I give you my word I will never force myself on her the way Rybank did. I will see to it your daughter never wants for anything, doctor, ever again."

"Except a chance to be happy, perhaps?"

"What do you mean by that?"

"My daughter is in love with another man, your grace. You can't tell me she's doing this willingly."

Stellan shook his head. "She tells me her young man has left Lebec to take up a position in Herino with the King's Spymaster, as his apprentice. Declan Hawkes has apparently chosen a career with Daly Bridgeman over your daughter. Hardly the actions of a lovesick young man wishing to take a wife. Anyway, Arkady assures me he is merely a good friend and not a consideration."

You foolish girl. You can't throw away your happiness for me. Not again.

Bary shook his head. "I'm sorry, your grace. I know you mean well, but I can't allow this."

Stellan stared at him in confusion. "I beg your pardon?"

"I can't allow it. I refuse you my daughter's hand."

The duke looked stunned. "Are you mad? I'm offering you a pardon, you fool. Your daughter will be one of the wealthiest women in Glaeba. She will have a life you can never give her. A life you cannot imagine."

"Unfortunately, your grace, I *can* imagine it. All your wealth, all the pretty baubles in the world, will mean nothing if my daughter is dying a little bit on the inside every day of her life." He shook his head and rose to his feet. "No. I cannot allow Arkady to give her body to yet another man to save me, no matter how well meaning that man is." Bary turned for the door and then stopped and glanced back at Stellan, hoping his smile would ease the duke's disappointment. "I know you're a good man, your grace. And I know you'd never deliberately hurt Arkady. But she's done enough for me. I won't allow her to throw her life away in another misguided attempt to ease my suffering."

"I think you underestimate how important this is to me," Stellan said, in a voice that Bary hadn't heard him use before. "And that you're suffering from the mistaken belief that I'm here asking your permission," he added, rising to his feet also. "I came today as a courtesy, doctor, to inform you that I will be marrying your daughter, and offering you a pardon as a wedding present to her, which nobody will think unusual or even unreasonable. I have already secured the king's permission for the marriage. You can't stop this happening, so you might as well accept it."

Bary glared at the duke, surprised at how determined he seemed. He'd always struck Bary as such an affable young man. The doctor shook his head stubbornly. "If you do this, your grace, I will go straight to the king. I will tell him what I know of you."

"You don't *know* anything, doctor."

"I know I treated a young man in your bed in the dead of night several years ago—a night when your own physician was available. You dispensed with his services not long after that, as I recall."

"That proves nothing," Stellan said.

"You had no need to call me that night, your grace, but your friend was sick and couldn't be moved and you couldn't risk him being discovered in your bed. So, I may not know anything for certain, but I *can* tell the king what I saw and let him draw his own conclusions."

Stellan considered this dilemma for a moment before he replied. "You do realise I have the power to lock you away and make sure you never see the light of day again?"

"Aye," Bary said. "But I also believe you're a good man, Stellan Desean, like your father."

Stellan barely hesitated before he shook his head. He looked rueful, but unrelenting. "Then I'm afraid you're a very poor judge of character, doctor. I am nothing like my father. And unless I have your word you will give this wedding your blessing and accept my pardon with your continued silence, the messenger I send to Lebec Prison with your pardon next week won't be bringing you back to attend the wedding reception at the palace; he'll be returning with the tragic news of your demise."

Bary shook his head. "I don't think you'll do that, your grace. I think you'll see the injustice of this and let my daughter out of this dreadful arrangement before anybody gets hurt."

Just exactly how wrong he was Bary discovered a few days later when they came for him, not to release him, but to throw him in a cell in the very bowels of Lebec Prison where, as Stellan Desean had threatened, he was unlikely to ever see the light of day again

PART I

HIGH TIDE

Deep into that darkness peering, long I
stood there, wondering, fearing,
doubting, dreaming dreams no mortal
ever dared to dream before.

"The Raven"
—Edgar Allan Poe (1809–1849)

Chapter 1

It seemed incomprehensible to Arkady that her father was still alive. Even more incomprehensible that Stellan had known about it all this time; that he'd lied to her so blatantly and so shamelessly.

She didn't believe it at first. It took hours after they threw her into the freezing cell in the tower of Lebec Prison before she would approach the bars dividing her cell from her father's in order to confirm the impossible truth. And when she was finally able to bring herself to confront him, she discovered she wasn't happy or relieved to see her father. She was angry. Blindingly, unreasonably angry.

How dare her father do this to her? How dare he let her believe all this time that he was dead? Arkady had grieved for her father. She had shed a river of tears for his loss. And all this time he was here, right under her nose, sitting in Lebec Prison. Kept here, not because of his crimes, but his misguided sense of nobility.

All he'd had to do was say nothing. His pardon was signed, sealed and only needed to be delivered. All Bary Morel had to do to save his own life was stand back and let his daughter marry a man who promised to give her wealth, a title and everything she could ever ask for. That her husband's fall from grace had brought her to this pass wasn't the point. That Stellan's troubles with the new king had taken her down with him, was unimportant. What gnawed at Arkady's gut was the stupidity of it. Her father's noble, and utterly futile, sacrifice. And her husband's mercilessness and willing complicity in the deception.

And then there was Declan Hawkes. Had he known of this and lied to her, too? Could the Duke of Lebec keep a prisoner confined for more than seven years without due process and the King's Spymaster know nothing about it?

Arkady couldn't believe Declan was a willing party to this. But then, she'd never have thought Stellan so ruthless, either. Or her father so stubborn.

"Are you planning to stay mad at me forever?"

Arkady glanced up from her bunk, shivering against the cold, her knees drawn up under her chin. "Yes."

"You must understand, Arkady . . ."

"Understand what?" she said. "That you'd rather have me think you dead? That your noble refusal to accept the opportunity to be free and well cared for, in perpetuity, not to mention a ducal pardon for your crimes, was for my own good?"

Her father was standing at the bars, holding them as if touching them somehow brought them closer together. He looked old now, in a way he'd never appeared in the past. His stubbled head was grey, his skin pallid and wrinkled.

"It was for your own good, my darling. Can't you see that? I would not have my own daughter sell herself to save me . . ." His voice faltered uncertainly.

"Again?" she finished for him. "Is that what you were going to say?"

He sighed. Arkady knew now that her father had learned about her deal with Fillion Rybank not long after his arrest. And he'd never said anything to her about it. Not a word; not in all the times she'd visited him in gaol. Not a single "are you all right?" Not a word about her courage, however misguided. Not even a thank-you for trying to save him.

Nobody else had been prepared to help him. Not his friends, not his colleagues, not the hundreds of people who owed him their lives, not even the Crasii slaves he'd been trying to help—the very reason for his arrest. Despite her anger, Arkady didn't really blame the Crasii. They had their own problems. The magically blended, half-animal, half-human creatures created by the Tide Lords didn't have time to be concerned by human troubles. The Tide was on the rise and they had no thought but pleasing their immortal masters, whom they were magically compelled to obey.

Her efforts to save her father from incarceration for six years by sleeping with the only man who could bear witness to his crimes was his failure as a parent. It had nothing, apparently, to do with Arkady.

Tides, but men are selfish creatures.

"Arkady, what that man did to you—"

"Turned out to be a complete waste of time," she said, refusing to look at him. "Did that ever occur to you, Papa dear, while you were sitting here in your lonely cell, rotting with quiet pride at the nobility of your sacrifice? Did you not, even for a moment, wonder that I might think I'd thrown my childhood away for no good reason, because in the end, nothing I'd done could save you?"

He shook his head, as if he was denying her right to feel that way. "I was the parent, Arkady. Your father. It was my job to save you. And I failed."

"So you decided a little penance was in order?"

His eyes misted with unshed tears. "I am sick with what you endured to protect me. Surely you can understand that when I heard of the deal you'd brokered with Desean, I couldn't stand by and let you make the same mistake all over again?"

She spared him an irritated glance. "You could have accepted Stellan's pardon and informed me of your disapproval in person, you know. Did that ever occur to you?"

Her father was silent for a time. Finally he said, "It sounds silly now, but to be honest, Arkady, I never thought he'd carry out the threat. Not really. I mean, even when they moved me to the cells on the lower levels, I thought the duke was just trying to frighten me into compliance. I couldn't believe it when you stopped coming to visit me. Or when I heard of the wedding. The Stellan Desean I remembered as a boy didn't seem the type to champion injustice to further his own interests."

"You met him a handful of times, Papa. How could you possibly think you knew Stellan well enough to call his bluff?"

"You thought you knew him well enough to accept his proposal."

She turned her gaze from him, wishing she could explain her reasons but knowing she was too angry to try. "Stellan gave me exactly what he promised, Papa. It was you who refused his offer."

"It's thanks to that man we're both here," he pointed out, angered by her intransigence. "How can you defend him?"

Arkady couldn't answer that question, because her father was right. Stellan's part in this miserable affair had been just as unconscionable as her father's. But somehow she found it easier to forgive her husband than her father. She understood what it felt like to do whatever you must to survive, and really, that's all Stellan had done. There would have been no other path left to him when he delivered his ultimatum to her father. By the time her father refused his pardon, Stellan had already been to the king and argued forcefully for permission to wed the common-born woman with whom he was supposedly in love. There was no backing down without causing a scandal of monumental proportions.

Stellan probably hadn't wanted to confine her father, Arkady thought, knowing him as she did. It was just that by the time Bary Morel took it into his head to defend his daughter's honour by refusing to stay silent, they were long past the point of no return. Stellan had his flaws, but indecisiveness wasn't one of them.

"I'm sorry, Arkady," her father said, pushing off the bars. "I thought I was doing the right thing. I thought you were in love with the Hawkes boy and that's who you wanted to marry."

Arkady smiled sourly. "You used to tell me Declan was a troublemaker who would come to no good. I distinctly remember you telling me I should stay away from him."

"He made something of himself in the end," her father conceded. "He had a responsible job. Did very well for himself in the king's service, I hear."

Ah, Papa, if only you knew what Declan has become.

"So you're telling me you would rather I married a penniless troublemaker than a wealthy duke?"

"If you were in love with the penniless troublemaker, then yes."

"Well, haven't you mellowed with old age?" She didn't mean to sound so bitter, but it was hard not to.

"I'm sorry."

"For what?"

"About Declan. I grieved for the lad when I heard he died in that fire in Herino a few months back."

Arkady turned her head to look at her father, as it dawned on her how little he knew of what she'd been doing this past year. How little he knew about her at all, really. When she thought about it, her father hadn't known what she was up to since she was fourteen. He had some idealised notion of her in his head. In his world, he worried Declan might lead her astray; that she was simply a victim of a series of men wanting to take advantage of her. He had no idea how strong she was, how every hard-fought battle had toughened her spirit until little could faze her. He knew nothing of the immortals. His problems seemed so immense to him, his perspective narrowed by the confines of his cell.

Who cared about whether or not she married well when the world might be coming to an end?

Arkady pushed off the pallet and climbed to her feet. It was time to start filling her father in on the state of the world.

"Declan's not dead, Papa," she said, approaching the bars.

He smiled at her sadly. "I know you'd like to believe that, darling, but—"

"But, nothing," she cut in. "I know he's not dead because I've seen him. Tides, Papa, I've slept with him. When I was in Senestra. Right after I got through being a concubine slave for a very nice young physician who turned out to be a callous murderer."

"Arkady . . ."

"You think while you sat in here, nursing your wounded pride, feeling guilty about what was done to me, that life came to a grinding halt? There's a whole world out there you know nothing about, Papa. The Tide is on the rise; the immortals are trying to take over the world. A couple of them are trying to take the Glaeban throne. There's a few more lining up to take over Caelum. Torlenia will be in the hands of a Tide Lord before the year is out. One of them wants to kill himself and doesn't care who he takes with him in the process. Oh, and it turns out Declan is one of them too."

She could see her father drawing back at her harsh tone, but she didn't care. She was done with his self-pitying depression. "So, who would you rather I married, in hindsight? The duke who made me rich and comfortable for a while, but whose downfall saw me sold into slavery as a whore? Or the troublemaker who, last I heard, was headed to Jelidia to meet up with the rest of his immortal brethren—where they've just released a madman from confinement so they can find a way to kill the Immortal Prince. All of which doesn't augur well for the rest of us, because I suspect nothing short of breaking the world in half is going to put an end to him."

Bary Morel stared at her in shock. "You're not making any sense, Arkady."

"Unfortunately, I'm making a lot more sense than I'd like," she replied. "And if you want to do something useful, instead of sitting there begging me to forgive you for being such a terrible father, why don't you help me figure out a way out of here?"

Bary shook his head. "There is no way out of here, Arkady."

"Not if you think like that, there isn't," she agreed.

"They will leave us here to rot," he said. "I know that for certain."

Arkady had learned the hard way that nothing was certain. "I don't think so, Papa. They'll come for us, sooner or later."

"They?"

"Perhaps I should have said *he'll* come for us, sooner or later. That's why you're here, you see. He's planning to use you to get at me."

Her father shook his head in confusion. "Who are you talking about?"

"The new Duke of Lebec, Papa," Arkady said, glancing toward the entrance to the chilly tower cells, as if by naming him, she might be calling him here. Thankfully, the door remained closed, as it did every day unless it was time for their meals to be delivered. "Stellan's former lover and the man responsible for the death of the King of Glaeba. The immortal Tide Lord, Jaxyn Aranville."

Chapter 2

The whole world seemed to shudder whenever another cathedral-sized chunk of ice broke off the ice-shelf and crashed into the freezing black waters of the southern ocean. The feline Crasii, Jojo, stumbled and took an involuntary step backwards, even though she was some distance from the edge and—at least for the moment—in no immediate danger.

"It's getting worse."

Declan turned his attention from Jojo to glance at the Tide Lord who had spoken, concerned to see her forehead creased with a frown. Arryl seemed uncomfortably worried about this unseasonal melting of the glacier.

"Tide's coming in fast," she said. Arryl wasn't, Declan was quite certain, referring to the water.

They had come here this afternoon, to the very edge of Jelidia, to witness the ice continent disappearing before their very eyes. Filled with an odd mixture of unease and guilty delight as the Tide continued its surging return, Declan had suggested the outing earlier in the day. On reaching the coast, he'd found his worst fears realised. The rising Tide was affecting more than the immortals; more than a newly minted immortal discovering the true meaning of a rising Tide for the first time. The whole of Amyrantha was starting to feel its influence.

Declan still couldn't quite believe the turn of events that had brought him here to this icy cliff with a clutch of legendary immortals as his companions. Not so long ago he had been a nobody, his only claim to importance his role as the King of Glaeba's Spymaster. But for an accident of fate—a fire in Lebec Prison in which he should not have been caught—Declan might have lived and died ignorant of his immortal heritage. But the flames had consumed him and that's when he discovered that he wasn't just Declan Hawkes, slum-child made good. He was the son, and the great-grandson of two powerful immortals whose bloodline was stronger than the flames, stronger than anything. He wasn't the bastard get of a Glaeban whore. He was a Tide Lord.

"Shouldn't we be moving back a little, my lord?"

Declan stopped pondering his strange fate long enough to glance over his shoulder at the fearful Crasii waiting behind them. Being out on the ice with the Tide Lords—who were immune to the vagaries of the weather—meant Jojo was forced to wear a coat. He could tell by her sour expression how much she hated wearing it, almost as much as she despised wearing boots. Her feet must be cramped, he guessed, and there was nowhere to rest her tail comfortably under the weight of the long fur jacket protecting her from the cold. But Jelidia was a bitter place. Even though it was summer here, and Lukys insisted it was getting warmer—a fact that seemed to be borne out by the breaking ice crashing into the ocean—it was still a bitterly *cold* place. So Declan insisted she wear the coat outside if she wanted to remain in their company. The feline shifted position again, undoubtedly wishing her masters would get over their fascination with the disintegrating coastline and return to the palace.

Not that the palace is much warmer, Declan thought, turning back to watch the breakup of the ice-shelf, although these days it was hard for him to tell. Declan had gained immortality, but along with that, he'd lost the ability to feel temperature extremes. It remained to be seen how many other things he'd lost the ability to experience.

"Bet she wishes we were back in Senestra," he remarked to Arryl. The poor creature had no option but to do as the Tide Lords commanded. But Declan wasn't sure if that meant the Crasii had also lost her ability for wishful thinking.

Arryl shook her head, sparing the shivering feline a brief glance. "She's not missing Senestra one bit."

"Really?"

"I think you'll find she's never been happier."

"How do you figure that?"

"The feeling of fulfilment she's enjoying simply by being in the presence of true immortals is enough to mitigate the worst discomfort." Arryl frowned. "Even the awkwardness of wearing boots. That's the tragedy of them, you know. That's the true weakness bred into them when they were created."

"Tell her to strip off and stand there until we're done, if you don't believe Arryl," Taryx suggested, stepping forward until he was right on the very edge of the cliff. The ice was raw and jagged where it had broken away and the ice behind it already riddled with hairline fractures that would soon expand to crack even more of the ice-shelf from the main ice-sheet. Taryx studied the cliff edge for a moment and then straightened, turning to look at Declan. "She'll happily freeze to death with a smile on her face, if you command her to."

The immortal leaned over to stare at the crashing ocean once more, ignoring the bitter wind that whipped his dark hair around his face. He wasn't as powerful as the other immortals, but he effectively ran the palace and certainly kept it intact. Taryx's gift was manipulating water. The ice-wrought Palace of Impossible Dreams remained standing and functioning, thanks to him. Declan wondered why he was doing nothing now to prevent the ice from breaking away from the coast, because if it kept disintegrating at this rate, in a few weeks the palace itself would be in danger.

"Might be a close thing," Taryx remarked loudly after a time, almost as if he had heard Declan's unspoken question.

"What?" Arryl asked in confusion. "The Crasii?"

Taryx shook his head. "I mean the Tide coming in. Thing's . . . *happen* . . . when the Tide comes in this fast."

Declan was afraid to ask what that meant. But he asked anyway, keenly feeling his ignorance about all things magical. "What things?"

"Things too horrible to mention," Kentravyon called in a rather dramatic tone. Tempting fate, he sat on the edge of the cliff a few feet away, his legs dangling over the rim as if he didn't have a care in the world.

"*What* things?" Declan repeated impatiently, more than a little fed up with these immortals and their cryptic responses to perfectly reasonable questions. *Why does immortality make things worse, rather than better?* he wondered. *Why does it seem to bring only cynicism and narcissism? Why all the sarcasm? Why doesn't it bring enlightenment? Or detachment from the material world? Some sort of universal awareness not available to mortal man?*

Tides, will I be like them in a few hundred—a few thousand—years?

A dark-haired, unremarkable looking man, Kentravyon was carving something from a chunk of ice he'd picked up on the way here, unconcerned, it seemed, about the imminent danger he was in if the ice beneath him crumbled into the ocean. Declan could feel him using the Tide to carve his statue, rather than more traditional tools, and from where he stood, it seemed to be taking shape as the head of a human.

"Things . . ." Kentravyon said with a shrug. "Cold places get colder, hot places get hotter . . . the rains move and deserts with them. Islands sink, mountains move, other lands arise . . ." As he spoke, little chips of ice flew randomly off his sculpture, hitting the other Tide Lords standing nearby, eventually prompting Arryl to ask what he was doing. She didn't seem surprised to hear about the effect of the rising Tide. But then, this wasn't the first time she had experienced one, so it wasn't the novelty for her that it was for Declan—if *novelty* was a word one could use to describe the potential disruption and perhaps destruction of all human settlement on Amyrantha.

"What are you doing?" Arryl asked.

"Creating the face of God," Kentravyon told her, yelling to stop the wind snatching away his words.

"How do you know it's the face of God?"

Kentravyon shrugged. "I just get rid of all the bits that don't look like me."

That remark evoked a sour laugh from Taryx who addressed the other two loudly to be heard over the wind, saying, "And to think, I thought being mad meant being inconsistent."

Kentravyon tossed the ice carving aside and climbed to his feet, turning to face the immortal who'd dared to insult him. "I am not mad. It is the rest of *you* who are misguided."

"I don't think I'm God," Taryx said.

Not yet, Declan thought, wondering if Kentravyon's delusions were the eventual fate of all immortals and one of the reasons Cayal was so anxious to die. Unbidden, another doubt crept into his mind. *Will I think the same way someday?* The notion scared him a little. *Will I one day find myself sitting on the edge of a disintegrating glacier, whittling away my time, thinking I'm omnipotent?* Declan glanced westward, to the ice-cliff some distance away, where a lone figure stood silhouetted against the overcast sky, his cloak billowing out in the harsh wind coming off the ocean until it was almost horizontal. Kentravyon noticed the direction of Declan's gaze and smiled.

"You don't want to die, either, I hope," Kentravyon said, peering at him curiously.

"No."

"Cayal wants it so bad he can taste it. I rather think that makes *him* the crazy one, not me."

Declan tore his gaze from Cayal's lonely silhouette to look at Kentra-vyon. "We're not allowing for the possibility that you're *both* lunatics, then?"

"You will come to accept the wisdom of my truth eventually," Kentra-vyon told him, with the sage air of someone who knew something nobody else did. "The Chaos Crystal will show you the way. As it always does."

"Assuming we ever find the damn thing," Taryx said, frowning.

"It's in Glaeba somewhere."

Declan looked at Kentravyon in astonishment. "You *know* where it is?"

Kentravyon shrugged. "It was stolen by the Cabal several thousand years ago. Not long before these other ungrateful sods here, ganged up on me and put me on ice." He glared at Arryl and Taryx for a moment before returning his attention to Declan. "I'd made a few mortal ene-mies by then, as well as immortal ones. They mistakenly thought they could use the crystal to destroy me."

"The irony, of course," Taryx added, "being that far from destroying any immortal, by losing the damned crystal they made certain we could never be gone from their lives."

Kentravyon turned to look at the Immortal Prince in the distance with a scowl. "Not going to be happy if I find he's managed to drown it at the bottom of one of the Great Lakes with his little tantrum over that wretched child."

Declan realised the Tide Lord was referring to the legend about the Immortal Prince, and how his tears of grief over the death of his mortal daughter, Fliss, had supposedly flooded the massive rift valley separating Caelum and Glaeba, turning it into the Great Lakes. He wondered what they'd do if the talisman they sought *was* buried at that bottom of the Great Lakes of Glaeba. The waterways were as large as an inland sea.

"So Maralyce is in on this too?" Declan asked, as it occurred to him why his own great-grandmother had made Glaeba her home. He should have suspected as much. "That's what Maralyce is looking for, isn't it? She's not mining for gold. She's looking for this wretched crystal of yours. Who else knows about this?"

"That's everyone," Kentravyon said. "Are you done sightseeing?"

"I've got another question," Declan said.

"There's a shock," Taryx muttered. Declan ignored him.

"You said 'as it always does.' You've used this crystal before?"

Kentravyon hesitated for the barest fraction of a second. "We've experimented with it in the past, yes."

"That's not an answer. I want to know how you *know* this crystal will even work," Declan said. "I mean, you're standing here telling us we have to find some talisman stolen by the Cabal. Well, I'm sorry. I was a member of the Cabal and Lukys was posing as one of the Pentangle. I never heard anything about a magical crystal capable of destroying an immortal."

It was Taryx rather than Kentravyon who answered him. "You heard about it every day, Declan. You just didn't know it, that's all."

Declan glared at him, waiting for him to elaborate.

"The Tarot, you fool," Taryx told him impatiently. "It was never about telling fortunes, any more than it was about documenting the story of the immortals. It was, and always has been, the key to the location of the crystal."

"You can buy a Tide Lord Tarot in any marketplace on Amyrantha," Arryl said, sounding almost as puzzled as Declan felt. "Why haven't you found it before now?"

"Because the Tarot has changed over time and a different version seems to surface after every Cataclysm," Taryx explained. "It's been embellished beyond recognition; endlessly amended to fit the romantic notions of good storytelling. Now—if you want the location of the Chaos Crystal—you need to get your hands on an original. Or at least a *copy* of the original."

"How?" Declan asked.

Kentravyon smiled. "Ah . . . and therein lies our dilemma . . ."

"I have another question," Declan said. "Lukys claims the process of focusing the Tide will kill any immortal standing too close to the portal when it opens. But how . . ." Declan stopped abruptly and turned toward the sea, his skin prickling with the now familiar feel of someone swimming the Tide.

Kentravyon and the others felt it too. Even Cayal straightened in the distance, raising his arm to shield his eyes from the glare of the sun. He sensed rather than felt another Tide Lord in the vicinity, one not standing with them on the ice.

Declan's voice faltered as he continued: ". . . How do you *know* the Chaos Crystal works?"

Before anyone could answer his question, the feline standing behind him gasped and turned toward the sea, falling to one knee as a wave rose unnaturally high on the water, racing toward them, gathering momentum as it approached. Declan couldn't see anybody on the wave. The burning sensation against his skin told him it was the magical Tide, rather than the oceanic one, driving the abnormal wall of water. As they watched, the wave quickly built up until it was almost as tall as the ice-cliff of the glacier.

Declan fought the urge to step back as the huge wave sped toward them. He knew—intellectually, at least—that it couldn't harm him, but his instincts had yet to adjust to immortality.

And then, without warning, the wave stopped—abruptly and unaccountably—at the very edge of the cliff.

"Maybe you should ask our visitor," Taryx suggested calmly, as a dripping figure dressed in a thin linen shift emerged from the still water, stepping onto the cliff like a grand lady emerging from a carriage, before the wave let go and tumbled down the ice-cliff with an almighty crash.

"Ask me what?" the newcomer said calmly, leaning her head sideways as she squeezed the excess water from her hair. She was a mature woman, dark-haired and well built, but Declan had never been able to pin an age on her. He supposed he should be surprised to see her—not to mention impressed by her dramatic arrival on a wave, no less—but Declan's senses were too overloaded, since arriving in Jelidia, to register such an emotion.

Kentravyon didn't seem surprised to see their visitor either. "Nice entrance, Maralyce," he said as she stopped before them. "Been practising that?"

"Don't be ridiculous," she said nodding a greeting to the others before fixing her gaze on Declan as she shook the water from her clothes. It was so cold, icicles were forming on her wet eyelashes as she spoke. "Hello, lad. See you found your way here. What is Taryx going on about? A question?"

"Your grandson wants to know how *we* know what the Chaos Crystal will do," Taryx said before Declan could utter a sound.

Maralyce shrugged, as if she wasn't in the least bothered by the question. Or, indeed, that there was anything untoward about her un-announced arrival on the back of a tidal wave. She took off her shift to wring it out, using the Tide to speed the drying process, revealing a fit and surprisingly shapely body. Declan blushed and looked away. This woman was his great-grandmother. Immortal or not, she had no right to disrobe so publicly, or to have a body like that at her age.

"We've done this before, Declan," Maralyce said, smiling at his dis-comfort. "It's how we first came to Amyrantha."

Her state of undress forgotten, Declan turned back to stare at his great-grandmother as the implications of her statement sank in and then glanced at the others to gauge their reaction. Taryx didn't seem sur-prised. Kentravyon was looking a little wild-eyed—which wasn't saying much because he looked like that most of the time—but, like Declan, Arryl seemed quite shocked.

"I think," Declan said slowly, his gaze swinging between Maralyce and Kentravyon, "you have some explaining to do."

Maralyce shrugged and then spied the figure standing over on the rise. She squinted a little and then turned to Arryl. "Is that Cayal over there?"

"Yes."

"What's he doing?"

"Wishing, I think," Arryl said sadly.

"For what?" Maralyce asked, pulling the now-dry shift back over her head.

"For death," Kentravyon replied. "What else?"

Chapter 3

The former Duke of Lebec, Stellan Desean, couldn't pinpoint the exact moment it had happened, but somehow, without even trying, he found himself fighting for a crown. He'd never meant to get into such a fight. Quite the opposite, in fact. His life—until recently—was dedicated to preserving the crown for his friend, cousin and king, Enteny Debree, and after his death, his rightful heir, Mathu.

A year ago, he would have given his life for Glaeba's king. The Tides knew he'd gotten himself into plenty of trouble over the years protecting Glaeba's heir.

That had all changed now. The life he imagined he'd be spending at the right hand of his young cousin, Mathu, guiding him as he grew into a worthy ruler, was a distant, almost forgotten dream. Falsely accused by Jaxyn Aranville of Enteny's murder and branded a traitor, escaping from prison during his trial had done little to help his cause. An escaped convict, these days Stellan was actively plotting against Glaeba's young king, an act that might have felt more like treason had he not known Glaeba's king was being manipulated by immortals bent on feathering their own nests. And so, to save his country from the blindness of its pliable young king, he was standing in the council chamber of the Caelish queen's palace. Here, surrounded by thick stone walls and tapestry wall-hangings boasting of long-ago victories over Glaeba he was discussing the most effective way to invade his homeland with a foreign army . . . a move that was proving to be somewhat problematic, thanks to the weather.

"Is the lake frozen solid?" the Queen's Consort asked. Lord Tyrone—or Tryan the Devil, for those who knew anything of the immortals—directed the question to nobody in particular. He'd married the Queen of Glaeba while her daughter was still missing, thinking it would gain him a crown, but under the complicated Caelish rules of succession, he had no chance of claiming the title now that Princess Nyah had returned. That didn't stop him acting as if he ruled the country, however, Stellan noted with concern.

"Not quite," Ricard Li, the Caelish spymaster, informed the meeting, moving to the map on the table to indicate the areas in question. He was wearing a sheepskin-lined jacket, his hands encased in sturdy leather gloves, and his breath frosted as he spoke. "The ice along the shore here is quite thin and there's still water flowing in a couple of places. We've sent amphibians under the ice-pack to test its thickness. We've lost several of them to hypothermia, and what the survivors report is not encouraging. If this cold snap keeps up, it'll only be a matter of days before you'll be able to walk all the way from Cycrane to Herino."

"I wonder if Jaxyn knows that?" Tryan asked, leaning back on the queen's red leather throne as if he owned it. Unlike the spymaster, he was in shirtsleeves, apparently oblivious to the icy air. Queen Jilna of Caelum was nowhere to be seen, confined to her rooms yet again after having sent yet another message to say she was feeling unwell.

Stellan wondered if her husband was drugging or poisoning her. Not enough to kill her, perhaps, but certainly enough to keep her out of the way of the immortals who had taken over her palace, and were well on the way to taking over her entire nation. With the queen's unexplained illness, Tryan was effectively ruling Caelum, with his mother and his sister, stepfather and stepbrothers all lined up behind him. Fortunately, the stepbrothers weren't here for this war council. Krydence and Rance had gone south to check how far the ice extended down the lake-shore and hopefully wouldn't be back for days.

"Of course he knows it," Syrolee said. The Duchess of Torfail slammed her teacup down so hard it almost broke the delicate porcelain saucer.

Warlock, the Crasii slave sent here by the Cabal of the Tarot to spy on the immortals, hurried forward to mop up the spill before resuming his position by the door. Stellan tried not to pay attention to him. The Cabal of the Tarot had been trying to find a way to rid Amyrantha of immortals almost as long as humans on Amyrantha had been aware of them. Although Stellan wasn't a member of the Cabal, he was sympathetic to their aims and wanted to do nothing to endanger their agent here in the palace.

"He's probably the one responsible for it."

Paying no attention to Warlock or what he was doing, Elyssa, Lord Tyrone's sister, had to lean to her left to see past the big canine wiping the table to make eye contact with her mother. "I've felt nothing."

Stellan assumed she meant she'd not felt Jaxyn working the Tide, which made this unbelievably cold winter a natural phenomenon, rather than the result of immortal interference. He could not admit to knowing that, however, because as far as these immortals were concerned, he was still ignorant of their true identities. And that was a problem, because the solution was obvious to Stellan, but without admitting he knew who and what they were, he couldn't suggest it.

"King Mathu is massing his forces for invasion as we speak," Ricard Li said. "As soon as the ice is solid enough we'll be facing a full-on attack by an overwhelming force of Glaeban warriors, many of whom are battle-trained felines."

"But how will he get them across the ice?" Elyssa asked. Although she was plain to the point of being unattractive, Stellan had discovered that of all the immortals in Caelum, she seemed the brightest. That made her more dangerous than she looked—something he was only just beginning to appreciate. Her nasty habit of murdering her lovers for causing her pain didn't do much to reassure him, either.

The Immortal Maiden hadn't earned her title frivolously, Stellan knew. According to Maralyce, her curse came from the fact that she'd still been a virgin when she was made immortal. The relentless and agonising regeneration that enabled these creatures to live forever applied to every part of their bodies. Her pain was never ending. Stellan wasn't surprised that it made her a little bit crazy.

But her brother, Tryan, was far more dangerous, Stellan thought, because he was so handsome, so agreeable on the outside, it gave no hint to the darkness within. Elyssa's mere presence set Stellan's teeth on edge, so he was usually on his guard when dealing with her. Tryan, on the other hand, was deceptively pleasant. *If he took it into his head to be rid of me, I wouldn't even know I'd been murdered until I looked down and saw my blood on his hands and the knife in my chest.*

"I'm sure Jaxyn will manage to come up with something," Tryan was saying with a dismissive wave of his hand. The how of an attack didn't bother him so much as the *when*.

"We can just wipe them out when they get here, can't we?" Engarhod asked. He was slumped at the other end of the table, an almost-empty jug of wine in front of him. *His idea of breakfast, probably.* Stellan thought that Engarhod didn't often contribute anything useful to the discussions.

Mostly he acted as if he just didn't care what the others were doing so long as it didn't interfere with his drinking. He was all but finished the second jug Warlock had fetched for him this morning. Stellan had never seen any man down the amount of wine Syrolee's husband could consume, and still remain standing.

"It's a pity there's no way to melt the ice," Stellan said with a sigh, wondering if he could prompt one of the others into seeing the solution without him having to spell it out for them. Thinking of Engarhod's breakfast made him realise he'd not eaten yet this morning. Nor would he get to eat until they were done here. If he didn't do something soon to move things along, this could drag on for hours. Immortals might be able to go forever without food, but he couldn't.

Tryan's lips pursed thoughtfully at Stellan's suggestion. "If we timed the melting right, we could drown their army, then sail ours across the lake and be in Glaeba before word even reached Herino Palace that their army was defeated."

Tides, that was easy.

Stellan nodded in agreement, hoping he looked encouraging but not too enthusiastic. "Perhaps if we send amphibians back under the ice to seek out weakness and built large enough fires along the fault lines, we'd be able to break up the ice—"

"You can't break up the ice with bonfires," Syrolee cut in. "That's a stupid idea."

"We *could* melt it, though," Elyssa said thoughtfully, staring at Stellan. "In theory."

Finally! Stellan thought.

"How?" Syrolee asked. "And I know what you're going to say, so don't bother. You do anything catastrophic, Jaxyn will respond in kind, and we won't spend the next High Tide ruling this damned country; we'll be rebuilding it."

Elyssa glared at her mother, as if she knew as much and didn't appreciate the reminder. For himself, Stellan was appalled to realise that the only thing staying the hand of these magicians was laziness.

"I meant we'd have to heat the ice; do it slowly."

Tryan rolled his eyes. "And how, exactly, does one melt a sheet of ice roughly the size of the Chelae Islands in a couple of weeks? That's about how long we have, I estimate, before Jaxyn gets here."

Stellan let out a dramatic sigh, hoping his next words wouldn't sound too contrived. "The mountains that gird the Great Lakes were volcanoes once. What a pity we can't just make one of them erupt . . . I mean, hot lava would do the trick, wouldn't it?"

Tryan and Elyssa exchanged a glance before answering. "I imagine it would do the trick very nicely. How do you expect us to accomplish it?"

The former duke shrugged, looking around the room at the Tide Lords and treated them to an ingenuous smile. "I was speaking hypothetically, of course. A fortuitous volcanic eruption controlled enough not to destroy us while saving Caelum from invasion, and yet powerful enough to facilitate our own invasion of Glaeba would be so unlikely it would almost make one believe in the Tide Lords."

"Be careful what you wish for, your grace," Elyssa warned with a thin smile as she rose to her feet. "Are we done here? I have something to take care of."

Tryan shrugged. "Do whatever you want. Desean and I will be going over the Glaeban defences for the rest of the morning. It'll bore you to tears, I'm sure."

"Then I'll see you later. Come, Cecil, let's go visit our babies." Warlock—or Cecil as he was known to the immortals—stepped forward at her command. Stellan marvelled at the big canine's patience, amazed that he'd not given himself away, even for a moment, the whole time he'd been here in Caelum. Elyssa nodded in Syrolee and Engarhod's direction. "Mother. Engarhod."

"Given that we're about to go to war, my dear," Syrolee said with a displeased frown, "I'd think you'd be able to find more useful ways of spending your time than playing with a litter of wretched Crasii pups."

Elyssa ignored the aside, turning on her heel to head for the door with Warlock obediently at heel. Stellan watched them leave, noted the simmering anger brewing in the eyes of the canine slave, and wondered how long it would be before the Cabal's Scard spy posing as a loyal Crasii finally snapped and brought them all undone.

Chapter 4

The grand entrance to the ice palace was a marvel of both architecture and magic. Tide-wrought beams constructed of translucent ice held up a vaulted ceiling, which was all but lost in the faint fog that lingered in the shadowed nooks and crannies of the vast building. The floors were darker, made of a substance that looked like granite, but proved, on closer inspection, to be polished permafrost. The temperature was warmer here in the main hall than outside—mostly because of the re-duced wind-chill—but that didn't seem to bring any comfort to the Crasii slaves who hurried to attend them. They were rugged up against the cold in furs and thick, sheepskin-lined boots, carrying trays with steaming cups of mulled wine for their masters. Declan accepted a cup and sipped it distractedly. His mind was on other things.

Maralyce's arrival in Jelidia worried Declan a great deal. His great-grandmother was not, in his experience, particularly interested in so-cialising with the other immortals. And he was quite certain she hadn't come here just to gawk at Lukys's fabulous ice palace. Her decision to abandon her mountain home in Glaeba and join the others here in Jelidia was as drastic as it was unexpected and, Declan feared, didn't augur well for the future.

Lukys used the excuse of seeing his guest settled to escape with Maralyce in almost indecent haste after they returned from the coast, leaving Declan staring at the others, wondering what the Tides was go-ing on.

Apparently he wasn't the only one finding that Maralyce's arrival was cause for concern. Taryx had wandered off on his own business, while Kentravyon had left them some way back on the ice, for reasons he felt no urge to explain. But Arryl was looking as worried as Declan felt.

"Have you considered the possibility, Cayal," Arryl remarked as Lukys and Maralyce, their heads close together in conversation, disappeared down one of the long broad halls of the palace, dwarfed by the majestic size of the building, "that Lukys's agenda is so far removed from what *you* want that he may have no interest in your problems at all?"

Still lost to the melancholy that had gripped him earlier as he had watched the ice disintegrating, Cayal seemed unconcerned about Lukys's motives. He'd said little on the return journey from the coast, other than to greet Maralyce as if he wasn't surprised to see her. He watched her leave with Lukys now, and then glanced at Arryl with a shrug. "What Lukys tells me about the Chaos Crystal makes sense, Arryl. If it focuses the Tide and it's the Tide that makes us immortal, then why shouldn't it be the Tide that unmakes us?"

"Lukys told me he had a way of effectively *putting an end* to an immortal," Declan said, downing the last of his mulled wine before handing the cup back to one of the waiting canine slaves hovering about. "I might be splitting hairs, but Arryl's right. He didn't actually say he could kill one."

Cayal glared at him for a moment and then stalked off without saying a word.

Declan looked to Arryl. "Was it something I said?"

"He doesn't want to hear you questioning the possibility that he might die soon."

"Do *you* want to die?" Declan asked, wondering why more of the immortals weren't afflicted with Cayal's particular form of madness.

"I get bored sometimes," Arryl said. "We all do. But I haven't run out of things to do yet."

"Cayal has."

"No," Arryl said. "Cayal wants to die because he's afraid he *might* run out of things to do, not because it's already happened."

"He should just do what I do," Pellys said, coming up behind them. "Make the memories go away." He'd been perched on one of the palace's many tall, thin spires when they arrived, something he seemed to do a lot lately. Declan looked over his shoulder to find Pellys walking toward them from the entrance, holding what looked like Kentravyon's incomplete carving, but that wasn't possible because the madman had tossed his handiwork into the sea before they headed for home several hours ago.

"What's that you have there, Pellys?" Declan asked. The Tide Lord was covered with a thin layer of snow and ice. Declan wondered if that meant he'd simply taken a dive off the tower, rather than climb down. If one didn't mind a short period of intense pain while one's broken bones healed, it was certainly the quickest way down.

"Kentravyon made it for me. He says it's the face of God."

Declan stared at the ice carving, shocked to realise it wasn't a human face but a perfectly formed skull constructed of ice. It was a little disturbing to think that was how Kentravyon saw himself.

"Do you recall anything about the time before you lost your memories, Pellys?" Arryl asked.

Pellys shook his head, studying the carving with great interest. "No. I mean, I *know* there was a time before then. But I don't remember any of it. So I must have started again. Cayal could do that. Then he'd be happy."

"I think there's the minor issue of causing a global catastrophe in the process," Declan reminded him. "Didn't you sink Magreth into the ocean when you lost your head?"

The Tide Lord shrugged. "That's the price you pay for peace."

"You call that peace?" Declan asked. "A lot of innocent people paid for your peace, Pellys, not you."

"And what if they did?" Pellys replied unapologetically. "Mortals are going to die anyway, Declan. I mean, it's not as if we're doing much more than giving nature a bit of a hurry-on." He put the skull in his pocket and smiled at them. "I like to watch things die."

Declan was chilled by Pellys's cheerful homicidal-mania. And anxious to be gone from it. He never knew what to say to Pellys. "I think I'm going to find Maralyce and ask what she's doing here."

"If she'll speak to you," Pellys warned. "She's a crabby old bitch."

"She'll speak to me," Declan said. "I'm family."

It proved harder to locate Maralyce than Declan anticipated. Although they had only left the main hall a few minutes ago, neither his father nor his great-grandmother was anywhere to be found when Declan went looking for them. Declan baulked when he thought of them as his relatives. Arguably, Lukys was older than Maralyce, but when one was talking of life spans that crossed millennia, he supposed one's chronological age wasn't really a consideration.

He'd expected to find Maralyce with Lukys in the expansive wing where the guest suites were located. However, he could find nobody in the cavernous white halls but the Crasii slaves brought here by Lukys to keep the palace running.

It was Jojo who finally located his great-grandmother for him. Although Declan could feel the others on the Tide, with so many of them gathered in the one place, he lacked the experience to sort one from another, or even determine the exact direction from where the sense of them was coming. Jojo, with her ability to sense a Tide Lord from across a room and her sharp feline sense of smell, was able to pinpoint the direction and informed him there were two immortals in the lower levels of the palace, somewhere to the east of where they were currently standing in the palace's massive entrance hall.

Declan ordered her to stay put and headed through the ice-carved halls, with their fanciful arches and impossibly beautiful polished-ice walls, into the lower levels of the ice palace, which he assumed was where the palace storerooms were located.

The labyrinthine underbelly of the ice palace was much more functional than the upper chambers, which seemed designed simply to overawe. The walls were much less polished down here and behind each burning torch a small hollow had formed in the wall where the flames had melted the ice. Every few feet, beneath each torch, was a cascade of frozen droplets forming a decorative frieze as the melting ice re-froze once the droplets had escaped the heat of the flames.

From the moment he'd first arrived here at Lukys's palace at the bottom of the world, Declan had wondered at the need for anything so massive. It seemed too pretentious for a man who liked to portray himself as a pragmatist.

Declan took another set of ice-carved stairs downward, the sense of the other two Tide Lords somewhat clearer now that the bulk of the ice forming the upper floors dulled the interference of the others. He followed the torchlit hall for some way, past the storerooms he was expecting. The flickering light reflected off the icy walls in a rainbow of fractured light. All the while Declan could feel the sense of Maralyce and Lukys drawing closer, even though the sensation remained oddly muffled.

And then, at the point where Declan had walked for so long he was starting to wonder if he was even still under the palace, he came to another staircase, glowing with a bright, faintly green-tinged light that seemed to come from everywhere at once.

As soon as he began to descend the wide, curved steps, the sense of the other two Tide Lords became clearer. He headed downward, on a seemingly endless descent, wondering how far below ground he was. Before he saw the other Tide Lords, however, he heard them, their voices funnelled to him with startling clarity by the unique acoustics of the curved stairs.

". . . going to be enough?" he heard Maralyce ask.

Declan stopped. He could feel Lukys and Maralyce on the Tide, but hoped they might be distracted enough by their discussion that they wouldn't notice him.

"It's nearly twice as many as we used last time," he heard Lukys reply.

"What are you talking about?" Maralyce sounded impatient. "The addition of Cayal and Declan isn't going to double the effect. Arryl and Taryx's contribution will be minimal at best. Even together, they won't make up the power of a full Tide Lord. If Medwen and Ambria had come with Arryl, as you claimed they would, then they may have made a difference . . ."

"I did invite them, you know. But they didn't want to join the party."

"They might have," she suggested, "if Cayal hadn't told them he needed their help to die. What was he thinking, telling them that?"

"He wasn't supposed to say anything of the kind," Lukys replied. "We had a very plausible story prepared about me wanting to conduct experiments on the Tide. Apparently, some mortal woman Cayal got involved with back in Glaeba let the cat out of the bag."

Maralyce was silent for a moment. "What are we going to do?"

Declan leaned against the icy, glowing wall, settling in to listen to what should prove a very enlightening conversation. "We need another Tide Lord."

"Then you're really expecting it to work this time?"

"I was thinking of recruiting Elyssa to our cause," Lukys replied, without actually answering Maralyce's question. "Particularly given the news you bring. Or rather, getting Cayal to ask her. She'd not lift a finger to aid you or I, but she'd walk through hell barefoot if she thought it might finally get Cayal into her bed."

"Why not Brynden?"

"Because he's a pompous, self-righteous, pain in the arse," Lukys's disembodied voice replied. "I'm not going to spend eternity listening to him go on and on about what we're doing wrong with our immortality."

"But surely, one of the others—"

"Who? Tryan? Jaxyn?" Lukys cut it. "Tryan's a sadistic narcissist and Jaxyn's a lazy, amoral bastard. Elyssa's a selfish cow, I'll grant you, but she's probably the best of a bad bunch for our purposes."

"I've always considered Elyssa little more than a self-centred child at heart," Maralyce said.

"We're all self-centred children at heart," Lukys said dismissively. "Aren't we, Declan?"

Declan sighed. He should have realised Lukys would know he was there. Pushing off the wall, he continued down the stairs, surprised to find a light ahead of him that seemed much too bright to come from a mere underground storeroom. He took the last few steps two at a time and emerged into a small antechamber that opened up into a vista that took his breath away.

"*Tides . . .*"

It wasn't a room. It was a cavern. Carved from the permafrost beneath the castle, the vast chamber stretched away into the distance, so far Declan was hard-pressed to figure out how far away the opposite wall might be. The massive hall was almost perfectly circular, the curved and ribbed walls nearly fifty feet high, lit by a ring of fire that seemed to be burning the very ice itself as fuel. At the very centre of the room there was a raised circular platform made of solid ice. Other than that, the immense chamber was empty.

Declan stopped and stared, his jaw slack.

After a moment, he turned from the remarkable sight before him and glanced to his right where Lukys and Maralyce were standing, just inside the entrance to the cavern. "What is this place?"

"My cellar," his father said, looking a little smug. "Impressive, don't you think?"

"What's fuelling the fires?"

"Methane trapped under the permafrost," Lukys said. "We hit a pocket when we were digging out the chamber." His father smiled. "Taryx blew his arm off when we stumbled over it, in fact. Put him out of action for days. It's contained now, of course, but there's probably enough gas trapped under the ice here to blow the arse out of Jelidia, if it escaped."

"So you set fire to it, naturally." Declan frowned. This is what being immortal did to you, he supposed. You spoke of catastrophic danger to every life on Amyrantha in vague, general terms, with no thought or care for the consequences to mortal existence. He was learning, however, that there was little use in pointing that out. "Where's the light on the stairs coming from?"

"It's a naturally luminescent moss," Maralyce explained. "It normally grows in some very dark and watery places. Lukys . . . encouraged it to grow here on the ice."

"Using magic?"

"No, Declan," Lukys said, a little impatiently. "I sat down and held a meaningful dialogue with it, and won over the entire species with the strength of my charming personality."

Declan turned to stare in awe at the chamber once more. "What's it for?"

Neither Maralyce nor Lukys answered him. He glanced over his shoulder at them. "Oh, come on, you know I overheard enough to realise you're up to *something*."

They glanced at each other before Maralyce answered his question. "When we activate the Chaos Crystal, it will open a portal to another world." He stepped forward, opening his arms wide. "This is where we'll do it."

Declan studied his father and great-grandmother for a moment, as something dawned on him that he probably should have questioned sooner. "Just exactly how old are you two?"

"Older than you can imagine," Lukys conceded.

"So you didn't become immortal when that meteor hit the ship near Jelidia, did you?"

Lukys shook his head. "No. Engarhod did, though. That part of the story is true enough. As is the story about the fire that destroyed the brothel in Cuttlefish Bay where Syrolee worked."

"And how did Engarhod become immortal? Is he another one of your random offspring?"

His father smiled. "Tides, I hope not."

"What makes *you* unique, Declan," Maralyce said, in a somewhat more conciliatory tone, "is that we can trace your ancestry back to the immortals who spawned you. But you're the exception, rather than the rule. There have been immortals out among the mortal population spreading their seed for thousands of years. The circumstances that give rise to a potential immortal are unlikely, but by no means improbable."

Declan frowned as another thought occurred to him. "That means there's a fair chance we're all related in some way," he said.

Lukys smiled widely. "Imagine that—Cayal might be your brother."

Declan had no desire to contemplate such an unsettling notion. He wanted answers to other questions. Answers he'd come to Jelidia to find. "So you find this crystal of yours, wait until the Tide peaks, step through to another world, killing Cayal in the process. Why? What's wrong with this world?"

"It's getting a little crowded," Lukys said.

"What's the real reason?"

Lukys smiled, but it was Maralyce who answered him. "There's quite a few more immortals on this world than is comfortable to co-exist with," she said. "And this lot in particular are somewhat . . . difficult."

"You mean Cataclysms *aren't* the norm among your kind?"

Lukys looked at Maralyce. "He gets the sarcasm from your side of the family, I think."

"And the brains," Maralyce shot back without even cracking a smile. "The stubbornness, however, is all yours."

Declan ignored their asides, determined not to be distracted from his purpose. Time was ticking on, the Tide was peaking, and he still had no real idea until now—when he'd stepped into this hidden fiery chamber beneath the palace—how Lukys intended to kill an immortal, other than his vague assurances that he could. "I don't believe the 'too many immortals here for comfort' excuse."

Lukys looked at him for a moment, as if debating something, and then shrugged. "It's time, Declan, that's why. We get one Tide in a hundred thousand years strong enough to power the Chaos Crystal. That Tide is on the way and if we don't leave, that's another thousand millennia on Amyrantha, with the likes of Syrolee reducing civilisation to rubble every time the Tide peaks."

"And what happens to the people of Amyrantha?"

"They get to be rid of at least half of us. Isn't that what the Cabal's been working toward all these years? Isn't it why *you're* here, pretending you care, when we all know you'd love nothing more than to see the end of every immortal you've ever encountered?"

Declan frowned. It was a little disturbing to think Lukys could read him so easily. "Suppose I don't want to go to this new world of yours?"

"Then stay here," Lukys said, unconcerned, the firelight on his face giving it a demonic cast that Declan thought quite appropriate. "Remain here and live happily ever after, for all I care. This is a one-way trip, son; we're taking the crystal with us. It'll be the only chance you'll ever have to leave here. As for what happens on Amyrantha, well . . . it won't be our concern once we're gone."

"Why are you so certain opening the portal will kill Cayal?"

"Because," Maralyce said, "he'll be holding the crystal when we focus the Tide."

Chapter 5

"You know, Chikita, this just might work."

"Yes, Lord Jaxyn. It's a brilliant strategy."

Jaxyn Aranville glanced behind him at the small ginger feline Crasii standing guard, something she was managing to do while standing close to the roaring fire, rather than near the lord for whose safety she was responsible. He didn't begrudge her the warmth. The council chamber was a cavernous room, almost impossible to heat effectively, and he didn't want her reactions dulled by the cold.

He didn't care much about her opinion. And, being Crasii, she didn't have any choice but to agree with him, anyway. Jaxyn still liked to hear her say it, though.

"Tell me how clever I am, kitten."

"You are the most brilliant military strategist who ever lived, my lord," the Crasii dutifully assured him, although she sounded less than convincing. Perhaps it was because she was following instructions. Or maybe her Crasii brain didn't really appreciate what he'd devised. Perhaps she lacked the intelligence to understand his genius.

And his plan *was* pure genius. For the first time in living memory the Great Lakes were frozen and any day now the invasion of Caelum could begin. Jaxyn leaned back in the king's throne he'd commandeered and studied the battle plans laid out on the council chamber's long polished table, well pleased with his efforts.

He'd solved the problem of what to do with the tender feet of the feline Crasii who made up the bulk of his attack force. He'd gathered enough troops at the various staging points he'd selected without raising the alarm in Caelum. By choosing major ports that were currently idle because of the ice, he'd managed to keep the Caelish believing his invasion force was stranded by the big freeze. The only thing holding up his conquest of the neighbouring kingdom was the last shipment of sheepskin boots he'd ordered from Tenacia. He'd had word the freighter carrying the boots had already docked at Solmain. Now it was just a matter of waiting for the cargo to arrive overland from the coast. It would take a good two weeks for the boots to get here, which meant for the first time in weeks Jaxyn had time to deal with a few other pressing issues he'd had to delay attending to until now.

"Getting a little ahead of yourself, aren't you, darling?"

Jaxyn glanced up to find Lyna standing by the chamber door. Rugged up in furs against the bitter cold, the tall, dark-haired immortal was posing as his fiancée and distant cousin, Lady Aleena Aranville. But there was little love lost between Jaxyn and his future bride. Theirs was an alliance of convenience that had nothing to do with trust and everything to do with avarice.

"What are you talking about?"

"You're sitting on the king's throne. Have you finally got rid of the irritating boy, or are you just trying it on for size?"

Jaxyn rose to his feet, in no mood to play Lyna's games. He eyed her fur cloak and raised a questioning brow. "What's with the bearskin? Surely you're not feeling the cold?"

"Of course not," she said, shrugging off the thick white cloak and draping it over one of the chairs at the other end of the table. "It's just everyone else is wandering around Herino like their balls are frozen solid. It looks a bit odd if we're dressed for a summery turn along the lakeshore." She walked the length of the long table in the centre of the hall, studying the diagrams and plans laid out on its surface as she walked. "Is it your doing?"

"Is what my doing?"

"This weather?" she asked. "Have you had a hand in this astonishing cold snap, or is it just coincidence that the day you decide to invade Caelum by marching across the ice, the Great Lakes conveniently freeze for the first time in living memory?"

Jaxyn smiled. "Don't you just love serendipity?"

"It's a risk, isn't it?"

"Not particularly," he said. "I haven't altered the weather. Just . . . encouraged it a bit. And it didn't need much. I've never felt the Tide rushing in like this before."

"I *meant* what if the others had felt you working the Tide?" she said, glancing up from the table. "Won't Tryan or Elyssa have felt what you were doing?"

He shook his head. "It was done in the smallest increments I could manage over a period of several weeks. I was very careful. They wouldn't have noticed a thing."

She smiled humourlessly. "Well, aren't you the clever one?"

"I'm glad you're starting to appreciate that."

"Will you win?"

"Of course."

"And what will you do with the others when victory is yours? Once you've taken the Caelish throne and murdered your old boyfriend. I mean, I assume that's what this . . ." she waved a hand to encompass the plans laid out on the council chamber table, ". . . is all about. You, getting back at your old boyfriend for making you look a fool."

Jaxyn scowled at her. "This is about securing a comfortable place to see out the next High Tide. If you don't like it, find someone else to sponge off."

Lyna smiled apologetically. "Now, now, dear, let's not be snippy. I was just wondering what will happen when we win, that's all. Syrolee's not going to hand over the kingdom she's earmarked for her new empire without putting up a fight. So you must have something to offer her that will make them back off. I mean, if it comes down to it, Tryan and Elyssa could wipe the floor with you, darling, if they combine their power once the Tide has peaked."

Jaxyn knew that. He also hadn't quite figured out the solution to that minor but important detail. He did not intend to let Lyna know that, however.

"There's no need for you to concern yourself with that," he told her. "If, and when, your input is required, I'll let you know. Are you packed?"

"Ah . . ." Lyna said, a little sheepishly. "About this trip to Lebec . . ."

"You're coming with me, Lyna. Don't bother trying to wheedle your way out of it."

"But why?" she asked, with a petulant scowl. "There's nothing to do in Lebec. The weather's awful. It rains all the time . . ."

"Lebec is two days north of us," he said. "The weather is exactly the same as here in Herino. And if you think for a moment that I'm leaving you here in Herino with Diala so the two of you can plot behind my back, you've another think coming. Besides, you're my betrothed. It would look odd if you didn't accompany me to Lebec."

"And what am I supposed to do while you survey your ducal holdings? Hold tea parties for the landed gentry?" She rolled her eyes with a heavy sigh. "Tides, you'll be wanting me to socialise with half-wits like Tilly Ponting next."

"Tilly Ponting isn't nearly as stupid as she'd have you believe," he warned, rising to his feet. "And you'd do well to at least pretend to care about the rest of the *landed gentry*, as you call them, until the Tide's high enough that it doesn't matter."

Lyna glared at him unhappily, then after a moment she shrugged. "I suppose. What are you going to do?"

"See to the estate. And to some other business in Lebec that I haven't had time to attend to until now."

"You mean your precious little deposed duchess, don't you?" Lyna asked with a sly smile. "The one I brought back from Senestra. She's a feisty little thing. Do you think the wait has softened her up at all?"

Jaxyn turned to the large map detailing his invasion plans that was laid out on the table and began to roll it up. "She's probably thought of nothing else but what I might be planning to do to her since she was confined in Lebec Prison. The wait may not have softened her . . ." He smiled wistfully for a moment. "It might well have driven her mad."

"You're such an evil little prick, Jaxyn."

He smiled even more broadly. Coming from Lyna, that was probably a compliment. "I have my moments."

"And what *are* you planning to do to her, now you've got her in your clutches? I can't believe you're going to take to her with a lash and a red-hot poker. You're long past getting a kick out of watching something suffer mere physical torment. Your tastes are much more sophisticated these days."

"I'm going to use her to bring Stellan to heel," he said.

Lyna smiled at him in a way he didn't much care for. "Ah, yes . . . It all gets back to the boyfriend, doesn't it?"

"The *boyfriend*, as you insist on referring to the traitor Stellan Desean, is currently residing in the palace of a foreign queen, urging her to invade us, so he can take the crown of Glaeba from its legally appointed heir."

"Unlike you," she said, trailing her finger along the table as she approached him, "who's currently planning to invade a foreign power so he can take the thrones of both Caelum *and* Glaeba from their legally appointed heirs and then appoint himself king of the whole blessed continent."

Jaxyn wasn't fooled by her scolding tone. "And the only reason you're striding the halls of this palace in all that finery and a snow-bear fur cloak, my dear, is because you're quite happy to go along with it," he pointed out, securing the map with a length of red ribbon.

"I didn't say I disapproved, darling," she said, leaning forward to kiss his cheek. "I just think I'm going to be bored witless in Lebec."

"Deal with it, Lyna. You're coming with me."

"Can I watch you interrogate the duchess?"

"No."

"Afraid I might be jealous?"

"More afraid you'll get in the way, actually."

"Will you tell me about it? *All* about it. I'll want every tiny little detail."

He sighed. "If that's what it takes to keep you hosting tea parties for the landed gentry, Lyna, then yes. I'll tell you every tiny little detail."

She took a step back from him. "Well, I'd better get packing then. When do we leave?"

"Tomorrow at first light."

"I'll be there," she promised. "And if you promise me at least one visit to watch you working on your little duchess, I'll even try to pretend I'm thrilled to be there."

Jaxyn wasn't amused by her attempts to manipulate him, but there probably wasn't any harm to be done by letting Lyna visit Arkady once. "We'll see," he told her, not quite prepared to commit to anything just yet.

"We will indeed," she agreed, before turning on her heel and flouncing out of the council chamber, stopping only long enough to retrieve her white snow-bear cloak on the way out. Jaxyn watched her leave and then turned to Chikita. Like the well-trained Crasii she was, the feline hadn't moved a muscle during the whole conversation, although noticing where she was now standing, Jaxyn did wonder if she'd been inching her way closer to the fire.

"Take this map to my office," he ordered, pulling a chain from around his neck from which a small key dangled. "Make sure it's locked in the cabinet, and then return the key to me. I'll be in the king's parlour."

Chikita took the map and the key and bowed low to her master. "To serve you is the reason I breathe," she said.

Damn right it is, Jaxyn thought. *And the world would be a much happier place if everyone on Amyrantha thought the same.*

Chapter 6

Lukys walked a little further into the fabulous ice chamber, admiring his own handiwork. He seemed inordinately pleased with himself.

Declan stared at his father's back, a little surprised. He wasn't sure what he was expecting, but it seemed wrong that all this effort had been expended to kill an immortal if all it would take for him to die was to have him holding a lump of rock at the critical moment. "Cayal will be *holding* the crystal?"

"Focusing the Tide into the Chaos Crystal is a tricky business," Maralyce said stepping up beside Declan. "You can't just lay it on the ground and hope for the best. It needs something organic holding it in place."

"Otherwise the magic just . . . bounces off," Lukys said, squatting down to examine some minute flaw in the ice cavern's polished surface that only he could see. He studied the ice for a moment and then rose to his feet. Declan couldn't help the feeling "bounces off" was not what Lukys originally intended to say.

Lukys looked around with satisfaction and then turned to Declan. "The ice walls should keep the magic contained and channel it back where it's needed."

Declan felt as if he was starting to get some hint of the bigger picture. "That's why you built yourself a palace here in Jelidia, isn't it?" he said. "It wasn't because you liked the idea of living at the bottom of the world in regal but isolated splendour. You needed to cover this up. You had to do something with all the ice you cut out of this chamber."

"He doesn't miss much, does he?" Lukys remarked to Maralyce.

"I did try to warn you," his great-grandmother replied. Declan wouldn't have bet money on it, but for once she sounded almost proud of him.

"Do the others know about this?" he asked.

"Kentravyon does," Lukys said. "He helped me build the chamber. And of course, Taryx, who disposed of all the ice we hollowed out, in a very aesthetically pleasing way, I have to admit. As for the others—well, we haven't really felt the need to involve anybody else at this stage."

"Were Kentravyon and Taryx around the last time you tried this?"

Lukys nodded, slipping his hands in the pocket of his vest. It was so cold in the chamber their breath frosted with every word. But Lukys was dressed in a plain white shirt, a simple knitted vest and linen trousers with sandals on his feet, which would have stuck to the ice had he tried to walk on it barefoot. "Kentravyon is one of the original immortals. Pellys, too, but I'm not sure he still has the ability to concentrate enough to be of use."

Declan wasn't sure how much of this he believed, but it seemed foolish to waste such an opportunity when Maralyce and Lukys were feeling so garrulous. He pointed to the platform in the centre of the chamber. "So this is where we put Cayal and the Chaos Crystal when we find it? On that? And then what? We all stand around chanting until Cayal explodes, opening a gateway to this other world you're planning to escape to?"

Lukys smiled, turning to glance at the altar. "Near enough. Of course, we have to find the crystal first. Or at least retrieve it. Which, thanks to my dear, dear friend, Maralyce, may happen sooner than we'd hoped."

Declan turned from the distracting vista of the chamber to look at his great-grandmother. This is what he'd come here to find out. Why she'd come here. Why she'd leave Glaeba, abandon her mine. "You've found it?"

"If only I had," she said with a sigh. "Alas, nobody has found it yet. But it seems Elyssa might know where it is. According to my spies, she's managed to get her hands on an original Lore Tarot."

"The one Taryx was talking about?" Declan asked, a sudden wave of guilt washing over him. His responsibilities to the Cabal of the Tarot were a burden that grew increasingly heavy, made worse by the fact that despite his noble intentions, he'd learned almost nothing useful since coming to Jelidia, except how to better control the magical Tide. Even now, standing here in the chamber where Lukys intended to kill Cayal, with his father actually explaining the details, Declan realised he was none the wiser.

And when did Maralyce acquire spies?

"When the Cabal stole the crystal from us," Lukys said, resuming his inspection of the floor. Declan supposed he was looking for cracks. He really wasn't sure. "They drew a map of where they hid it and then buried the map within the Lore Tarot so only a few key members of the

Pentangle would know about it. And then they copied the Lore Tarot, both correctly and incorrectly, and spread it around like chicken feed, to further confuse the issue." Lukys squatted down again, brushed away a speck too small for Declan to see from this distance, and then rose to his feet and resumed his walk toward the altar, his head bent as he studied the floor while he walked.

"Is that why you joined the Cabal?" Declan called after him, his voice echoing off the walls, thinking of a meeting held long ago around Tilly Ponting's table in Herino, where this man had sat there and pretended he was just as desperate to find a way to kill an immortal as they were.

"Partly," Lukys called back. He looked up, smiling. "But mostly, I have to say, because it was rather fun, Declan. I quite liked being Ryda Tarek, respected gem merchant from Stevania, noble member of the Cabal of the Tarot. It was almost as much fun as when Cayal and I joined the Holy Warriors."

Had he been closer, Declan might have been tempted to slap that smug look off his face. He wanted to rail at every member of the Cabal for being such fools and allowing themselves to be taken in by Lukys. The Tide Lord turned back to his inspection of the floor, moving farther and farther away from Declan. Suspecting Lukys had lost interest in explaining anything further, Declan turned to Maralyce. "How do you know Elyssa has the map?"

"You'd be surprised what I know."

"Nothing would surprise me about you, Granny," he said. "But how do you know she has the map?"

Maralyce looked as if she wasn't going to answer him, and then shrugged. "I think I've mentioned before what a remarkable source of intelligence Clyden's Inn can be. It's a favourite meeting spot for the Cabal's spies, and young Lord Aleki Ponting, righteous freedom fighter for the cause, seems to labour under the misapprehension that it's a safe place to do business. I overheard one of his men reporting to him. Apparently, your Cabal has a Scard in Elyssa's service. He's the one who passed the information on to the Cabal." And then she frowned, putting her hands on her hips. "And if you ever call me granny again, my lad, I will make you sorry you ever drew your first breath."

Declan bit back a smile. He wasn't sure what Maralyce had in mind, but if looks could kill . . . well, it was a good thing he was immortal.

"Do the Cabal realise the significance of what she's found?" Declan asked. He knew the Lore Tarot was important, but the knowledge that it contained a map of the location of the Chaos Crystal was lost to history. Certainly, the idea that the Chaos Crystal was the key to getting rid of the immortals would come as news to them.

Assuming he could find a way to get word to them from this isolated palace.

"I doubt it," Maralyce said. "In fact, when he was reporting it, your Cabal fellow seemed to think it quite secondary in importance to his other news."

"What other news?" Declan asked.

"It was about your friend," Maralyce informed him, with no inkling, Declan decided later, of the blow she was about to deliver. "The one Cayal brought to my claim after he escaped the Glaebans. Arkady . . . whatever her name was . . . You know, Stellan's wife? The pretty duchess?"

It was a good thing he *couldn't* die at that moment, Declan thought, because he suspected his heart had stopped beating. "Yes, I know who you mean."

"She was captured in Senestra, it seems, a couple of months ago. I'm not sure what you said to him after I left, but Stellan Desean has been very busy since he left my claim. He's turned traitor to Glaeba and is now aiding the Caelish, last I heard, which means he's allied himself with Syrolee and her clan. The consensus seems to be that King Mathu—and by that, I suppose I really mean Jaxyn and Diala—will try to use Stellan's wife as leverage to make her husband back down."

Declan stared at her in shock. "Jaxyn has Arkady?"

"So I believe."

"Where is she?"

"Residing in Lebec Prison awaiting trial, as I understand it."

Declan felt the bottom dropping out of his world. *Tides. This is my fault. I should never have left her. I should have insisted we stay in Port Traeker until we'd tracked her down. I should never have left the Outpost with Arkady still angry with me . . .*

"Declan?" Lukys called. "Come here. I want to show you something."

"I have to leave," he said with a shake of his head.

"Leave? And go where?"

Declan glanced at Maralyce who seemed to understand his haste, before he turned to Lukys and called, "I have to go back to Glaeba." And then he added in a voice meant for nobody but himself, "I have to go to Arkady."

Chapter 7

Arkady wasn't surprised when Jaxyn came to visit, only that he'd taken as long as he did to get around to her. It seemed the pressures of stealing a crown were more important than tormenting an old adversary. That, or he was hoping to sharpen her fear by making her chew her insides out with anticipation before he got there.

She spent nearly two weeks doing just that, although it wasn't herself for whom Arkady feared. Jaxyn was far too sophisticated to gain pleasure from simple torments, so she doubted he would arrive with a branding iron or a handful of wood-slivers to insert under her fingernails.

Physically torturing Arkady would be much too easy for a world-weary Tide Lord. Her pain would offer no challenge to him at all. And when all was said and done, Arkady wasn't even sure torturing her was Jaxyn's ultimate goal any longer. With Stellan raising an army against him, Arkady knew she had other uses now. She had value beyond that of a means for slaking Jaxyn's jaded palate.

The leverage he had over her, Arkady was loath to admit, was her father. It was for that reason he had been moved here, into the cell beside her. Perhaps even the reason they had been given so long alone to make up for lost time. Arkady had grieved for her father and believed him dead. For his torment to affect her now, Arkady had to accept that he was alive. She had to fear his loss, and his humiliation, all over again.

Only then would she truly suffer.

The prospect left Arkady wondering if there was anything she could offer Jaxyn that might encourage him to leave her father alone. She could offer him her body, she supposed, but he may no longer be content with that. And if he was planning to use her against Stellan, he may not even want it.

Besides, how many times could she wriggle out of a sticky situation by letting a man have his way with her? She'd done it to save her father from Fillion Rybank—for all the good it did. She'd have laid down for Stellan in a heartbeat, had he ever asked it of her, to save her father from prison. In fact, the very nature of their arrangement had been that she was meant to provide him with an heir. And in Senestra,

Arkady had offered herself to Cydne Medura with barely a moment's hesitation to save herself from being passed around the crew of a slave ship.

Arkady was quite appalled at the tally, when she thought about it. For a woman who prided herself on her intelligence, who resented any implication that she'd achieved success simply because she was a beautiful woman, or married to a rich and powerful man, she'd acquired a terrible history.

It was time to break the cycle. Arkady was smart, she was a cool head in a crisis and if she couldn't outsmart a wretched immortal, then she didn't deserve to survive.

And she had something Jaxyn might want.

"Could you stop that infernal pacing, Arkady? It's driving me to distraction."

She glanced through the bars at her father, considering him with the cold eye of a woman planning to take down a Tide Lord. "I'm sorry," she said, but she didn't stop pacing. It helped keep her warm, if nothing else. She wore only the shift she'd travelled here from Senestra in, and it was icy in the tower cell where they were incarcerated. This unnaturally cold winter bothered her, but Arkady didn't know if it was normal, the result of the Tide coming in, or something a Tide Lord had caused. She pulled the thin woollen blanket around her shoulders more tightly. "I keep worrying about what will happen when Jaxyn Aranville turns up. The thought doesn't exactly lend itself to peaceful contemplation."

"Perhaps this new Duke of Lebec will be more accommodating than . . . your husband?"

Arkady looked at her father and shook her head in amazement. "I hope you're not trying to be funny, Papa."

Bary climbed slowly to his feet and walked to the bars dividing their cells. Her father walked stiffly these days. He also had the thin blanket from his bed wrapped around his shoulders to ward off the bitter cold. "Stellan Desean has proved himself a liar and a traitor, Arkady. To you *and* to his country. Perhaps the new king has awarded Lebec to a man with some moral fibre. A man we can reason with. Maybe we can even appeal to his better nature."

"Jaxyn doesn't have a better nature, Papa," she told him, a little more harshly than she meant to.

"You don't know that . . ."

"Yes," Arkady said emphatically, "I do." She stopped pacing and turned to look at him. "And before you get too enchanted with the notion of appealing to Jaxyn Aranville for clemency, just remember he was Stellan's lover for over a year before we left for Torlenia. The moment our backs were turned, he lied about every day he spent in Lebec, arranged the death of the King and Queen of Glaeba and had my husband blamed for it."

Her father shook his head in denial. He'd had years to incubate his woes. He blamed Stellan for his predicament, and was unwilling to contemplate any point of view that cast the former Duke of Lebec's actions in a favourable light. "Are you so certain Stellan is innocent?"

Arkady laughed humourlessly and stopped in front of the bars. "Innocent? I've come to the conclusion there is no such thing. But I can promise you he is not a traitor. And if, as the guards are claiming, he's gathering an army to invade Glaeba, you can be sure it's because he believes such an act would be in Glaeba's best interests."

Bary Morel shook his head in puzzlement. "I cannot comprehend your continuing faith in that man, Arkady. After what he did to you, to me . . ."

"You did it to yourself, Papa."

Her father's eyes seemed haunted. "How can you say that?"

"You could have walked away from here seven years ago, a free man. All you had to do was keep your mouth shut and smile approvingly as I married the richest duke in Glaeba. What was so hard about that?"

He stared at her as if she was a stranger. "I cannot believe how cold and hard you have become, Arkady. What happened to you?"

A great many things I have no intention of sharing with my father, Arkady replied silently. It was doubtful he would have heard her reply, even if she had responded aloud. His mind was already made up, the blame placed, and it wasn't anywhere near his own shoulders.

"Desean has done this to you, hasn't he? For that alone, I despise the man."

She was tempted to point out that it wasn't Stellan, but her own father who had driven her to such a pass. Right up until Arkady met the Immortal Prince, every man she'd ever slept with, every move she'd ever made, had been designed to protect her father or his memory. And now, here he was, trying to make her feel guilty for wanting to help him.

Arkady never got a chance to berate him further, however, because at that moment the outer door to their tower cell chamber opened and Jaxyn Aranville walked in.

Jaxyn smiled when he saw Arkady, glancing around approvingly at the rough granite walls. He wouldn't be feeling the bitter cold himself, but he'd know how bad it was for her and her father.

Arkady turned to face him, her arms crossed, clutching the scratchy grey blanket against her body. Bary stepped away from the adjoining bars and also turned to face their visitor, who was accompanied by a single feline Crasii. Arkady thought she looked like the feline Stellan had won in that bear-baiting he'd attended with Mathu and Jaxyn, a lifetime ago, back when Stellan was the Duke of Lebec, Mathu a like-able young prince and Jaxyn just annoying rather than dangerous. The feline took post by the door, her expression inscrutable.

"Your grace," her father began, "it's so good to see you again. If you could—"

"Shut up, fool," Jaxyn ordered, without even glancing in her father's direction. His eyes fixed on Arkady, searching her face for some indica-tion she was near breaking point.

Arkady had no intention of giving him the satisfaction.

"Well," she said as he approached. "If it isn't the legendary Lord of Temperance. I met some of your followers in Senestra, you know. They were a universally dour lot, with no personality and absolutely nothing in the way of charm or charisma. So I guess it's true that like attracts like."

Jaxyn seemed amused. "Ouch! Such cutting insults." He spared her father a look and smiled even wider. "Do you like the gift I left for you?"

"Is that what you call locking my sick father in a bare tower cell in the middle of winter with a single blanket so he can slowly freeze to death? A gift?"

"Absolutely," he said, stopping in front of her cell. "Aren't you grate-ful? I found your most beloved possession for you, Arkady. Brought him back from the dead. You should be weak-kneed with gratitude for my kindness."

"Words fail me," Arkady agreed in a tone that was anything but gracious.

Jaxyn was in a rare good mood and didn't seem to mind her sarcasm. "Who'd have thought Stellan, The Tiresomely Righteous, would lock the poor fellow up and throw away the key?"

"You'd have done the same in his place."

"No, my precious, I wouldn't have. I would have killed your wretched father without hesitation and been done with him. Typical of Stellan, though, don't you think? Even when he's being ruthless, he lacks the balls to go all the way."

"Your grace . . ." her father began again.

Jaxyn raised his arm and her father flew backwards across his cell, slamming into the far wall. With a grunt, he slid down the rough wall, winded and gasping.

Arkady didn't move; didn't react. More than anything, Jaxyn wanted a reaction from her. That was why he was here. She wasn't going to play his game. She squared her shoulders and spoke with all the withering scorn she could muster. "Immortality . . . control of the Tide . . . and the best you can do, Jaxyn, is throw a feeble old man around? Perhaps that's why Cayal is so much more revered than you among the general populace. He, at least, doesn't lack for imagination."

Mention of the Immortal Prince got a response from him. Jaxyn's eyes flashed dangerously for an instant. It wasn't much, and Arkady only noticed it because she was looking for his reaction, but it was there. "You think I care what the unwashed masses think of Cayal?"

"I think it irks the Tide out of you that he's considered a legendary lover and you're worshipped as the god of restraint and self-control."

"I didn't come here to discuss Cayal with you, Arkady." He stepped a little closer to her cell.

Arkady held her ground, resisting the urge to retreat from him. "Really? Then why did you come, Jaxyn? To torture my father? To get at me? I can't imagine why you'd bother. Or that you have the time. Aren't you on the brink of war?" She smiled as another thought occurred to her. "Or do you think you can use me to stall Stellan? You must know by now that he's not the pushover you thought him to be."

Arkady glanced at her aghast father uninterestedly, hoping her apparent lack of concern was believable. "The man who so callously incarcerated a sick old fool to hide a secret about himself, isn't going to stop his plans to take Glaeba's throne just because you're threatening to harm the woman he was pretending to love."

Jaxyn looked at Bary curiously for a moment and then fixed his suspicious gaze on Arkady. He didn't seem to be buying her lack of concern. "I might be interested in discovering how far you'd be willing to go to protect your father."

She shrugged. "If you think I'm going to roll over and die on your command to protect the man whose actions ultimately led me to this sorry pass, you've badly misjudged me as well." And then she added, turning away from him, "Not to mention passing up a chance for some really useful intelligence."

There was a moment's tense silence before Jaxyn took the bait. "What intelligence?"

Arkady let out a sigh of relief she hoped Jaxyn didn't notice. She'd not been sure he'd bite, but it was all she had. Her only way out of here. Her only chance to save her father that didn't involve throwing herself at yet another man.

She turned to face him. "I want your word that I'll be released, as well as my father."

"Your husband is leading an army against Glaeba, Arkady. Even if I was inclined to, I can't just let you walk out of here."

"I know that," she said. "But there's nothing wrong with house arrest. You can confine my father and I to Lebec Palace until the war is done, where we can at least be warm and comfortable. There's no reason for us to be freezing to death here in Lebec Prison while you squabble with the Empress of the Five Realms about who's going to own the continent."

"Is there anything else?"

"A pardon for my father."

"What do you want? Personally?"

"The freedom to leave Glaeba when the war is over. With sufficient means to keep me in the manner to which I was once accustomed."

Jaxyn looked unimpressed by her demands. "If you know something important enough to warrant such a concession, Arkady, why don't I just torture the information out of you now, and have a little fun in the process?"

Arkady took a step closer to the bars. "If you try to harm me or my father, I will kill him and then myself. I learned quite a bit in the slave pens of Senestra, Jaxyn. Don't make the mistake of thinking I lack either the will or the means to do what I threaten."

He studied her in silence for a moment, but Arkady couldn't tell if he believed her or not. Finally he said, "And what do I get in return for this remarkable generosity?"

"In return, I'll give you the information you need to rule the world."

He laughed. "You? You'll give me the chance to rule the world. How?"

Arkady took a deep breath. *Here goes nothing.*

"I can tell you," she said, "where the rest of the Tide Lords are hiding."

Chapter 8

"My lady, did you want help with your packing?"

Arryl looked up from the book she was reading by the glow of a lantern that sprayed a rainbow of light on the wall behind her, thanks to the prism-cut walls of her bedchamber. The chamber was huge, built on the same scale as the rest of the palace, with vaulted ceilings and polished walls and floors, softened by colourful scattered rugs from all over Amyrantha.

"Packing, Tiji? Why would I be packing?"

"Aren't you going with the others, my lady?"

"Going where, dear?"

"To Glaeba?" Tiji said, stepping onto the nearest rug with a frown. It was never a good idea to stand on the ice floors for too long, no matter how thick one's boots were. "Declan is leaving."

"Why?"

"The same old thing."

Arryl smiled and put down her book on the wooden side table beside the elaborately carved bed that Tiji was sure must have been imported from Caelum where such intricate designs were popular. "You know him better than I do, Tiji. Just what constitutes the *same old thing* for Declan Hawkes?"

"The duchess."

Arryl looked at her blankly.

"Arkady Desean."

"The young mortal woman who seems to attract immortals like flies to flypaper? What's she done now?"

"She's been captured by Jaxyn and taken back to Glaeba."

Arryl nodded in understanding. "Ah, and Declan wishes to follow so he can rescue his damsel in distress. You sound as if you don't approve, Tiji."

The little chameleon pulled a face, annoyed Arryl could read her so easily. "He's always getting into trouble because of her. I think he should leave well enough alone."

"But you're afraid he won't?"

"I absolutely know he won't."

The immortal smiled. "And what, Tiji? You want to go along to protect him?"

Tiji wasn't amused by the immortal's patronising tone. "I don't think it's Declan that needs protecting, my lady. It's all the other people they're likely to run across."

"They? What they? I thought you said it was just Declan leaving in search of his damsel in distress?"

"Kentravyon and Cayal are going with him," Tiji told her.

That got Arryl's attention. "*Kentravyon* is going with him?"

"And Cayal. He and Lukys and Maralyce have been arguing about it for hours, but I think Cayal's finally agreed to it."

"What have they been arguing about?"

"I'm not sure. Something to do with Elyssa. I think she has something that will help find this crystal Lukys keeps talking about. Or she knows where it is. Or something like that. I didn't hear all of the argument. Just enough to know I don't like the sound of it."

Arryl rose to her feet and reached for her shawl, which was draped over the arm of her chair. Tiji wondered why she bothered. It wasn't as if she felt the cold in this place, unlike her chameleon servants, who were rugged up so tightly against the cold they could barely walk.

"I think we should have a word to Lukys about this."

"Shouldn't you talk to Declan?"

"Whatever for?"

"So you can tell him not to go. All that ever happens when he gets near that woman is trouble." Tiji felt a little guilty for speaking that way about Arkady. She actually quite liked the former duchess. But she couldn't help the feeling that Arkady was somehow responsible for Declan's immortality even though, logically, she knew that couldn't possibly be the case.

Arryl didn't seem in the least bit bothered about the Duchess of Lebec, however. She had other things to worry about. "Declan can follow his woman to the ends of Amyrantha for all I care, Tiji. It's Kentravyon I'm worried about."

"But, my lady . . ."

Arryl stopped and put a comforting hand on Tiji's shoulder as she passed her on her way to the door. "I sympathise with your fears, Tiji, but Declan Hawkes is not my concern. You have no concept of the trouble Kentravyon can cause."

Without waiting for Tiji to respond, Arryl left the chamber in search of Lukys, leaving the little chameleon standing there wondering if she wouldn't have been better off staying in Senestra and learning to deal with her own kind than foolishly believing she could achieve anything by following a bunch of wretched Tide Lords to Jelidia.

Arryl was only gone for a few moments before Tiji decided to follow her, to hear what she had to say to Lukys. Perhaps, if Arryl could convince Lukys this ill-advised expedition to Glaeba was a bad idea, Declan would rethink his absurd notion about going off in search of Arkady. Tiji's plans hit a snag, however, when she ran into Azquil in the wide hall outside Lukys's chamber.

There were times when Tiji looked at Azquil and felt nothing but gratitude towards the chameleon Crasii who had kidnapped her off the streets of Elvere and brought her back to her own people. There were times when she thought she might burst with the love she felt for him.

And there were times she considered him a blind fool for believing any good could ever come from serving an immortal. Now, was one of those times. Acting just like the good little minion he kept insisting he wasn't, her companion was on his way back to Lady Arryl's room with a fresh set of linens for his mistress's fur-lined bed.

"Tiji? What are you doing?"

"Eavesdropping," she said, inching a little closer to the entrance of Lukys's private chamber. There were no doors in the ice palace, and with a staff of mostly slavishly loyal Crasii to wait on them, the immortals had little need to worry about being overheard.

"You can't eavesdrop on the immortals," Azquil hissed, trying to pull her away.

"Sure I can." She shook him off and moved a little closer to the opening. The air reeked of suzerain, making her want to gag.

". . . sending Kentravyon into the middle of a brewing war is a recipe for disaster," she heard Arryl telling someone. Although she could smell the suzerain, Tiji wasn't sure who else was in the room until she heard Cayal agreeing with Arryl.

"That's what I've been trying to tell them," the Immortal Prince replied.

"I disagree," another female voice said, which Tiji guessed belonged to Maralyce. "To ensure Elyssa's cooperation, you're probably going to need to help her win the war against Jaxyn."

"I don't need Kentravyon for that," Cayal said. "I can beat that little prick with my eyes closed. Who's he got helping him, anyway? *Diala*? She's hardly a threat to a Tide Lord."

"Don't forget Lyna is in Glaeba too," Maralyce said.

"Still nothing and nobody I can't handle on my own. And, I suppose, if worse comes to worst, the Rodent will be there to lend a hand."

"Exactly," Arryl said. "So why are you letting Kentravyon go with them? With the Tide coming in the way it is, the mere presence of that many immortals in one place is likely to cause trouble."

Tiji wasn't sure what Arryl meant by that, but even though she couldn't see him, she could hear the smile in Lukys's voice when he replied. "I do appreciate your confidence in me, Arryl, my dear, but why do you assume for a moment that I have any control over Kentravyon? He's heard Declan is leaving for Glaeba. He knows Elyssa is in Caelum and has the location of the Chaos Crystal. He also knows the only living soul she's likely to give it up to is our very own Immortal Prince. Kentravyon would like to move on, and he trusts neither the suicidally-depressed Cayal nor the dangerously inexperienced Declan Hawkes to retrieve the crystal before the Tide peaks and our chance is lost for another hundred thousand years."

"He thinks he can do better than anyone else, I suppose?"

"The man thinks he's God, Arryl," Maralyce pointed out impatiently. "Of course he thinks he can do it better than anyone else."

The little chameleon smiled. Even to Tiji, that sort of logic, however misguided, made perfectly good sense.

"Come on, Tiji," Azquil urged in a whisper, tugging at her sleeve. "Come away before someone comes out here and catches you spying on them."

She shook him off, anxious to hear the rest of the conversation. A part of her wanted Arryl to convince the other suzerain to stay here in Jelidia. Another part of her wanted Arryl to agree to go with them. If Arryl left the palace, Azquil would want to follow his immortal mistress to Glaeba and Tiji could finally get out of this cold miserable place too.

"Things are unstable enough already. This is going to cause nothing but trouble," Arryl predicted. Although she was inside the chamber where Tiji couldn't see her, there was no mistaking her voice.

"Trouble we won't be around to add to," Lukys replied, in a tone that sounded like a man soothing a skittish horse. "We're not just leaving because we're bored, Arryl. We're doing the mortals of this world a favour. No world can flourish with so many immortals on it, constantly vying for power. You saw that yourself the other day. Look what having this many of us here with the Tide returning is doing to Jelidia."

"Perhaps you should do what Kentravyon suggested to me once," Cayal said. "Each one of you should find your own galaxy to rule."

"Didn't he mean his own *world* to rule?" Arryl asked.

"No. I'm pretty sure he said galaxy."

"Kentravyon's desire to rule a galaxy notwithstanding," Lukys said in an eminently reasonable tone, "it gets down to this: we need the Chaos Crystal. Elyssa has the means to find it. You, Cayal, if you can swallow your pride—and perhaps your gag reflex—have the ability to get the information from her. Declan, for his own reasons—and they're reasons I don't necessarily agree with, I hasten to add—is heading in the same direction. Between the two of you, if you can manage to cooperate, I think you'll find you have the power to rein in Kentravyon's excesses, should he get a little fractious on the way."

"Me and the Rodent?" Cayal said sceptically. "Working in concert? Even if I was willing to do anything in concert again with that insufferable bastard you spawned, Lukys, the last time we iced Kentravyon it took half-a-dozen of us to bring him down."

"It took that many of us to *immobilise* him," Lukys said. "That's not what's needed here. You just need to keep him . . . reasonable. I'm sure you and Declan have enough power between you to be able to curb his enthusiasm if the need arises."

Tiji frowned. Just how powerful *was* Declan, now he was immortal? It was no secret Cayal was among the most powerful Tide Lords to have ever walked Amyrantha. The Great Lakes of Glaeba were testament to that fact. But Kentravyon was not an immortal to be trifled with, either. If Lukys thought Declan and Cayal between them could control the mad Tide Lord, that must mean Declan was either *as* powerful—or even *more* powerful—than Cayal.

Together, the two of them would be unassailable.

Will power corrupt Declan, the way it's corrupted the rest of them? Tiji wondered. *And where does Arkady figure in all this?*

Declan was in love with her. Cayal was obsessed with her. Would she come between them, even if she wasn't actually around, preventing them from controlling a madman's wrath, which could easily result in the death of millions? Or would the spectre of a mortal woman both men wanted, but neither seemed to be able to hold, actually save humanity from the frightening possibility of the two most powerful Tide Lords on Amyrantha combining their power, which might result in something even worse for the mortals of this world?

"Tiji!" Azquil hissed, tugging her backward much more forcefully than he had the first time. "Come away from there, now!"

"This is going to end badly. You know that, don't you?" Tiji heard Cayal predict, as Azquil decided to take matters into his own hands and physically pull her from the entrance.

For the first time she could remember, Tiji found herself agreeing with Cayal, but if any of the other immortals in the room answered him, Tiji didn't hear them. Azquil, his arm firmly around her waist, dragged her backward, her booted feet sliding on the icy floor as he pulled her away, down the hall toward Arryl's suite.

Tiji wasn't strong enough to fight him, and yelling at him would have given away her presence, so she settled for passive resistance, making him drag her all the way, her arms crossed grumpily, thinking, *This is going to end badly, Azquil. You know that, don't you?*

Chapter 9

"Can you swim, Rodent?"

Declan stood on the edge of the crumbling glacier staring out over the roiling sea and decided not to dignify Cayal's idiotic question with an answer. They were standing on the very edge of Jelidia once more, staring into the setting sun, facing several thousand miles of ocean between the Tide Lords and their destination. Declan had no notion of how they were supposed to cross the ocean to reach Glaeba on the other side of the world in the opposite hemisphere. There was no ship waiting at anchor for them. The vessel they'd commandeered in Port Traeker to bring them here was long gone, and it was too early in the year to flag down a passing fishing vessel, even if the likelihood of chancing across such a ship wasn't such a remote possibility. Nonetheless, Declan was quite certain they weren't standing here for the good of their health.

One way or another, Declan figured, either Cayal or Kentravyon had a way of crossing the ocean. He sincerely hoped they weren't planning to do it the same way Maralyce had arrived from Glaeba.

At the sound of an agonised yelp, he looked over his shoulder to see what Kentravyon was doing. To his disgust, the immortal was working his way down the line of dogs that had so diligently pulled their sled to the coast, breaking their necks as he went, leaving them lying on the ice, still in their harnesses.

"Is it really necessary for him to be so . . . enthusiastic about it?"

"You'd rather we left them here to starve after we're gone?" Cayal said beside him, apparently unaffected by Kentravyon's grisly task.

"Maybe we *should* have just let them go."

"And they'd still starve, or fall down a crevasse and break something only to suffer a slow painful death over several days. Or they'll hang around the coast in the hope of finding fish to eat and be taken by a sea lion. Tides, Rodent, and you accuse *us* of lacking compassion." Cayal turned, heading back to where Kentravyon was killing the last of the dogs. Declan winced again, glad Tiji hadn't come with them. She'd never forgive him for standing by and doing nothing about this. Even worse, she'd be mortified to realise Declan could see the necessity of not leaving the dogs here alone, however distasteful Cayal's logic.

Of course, there was nothing compassionate or humane about the gleam in Kentravyon's eye as he volunteered to do the deed, which was what sickened Declan most.

With some reluctance, Declan followed Cayal back to the sled. He'd wondered why they'd brought it and figured he'd finally find out now the dogs were taken care of. Kentravyon was pulling a large bundle from the sled. He sliced through the ties holding the package and with Cayal's help, unrolled the bundle onto the ice. Declan stared at it for a moment and then looked at the two Tide Lords.

"It's a rug."

"Lukys is right, you know," Cayal said to Kentravyon. "The lad certainly doesn't miss much, does he?"

Declan ignored Cayal, directing his next question to Kentravyon. "We're going on a magic carpet ride, are we?"

"Don't be stupid," Kentravyon said, straightening out the edges. "There's no such thing as a magic carpet."

Declan wasn't sure he believed that. Many nations on Amyrantha had legends of Tide Lords with flying carpets, particularly in the Commonwealth of Elenovia where they had a whole festival devoted to their rug industry and the flying carpets of legend. There was even mention of one in the Tarot somewhere. "What's this then?"

"A carpet," Cayal said. He retrieved his pack from the sled and tossed it onto the rug. "That we're going to ride. Using magic."

"How is that not a magic carpet ride?"

"The carpet is just an ordinary rug," Kentravyon said, tossing his own pack onto the rug before taking a seat on it and crossing his legs. "The Tide is what will move it along. It's that or riding the waves like Maralyce did, which is messy."

"Why messy?" Declan asked, thinking it an odd description. Wet, maybe, or unpleasant, but *messy?*

"Because we're heading toward civilisation," Cayal said. "Not a good idea to make a tidal wave and ride it into a populated region when you're trying to be inconspicuous, Rodent."

The ground rumbled as another chunk of ice broke away from the coastline and splashed into the water far below. "You two coming,"

Kentravyon asked, "or are you just going to stand there admiring the view?"

Cayal needed no further prompting. He sat down on the rug facing Kentravyon, crossed his legs in a similar fashion and then looked over his shoulder at Declan, as he moved his pack around behind him so he could lean against it. "It's this or swim, Rodent."

With a great deal of trepidation, Declan stepped forward and dropped his pack onto the rug. A part of him was fascinated by this mode of transport, another part of him unable to shake the feeling these two were having a wonderful time at his expense. Was this a prank that would follow him into eternity? Would his acceptance of a magic carpet be laughed about for aeons—the brand new, gullible Tide Lord who believed a rug could fly? He sat down facing Cayal and Kentravyon, cross-legged as they were, filled with apprehension.

"What now?"

"Hang on," Kentravyon said.

Before Kentravyon had even finished speaking, Declan was thrown backwards. He felt the surge of the Tide as the rug took off across the ice and sped straight over the edge of the cliff, plummeting towards the ice filled water below. Declan bit back the urge to scream, his senses still not adjusted to the notion that he couldn't die and was in no immediate peril. Cayal and Kentravyon were both grinning at him as they plummeted toward the ocean, either exhilarated by the fall or amused by Declan's reaction it—he wasn't sure which and didn't much care to find out. The ocean rushed toward them, so deep here the water appeared black, soaking up the twilight. At the last minute, and with only inches to spare, the rug levelled out, missing a freshly broken chunk of ice the size of a house by a whisker. Somehow, they stayed above the water, dodging icebergs, skating over the whitecaps as if the ocean was made of glass and the rug a sheet of polished metal skimming downhill over the waves.

Even more miraculously, Declan stayed aboard. The icy spray of the ocean stopped just short of them, hitting an invisible wall and falling away before it could reach them. His skin tingled, a reaction to being in such close proximity to Kentravyon swimming the Tide. Declan guessed he was also using it to protect them from the spray, while propelling the rug over the water at a speed that left him gasping.

Within minutes, the tall, crumbling ice-cliffs of Jelidia were a blur on the horizon, yet the rug stayed flat and dry and after a few moments, Cayal stretched out, using his pack as a pillow.

"Wake me when you want a break," he told Kentravyon, before closing his eyes with his arms folded across his chest. The ocean rushed beneath them silently, not so much as a breath of wind ruffling the hair of the three Tide Lords riding the magically-propelled rug.

The madman nodded and looked at Declan oddly. "*What?*"

"Nothing. I just wasn't expecting—well, this . . ."

"Tides, you didn't think I was going to make it fly, did you?"

"Of course not."

Kentravyon smiled and leaned forward a little. "Do you want to know how to do it?"

"Yes, I would."

"Then do what the rest of us had to do," he said unsympathetically. "Figure it out for yourself."

Declan frowned, but supposed he shouldn't be surprised. Kentravyon wasn't renowned for his social skills. "Does Cayal know how to keep us afloat?"

"Says he does," Kentravyon said with a shrug. "Probably doesn't do as well as me. Nobody is ever as accomplished as God."

Until he made comments like that, it was easy to forget Kentravyon was mad. Declan had his doubts about that. Kentravyon seemed quite rational most of the time. He supposed it came down to one's definition of mad. *Did a man have to be drooling and incomprehensible to be called a lunatic? Or did he just have to believe he was God?*

According to Cayal, Kentravyon's madness resulted from swimming too deep into the Tide, losing himself in it so much that he never really came back. The circumstances of his downfall remained disturbingly vague, leaving Declan with the impression that Cayal hadn't told him the details, not because he was holding back on purpose, but because he simply didn't know himself.

"Are you the best at everything?" Declan asked, figuring it would be safer to broach the subject of his madness in a roundabout fashion.

"Yes, Declan, I am," Kentravyon replied. "That's why I'm God."

"Is there no room for other gods in your pantheon?"

Kentravyon shrugged. "I suppose. Provided they kill me first."

"But you're immortal."

The mad Tide Lord smiled, confirming Declan's suspicion that he wasn't as mad as he liked people to believe. "Well, that takes care of that then, doesn't it?"

Despite himself, Declan smiled. Then he glanced across at Cayal's reclining figure, unsure if the Immortal Prince was really sleeping or just resting with his eyes closed, while listening to their every word. "Do you really think Lukys has found a way to kill a Tide Lord?"

"The others have never come through when we did it before."

That piqued Declan's interest. "The others? What *others*?"

"The immortals we've left behind whenever we cross the rift." Kentravyon rolled his eyes impatiently. "Tides, lad, did you think that with millions of years behind us, and millions more ahead of us, the best the Tide can do is produce immortals the calibre of Engarhod?"

Declan stared at him, a little stunned by the idea. He had enough trouble trying to comprehend the notion that he might live for thousands of years. The realisation that he might one day count his life in a span of millions of years had never even crossed his mind, until now. *Tides, no wonder Cayal is looking for a way to die.*

"Are you telling me that you—and Lukys . . . and Maralyce—that you're *millions* of years old?"

"Who knows?" the madman said with another shrug. "I don't bother keeping count any longer."

"But you came through this rift from another world, didn't you? From a world just like this one?"

"Well, it wasn't *exactly* like this one," Kentravyon said. "Had more water on it, for one thing. And it was warmer. And no people, which was a bit of a bore after a while. We had a few species that were kind of intriguing, but they didn't really live long enough to be useful. Something in the air, Lukys postulated, that kept them dying young. It was very picturesque, though, as I recall. The whole world was like a riotous garden with creatures the size of sailing ships. And they had these really delicious little molluscs you could only find up around the Fianca Inlet—"

"How many worlds have you *actually* been to, Kentravyon?" Declan cut in, fearing he'd lose the madman's attention if he started reminiscing about long forgotten culinary delights.

The older man shrugged. "I don't know. Must be a few. I was just a lad when I was made immortal."

Declan studied him for a moment. He looked to be a man in his early forties. Lukys seemed to be in his late-thirties, Maralyce a woman nearer fifty. Declan had always assumed that was the age they were when they'd been immolated. That the immortals might be ageing, however slowly, was something he'd never considered before.

Declan glanced over at Cayal's reclining figure for a moment. He'd been alive for the better part of eight thousand years and didn't look a day older than he had when he was made immortal at the age of twenty-seven. How long must the others have been alive to have visibly aged?

"Who were the others?"

"What others?"

"The other immortals you left behind when you came through the rift?"

"I don't remember their names."

"Did they really die?" Cayal asked, opening his eyes to look at them. Apparently he'd not been asleep after all.

"I suppose they did. I mean, there wasn't much world left after the rift closed. None of them have ever come after us complaining about it, that's for certain."

Declan frowned, wondering if he'd misheard Kentravyon. "What exactly does 'there wasn't much world left' mean?"

Kentravyon treated Declan to a baleful glare. "What I *said*," he replied, speaking slowly as if Declan was too stupid to understand what he was saying. "It takes a lot of Tide energy to open a rift between worlds, you know. Anything in its wake when it snaps shut is usually destroyed."

Cayal gave up all pretence of being asleep. Rolling onto his side, he pushed himself up on one elbow and stared at Kentravyon. "You mean that's how Lukys is planning to kill me? By destroying Amyrantha?"

"Well, yes, I suppose he is," the Tide Lord told him with a shrug.

Declan was too stunned to speak. And so was Cayal, it seemed, for a moment or two. And then the Immortal Prince lay back down and adjusted the pack he was using as a pillow into a more comfortable position.

"Well," he said, settling himself down. "That explains a few things."

Then he closed his eyes again and said nothing more, leaving Declan staring at Kentravyon, the ocean rushing by beneath their flying carpet, trying to deal with the realisation that he'd discovered what the Cabal had been trying to learn for several thousand years.

He knew the secret of killing an immortal. It wasn't opening a rift that would kill them. It was closing it.

Of course, there was one tiny complication that made the information less than helpful—apparently, it would kill every living soul on Amyrantha if they tried it.

Chapter 10

"They're so pretty."

Boots grimaced at her immortal mistress. Warlock hoped Elyssa would think it a smile. Outside the frosted-over windows, another storm battered the thick stone walls of Caelum Palace. It was warmer inside, but not by much, although naturally the immortals barely noticed the cold. Why else would Elyssa take it into her head to set off on another expedition in this weather?

"Thank you, my lady."

"Are they feeding well?"

"Very well, my lady."

"You'll take good care of them while we're gone, won't you?" They were sitting on a rug on the floor in the centre of the suite of rooms Elyssa had claimed. This outer reception room, being slightly smaller, was a little easier to keep warm. The heavy red drapes helped, as did the thick rugs on the floor, but the furniture was cumbersome and uncomfortable. At least it looked uncomfortable. No canine slave would ever sit in the presence of an immortal to find out. Warlock glanced at Boots with concern. She was trembling, but it had nothing to do with the bitter cold.

Hopefully, the Immortal Maiden didn't realise that and would put Boots's shaking voice down to the temperature.

Boots nodded. "Of course, my lady."

"If they need anything, speak to Lord Stellan. I've asked him to keep an eye on you until I get back. He'll make sure my brothers don't decide to claim you while I'm gone."

She said *brothers* rather than *brother*, which meant Elyssa was referring to her stepbrothers, Krydence and Rance, as well as her blood-brother, Tryan. Warlock wondered if it was a slip of the tongue. Her stepbrothers were here posing as friends of the family, after all, not members of it. Or maybe Elyssa simply didn't care any longer, secure in the knowledge that no Crasii could ever betray her true identity.

"I'll serve Lord Desean as I would you, my lady," Boots promised.

Several days ago Warlock had almost fainted with relief when Elyssa had announced to him that she would entrust the protection of Boots

and the pups to Stellan Desean, as she was leaving to take care of something to do with the defences they'd devised to protect Cycrane from an
invading Glaeban army. Elyssa had made a gift of Boots and the pups to
the Glaeban duke—in quite a showy ceremony—as a token of her thanks
for his help in prosecuting the war against his evil countrymen who had
stolen her precious niece-by-marriage from Caelum.

Her generosity had nothing to do with Stellan, and Elyssa couldn't
have cared less about Nyah. Warlock knew that and so, he suspected,
did Desean. Awarding Boots and the pups to Stellan Desean was meant
purely to stop her brother getting his hands on something she owned
and feared he coveted.

It was no mean feat to convince the Immortal Maiden that the first
thing Tryan would do after they left was claim Boots and drown her
pups as an inconvenient nuisance, mostly because the threat was a complete fabrication. Tryan had lost all interest in Boots and her litter after
Elyssa had claimed them on the Cycrane wharf when they first arrived
in Caelum.

But it served Warlock's purpose to keep Elyssa believing her brother
still had some interest in them, so when Stellan expressed concern for
the pups while Elyssa was away, it had taken very little persuasion to
have the discussion end in the Immortal Maiden granting foster care of
her youngling Crasii to Stellan, in order to protect them.

Even so, it was a very fragile protection Warlock had arranged for
Boots and the pups. If another immortal took it into his head to be rid
of them, neither Stellan Desean nor anybody else on Amyrantha could
stop them. Protecting his family from the immortals wasn't the point,
however. As soon as Warlock and Elyssa were gone from Cycrane—with
the work parties they were sending out to the tar seeps—Stellan had
promised to find a way to get Boots and the pups out of the palace and
back home to Glaeba.

Warlock had no idea how Desean would manage such a feat, given
the lake was frozen and they were on the brink of war. He couldn't afford to dwell on the problem, either. Desean had promised he'd get the
pups and Warlock's mate away from here and that was all that really
mattered.

"You may go now." Elyssa climbed to her feet, dismissing Boots with
a wave of her hand. She turned to Warlock. "You have a few moments

to say goodbye to your mate, Cecil. Take my babies back to the kennels and meet me in the courtyard. I want to get away within the hour."

"To serve you is the reason I breathe," he said, bowing low, before bending down to scoop up the two male pups into his arms. Holding their daughter Missy, Boots stood up, bowed to their mistress too, and then opened the door, anxious to leave Elyssa's chambers before the immortal changed her mind.

As soon as the door closed behind them, they hurried down the hall toward the servants' stairs, saying nothing until they reached the safety of the landing on the floor below.

"How long do you think you'll be gone?" Boots asked in a low urgent voice, stopping to face him.

"Long enough for you to get away from here," he assured her. "Lord Desean knows of a ruin on the lakeshore north of the city. Nobody has been there in years. You'll be safe there until he can find a boat to take you across the lake."

"The lake is frozen solid, Farm Dog," she reminded him, rocking Missy gently to stop her from fretting.

"Then you'll have to wait until I return, and I'll—"

"You mustn't!" she cut in. "Tides, Warlock, if you come looking for us, Elyssa will know something is amiss. You must do as we agreed. Once we're away from here, Lord Desean will tell the suzerain I perished with my pups in the snow. You need to act as if we really *are* dead when you get the news, not come looking for us and give the game away."

Warlock looked down at his sleeping sons in his arms, wishing there was something better he could do to protect them than effectively abandon them in a foreign country. But Boots was right. Stellan Desean could spin a tale about the regrettable death of a few Crasii slaves and nobody would think to doubt his word. This was a one-off chance and he couldn't afford to do anything that might jeopardise his family's safety. He'd done enough of that just by bringing them to Caelum.

"You will be careful, won't you, Boots? I think Desean can be trusted, but there are others—"

She put a finger to his lips, shaking her head. "We'll be fine, Warlock. With the pups away from the suzerain, we have nothing to fear."

"As long as we can *keep* them away from the suzerain."

"Well, that's your job now. If this talisman Elyssa seeks is of any use to the Cabal, maybe we'll live to see an end to the immortals."

Warlock was almost afraid to hope for that, but Boots was right. The Cabal had been very interested to learn that Elyssa was seeking some long-lost Tide Lord talisman. His orders were to stay as close to her as possible, to discover what it was. The upside of his new orders was that everyone seemed to have forgotten about assassinating Stellan Desean. He had no further orders from Jaxyn, either. Perhaps he figured Warlock's value as a spy had been undermined by Elyssa, and had found other ways to make mischief.

Or maybe he had other reasons to keep Stellan alive.

Either way, in less than an hour it would no longer be Warlock's problem. He was heading out of the city with Elyssa, which would give Boots and the pups a chance to get away.

And that, in the end, was all he cared about.

"You will be careful, won't you?" he asked her, searching her face for reassurance. Her big dark eyes were shining, but she was too well practised at hiding her emotions to give much away. "I'll come for you, Boots," he promised. "Someday, when this is over, I'll find you and the pups and we'll make our own Hidden Valley somewhere. We'll find a place where we'll be safe and no suzerain can bring harm to our babies."

She smiled wanly. "You honestly expect me to believe that, don't you?"

"I mean it, Boots."

"I know you do, Warlock," she said, leaning forward to kiss his cheek, her tail wagging gently. "That's what makes you so damned infuriating."

She kissed him again, this time on the mouth, and then relieved him of the pups, somehow managing to hold all three of them safely. Warlock still wasn't sure how she managed that.

"Boots . . . I . . ."

"Go, Farm Dog," Boots said without rancour. The name had long passed from an insult to a term of affection between them. "Go save us from the suzerain."

"Tell my pups about me."

"Tell them yourself," she said. "When you find us again."

Warlock nodded, afraid to say anything more for fear he'd choke on the lump in his throat. He leaned forward, kissed each of the pups in turn, then with a last lingering look at his family, he turned and headed back up the stairs to help Elyssa with the last of the preparations for their journey south to the tar seeps.

Closing his eyes for a moment he took the stairs two at a time, hoping to preserve the image of Boots and his babies in his mind forever.

Chapter 11

By the third day of their magic carpet ride—Declan couldn't help thinking of it as anything else, despite the objections of the other immortals—he felt he'd learned enough to try controlling the Tide by himself. The other Tide Lords, who'd been sharing the duty of keeping the carpet moving and afloat between them, were more than happy to allow him a share of the load.

It proved to be a balancing act, Declan discovered when he tried it; a delicate equilibrium between drawing enough of the Tide to keep them magically skimming the waves at a pace that ate up the miles and protected them from the spray, while not causing anything more than the most local disturbance in the surrounding elements.

Declan was rapidly learning why mastering the Tide was such a hit-and-miss affair, and why each Tide Lord was required to find his own way. Although they were performing the same feat, there were subtle differences between the way Cayal rode the Tide and the way Kentravyon did it. That left Declan wondering whose way he should try—a somewhat problematic decision, given one of them was mad and the other suicidal.

Still, when Cayal offered to let him try, Declan didn't refuse the opportunity. This was a skill worth acquiring, this ability to circumnavigate the globe at speed, and something he was quite sure the Cabal knew nothing of. The histories spoke of Tide Lords wreaking local havoc, it even spoke of magic carpets, but nowhere did the Lore mention that the Tide Lords weren't bound by the rules of mortal men when it came to the speed with which they could cross the world.

Declan's first attempt at keeping them afloat on the Tide resulted in an icy dunking for all three immortals, something neither Cayal nor Kentravyon intended to let him live down any time soon. To add to his woes, Declan had lost his pack in the dunking, although Cayal had somehow managed to hang on to his.

Kentravyon had taken to glaring at him, sitting cross-legged on the now soaking rug, as Declan struggled to master the Tide. This was only slightly less disconcerting than Cayal's constant attempts to interfere, telling Declan to pull this way or that, until he was tempted to dunk them in the water once again, just to shut Cayal up.

"Keep it level," Cayal warned for the thousandth time. Declan wondered how long it would take him to master this flying carpet business enough to tip just the one corner Cayal was sitting on, in the water.

"I *am* keeping it level," Declan said. He'd been at it now for a couple of hours, and was starting to feel like he was getting the hang of it. Of course, the downside was that Declan had never ridden the Tide for so long before. His skin was on fire and he feared that soon he'd be as crazy as Kentravyon from the ridiculous ecstasy of it. He understood now why neither Cayal nor Kentravyon had objected to him learning how to do this. Riding the Tide for extended periods was beyond draining. It left one feeling bereft, ultra-sensitive and more than a little lustful.

And they were still thousands of miles from Glaeba.

"If you manage to keep us heading northeast," Cayal told him several hours later, when Declan was on the point of collapsing from the relentless thrill of the Tide, "we'll be able to make landfall in Stevania tonight."

It was raining heavily, the sky ashen and overcast, and occasionally split by lightning. Falling rain pockmarked the roiling water surrounding them. No raindrops fell on the immortals, however. After a shaky start, Declan had finally figured out how to protect them from the elements just as Kentravyon had done, so they travelled in a bubble of calm through the storm, untouched by its fury.

Cayal seemed to be in a rare good mood, perhaps still riding the exhilaration of the Tide left over from his own stint as their magical guide.

"There's a small settlement on the coast near here named Blackbourn," he explained. "It's not much more than a fishing village really, but it has quite a serviceable brothel staffed by some tireless young ladies who deserve our special attention. A day or two's recuperation there, and we'll be on our way again."

Declan looked at Cayal, wondering. He'd thought he was the only one ready to explode from the aftereffects of this extended journey on the Tide.

Cayal must have guessed the direction of his thoughts. "What, you think it gets better with time?" He shook his head. "It gets predictable, Rodent. It even gets tolerable. But it never gets better."

"Even for someone as old as him?" Declan asked, jerking his head in Kentravyon's direction. The older—perhaps millions of years older—Tide Lord had stretched out on the damp rug. He'd shed his wet clothes and was lying naked on his back, apparently asleep. Given he could have dried his clothes and himself instantly using the Tide, Declan got the feeling Kentravyon was soaking up the ocean's vastness as a reaction to being trapped in the ice for so long.

"He's mad, so I'm not sure his opinion counts."

"And Lukys?"

Cayal shrugged. "What? You think he went out and got himself an energetic young wife just because she can cook?"

Declan frowned. "Tides, here I am thinking you're all bent on ruling the world and it turns out you just want to get laid."

"Disappointing, isn't it?" Cayal looked at Declan for a moment, amused about something. "Didn't you ever wonder how Syrolee and her lot got involved in all this? We immortals spend an inordinate amount of time hanging around brothels, Rodent. In fact, when all is said and done, we're really rather ignoble creatures."

"I had that much worked out a long time ago."

Cayal smiled at his dilemma. "And yet here you are—one of us—riding the Tide as if you've been doing it all your life, and ready to implode from the ecstasy of it all. What a journey you have ahead of you, you unsuspecting fool, trying to reconcile your narrow-minded mortal sensibilities with the reality of your immortal situation."

"I suppose *you* had no trouble at all with adjusting when you were made immortal?"

"I did go through a period of thinking there might be a purpose in my fate. But I never suffered from the delusion that there was anything particularly decent about me," Cayal said, shifting to a more comfortable position. "Tides, by the time I became immortal, I'd already killed my best friend, been dispossessed, exiled, and lost everything I ever owned or loved." The Immortal Prince cocked his head to one side and studied Declan for a moment. "Kind of where you're at right now, isn't it?"

"What makes you so sure I've killed anyone?" Declan asked, not wishing to dwell on what—or who—he might have lost. He wasn't all that enamoured of Cayal pointing out the similarities between them, either.

"Are you kidding? Weren't you the King of Glaeba's Spymaster? I'd be surprised if you'd *only* killed one man."

He had a point, although Declan had no intention of admitting it. "Do we have time," he asked, "to stop along the way?"

"We can keep going without a rest if you want—provided you have a hankering to end up like him," the Immoral Prince said, glancing over at Kentravyon. "Moderation in all things is the key to swimming the Tide and staying sane, Rodent."

"Why do you care?" Declan asked, curious to hear Cayal offer such sage advice. Actually, it seemed strange to hear Cayal offer any advice that wasn't designed to aid his cause in some way. "You'll be dead soon. What difference does it make if the effort of getting you to your goal drives you, or anybody else, crazy?"

"I might go mad and change my mind about wanting to die," Cayal said. "And that *would* be a crazy thing to do."

"Does it bother you that your efforts to die might destroy Amyrantha?"

"No."

Declan found that hard to believe. Of course, given the source of the information, he wasn't certain Kentravyon's prediction about the end of the world deserved any credit, but still . . . it was something to consider. "Are you trying to tell me it doesn't bother you in the slightest that your quest for death may kill millions of people and destroy a whole world in the process?"

"*My* quest for death isn't going to kill anybody," Cayal replied. "According to Kentravyon, Lukys closing his rift is what will do the damage. He's the one who wants to move on. I'm simply going along for the ride. So before you start pointing the finger at me, Rodent, look a bit closer to home. If he's right, then it's *your* father who's planning to destroy Amyrantha, for no better reason, I gather, than he has itchy feet. Worse—if you believe the madman over there—this isn't the first time he's pulled this trick, either." Cayal lay back down on the rug, folding his arms behind his head. "Amyrantha's blood will be on Lukys's hands, not mine, if it goes awry. And yours, too, if you decide to help him."

"If I don't help Lukys open his rift, *you* don't die," Declan pointed out.

Cayal turned his head to stare at Declan, smiling. "And isn't *that* little dilemma just going to eat you up inside until the very end of time? What's a noble man to do, Rodent? Kill the man who stole his woman and then drove her away? A very satisfying act, which might, somewhat inconveniently, destroy the whole world? Or do you refuse to help? Make the bastard who caused you all this grief live forever, and then suffer his presence into eternity, long after Amyrantha is a cold and lifeless rock and Arkady nothing more than a dim and distant memory?"

Declan had no answer to that, because Cayal was right. The choice before him was eating him up, and he had no idea what he was going to do about it.

Chapter 12

"They're here," Arkady said, pointing to the map of Amyrantha Jaxyn had unrolled across the exquisitely carved desk that had once belonged to her husband.

Jaxyn looked at the position on the map she'd indicated for a moment and then looked up, his doubt written clearly on his face. "In Jelidia?"

"Lukys has built a palace down there. It's huge, apparently, and very beautiful, according to Cayal. Taryx helped him build it. Cayal said Pellys calls it the Palace of Impossible Dreams."

"So Pellys is down there too?"

Arkady nodded. "Along with Taryx, Arryl and Kentravyon." She didn't mention Declan. Jaxyn didn't know of Declan's new status as an immortal and she couldn't see any benefit in telling him just yet. Besides, it meant she still had something she could hold back; one last bargaining chip if things went awry.

"What about Medwen and Ambria? Are they still in Senestra?"

Arkady nodded. "How did *you* know they were in Senestra? I thought that was supposed to be a secret?"

"Worst kept secret in history," Jaxyn said with a shrug. "You say Kentravyon's awake again? On purpose?"

Arkady hesitated, wondering if it was really such a good idea giving Jaxyn so much information. And then she thought of her father sleeping in a real bed this night for the first time in over seven years, and the guilt evaporated. She owed the immortals nothing. "Lukys revived him a couple of months before I saw Cayal in Senestra. Cayal says it has something to do with the power needed to help him die once the Tide peaks, but I'm not sure he was entirely convinced of that himself."

Jaxyn leaned back in his seat—the seat that had also been Stellan's—rubbing his chin thoughtfully. Outside, a gentle snow was falling; an unusual event for Lebec at this time of year. But then, the whole country was in the grip of a winter like no other. Arkady had her suspicions about who was responsible for that, too.

"Do you really think Lukys has found a way for Cayal to die?"

"How in the Tides do you expect me to know the answer to a question like that?" Arkady said, stepping back from the desk. It felt so strange to be standing here in the palace again, in Stellan's private sanctuary, with Jaxyn Aranville sitting there, acting as if he owned the place.

Jaxyn smiled. "Fair enough. I wonder what they're really up to down there."

"Here's an idea, Jaxyn. Why don't you abandon your quest for the Glaeban throne, call off the war and go down to Jelidia and ask?"

Jaxyn's smile faded. "You dare a lot, taking that tone with me."

"So kill me. You're going to eventually. Why drag it out?"

He studied her sceptically for a moment. "You don't mean that. I know you, Arkady. You want to live."

"In a world ruled by Tide Lords? Death may be preferable."

"Tides, do you really think we're that bad?"

Arkady took the seat opposite Jaxyn, leaning back in it as if she hadn't a care in the world. It was an act, of course, but Arkady had learned one thing in the past year: men—tyrants—like Jaxyn could smell fear. "So far, Jaxyn, you've murdered the previous King and Queen of Glaeba, accused my husband of the crime, had him stripped of his title and declared a traitor, stolen everything he owned, started a war with our closest ally and arranged to have your minion marry our new king. And that's just been in the last year. How long does a High Tide last? Centuries?"

"And yet here you sit, daring to taunt me. Perhaps you do have a death wish, after all," Jaxyn observed.

She pulled the spotted fur coat she'd been given on leaving Lebec Prison a little tighter around her shoulders. Even with a blazing fire going, it was still freezing in Stellan's study. "You need me, Jaxyn. If not for what I know of Cayal's movements, there's still the chance you can use me to gain leverage over Stellan."

"I'd not put too much store in that notion," Jaxyn warned. "Stellan may care what happens to you, but I'm fairly certain nothing would concern Syrolee and her family less than the fate of Stellan's long-lost wife. And it's Syrolee who's pulling your husband's strings these days over on the other side of the lake, my dear. You can be certain of that."

Arkady feared Jaxyn was right, but she was reluctant to agree with him. She never got the opportunity in any case, as their discussion was interrupted by a knock at the door, followed by Lady Aleena letting herself into the study. Dressed in the finest silks—the cold did not concern her—and draped in the Desean family rubies that had once belonged to Arkady, the woman was tall and dark-haired and the candelabra she carried lit the angular planes of her face, highlighting her finely sculpted cheekbones.

Jaxyn's fiancée eyed Arkady curiously for a moment and then looked at Jaxyn. "Not interrupting anything salacious, am I, dearest?"

"Not at all," Jaxyn told her expansively. "Arkady and I were just discussing her future."

"Oh," Aleena said. "She has one, does she?"

Arkady forced a smile at the woman posing as Lady Aleena Aranville, reminding herself that this woman had been a whore in a sea port brothel before she was immortal, which probably accounted for her manners—and her desire to wear every single ring and bracelet Arkady had once owned, all at once.

Admittedly, Arkady had demonstrated rather less moral fibre than a whore herself in recent times, but at least she could console herself with the thought that she'd done what she had out of necessity. Lyna, Arkady had discovered on their journey together back from Senestra, had been a whore—and often returned to that occupation when she was hiding during low Tides—because she liked it. Her reasoning totally eluded Arkady. Despite sharing a cabin on the trip from Senestra during which time Lyna was at least civil, if not exactly friendly, Arkady still didn't trust her or her motives.

Jaxyn wasn't going to be drawn on Arkady's fate, however, not even by his betrothed. "Well, that remains to be seen, my dear. Have you settled in our other guest?"

"Doctor Morel is resting comfortably in one of the guest rooms under guard as you requested," Lyna assured him. "Although he's not very happy about his new living arrangements."

"Is something wrong with his accommodation?" Arkady asked.

"Considering where he's come from recently, not a damned thing," Lyna said. "I gather his objections are on moral grounds. I do believe your father thinks you're a shameless whore, Arkady."

"And you did nothing to disabuse him of the notion, I gather?"

The immortal shrugged. "It's not up to me to remedy your father's misconceptions. Assuming they *are* misconceptions. Apparently you have quite a history of opening your legs to get what you want."

Arkady caught sight of Jaxyn's amused expression and wondered if he hadn't deliberately staged this scene to test her mettle. She had been through enough lately, however, for mere insults to bounce off her skin like raindrops off an oiled cloak. She smiled at Lyna. "A skill I'm sure you're also expert at, my lady," she replied with acidic sweetness. "Perhaps we can compare notes sometime."

Lyna wasn't amused. "Death is very final, Arkady. Don't make me show you that the hard way."

"We were just discussing Arkady's mortality," Jaxyn said, leaning back in his seat with a smile. The bickering between the women apparently entertained him a great deal. "It seems she's rather anxious to provoke one of us into doing her in."

"Tides," Lyna said. "What a waste. Still, I suppose that explains your father's message."

"What message?"

"He said to tell you not to worry about the future. And something about him being the parent for once and it being time he did his job." She shrugged. To her, the message was of little consequence. "You're very lucky, you know. My father sold me to a brothel when I was twelve. He wasn't interested in saving me at all. Will we be three for dinner, Jaxyn? Or doesn't Arkady's house arrest extend to her eating with the family?"

"Don't be so catty, Lyna," Jaxyn said, still smiling. "It's not nice to taunt our guest with what she's lost. You're not too tormented being back here in Lebec Palace, are you, Arkady? Surrounded by all these pretty things you no longer own?"

Arkady didn't answer because she wasn't really listening. Something about her father's message bothered her, although she couldn't put her finger on it. "Did my father say anything else, my lady?"

Lyna shook her head. "Nothing of consequence. You'd think he'd be a little more grateful, though. I mean . . . the stupid bastard was rotting in Lebec Prison until a few hours ago. Now he gets to see out the war on a feather bed. Some people are just never happy."

"I think I'll go and see to him," Arkady said, rising to her feet.

"I think I'll go and see to him, please, your grace, is what you really meant to say, isn't it?" Jaxyn asked.

Arkady glared at him.

"You're under house arrest, Arkady," he reminded her. "You'll not be taking a piss without my permission. Now, if you want to see to your father, ask. Nicely."

Tides, Declan, Arkady prayed silently, quite certain there was nobody listening to her prayer. *If you ever do manage to find a way to kill an immortal down there in Jelidia, can you please put Jaxyn high on the list of Tide Lords you intend to do away with?* She said nothing aloud, however, knowing Jaxyn was just looking for any excuse he could find to punish and humiliate her.

"May I go and see to my father, please, your grace?" she asked through gritted teeth. Arkady wasn't as bothered by the request as she appeared. In truth, this was just a word game, and there were far more dangerous games she could be playing with Jaxyn Aranville. If he thought having to ask his permission irked her, however; if he thought it was tearing her up inside to kowtow to him, then he would—for a while at least—confine his torments to such relatively simple and harmless games. Her father's safety might well hinge on Jaxyn's belief that he was torturing her with words and didn't need to move on to something more substantial to achieve his goal.

"You may," Jaxyn said, after deliberating on the request for a moment or two for dramatic effect.

"Thank you, your grace," Arkady said, bowing to him with obvious reluctance. She crossed the rug and stopped in front of Lyna. "May I borrow your candelabra, my lady, to light my way?"

Lyna handed her the silver candleholder and stepped back from the door. "He's upstairs. Third door on the left."

"I know the way, my lady."

"I'm sure you do," Lyna said with a smile. Before the immortal could add anything else, Arkady stepped into the hall and shut the door on her.

Taking a deep breath and putting Jaxyn Aranville and his wretched fiancée out of her mind, Arkady hurried down the hall toward the main staircase, still worried about her father's cryptic message. What had he meant by telling her not to worry about the future? The message about him being the parent for once and it being time he did his job was equally puzzling.

What does he think he's going to do? Call Jaxyn out? Challenge him to a duel?

Although she'd spent a lot of time during their incarceration trying to explain the Tide Lords to him, she knew her father didn't really believe her. She didn't even blame him for that. Magic and immortality were not easy concepts for a man of science to grasp.

Tides, Cayal had to chop a few fingers off to get me to believe him.

The guards on her father's door offered no resistance when she demanded entry, so she assumed Lyna hadn't instructed the felines to forbid her from seeing him. The tabby on the right produced a key from her belt pouch and opened the door, standing back to let Arkady pass. The room was dark and cold, lit only by a smudge of glowing coals in the fireplace to Arkady's right. The large four-poster bed against the far wall had its heavy brocaded curtains drawn against the chill.

"Papa? Are you asleep?"

There was no answer. Arkady smiled at her own foolishness, thinking there was never a more ridiculous question than asking a sleeping person if they were asleep.

"Papa?"

She walked to the bed and put the candelabra on the side table, deciding that if her father really was asleep, she wouldn't disturb him now. It had been a fraught few days since Jaxyn had first come to visit them, and he was very uncomfortable with the deal she'd brokered to secure their release from prison and into house arrest in Lebec Palace.

Part of the problem, she knew, was that her father couldn't understand why Jaxyn would be interested in the location of the imaginary Tide Lords—despite Arkady assuring him that Jaxyn was one of them—so her deal with him didn't make sense. Bary Morel assumed the deal must involve something far more tangible. He believed she'd offered herself to Jaxyn to save them, as she had with Fillion Rybank and Stellan Desean, and it didn't seem to matter what Arkady told him, nothing was likely to disabuse him of that notion any time soon.

"Papa?" she again asked in a whisper. It wasn't surprising that he was already unconscious. This was the first time in years her father had slept in a proper bed with proper linen sheets and with blankets that weren't flea-bitten. Carefully, she leaned forward and pulled the curtain near the head of the bed back a fraction, to check if he really was sleeping. It was impossible to make out anything in the dark cave created by the closed curtains, so she let it fall back into place, deciding he must be asleep and there was nothing so important that it couldn't wait until morning. She picked up the candelabra and turned toward the door, bumping against her father's foot hanging down by the edge of the bed as she moved.

Thinking he may have turned in his sleep, she put the candelabra back down on the side table. This time she opened the curtains in the middle, expecting to find a somnambulant man twisted up in sheets and blankets in which he wasn't used to sleeping.

Instead, she found herself face-to-face with her father's midsection.

It took a moment for Arkady to realise what she was seeing, and why. Then it hit her and she cried out for the guards. She grabbed her father around the legs with both arms, trying to lift his dead weight, sobbing angrily as she tried to pull him down and lift him at the same time.

The felines on guard outside were quick, responding in a matter of seconds. Her father let out an agonised gasp as they released him from the crisp sheets he was supposed to be sleeping on; sheets he'd torn and twisted into the noose around his neck.

Tears streaming down her face, Arkady let him go and stepped back to allow the felines a chance to cut him down. His face was bloated, his neck bruised, his extremities already purpling with blood. One of the felines ran for the door, calling out for help.

Arkady stared at her father, speechless with shock as they laid him on the floor. She was a little surprised to find she wasn't distressed so much as angry—angry beyond belief at her father's selfish arrogance.

Bary Morel's brilliant solution to how to save his daughter was to remove himself from the equation.

It would have made a twisted sort of sense to her father, she supposed, even though it was a gesture of such utter futility that Arkady wanted to kill her father herself for even contemplating the notion, let alone attempting to carry it out.

"What's all the commotion about?" Jaxyn demanded from the doorway, arriving on the heels of another couple of felines who had come to investigate the guards' cries for help. The Tide Lord walked across to where Bary Morel was lying on the floor and studied him for a moment. "Tides. The old fool tried to kill himself."

"Ever the sharp observer," Arkady said caustically. Her father was barely breathing.

"Why would he do that?"

"To save me from you."

Jaxyn looked at her oddly. "Where's the sense in that? If he wanted to save you from me, he'd have been better served killing *you*."

"If you're planning to share that pearl of wisdom with him," Arkady said, looking down at her father's lifeless body, "perhaps you might take the time to heal him first?"

Jaxyn hesitated for a moment, staring down at her father's unconscious form, and then he smiled.

"Beg me to do it."

"All right, I'm begging you," she said emotionlessly. Inside she wanted to scream at him. Her father didn't have time for Jaxyn to play these stupid games.

"No, I mean I want you to *actually* beg me. On your knees."

Arkady stared at him for a moment and then did as he asked. She fell to her knees and lowered her eyes. "Please, my lord. Will you save my father?"

He smiled. "Tides, you actually hesitated then, didn't you?"

Fortunately, she didn't have to answer him. Jaxyn must have realised how little time there was before her father was beyond the intervention of even a Tide Lord. Before she could respond or be asked to beg him again, he knelt beside her father, and placed a hand over his bruised neck. Bary Morel convulsed with pain, even though he was out cold, but Arkady was relieved to see his skin tone visibly improving a moment later. Then he took a deep shuddering breath and his posture relaxed a little as he began to breathe normally.

Arkady tried not to look too anxious or relieved, aware of what a narrow escape this had been.

"Thank you," she said, still on her knees, as Jaxyn rose to his feet.

"You may not think it was such a good deed once you've thought this through, Arkady," he said. "I mean, the old fool wants to kill himself and you just stopped him from doing it."

"I know you didn't have to save him."

The Tide Lord smiled. "Yes, I did. You see, now you're going to have to explain it to him. You're going to have to explain how it is that he's alive. How it is that now I can *truly* use him to torment you. You can tell him all the ways I can cause *you* pain by making *him* suffer. And how he's *going* to be suffering, Arkady, because when he was on the cusp of death, *you* begged me to save his life."

Jaxyn spared her father another glance as he began to moan softly at the Tide Lord's feet, then he turned and strode from the room. Still on her knees, Arkady crawled across the rug to her father, pulling his head onto her lap, wondering if Jaxyn and her father were right. Maybe she should have let him die.

But Arkady had lost her father once already. She wasn't ready to lose him again so soon. Tears streaming silently down her face, she held her father close, filled with a sense of such helplessness that it almost overwhelmed her.

Chapter 13

"What happened here?"

The scene that confronted the Tide Lords when they reached Black-bourn just on dark was one of almost utter devastation. Flattened trees littered the landscape and the ground was drenched, small puddles filling every low-lying surface. It was hard to tell how far the damage extended, but everywhere they looked, the jetsam and flotsam of a devastating tidal wave lay about them, reaching far inland—certainly as far as they could see in the darkness.

They'd landed on the beach just south of where the town should have been. By Declan's estimation, they had travelled almost 2000 nautical miles in just over three days. His head was pounding, his skin felt as if it was covered in fire ants. Kentravyon had taken over guiding them several hours earlier. He brought them in to land with consummate skill, the rug settling gently on the wave-ravaged beach with barely a flutter as he let the Tide go.

"We happened," Cayal said, as he stepped off the rug.

It was almost completely dark, an early full moon already on the horizon. They were just out of sight of the fishing village that should have been located further along the beach. Given the look of this place, Declan wasn't hopeful they'd find much of anything at all. Or anybody.

"What do you mean—we happened?"

"Tide's up," Kentravyon said, peering into the darkness. A steep cliff loomed over the small cove, reaching up into a night that was silent and dead. Under normal circumstances, it would have been filled with the chattering of a million cicadas and other creatures of the twilight. There was nothing. Everything here was dead or had fled the rising water.

"This is the remains of a tidal wave," Declan said, squatting down to pick up what looked like the broken leg off a child's wooden doll. There was no sign of any people, no bodies, nothing. Had they all been washed out to sea? How many people had lived here? "Nothing magical did this."

"Not directly," Kentravyon agreed. "But the Tide, in its own way, is an element like any other. You mess with one it affects all the others."

"You mean us riding the Tide caused this?"

"It's hard to say for certain, but it's likely, given there haven't been any undersea quakes in the past few days," Cayal said, walking a little way up the beach toward the tree line which was now a series of broken-off stumps.

Moonlight filtering through the clouds lit the darkened beach, making the spectre even more depressing. Adding to his woes, Declan's skin itched like he was allergic to air, and he was finding it hard to stand still. "I thought you said this wouldn't happen? You said that's why we had to ride the magic carpet, because to ride the water itself was too dangerous."

"Actually, nobody said it *wouldn't* happen. We just said riding a tidal wave in the direction of a populated area wasn't a good idea." Kentravyon looked around curiously. "It was probably you, Declan. You splash around in the Tide like a child playing in the shallows at the seaside and with about as much finesse. Still, we all have to learn, I suppose."

Muttering to himself and shaking his hands as if to rid them of pins and needles, Kentravyon wandered off into the darkness, leaving Declan overcome by guilt—and trembling like a drunkard who couldn't recall when he'd had his last drink. He tried to ignore the shaking. *Tides, how many people died here because I'm in a hurry to get back to Glaeba?*

Appearing much calmer than Declan felt, Cayal turned inland, studying the devastated terrain. "Look," he said after a moment. "Up there."

Declan turned to look in the direction Cayal was pointing. On the cliff top behind them, there was a light. It seemed to be waving back and forth like a signal. "The survivors must have taken shelter on higher ground."

"They're signalling us."

Cayal nodded and started out toward the cliff. "If anybody asks, we're off a boat moored out in the Bight."

"Will they care?" Declan asked, hurrying to catch up to him.

"This is—was—a small village," Kentravyon said, falling in beside Cayal and Declan as they picked their way across the saturated sand and debris toward the cliff. "People in places like this are suspicious of strangers."

That seemed a fair call, but there were other, more practical things to deal with before they started worrying about their cover story. "We're going to help them?"

"I have money."

"These people have lost their homes and their livelihoods," Declan said. "They'll need food and shelter and probably fresh water. Money isn't going to help."

"What do you want us to do, then?" Cayal asked impatiently. "Go up there and announce we're the Tide Lords of ancient legend, come to aid them in their hour of need?"

"You know, Declan, that might be just the thing," Kentravyon said, looking over his shoulder at them—entirely too pleased at the prospect.

Declan glanced at Cayal, wondering what he was thinking. It was hard to tell. There was a look in Cayal's eyes that said he was suffering just as much from the effect of too much exposure to the Tide as Declan. Kentravyon seemed quite calm, but that wasn't actually very reassuring.

"Do you speak Stevanian?"

"Not really. A few words, maybe."

Cayal nodded and turned to Kentravyon. "If we help them, their gratitude should be . . . substantial."

"Gratitude?" Declan asked. He stared at Cayal for a moment and then shook his head in disgust when he realised what the Immortal Prince had in mind. "You're going to offer them help in return for what—sexual favours?"

"You're the one who thinks they won't be interested in money."

Declan wished he had a response that didn't sound quite so hypocritical. Cayal was right: they had stopped here because the Tide was consuming them and they needed to relieve the tension. That a tidal wave had devastated the village before they arrived—and had possibly been caused by them into the bargain—hadn't altered their basic and urgent need.

It just felt so wrong.

Kentravyon could obviously see what was bothering Declan and was completely dismissive of it. He shrugged and stopped for a moment, looking up at the cliff tops behind the hinterland.

"Do whatever you want. I'm going to visit the temple."

"Do they have a temple here?" Cayal asked.

"I told them to build one the last time I was here. It should have been high enough to escape the waves."

Declan glanced worriedly at Cayal before he answered Kentravyon, wondering if the madman realised that the last time he'd been here was probably several thousand years ago. "There's been a couple of Cataclysms since then, you know. I wouldn't get too fixed on the idea that they remember you."

Kentravyon glared at him. "I am God. Of course they will remember me."

"You do whatever you want, Kentie, my old friend." Cayal grabbed Declan's arm and pulled him away from Kentravyon, pushing him in the direction of the cliff and whoever was signalling them. "The Rodent and I are going to do good deeds and save the day, and hopefully ourselves. See you in the morning. And remember, gods are a lot easier to venerate if they're easing their worshippers' pain, not contributing to it."

"Hang on—" Declan began, not liking the idea of leaving Kentravyon to his own devices, but Cayal gave him no chance to say anything further. He put himself between Declan and Kentravyon and shoved him, none too gently, further along the beach.

Declan pulled free of Cayal and turned to face him. "Tides, Cayal, aren't you going to stop him?"

"Why should I stop him?"

"We've done enough damage here. If he goes up there and they haven't built a temple to him . . ."

"He'll be peeved. That doesn't make him homicidal. He'll probably start preaching to anybody who'll listen, truth be told, which—I will grant you—is a cruel fate indeed, but hardly a problem. Leave him be."

"Lukys told us to stop him doing anything stupid."

"And if he starts doing anything stupid, we will. In the meantime, we let it go. Kentravyon, the Tide . . . all of it."

Declan stared back over Cayal's shoulder, certain no good could come of letting Kentravyon out of their sight. He felt out of sorts, uneasy, but he couldn't tell if his premonition of impending doom was real, or a consequence of riding the Tide for so long.

He watched Kentravyon's retreating figure, wondering how a man could command so much power and yet feel so helpless, all at the same time.

He turned to Cayal. "I need a drink."

"You know, Rodent," Cayal said, shouldering his pack and turning for the village, "this may be the first time in living history you and I are in total agreement."

Chapter 14

The survivors had gathered on the cliff top, a motley bunch of some two hundred men, women and children, sitting around in small groups, all wearing the blank-eyed stare of people too overwhelmed to know what had happened to them. The arrival of strangers had an odd effect. As Cayal and Declan reached the top of the escarpment, some of the people turned from them, fearing they were simply more survivors wanting to share what little they'd managed to salvage from the deluge. Others, particularly the children, clustered around the strangers, asking for help. At least Declan assumed that's what they were asking. Even if he didn't speak the language, he could see the pleading in their eyes.

And then a woman approached them, perhaps the grandmother of some of the younger children. She shooed the children away and said something in a rapid stream of words Declan didn't understand. He guessed she was asking for something, because she pointed to the children. Even in a language he didn't know, there was no mistaking the desperate look in her eye or her pleading tone of voice.

"What's she asking?"

"For water, I think," Cayal said. "My Stevanian isn't what it used to be."

"Are these all the survivors?"

Cayal asked the woman the question in her own language and then shook his head. "She said the wounded have been taken to the temple."

"It's still here, then," Declan said, relieved to hear the news. The last thing they needed was Kentravyon getting snippy because his temple had been washed away. "Can we help them?"

"How, exactly?" Cayal asked.

Declan looked around in the darkness at the clustered survivors. Other than a few torches offering flickering illumination, there were no fires. He supposed that meant any firewood they'd been able to find—assuming they'd even thought to collect any—was too wet to burn.

"We could try drying out some firewood for them, couldn't we? Organise fresh water?"

"From where?" Cayal asked, looking a little dubious. "Their wells are probably filled with sea water."

"Can't we get rid of the salt?"

Cayal stared at him for a moment, his expression thoughtful. "Using the Tide? I suppose we could, now you mention it."

Declan couldn't believe how relieved he was to hear it. The burden of guilt that came with the realisation he may have caused this disaster was proving quite a bit more than he'd bargained for. "How do we do it?"

"*We* won't be doing anything of the kind," Cayal said, shaking his head. "Desalinating water takes a level of finesse you can't even imagine yet." Without waiting for Declan to respond, he turned and spoke to the older woman for a moment, who nodded with relief and then beckoned another young woman forward. Cayal turned back to Declan. "She's sending her granddaughter with you to find some dry wood. She doesn't know who we are, just that we've offered to help, so try not to be too obvious about it."

"Why didn't you tell them you're a Tide Lord?"

"Because for one thing, they probably wouldn't believe me, and for another, we don't have time. So go and just pretend you're really good at collecting dry wood. I'll see what I can do about their well, and then we can get some rest . . . and maybe," he added, eyeing off the pretty, albeit blank-eyed, young woman who had come forward to help Declan with the firewood, ". . . score a little bit a *gratitude*, too. Either way, by morning we'll be gone, with a bit of luck, and these poor sods will be none the wiser."

Declan took a step forward. "We should check on the wounded in the temple, too. We could heal them."

Cayal stopped him from taking another step by grabbing his arm. "Steady on there, Rodent. Kentravyon's already on his way to them. Leave him be. You'll spoil his fun."

Cayal had a point. And Declan needed to do something, he'd been standing still for far too long. He turned to the girl, whose eyes were dull with shock and grief. "Ask her what her name is."

Cayal questioned the young woman in Stevanian and then turned to Declan after she answered him. "She says it's Gasandra."

"Tell her we're here to help."

"I already did. Go fetch the firewood, Rodent. I'll fix the well, and if it doesn't take too long, I may even see what I can do about food."

Declan wasn't sure he believed Cayal's apparent willingness to aid these people, but there wasn't much he could do about it now. If he started questioning Cayal's motives, the immortal might decide not to help out of sheer perversity, so Declan turned to Gasandra and pointed inland. The girl nodded and turned to lead the way, leaving Declan with the uneasy feeling that this was all too easy; the willingness of Cayal and Kentravyon to aid the survivors of a tidal wave they'd probably caused was completely out of character for both of them.

Chapter 15

The next few hours passed in a blur for Cayal. They'd stopped here in Blackbourn to rest from the incessant drain of the Tide, only to have the Rodent insist they help the survivors of the tidal wave they'd almost certainly caused. Even his immortal regenerative ability strained to cope with the demands he was making on his stamina. Cayal remembered when he used to behave as Hawkes was now; when guilt was the only emotion he truly understood, and he was driven by little more than the need to assuage it.

The Rodent still hadn't figured out who he was or what he could do. So he was clinging to what he did know, trying to convince himself as much as the others that he still retained his humanity.

Good luck with that, Cayal thought.

Helping others to help himself. Poor sod didn't realise yet that even now, he was turning into what he most despised. He was already helping others in order to help himself. Such was the selfishness of all immortals.

By dawn, Cayal had desalinated the two wells that had supplied the village before its destruction by the rising water. It was a simple matter really. Tide magic was elemental and separating salt from water was a relatively uncomplicated task.

He had little time to savour his good deed, however. With the sky already beginning to lighten, the air crisp with the chill of the departing night, Cayal turned and headed for the temple, wondering how Kentravyon had fared. Cayal had not checked on him for hours. Nor had he heard anything. The wounded were there, according to the villagers sheltering on the escarpment. Maybe . . .

Cayal's thought was cut short by an enraged scream, followed by a crash so powerful it made the ground shake. He traded a surprised look with the lad who had been sent to show him the location of the wells amid the wreckage of the little town. He looked up in time to see a block of masonry tumbling down the cliff above him. The large granite block crashed and bounced down into what was left of the devastated village.

"Look out!"

Cayal looked up. A second massive block was almost on them. Reflexively, he redirected it with the Tide, forcing it to make a sharp turn to the left. It tumbled down to land harmlessly in the water near the stumps of the town's single wooden jetty.

Cayal swore savagely for a moment and then broke into a run, scrambling up the cliff face until he reached the top. The scene that greeted him was completely unexpected. Kentravyon stood in the middle of the wounded—perhaps forty or fifty of them laid out in neat rows—confronting a very furious Declan Hawkes who looked utterly enraged. This surprised Cayal, because he'd assumed the blocks hurtling off the cliff had come from Kentravyon.

"Tides, you almost flattened me, you fool!" he exclaimed, walking into the centre of the temple. If these people had built it on Kentravyon's command, they must have done it eons ago. The place was a ruin, barely more than a few moss-covered pillars holding up a fading memory of the past. "What the hell is going on?"

"He killed them."

Cayal stared at Declan for a moment and then looked around at the unnaturally silent wounded laying about the ruins. Every one of them was silent, their arms crossed over their chests, their eyes open and staring, as dead eyes always were. It was only then that he realised what Hawkes meant.

"I eased their pain," Kentravyon corrected, as the dreadful truth sank in. "And this ungrateful whelp is abusing me for it."

Cayal looked around, frowning. "They're all dead, Kentravyon."

"Gods are a lot easier to venerate if they're easing their worshippers' pain, not contributing to it. That's what you said. That's what I did. Their pain is eased. They will suffer no more."

Cayal glanced at Declan. He could feel the barely leashed anger from where he was standing, which was worrying because the Rodent was fair trembling with the Tide, the ripples he was making on it both erratic and dangerous. They'd stopped here to let the Tide go, and ended up using it even more. If Cayal was feeling the strain, Hawkes—so unused to the sensation—would be feeling it tenfold.

"Say 'I told you so,' Rodent, and you *will* regret it."

Declan shook his head, his fists clenched by his side so tight his knuckles were white. "What do we do?"

Cayal shrugged. "Get out of here before someone comes to check on the wounded, is my suggestion."

"But he's killed them all!"

"All the more reason to get the hell away from here."

Kentravyon shook his hand. "We're not going anywhere until this disrespectful nobody apologises."

"*Apologises?*"

Hawkes's refusal to give Kentravyon what he wanted infuriated the older Tide Lord. Cayal felt the Tide surging around him. Another block of tumbled masonry was suddenly hurtling across the ruin, over the neat rows of the dead Kentravyon had so carefully laid out.

Cayal ducked reflexively as the boulder flew over his head to land far below in the water behind them. Some of the survivors—who'd probably come to see what all the fuss was about—were in a panic. There were screaming people running everywhere. Cayal wasn't sure if they were panicking over the flying masonry or the dead they were beginning to discover.

It was time to leave. But neither of the other two seemed to realise that. The Rodent was too angry, Kentravyon too full of divine indignation.

This is why I want to die.

The thought flashed through his mind, reminding him of the countless times he'd seen this very situation before. The details might be different, but the result of two opposing Tide Lords, both thinking they were in the right, was always the same and always bad for any mortal unfortunate enough to be in the vicinity.

Possessing the only clear head amongst them, Cayal looked around for something large and flat to take the place of their rug. Their magic carpet—as Hawkes insisted on calling it—was back on the beach south of the town. For what Cayal had in mind, he didn't have the time to retrieve it. Another block hurtled past him and crashed into what little was left of the village below. There Cayal spied something that might suffice, that might even perform better than their missing rug.

Cayal turned his back on the warring immortals, and then, using the Tide, he lifted a large—albeit somewhat tattered—section of thatched roof that had been standing on its edge against the cliff, displaced by the tidal wave. He jumped off the cliff as it rose from the ground, leaping aboard the roof-section and soared out to sea. He felt a surge on the

Tide behind him . . . or rather, a confused series of them. Kentravyon
and Hawkes were settling their differences. Hawkes was using raw
power and absolutely no finesse to divert the blocks and send them back
the way they'd come.

Cayal's blood sang with the Tide, and for a moment he remembered
what it was to want this, not to dread it.

And then he pushed the thought aside, skimming the tattered roof-
section out over the water so far the land became a blur of the horizon.
Once he was far enough out to be lost to sight, he banked to the left, heading back toward the coast in a wide circle that would bring him around behind the other two Tide Lords. There was no way to stop either of them
feeling Cayal's manoeuvring on the Tide, but hopefully Hawkes would
keep Kentravyon distracted long enough for Cayal to reach them.

The water sped beneath Cayal in a grey-blue blur that soon changed
to a rushing green smear as he reached the coast and headed inland.

With the wind rushing through his hair—he wasn't wasting Tide
power on protecting himself from the elements—Cayal banked again,
heading back to Blackbourn, riding his thatched roof like the children
of the Chelae Islands, riding the waves off the beach of their homeland.
He could feel the other immortals in the distance, battling each other
on the Tide. It felt like a fairly even fight, which meant the Rodent was
managing to hold his own. The thrum of the Tide cantillated through
him, the exhilaration of riding it so wantonly enough to make him forget the reason he was here. Then another surge on the Tide, erratic and
dangerously close, reminded him of his purpose. Cayal banked his
thatched platform again and headed back toward the coast; back toward
what was left of the village of Blackbourn. And Kentravyon.

The mad Tide Lord didn't see him coming. He had his back to Cayal
and, in any case, was too engrossed trading missiles with Hawkes, who
was proving to be a disturbingly quick study when it came to manipulating the Tide. Cayal bore down on him, catching sight of the ruined
temple on the cliff top as he approached.

He was barrelling toward Kentravyon at a dangerous speed, determined to reach him before he had time to register what was happening.
At the last minute, Kentravyon must have noticed the disturbance on
the Tide behind him. He glanced over his shoulder in time to register
shock as the roof-section took him in the back of the knees, knocking

him off his feet and backwards onto the thatching. Cayal sped on, aiming the roof at the Rodent next, but the Rodent wasn't as stupid as he looked. He could see Cayal coming and he threw himself onto the platform as it approached, rather than be barrelled over by it as they passed.

Kentravyon struggled to sit up as they climbed into the morning sky at a speed that soon took them far from the Stevanian coast. Cayal could feel Kentravyon's irritation, feel him drawing the Tide to himself to retaliate, the Rodent's equally furious response building up in reply. Before the mad immortal or the dangerously inexperienced Rodent could do anything about it, however, Kentravyon's fist connected squarely with Hawkes's jaw. He fell backward, arms and legs flailing, as he tumbled from the platform and into the icy water beneath.

Cayal slowed his thatched craft and banked again, looking at Kentravyon in surprise. Then he shook his head in wonder.

"All the power of the Tide is yours to command, Kentravyon, and you decide to take on another Tide Lord with your *fist*?"

Kentravyon was grinning, unable to quash the exhilaration he was feeling from swimming the Tide. He was on his knees, still trying to find his balance on the thatching. "It worked, didn't it? He wasn't expecting it. He's let the Tide go. And he needed cooling off. Not handling this at all well, if you ask me."

Cayal realised Kentravyon was right. The shock of someone belting him in the face had had the desired effect on Hawkes. Cayal glanced over the side and spied the Rodent bobbing up and down in the water, no longer swimming the magical Tide, too preoccupied, apparently, with treading water on the more mundane one.

"He's going to be pissed at you, Kentravyon."

"He already was."

Kentravyon had a point. Cayal glanced down at Hawkes again and then grinned. "Wonder how long it would take him to find us again if we left him down there?"

For a moment, Kentravyon grinned back at Cayal like a conspirator. "I'm game if you are."

Cayal considered the very tempting prospect of leaving the Rodent down there, bobbing in the ocean, thousands of miles from anywhere significant. Then he sighed and began to lower their thatched platform toward the water. "We'd better not," he told Kentravyon. "For one thing, we need him to open the rift when we get back to Jelidia. For another, he's likely to decide to solidify the sea, or something equally disastrous, so he can walk back to dry land. Amyrantha isn't quite ready for another Cataclysm just yet."

Kentravyon looked at him askance. "You're willing to destroy the planet in order to take your own life, Cayal, but you're worried about another Cataclysm? And people call *me* the crazy one."

"You're worse than the Rodent. And you said you didn't know for certain that opening the rift will destroy Amyrantha," Cayal said, getting a little tired of everybody's constant attempts to make him feel guilty about wanting to die.

Kentravyon didn't answer him. They'd reached the water and Hawkes was swimming toward them, looking very unhappy. Cayal leaned forward and helped him clamber aboard.

"Enjoy your dip?" Cayal asked, not sure what Declan was planning to do next. He hadn't taken hold of the Tide again, which was reassuring.

He wasn't pleased, though, and his jaw was bruised, although it was healing as they spoke. Kentravyon must have hit him hard.

"That was your idea of helping, was it?"

"You two were randomly throwing granite blocks around," Cayal reminded him. He levelled the platform and began to move it over the wavetops toward Torlenia. "You ready to move on now . . . *God*?"

"You mock me at your peril, Cayal."

"No, I don't, Kentravyon. Although it would be nice to think you really were as divine as you think you are."

"Why do you wish for that? Even now, knowing I am God, you do not worship me."

"No," he agreed, taking a seat on the thatching. "I don't. But that's not because I don't believe that *you* believe you're God. It's because if you really *were* God, Kentie, my old friend, we wouldn't have to go to all this trouble because you'd already have the power to help me die."

Kentravyon didn't answer him. Hawkes said nothing either, as they sped east. He just sat there, dripping and glowering, and wrestling—Cayal had no doubt—with his own internal demons.

Chapter 16

"She's gone!" Lyna announced, slamming the door behind her.

Jaxyn looked up from the map he was studying in what had once been the elegantly decorated study belonging to Stellan Desean. He was still debating the best way to approach Caelum. Should he concentrate his forces on Cycrane, or spread them thinner and attack even more of the coastline simultaneously? It was a tricky problem. And he certainly wasn't in the mood for Lyna, whose role as his fiancée was becoming increasingly irrelevant. Soon he would be in a strong enough position to be rid of her entirely.

But for now, he was required to humour her. "Who is gone, my dear?"

"Your precious little duchess."

Jaxyn swore under his breath and pushed the map aside. "How long?"

"Since she fled? Only an hour or two, I gather." She crossed the room and then stopped at the desk, putting her hands on the edge of its polished surface and leaning forward until she was only a few inches, from his face. Lyna's breath frosted as she spoke. Impervious to the weather, like all immortals, Jaxyn hadn't bothered to light a fire and the room was icy. "I warned you it was stupid to let them have the run of the palace."

He didn't move, or even lean backward. "I believe you merely remarked it might be unwise."

"Turns out I was right, however much you want to quibble about semantics."

"Did the old man go with her?"

Lyna nodded. "Of course. She'd not leave him behind. Family loyalty and all that. Tides, she's as tiresomely loyal to her family as any one of Syrolee's clan."

"Then they won't have gone far. In fact, I can pretty much tell you where they'll be heading." He rose to his feet, forcing Lyna to move back.

She was sceptical of his boast. "You think you know your little duchess so well?"

"I know her history," he said, walking around the desk. "She has few real friends she can turn to, particularly within reach of the palace."

"She's long gone, Jaxyn. You've lost your leverage and any use she might have been in bringing her husband to heel, because you're always thinking with your cock instead of your head."

The temptation to slap Lyna was almost overwhelming. Fortunately, Jaxyn understood the futility of such a gesture, despite the momentary gratification he might have gained from it. He stayed his hand, sneering at her instead.

"She'll be back in the palace by nightfall," he said, crossing the elegant rug to reach the door. Jerking it open, he turned to his increasingly unnecessary fiancée. "And now, if you don't mind, I'm busy."

"Want some help getting them back?"

"They won't get far in this weather."

Lyna glanced at the two tall windows flanking the fireplace and the clear skies beyond. The day was a rare one in Glaeba—bright and clear, although there was little warmth in the winter sunlight. "There's nothing threatening about the weather."

"Not yet there isn't," Jaxyn agreed. And then he smiled. He couldn't help himself. "Give me an hour, and then we'll see how far they get."

Jaxyn was as aware as any other Tide Lord of the danger of messing with local weather patterns. It was that, as much as his desire to remain undetected, that had forced him to be so cautious when he froze the Great Lakes. Although it was necessary to freeze the lakes in order to facilitate his invasion of Caelum to rid himself of Syrolee and Engarhod—and the threat of having two equally powerful Tide Lords, Elyssa and Tryan, residing on the same continent at High Tide—he had done it very slowly.

This was a somewhat different situation. He didn't need a big storm. Just a very small and localised one and, while it would have consequences elsewhere, they were nothing he couldn't deal with.

One of the Crasii grooms brought his saddled horse around from the stables, its shod hooves clacking loudly on the cobblestoned pavement at the front of the palace, as Jaxyn drew on the Tide. It was not enough to alert any other immortal—except Lyna who was in the vicinity and knew the reason for the storm—but enough to make storm clouds gather overhead with unnatural speed. He had done much the same the day he called up a localised storm to sink the royal barge, killing King Enteny and Queen Inala. He turned the horse for the gates and set off at a trot, the temperature already dropping.

With the sky darkening as he rode, Jaxyn's storm ran ahead of him, heading for the one place he was sure Arkady and her father would take shelter—Clyden's Inn; home of that annoying one-armed miner-turned-tavern keeper. A place where it was easier to find a rumour than a meal. The only place near Lebec Palace Arkady and her father might reasonably reach in a couple of hours on foot.

He might be wrong. Arkady and her father might have headed across country to the city, but he doubted it. Arkady had it in her to traipse across the countryside through knee-deep snow, but her father wasn't a young man. Although Jaxyn had healed him after his suicide attempt—and by default probably restored his health to the best it had been in years—he'd been incarcerated for a long time. Bary Morel didn't have the stamina to handle a cross-country flight and Arkady would not risk him failing or succumbing to hypothermia.

No, Jaxyn reasoned, *the safest haven is also the easiest to reach. Clyden's Inn.*

By the time the crossroads came into sight, the storm, localised though it was, had already whipped up a frenzy of sleet, rain and ice. Visibility was down to a few feet. Wind-driven snow sliced almost horizontally across the road. The wind-chill factor was bordering on fatal to any mortal caught out in the storm. The trees beside the road bent over so far they seemed to be bowing to Jaxyn as he rode past. For a fleeting moment, he wondered how much collateral damage he was causing. Would the storm abate when he was done, and expose fields littered with dead Crasii caught in the tempest?

Jaxyn hoped not. It would be damned inconvenient to lose skilled farm workers just to retrieve Arkady and her wretched father from a tavern.

The inn and the countryside around it were suffering badly from the blizzard when Jaxyn arrived. He dismounted, extending his magical protection to include his mount. He didn't want the horse dropping dead, leaving him no choice but to walk back to the palace. As he approached the door, the wind howled around the walls of the inn. The air was white and the Tide tingled along every nerve he owned. Perhaps, if Arkady *was* here, he'd be able to relieve the tension by using her to assuage his lust.

The thought wasn't as attractive as it might once have been. Arkady's value to Jaxyn, in the current political climate, required her to remain whole and unharmed. This was the main reason he'd agreed to house arrest for her and her father in the palace. Raping her to ease a momentary urge would rob him of his bargaining chip. Stellan had already surprised Jaxyn once with the lengths he was willing to go to when he felt betrayed. Who knew what he'd do if he found Arkady harmed by the lover he was still smarting over?

A loose corner of the inn's shingled roof was banging relentlessly in the wind as he reached the door, accompanied by a swirl of icy sleet. He hammered on the door with his fist, but it remained determinedly closed. That told Jaxyn a great deal. Mortals would not leave a lone traveller out here in this blizzard to die.

Which meant they must know the traveller banging on their door *couldn't* die.

And that meant there was something or someone inside they wanted to protect from him.

Jaxyn took a deep breath. The Tide surged around him. The wind picked up and the temperature dropped even lower, the sleet falling so hard and sharp now that it scoured the bark from the unfinished logs from which the inn was constructed. A moment later, the loose corner of the roof ripped off, exposing the beams underneath. He thought he heard a scream coming from inside the building, but he might have imagined it. In any case, no matter how desperate, their mortal cries for help would be torn away by the wind before anybody could hear them.

"I know you're in there!" he called, using the Tide to amplify his voice so they would hear him over the screaming wind.

There was no answer, but he was hardly surprised. And in a way, he was glad of it. With the Tide nearing its peak, the exhilaration of allowing the magic to sing through his veins was something he hadn't experienced fully for a thousand years. This is what it was to be a Tide Lord. This was the glory of it, the seduction of omnipotent power.

Without another word, he blew the inn door off its hinges, exposing the interior of the tavern to the storm. He stepped inside and glanced around. There were several wizened old miners cowering in one corner, the one-armed tavern keeper, Clyden Bell, standing in the other, his arm protectively around a lad of about fifteen, who was wearing an apron and a look of abject terror.

There was no sign of Arkady or her father.

"I know you're here, Arkady," he called, as another piece of the roof let go, allowing the sleet and ice into the taproom. "Come out now and I won't kill anyone!"

There was no response. Jaxyn wondered if he'd misjudged Arkady. Had she outwitted him again? He was on the verge of believing she might have, when the tavern-boy gave the game away by shouting at him, "They're not here! We haven't seen them!"

"I didn't ask if you'd seen *them*," Jaxyn said with a smile as another part of the roof let go. Clyden Bell seemed terrified, the young lad even more so. The miners in the other corner were paralysed with fear.

"The boy dies first, Arkady," he called again. "But only after I've used him to assuage my need. Are you going to listen to his screaming while I take my pleasure, or come out here and stop it?"

"Lay one hand on the lad . . ." Clyden began, stepping forward bravely.

Jaxyn never heard the end of the threat. He picked Clyden Bell up without a thought and slammed him into the stone fireplace so hard he could hear the old man's bones shattering even over the storm. "Lay one hand—that's quite amusing, coming from you."

The young lad cried out in horror as Clyden's limp body dropped to the floor. Jaxyn ignored him for now. He held his arms out wide, calling out into the storm that was, bit by bit, un-roofing the inn. "Look what you've done now, Arkady. All this death, doom and destruction. It's your fault. You made me do it."

"Liar."

He turned to find her standing behind him. Arkady and her father must have been hiding beneath one of the tables near the door. He smiled and let the storm go; even a Tide Lord needed their wits about them when dealing with this woman. Her father slowly climbed to his feet beside her as Arkady stepped forward.

Drenched and frozen though she was, she seemed uncowed. Arkady slapped his face with considerable force, her eyes glistening with un-shed tears.

"Again," he said with a leer, as the wind died down now he'd let go the Tide. "Harder."

"You make me sick."

"And you made me ride all the way out here to find you," he said, glancing at the pale, shivering figure behind her. Bary Morel seemed resigned, the fight drained out of him by the cold. "Can't have done the old man any good. And now you've gone and killed your old friend, too," he added, glancing over his shoulder at Clyden's body and his weeping apprentice. "And after you gave me your word you'd be good."

Arkady had no answer to that, which disappointed him a little and made him angry. His blood was tingling as the Tide drained away, his skin itching, his flesh crawling with the need to release the tension.

For a long, considering moment, he stared at Arkady, debating the need to keep her whole against his need to relieve himself.

Prudence won. Barely. He needed Arkady whole and unharmed, and despite his threat, he wasn't so far gone that some unwashed tavern-boy offered much of an alternative.

Jaxyn drew the Tide to himself again, wrapping Arkady and her father in bonds of air—a technique that took enough concentration to stave off his carnal needs for the time being. Without another word he forced both of them out of the door and into the storm which was dissipating almost as quickly as it had gathered.

With these two walking behind his horse, it would take an hour or so to get back to the palace. An hour drawing on the Tide to keep them bound. An hour to relish the Tide and bask in its magical glow.

And when he got back to the palace . . . well, it was a good thing Lyna was there.

Perhaps it was time she earned her title as his betrothed.

Chapter 17

It took a week to cross the ocean from Stevania to Torlenia. The three Tide Lords took turns riding the Tide, keeping their thatched vessel skimming over the waves. Declan's blood was constantly on fire from the strain of it, but he was growing accustomed to the feeling. As Cayal had said when they first let Declan ride the Tide to keep their magic carpet afloat: *It gets predictable. It even gets tolerable. But it never gets better.*

Declan had discovered that for himself in the past few days. Although he felt as if raw lava was running through his veins, he'd also found some point at which it became bearable. Somehow, you just had to step away from it and let it go.

It was that, or lose your mind, he decided. He stared at Kentravyon out of the corner of his eyes, still numb with what the madman had done. Although they hadn't spoken of it again, Declan saw those lines of dead laid out in the ruined temple every time he closed his eyes.

It was a good thing sometimes, he decided, that immortals didn't need to sleep, and with it, face their dreams. Or their nightmares.

Declan was contemplating this interesting phenomenon as he rode the Tide toward the Torlenian coast, the smudge of brown on the horizon growing rapidly larger in the distance as they sped toward it. Both Kentravyon and Cayal were lying on the thatched roof beside him— Cayal on his back with his arms folded behind his head, apparently asleep, and Kentravyon on his belly, his head hanging over the edge of the thatching, Tide fishing.

Tide fishing was a game Kentravyon appeared to have invented for the sole purpose of entertaining himself on this trip. As if the incident in Blackbourn had never happened, he would hang over the edge of their fragile platform, using Tide magic to keep himself balanced, one hand dragging in the water. His plan, as far as Declan could tell, was to catch fish. This was an almost impossible task, given the speed they were travelling and the fact that for there to be any chance of him even seeing a fish, let alone getting a hand to one they needed to be passing directly over a sizable school. He would occasionally direct Declan this way or that in the hope of finding a school near the surface, but so far he'd done little more than brush a few fish in passing with his fingertips. He didn't seem to mind the impossibility of the task, or even the silliness of it. It gave him something to do, and the more impossible the task the better. He was immortal, after all. Impossible tasks had the advantage of taking longer, and therefore keeping one amused for longer.

At least, that's how Kentravyon had explained things to Declan. And it was better than murdering wounded innocents.

"A little to the left!" Kentravyon ordered, without looking up from the water. "I almost had one then."

Declan shook his head, thinking that highly unlikely, but he did as Kentravyon asked and banked their magic thatched roof-section (a mode of transport Declan decided was not nearly as romantic as a magic carpet), a little amazed at how easily he could make the roof turn now he'd had a bit of practice.

And then, without warning, the platform shattered, Declan lost his grip on the Tide and hit the water like it was made of cobblestones. He had time to wonder what they'd hit before being swamped by the waves. Stunned and reeling from his sudden disconnection from the Tide, Declan fought his way to the surface and looked around, spitting out salt water, trying to figure out what had happened. The other two immortals were bobbing in the waves a few feet away. Cayal's expression was thunderous. Kentravyon, on the other hand, was looking delighted. He was clutching a large silver fish over his head, which wriggled and fought in his grasp. "I caught one! Look! I caught one!"

"Tides, Rodent, what did you do that for?"

"I didn't do anything," Declan said, ignoring Kentravyon. "It was as if we slammed into a wall or something."

Cayal made a noise of disgust, then turned and began to swim toward the distant shore as the last remnants of their thatched roof-section sank below the waves. A few moments later, still clutching his prized fish, Kentravyon did the same. The Tide Lords neither asked for a further explanation nor bothered to reprimand Declan for his carelessness. Puzzled by their odd behaviour, Declan eyed the coastline warily, thinking it was almost too far to swim. But then, what was too far, now he was immortal? In theory, he could survive here forever.

Declan struck out after Cayal. If Kentravyon or the Immortal Prince knew what had caused their accident, they weren't saying. But there was something in the way neither of them questioned Declan's assertion that he'd simply slammed into something, that made him think they knew what was going on.

Perhaps, if one of them was feeling generous, they might eventually tell him what it was.

"What do you think happened?" Declan asked, as he emerged from the water a couple of hours later. The effort of swimming ashore through the breakwater had cooled his blood somewhat, making it easier to concentrate on their immediate dilemma. He still had no idea what had toppled them, and was hoping the others had some inkling. Kentravyon and Cayal were sitting on the deserted beach waiting for him. He had no idea where in Torlenia they were, other than a rough guess they were somewhere on the northern coast.

The others already had a fire going and had stripped off their wet clothes. *Why did they not use the Tide to dry them?* Declan wondered. Bedraggled and soaked to the skin, his boots squelching, Declan began peeling off his own shirt as he approached the fire.

Cayal was sitting naked on the sand beside the fire. He looked up, squinting into the sun setting behind Declan. "You weren't paying attention, is what happened."

"It felt like we hit a wall."

"What we hit, Rodent," Cayal said, "was a trip wire. Or the magic equivalent of one, at any rate."

Declan's brows drew together in confusion as he pulled the shirt over his head and wrung it out. "A magical trip wire? Who would set . . . ?" He stopped as he realised the answer to his question without having to complete it. "Brynden?"

Kentravyon nodded. He was also naked, his clothes spread out over the nearby rocks, drying in the remains of the day's sun. He was scaling the fish with a small dagger from his belt. Apparently his prized catch was going to be this evening's dinner. "Tide's coming in fast this time. Didn't think it'd be up high enough for something like that yet."

"But how could he know we were coming?"

"He wouldn't know," Cayal said. "He'd have set it around the whole continent. It's not that impressive a feat really—just a very thin magical barrier a few feet high, a couple of miles off the coast. The effort it takes to ride the Tide the way we've been doing means you probably wouldn't even feel it—unless you were paying attention. And clearly, you weren't paying attention."

"If you thought there was a danger of something like this happening, Cayal, why didn't you warn me?"

Cayal shrugged. "I should have, but I keep forgetting how stupid you are. Sorry."

Quashing the desire to even the score with Cayal using his fist, Declan decided to let that one pass. He turned to Kentravyon. "So if Brynden set a trip wire, then he'll know we're here?"

"Without a doubt," Kentravyon agreed.

"What will he do?"

"Depends on what else he's got going on here in Torlenia, I suppose," Cayal said before Kentravyon could respond. "He won't know who's tripped his alarm, just that somebody has. He might not even come to investigate if he's otherwise engaged."

"He might send Kinta," Kentravyon suggested. "She's a fierce warrior, is our Kinta," he added with a smile. "If I ever decide to take a goddess, I could do worse than her."

"Don't bother," Cayal said, with an edge of bitterness in his voice. "She's not worth the trouble. Believe me, I speak from experience."

Kentravyon looked at him curiously. "Lukys mentioned Kinta when he was bringing me up to date on everything I've missed these past few eons. You stole her from Brynden, didn't you? Or kidnapped her? Or something like that?"

"I didn't steal her. She was the one who wanted to leave Brynden."

"That would not have made him happy."

Declan couldn't help but smile at Kentravyon's mild observation. He sat down and began working off his sodden boots. "That's something of an understatement, I hear."

Cayal glared at him. "You weren't there, Rodent, so why don't you keep your flanking unwanted opinion to yourself?" The Immortal Prince turned to Kentravyon. "Whatever way this plays out, we'd be well advised to be gone from Torlenia before he does come looking for us, though. You're right about how fast the Tide is coming in. I don't know that we've got the time to indulge in a pissing contest with Brynden."

The older man sighed regretfully. "What a pity, Cayal, that you wish to die right at the point where you appear to have gained some wisdom."

"How do we keep going?" Declan asked.

Cayal looked at him with a puzzled expression on his face. "What?"

"We need something to ride, don't we?"

"Yes."

"Well, the roof-section is gone, the carpet's back in Stevania, and there doesn't seem to be much here," Declan said, indicating the barren rocky landscape, "from which to fashion a raft."

"Kentravyon's got a dagger. We could skin you alive and use your hide stretched over a couple of bits of driftwood. I mean, you're the biggest one here, Rodent, so it makes sense to have you volunteer for it. And it's not like your hide won't grow back in a day or so. Might be a bit painful, though. What do you think, Kentravyon?"

The madman smiled. "I think you've been anticipating an opportunity to make a suggestion like that ever since we left Stevania."

Cayal grinned back at him. "Doesn't mean it's not a good idea."

"It's a stupid idea," Declan said, finally getting off his right boot. "Why don't we just use Kentravyon's cloak?"

Cayal seemed rather disappointed at the suggestion and looked to Kentravyon, hoping, Declan suspected, that he'd refuse. "You don't have to give it up, you know, old boy. The Rodent's hide is plenty thick enough for our needs."

"Perhaps," Kentravyon agreed, "but the time he'd take to heal is time we don't have."

Declan found it more than a little disturbing to think the only thing stopping Kentravyon from agreeing to Cayal's ludicrous plan was the idea that the healing process required to recover from being skinned alive might slow them down a bit. He remembered the lines of dead on the cliff top in Stevania. *Tides, but these creatures are callous monsters.*

What does that make me?

"Then it's settled," he said, making sure they had this clear in their minds and it didn't involve him being skinned. "We move on, using Kentravyon's cloak. When we get to Elvere, we can find something a bit more suitable."

"We won't be stopping in Elvere," Cayal said. "Or anywhere else in Torlenia if we can help it. Next stop after this will be the Chelae Islands."

"But first we eat!" Kentravyon declared, holding up his gutted prize.

"There's not enough meat on that wretched thing to feed a starving child, Kentravyon," Cayal pointed out with a frown.

"Then it's a good thing there are no starving children here," Kentravyon said, tossing the fish into the flames. It hissed and smouldered for a few moments, the stench of burning scales making Declan glad he didn't have to eat if he didn't want to. If his survival had depended on that one small charred fish, he'd be in big trouble.

"If we're so pressed for time," Declan said, tugging on his left boot, "do we have time to eat?"

"We have time," Cayal said. "Unless Brynden's hiding over the next ridge, he's unlikely to find us before morning."

"*Unlikely?*"

"There always a chance, Rodent, however unlikely. I mean . . . look at you."

Declan pulled off his other boot and emptied the water out of it before answering. "If you're looking to figure the odds, Cayal, you might want to wonder what the chances of me helping you anytime soon are going to be, if you keep trying to piss me off."

Cayal didn't seem too bothered by Declan's warning. "Maybe I'm trying to make *sure* you want me dead."

"Making you suffer seems like a lot more fun right now, Cayal."

"You'll change your mind," Cayal told him confidently. "Come the crunch you'll look at me and realise everything in your world would be better if I'm dead."

"And you're counting on that?"

"Like it was—" Cayal stopped abruptly and looked around.

Declan felt it too—the ripples on the Tide that indicated another immortal was approaching. They both jumped to their feet, although Kentravyon paid no attention to the disturbance, too interested in his fish.

"That way," Cayal said, pointing inland.

Declan turned, squinting into the darkness that was slowly overtaking the land. "Can you tell who it is?"

Cayal shook his head. "It's not Brynden. The ripples aren't strong enough."

"Kinta then?"

"Probably."

They waited as the immortal drew closer, her presence humming along Declan's still hypersensitive veins as if they were taut wires singing in a high wind. A few moments later, a chariot appeared on the top of the dune behind them, pulled by a matched pair of greys. The person driving the chariot wore a shroud in the Torlenian fashion, which led Declan to assume that it was a woman. She brought the chariot to a stop and looked down over the beach for a moment, before turning the horses into the dune and plunging down the slope toward them.

The men waited for her as she drove toward them on the damp sand. After stopping the horses a few feet from their fire, she alighted from her chariot, but made no move to identify herself. Dark eyes through the slit of her embroidered shroud took in Cayal's naked figure with barely a second glance, spared a curious look at Kentravyon sitting on the sand roasting his fish and then she turned her attention to Declan.

Lifting the shroud to reveal a statuesque blonde woman wearing a tooled and gilded leather breastplate and a short leather warrior's skirt, she stared at him, frowning.

"I am Kinta," she said in Torlenian. "Consort to My Lord Brynden, the true Imperator of Torlenia. I know who these two are and the trouble they bring with them. Just who the hell are you?"

Chapter 18

Kinta proved to be everything Cayal's reports about her claimed—and then some. She was a tall woman, easily as tall as Arkady, but much more statuesque, her body forced into its optimum form by her immortality. She was beautiful, regal and thunderously angry, both at the intrusion into Brynden's realm by these uninvited guests and the realisation that someone was out there making new immortals. It was only on hearing that he was Lukys's son and Maralyce's great-grandson that she seemed to begrudgingly accept, if not Declan himself, then at least the truth of his origins.

"Brynden will not be happy when he hears of this," she said to Cayal, after Declan got through explaining how he'd been made immortal accidentally in the Herino Prison fire. "To think you've been lying to us all this time . . ."

"Hey, I wasn't lying to anybody," Cayal objected. "Tides, Kinta. Do you think I would have drowned Glaeba trying to put out the Eternal Flame if I'd had any idea that it *wasn't* the Eternal Flame? Where is the noble champion of double-crossing traitors, anyway?"

"He's back in Ramahn," Kinta told them with a frown, clearly not pleased by Cayal's description of her lover. "I'm only here because the coast was hit with a tidal wave." She shook her head as she made the connection. "Tides, I should have guessed one of you was behind this. Do you know how many of our people have died this past week?"

"Probably just as many as died in Stevania," Declan said, his guilt growing more burdensome by the moment.

Kinta shook her head. "Chintara—the real one . . . her family seat is not far from here. I was here seeing what we could do for the survivors. When I felt the barrier breached, I knew Brynden would want me to investigate."

"So Brynden's moved on the Torlenian throne then?" Declan asked. He was wondering if this woman had murdered her young unsuspecting husband herself or waited until Brynden returned and had him do the job for her—an act that seemed at complete odds with a woman who would cross a continent to aid the survivors of a natural disaster.

Kinta nodded, perhaps not picking up the edge in Declan's voice. "The Imperator fell ill, and during his illness a great change overcame him. He emerged from it a different man."

"Changed from the real Imperator to Brynden, you mean?" Cayal said. He shook his head for a moment, smiling wryly. "Tides, that sanctimonious bastard is worse than you, Rodent. He lectures *me* about morals and then commits regicide to put himself on the Torlenian throne. What a hypocrite."

"What Brynden has done will aid all Torlenians and lead them to a better life," Kinta insisted. "And there was no bloodshed."

"Not counting your poor husband," Kentravyon reminded her, which surprised Declan because the madman didn't seem to be taking much notice of their conversation.

Kinta glared at Kentravyon, but didn't respond to his interjection. "The people are rejoicing in their new monarch's strength and purpose."

"Only because they don't know he's replaced the old one," Cayal said. "But, you know what? He can have Torlenia. He can have the whole flanking world, for all I care. We have business in the north, so . . . nice seeing you again, Kinta, but if you don't mind, we'll be on our way." He turned his back on her, snatched his trousers from the rock where they were laid out to dry and began to get dressed.

"You're not going anywhere without telling me what you're up to," she said. "And explaining what *he's* got to do with it," she added, pointing to Declan.

Declan was getting a little fed up with trying to explain his very existence every time he ran across a new immortal. Kinta was proving to be particularly trying. Not that he really blamed her in this case. Finding a new immortal in the company of Cayal and Kentravyon probably did nothing but deepen her suspicions about him, particularly given the trouble they'd caused her people on their way here.

Cayal straightened and turned to look at her. "It's none of your damned business what we're—"

"Just tell her, Cayal," Declan cut in.

"She doesn't need to know."

"She doesn't *not* need to know, either," he said. "And if you don't tell her the truth, she'll go straight back to Brynden and tell him about us, and then he'll be after you and we'll have to deal with him too. Tell her, for the Tides' sake."

Kinta looked at Declan with something close to respect. "You speak sense, Declan Hawkes. Perhaps the fates chose wisely, making you immortal."

"The fates had nothing to do with him becoming immortal, Kinta," Cayal said. "Mostly it was Lukys and his breeding program."

"What are you talking about, Cayal?"

Cayal stared at her for a moment and then he shrugged, as if he'd come to a decision about something. "Why don't we sit down?" the Immortal Prince suggested, with a resigned sort of sigh. "I'll tell you the whole sorry saga, starting with the startling news that about eighty years ago, Maralyce had another baby . . ."

When Cayal had finished bringing Kinta up to date, she frowned. It was completely dark now and they were all sitting around the driftwood campfire on the deserted beach. Apparently paying no attention to their discussion, Kentravyon was nosily sucking the bones of his fish clean on the other side of the fire. The night was silent, but for the soft susurration of the sea behind them.

"But if all it takes to create an immortal is to be more than half immortal to begin with," she said, her forehead creased with concern, "that throws into question everything we know or believe about ourselves and where we come from."

"Tell me about it," Cayal agreed heavily.

"It means you're all related, actually," Kentravyon said, tossing away the last of his fish. He wiped his hand on the sand and then looked at the three of them across the flames, smiling.

"What do you mean?" Kinta asked. She didn't seem to think there was anything to smile about.

Declan understood immediately what Kentravyon was getting at. "He means that if only a few immortals came through the rift in the first place, then any subsequent immortals must be their offspring."

Kinta shook her head. "That is not possible. My mother was an honourable woman, my father a chieftain in a village rarely visited by strangers. There is no way I can be the bastard get of some random immortal who just happened to be passing through. Nor could Brynden."

Kentravyon, now he was done with his fish, seemed to be a little more interested in the discussion. He moved closer to the fire and assumed something of a lecturing tone. "Actually, Kinta, my dear, given that you and Brynden both came from the *same* isolated village in the middle of Fyrenne, the chances are pretty good you're a tad more closely related than is socially acceptable."

Kinta looked mortified to receive that news, but it was Cayal who was shaking his head in denial. "This is nonsense. If what you say is true, then who are you claiming fathered me?" he asked. "My mother was the Queen of Kordana."

Kentravyon shrugged. "Tides, how should I know? I heard Pellys was hanging around Kordana there for a while, so maybe it was him. I *do* know your mother didn't die in childbirth. I hear she was done in for infidelity."

"That's ridiculous!"

"Well, you'd know, Cayal," Kentravyon said with a shrug. "But when you think about it, it fits. I mean, your sister always hated you, didn't she? And as the Queen of Kordana after your mother died, she'd have known the truth about you."

"I was exiled because I killed a man, not because I was a bastard."

"You may be right," the older man said. "But you *are* immortal now, so somewhere along the line, my lad, you have more than one immortal ancestor. That's fact, not speculation."

Declan watched Cayal with interest; he was still shaking his head in disbelief. Declan found it fascinating to see how these immortals were reacting to the news they were not who they thought they were. He had no such problem. He'd always known his grandfather was a Tidewatcher and, as such, had accepted, without really thinking much about it, the notion that he had immortal ancestors. To discover his father was also immortal was hardly news, either. He'd grown up knowing his mother was a whore and he could have been fathered by any one of numberless men.

But these immortals had thousands of years behind them believing they knew everything there was to know about themselves. Learning they might be wrong had really knocked the wind out of their sails.

"Why has nobody mentioned this before?" Cayal asked.

"What's to mention?" Kentravyon said. "It's of little mind who fathered whom, Cayal. I mean, young Declan here is a bit of an odd case, because he knows who his immortal ancestors are, but what difference would it make to the rest of you?"

Kinta smiled suddenly, although it wasn't a pleasant smile. "If Pellys fathered you, Cayal, that makes Tryan and Elyssa your brother and sister."

"Why?" Kentravyon asked, looking puzzled.

"Everyone knows Pellys fathered those two."

Kentravyon shook his head. "Unlikely. Or at least he wasn't completely responsible. I see the hand of Lukys and Coryna in the mess that resulted in Syrolee and her lot. You don't get a cluster of immortals like that happening by accident."

"Do you mean Coron the Rodent?" Declan asked, thinking Kentravyon had mispronounced the name.

The immortal smiled cryptically. "Coron wasn't always a rat, you know."

"But Coron's dead," Cayal said, frowning.

Declan didn't blame Cayal for looking worried. He was on this journey because he believed Lukys had found a way to kill an immortal and had proved it by killing Coron, the only immortal to have taken animal form. He didn't want doubts thrown on his beliefs now.

"How?" Declan asked. "How exactly did he kill the rat?"

"I don't *know* how," Cayal snapped. "I just know he's dead and Lukys can make me dead the same way, once he gets his hands on this Chaos Crystal Elyssa's found."

"Yes, but . . ." Declan said, the flaw in Lukys's story so screamingly obvious he couldn't understand why nobody but him could see it. "If you need the Chaos Crystal to kill an immortal, how did he do away with the rat if he doesn't *have* the crystal? I mean, even Kentravyon says he's not sure opening a rift with the Chaos Crystal will kill you. And you'd think they'd know by now, because they've done it a few times before, I gather?"

"Plenty of times," Kentravyon agreed cheerfully.

"Rift?" Kinta asked. "What rift?"

"Lukys has offered to kill Cayal by opening a rift to another world," Declan told her. "There's a risk that opening this rift will likely destroy

Amyrantha, mind you, but that doesn't seem to bother Cayal. Or any-body else involved in this venture either, now I come to think of it. They're on their way to visit Elyssa who has apparently discovered the location of the crystal Lukys requires to channel enough of the Tide to make it happen." He glanced at Kentravyon and Cayal. "Did I miss any-thing?"

Kinta glared at them. "Why were Brynden and I told nothing of this plan to open a rift to another world?"

Cayal rolled his eyes impatiently. "Tides, Kinta, why do you even ask? Last time I ran into Brynden he tried to flatten us with a meteor. No, actually that was the time *before* last. The *last* time he sold a friend of mine into slavery just to piss me off. And, for your information, I *did* mention opening the rift to Brynden. I even asked for his help. That's about the point he told me to go screw myself."

"She was a friend of yours too, my lady," Declan added. He doubted that Kinta had yet made the connection between the Ambassador of Glaeba's wife who she'd helped escape from Ramahn a year ago, and the mortal woman Brynden used to take his vengeance on Cayal. "And the reason I'm on this journey. I am hoping to find her."

"Find who?"

"Arkady Desean."

Kinta looked at him in surprise and then turned to Cayal. "*Arkady* was the lover Brynden punished to get at you? Tides . . . I mean, she told me she'd met you, Cayal, but I never realised . . ."

"She's not my lover," Cayal said. He jerked his head in Declan's direc-tion. "Well, not any more. Arkady belongs to him now. At least she did—until she found out we'd come to an amicable agreement about her fate between us, which she didn't seem to think was very gentlemanly—"

"Enough!" Kinta cut in, her ire rising. "Tides, you're making my head ache. You say you told Brynden of your plan to open this rift, even though it might result in the destruction of this world?"

"Well, I didn't really go into details . . ."

"That figures."

Cayal looked quite wounded by her tone. "Hey, I didn't even know the bit about destroying Amyrantha until a few days ago. And I'm still not sure I believe it either."

Kinta fixed her gaze on Kentravyon. "Is it true?"

He shrugged. "Don't know. Never gone back to any of the other worlds we left behind to find out."

"Other worlds?" Kinta said, looking even more confused. "What other worlds?"

"The *other* worlds," Kentravyon said. "The ones before this world. You know . . ."

"No, Kentravyon, I don't know," Kinta said, frowning. "The last I saw of you was when we all banded together to immobilise you, because the only thing we immortals have ever agreed upon is that you're too dangerous to leave running around unsupervised. And yet, here you are, with a new immortal playmate at your side, off to fetch some crystal that will allow you to destroy Amyrantha." She stared at the three of them. "I want an explanation."

"I told you, Kinta—" Cayal began.

"Not from you," she cut in, turning her attention to Kentravyon. "From him."

The immortal looked quite shocked to be singled out. "Me? Why me?"

"Because you're the one who claims to know about these rifts to other worlds, Kentravyon," Kinta said. "You're the one who's saying that opening one will destroy Amyrantha. I want to know how you know that."

"Lukys is the one you need to talk to. He knows more about it than I do."

"Lukys isn't here," Kinta pointed out. "And even if he was, you're the one who claims to be God."

Declan watched Kinta warily, glad he wasn't on the receiving end of that stare. Although of the four immortals here she commanded the least power, she was not—he decided—someone to be trifled with.

"I *am* God," Kentravyon agreed simply.

"Which brings up another interesting question," Cayal said, looking at Kentravyon thoughtfully. "Who made you God, anyway?"

Declan shook his head at the futility of trying to get a rational explanation from a madman suffering delusions of divinity.

Tides, a few hours ago this man was giggling like a schoolgirl, trying to catch fish with his bare hands.

Declan was about to mention this aloud when Kentravyon said, "Of course, if Coryna hadn't started looking for a way to transfer her consciousness into a younger body, things might have turned out differently. We wouldn't have half the immortals we've got now for one thing, and Lukys wouldn't be so anxious to find a way to be rid of them all."

Declan, Kinta and Cayal were all silent as they digested that unexpected statement. It was Declan who finally asked the question they all wanted answered.

"Who are you, Kentravyon . . . really?"

"And who, in the name of the Tides," Kinta added, "is Coryna?"

Chapter 19

My name was not always Kentravyon. To be honest, I can't remember what it was originally. I was made immortal as a youth. I might look like a mature man now, but that should give you some notion of how long I have been alive. You, who've not collected, so much as a wrinkle or a grey hair in eight millennia, can't imagine what it must take for an immortal to age. Lukys is even older than I am and was little more than a lad when he met the Eternal Flame. Coryna and Maralyce—well, they are the oldest of us all.

I know what you're going to say, Declan. The Eternal Flame is a lie. You were made immortal with nothing more than a falling beam in a burning building. But it's an old habit to call it that. Fire—and fire only—is what makes us. It is the process of immolation that makes us immortal.

Provided—so we've discovered—you have the right ancestors, of course.

And that makes it difficult, you know, because it's next to impossible to keep track of these things. Mortals flash past us like sparks in the night from a fire stoked into life. You plan to keep track. You know your seed is strong with a life-force no mortal can match. But you can't stay in one place for too long, or people start to notice you. So you move on, never really sure which child is yours . . .

Until young Declan here—and it was a stroke of luck, not planning, that he learned the truth. Even so, it's rare for one of us to push the matter so far. It is no easy thing being immortal and those of us who understand that would not willingly bestow godhead on another unless there was a compelling reason to do so. Lukys tells me he was going to let you live and die in peace. But you found a fire without help from us, and discovered our secret.

Except there is no secret about who we are. We are what *you* will become.

By "we" I mean those of us not of this world. There were five of us who stepped through the rift during the last King Tide. Me, Maralyce, Pellys, Lukys . . . and Coryna. There were more of us, once, but only six of us inhabited the last world we called home. Tameca stayed behind when we left it. Like you, Cayal, she'd had enough. It was her time, she believed, to die. She held the rift open for us, and the last one through almost never survives. So you see, Lukys is not lying to you about that. If you anchor the rift, you'll more than likely not survive the closing of it.

The rest of the immortals who make up that silly Tarot the mortals of this world have invented are of this world, which is something we try to avoid as a rule. We haven't even been here that long. Although by your standards, at any rate, I suppose we have. So a certain mixing of the bloodlines is inevitable. It's not good that there are so many immortals here. That's part of the reason it's time to move on.

So, we're not who you think we are. We came here before there were people, before there was much of anything, really. Tides, the ham-fisted way you amateurs found to make the Crasii made us cringe. You have no concept, none of you, of how to truly manipulate the stuff of life, or the patience to sit back and wait for it to happen. The game is one that requires infinite patience. To set something in motion, tweak it a little here and there, until you have a whole world that is so finely crafted, so gloriously interconnected, that every living thing on it is interdependent on every other living creature. That's not science—it's art.

That's what it is to be God. But none of you understands that. Yet.

And your stupid power games. Tides, we watch Syrolee and her family jostling to rule some backward kingdom and it makes us want to weep—not for the power they seek, but that they are willing to settle for so little. They seize an empire and think they're kings. With a little more finesse, they could be true gods.

Like me.

But I digress. You asked about Coryna . . . or Coron . . . whatever you want to call her. She has many names on many worlds and on most of them she is a goddess. I don't know how long she has been alive, but I do know this much—she has been alive long enough for her to worry that she is growing old.

I'm not sure what started her worrying about it. Perhaps she thought if her beauty faded, Lukys's heart might start to wander. I can't imagine why she'd be concerned about that. There is no limit to what Lukys will do for Coryna, no length to which he is not prepared to go, no sacrifice too great, no deed so foul that he'd not perform it willingly if she commanded him.

I've witnessed many great love affairs in my time, more than a few that became legend on their worlds, but there is nothing in either the mortal world or fiction to compare with the dedication Lukys has for his lover. You need to remember that, children, because even when you *think* he's helping you, everything he does, every thought he has, every move he makes, is in some way connected to her.

I include my own ice-bound incarceration in that. You thought you were helping to contain me because I'm insane, I suppose. Lukys tells me that's the story he fed you all. Truth is, Lukys was more interested in what a few thousand years in the ice would do to an immortal. My social experiments with xenophobia and monotheism had little to do with it, other than giving him a plausible excuse to co-opt you to his cause. This time, in order to gain your cooperation to channel the power he needs, he's offering Cayal a chance to die. I don't doubt for a moment that he intends to honour his promise, mind you. But it's not the only reason.

The true reason is Coryna.

Remember that—nothing Lukys does is ever for the reason you think it is.

And that includes coming to Amyrantha. Lukys said this world would be easier to manipulate, but it was Coryna's fear of growing old that brought us to Amyrantha, not anything else we might have gained from coming here.

The last world we inhabited was nothing like this one. It was warm and vibrant and we treated it like our personal playground. We built creatures to keep us entertained—from the tiniest insects to behemoths the size of sailing ships. Not in the clumsy way you constructed the Crasii, but with finesse—with the smallest of changes on the most minute level and then we let nature take its course. It was indescribably diverse and beautiful, our immortal playground, and we lived in relative peace with it and each other for a very, *very* long time . . .

And then we grew bored. It happens . . . always happens . . . and we started to recall worlds before this one, and what it had been like to have creatures made in our own image to interact with . . . someone other than ourselves to talk to. The veneer of paradise began to fade once we began to recall what that was like.

We started to hunger for another challenge.

We weren't really planning to move on, that I recall. We were just fidgety and bored and talking about it really, but then the Tide came in and it was going to be a King Tide and Coryna reminded us that if we didn't move now, we'd not be able to move again until the next King Tide and that might be a thousand or a hundred thousand years away.

So we dusted off the Chaos Crystal, opened the rift, and stepped out on Amyrantha.

We brought enough creatures and vegetation with us to get things moving on this world without having to start again from scratch, and before long—at least by our definition of *before long*—we had a world able to sustain human life. After that we did what we always do—we let nature take its course.

I'll admit we didn't leave *everything* to chance. We all contributed our own seed to create our very own race of mortals made in our image, so in a way, every human on Amyrantha is descended from one of us. The spark is dim in some, but in others it burns a little brighter. I suppose that's the reason we ended up with so many of you. After the accident in Cuttlefish Bay that resulted in Syrolee, Tryan, Elyssa, and the rest of them, it became apparent that our carelessness had created a pool of potential immortals who were going to cause us problems if we didn't limit their numbers. Tides . . . and then Diala started trying to make them *deliberately*, and things got really messy there for a while.

We thought about stopping her, but Lukys advised against it. I know Maralyce was all for it, and so was Pellys. At least until Cayal cleaved his head from his shoulders. It's not the first time he's done that, either, which is why he's such a simpleton. Each time a little less of him grows back, I fear. And if you'd bothered to ask about the consequences, Cayal, we could have told you the danger you were courting by trying to decapitate an immortal. But you didn't ask, did you? Too busy play-ing the noble friend and hero to stop and think about the consequences.

Tides, there is nothing worse than a well-intentioned immortal.

Anyway, after the others were made immortal and Diala started her minion-making, we worried what it would mean if we revealed the truth about the Eternal Flame—which was Engarhod's idea, I believe.

He took what Lukys told him about fire making him immortal quite literally. The flame that Cayal extinguished in Glaeba started out as a remnant of the ship destroyed near Jelidia several thousand years before, I believe; the same flame that burned down the brothel in Cuttlefish Bay.

Lukys was living in Cuttlefish Bay. He was on that ship to Jelidia because of Coryna.

But I'm getting ahead of myself. I was talking about how the story of the Eternal Flame got started. Cayal had his tantrum and rid us of the Flame eventually, which was a blessing to those of us who knew the truth, and that was the end of any new immortals for a while. That you are here now, Declan, and can trace your ancestry, means Lukys is tampering again, trying to make a new immortal.

That is because of Coryna, too.

And he has Maralyce helping him, I don't doubt, even though she'd probably deny it. Her devotion to Coryna, while not as obsessive as Lukys's love, is every bit as strong. If Lukys needed Maralyce's help to make more immortals, she'd have given it, if it meant restoring Coryna.

You see, Maralyce is Coryna's twin sister.

I'll tell you something else you may not realise. Declan, you were never going to be made immortal—not because Lukys was feeling generous, but because you're male. Lukys is looking for a female body—young, beautiful and worthy of his queen. Whatever he told you, Declan, whatever web of lies Lukys wove to convince you, he never intended to make you immortal. The truth is, you were out of contention from the moment you emerged from the womb and someone announced, "It's a boy!"

Which brings me to Coryna again, and how she was afraid of growing old.

We'd speculated in the past—any number of times—on the possibility of transferring one's mind into a different body, and once Lukys got the idea, he started to study the practicalities of it. When he announced he thought he had the problem solved, Coryna decided she'd like to try it. I suppose it gave them something to aim for. A hobby, if you like; a puzzle that would fill their waking hours for countless eons to come . . .

I know what you're thinking; I can see it in your eyes. If we're already immortal, we already have bodies that cannot be harmed. What purpose would there be in changing form? You only think that way because you are defined by the brief time you've been alive. Live for a few million years more, and then start to wonder if there is anything else to be experienced. Then you'll begin to understand the allure. Decide you'd like to spend time as a different gender—just to see what it feels like. Or perhaps experience the world as an animal. Or a creature adapted to an environment so unlike the one you are used to that your very perception of the universe is altered.

These are the thoughts that occupy immortal minds left idle for too long.

Some of us go mad.

Some of us start experimenting.

We had long speculated about transferring consciousness between bodies. In theory, it seemed plausible; the practicalities, however, were a little more problematic.

If you're going to transfer the mind from one immortal's body into another, the first problem you face is that you can't use another immortal body, even if you could find an immortal willing to surrender their own consciousness to make room for a new one. The same magical protection that prevents any harm coming to an immortal prevents the transfer from taking place. So, even after we'd worked out how to effect the transfer, we were stuck with the significant problem of *where* we could transfer the consciousness.

The obvious answer to that is to use a mortal mind, but with a mortal mind comes a mortal body. We who *want* to live forever have no wish to surrender our lives for a few brief moments of joy in someone else's form. And we learned the hard way that there is no going back.

There was no meteor that conveniently struck Engarhod's ship near Jelidia, that only he, Lukys and the rat survived. Lukys spun that story when Engarhod regained consciousness. And being little more than a simple fisherman, the man swallowed every word of the tale—after Lukys's tampering had immolated him and destroyed the ship. If you want a measure of how gullible Engarhod and Syrolee are, they believed the story then, and have never thought to question it since.

The truth is far more simple. The Tide is strongest near the magnetic poles, although I doubt even Lukys knows why. He needed to be near the pole to attempt the transfer of Coryna's consciousness into a new, younger, body.

It was High Tide by then. He, Maralyce and Coryna had been studying and planning and fiddling with bloodlines for centuries, thinking they had everything in place to effect the transfer. Engarhod, as far as I know, wasn't chosen for any other reason than he was a competent sailor—just a man in the right place at the wrong time.

Coryna travelled on the ship as its cook, and the body they'd chosen as a replacement for her went along—quite unsuspectingly, I assume—as Lukys's mistress. Her name was Taya, if I recall it correctly. She was Lyna's sister, in case you're wondering, which is one of the reasons I always found that woman so damned attractive. Perhaps it's the idea that she could have been Coryna that makes her so desirable. Or maybe it's just the idea of taunting Lukys with his failure . . .

It doesn't really matter. Either motive serves me just as well. The irony is they chose the wrong sister, you see. The one they left behind was the one they should have taken. It was Lyna, not Taya, who had the potential to become immortal.

Lukys and Coryna had been living in and around Cuttlefish Bay for quite a while by then. They owned most of the fishing fleet working out of the harbour, including Engarhod's ship. Lukys—in typical fashion—was posing as his own father and son. He had everyone convinced he was two different people, and when he finally embarked on the trip to Jelidia to test his theories, he was able to spin some nonsense about being the reluctant eldest son, more interested in astronomy than trade. It also gave him an excuse to take the measurements he needed before attempting the transfer, without Engarhod or his crew asking too many questions.

You know what happened, of course. The whole thing ended in disaster. Lukys destroyed the ship with the amount of Tide magic he and Coryna tried to channel while extracting her consciousness from her body. Taya was one of the first to die. Engarhod survived, but his immortality made transferring Coryna's mind into his body impossible. Coryna's original body was lost in the wreck and nowhere to be found. For all I know it's still floating around the depths of the southern oceans somewhere, mindless, thoughtless and devoid of all awareness; a regenerating source of nourishment for any meat-eating fish who happens by.

Lukys was desperate when he realised what had happened, terrified that if he left it more than a few seconds, he would lose not only Coryna's body, but her consciousness as well. And then he spied it—the only other creature who'd survived the explosion. A ship's rat, of all things. Lacking sentience, it had neither the wit nor the will to fight him. Desperate by then and with nothing left to lose, Lukys did the only thing he could think of—he rammed Coryna's fading consciousness into the rat.

Thus was Coron the Immortal Rodent born. We're not sure why the rat survived, or how it achieved immortality. It might have been one of those one-in-a-million things, or there might be some mechanism in play that we've never considered. Coryna has enough awareness to know who she *should* be, but neither the power nor the ability to act upon it while she remains in animal form. If she is to be rescued, it'll be one of us who saves her.

Trapped as a rodent, Coryna cannot save herself.

And I will tell you now the reason why Lukys has been making more potential immortals with Maralyce's help, and built himself a palace near the southern magnetic pole of Amyrantha. There is a King Tide coming. He may mean to keep his promise to you, Cayal, to end your sorry existence—just as he may well honour all the other promises and compromises he's been forced to make along the way to achieve his goal. But they are secondary considerations.

Lukys has a fresh young female body—a potential immortal—waiting in the wings, and he's experimented enough over time now to be reasonably certain of success. Coryna grows impatient so he's leaving nothing to chance. To draw the power required to restore his lover to a human body, he's gathering every Tide Lord he thinks he can trust to aid him in his quest. And that includes waking me—even knowing how pissed I would be that he froze me in the first place.

Lukys judges people well. I'd not lift a finger to help you die, Cayal, if that was the only reason we were doing this. But to bring Coryna back—to see if Lukys can actually make this work. Well, for that, even I am willing to put myself out a little. And we're going to make dammed sure we've got sufficient power this time by using the Chaos Crystal, which means we can channel the Tide magic from more than one world at a time.

We'll open a rift, sure enough, when the Tide peaks. But it won't be to give you the death you crave, Cayal.

It will be to give Coryna life.

Chapter 20

"Did you never ask Lukys for proof that Coron was dead?" Kinta asked Cayal some time later.

Kentravyon had wandered off somewhere, leaving the others walking along the dark beach trying to digest everything he'd told them. Declan's head was still reeling; he couldn't imagine how the other two felt. The first glimmer of sunrise was beginning to lighten the sky to the east, the air was cold and the tide was coming in. They would have to move soon or be swamped by it—an ironic analogy of the magical Tide that wasn't lost on Declan.

"Of course I asked for proof," Cayal said. "He showed me a dead rat."

"And you just assumed it was Coron?"

Cayal glared at him. "Don't take that tone with me, you inbred little prick. Why wouldn't I believe him? He's not wandered more than five feet from that wretched rat in eight thousand years. Why is it so hard to think that when he showed me its corpse and told me it was his pet and there was no sign of the live Coron, I believed he was telling the truth?"

"I'd have believed him," Kinta said, surprising Declan by siding with Cayal. "The question is, do we believe Kentravyon?"

"He's mad," Cayal said.

"What he told us had a certain ring of authenticity," Declan said. "And it fits with what we know."

"Well, it would, wouldn't it?" Cayal said. "You've been alive for how long? Not quite thirty years? Yes, I can see how that would equip you with all the knowledge you'd need to make a sound and rational judgement on the fate of the immortals. I bow to your superior knowledge, O Great and All-knowing Spymaster."

"Stop it, Cayal," Kinta said impatiently.

"Or what?"

Kinta didn't answer him, turning to Declan instead. "What are you going to do now?"

"Continue on to Glaeba," he told her. "For me, nothing has changed. I'm trying to find Arkady. What about you?"

"I need to talk to Brynden. Tell him what Kentravyon said. It will . . . bother him, I think."

"That's something of an understatement," Cayal said, with a short, bitter laugh. "It's going to knock the stuffing right out of our brave and noble warrior. Imagine what it's going to feel like—after all that time he's spent looking for the true meaning of immortality—when he discovers it's all about the rat. Tides, it's a good thing he is immortal, because otherwise this news *would* kill him."

"And what about you, Cayal?" Kinta asked. "Do you intend to aid Lukys in his quest to restore Coron to human form?"

"Why not? If it means I die in the process, he can transform a whole flanking chorus line of Jelidian snow bears into dancing girls for all I care."

"Kentravyon's right about one thing," Declan noted. "Lukys is a brilliant judge of what motivates people."

"What do you mean?"

"I mean, look at you. You're nodding and saying 'Well, isn't that interesting,' but nothing's changed so drastically that you're threatening to pull out of the deal. You're still willing to open the rift for him, despite the risks. Cayal still wants to die. Kentravyon seems to want to help just because he's curious. Lukys's motives may be noble enough that Brynden won't try to interfere, even when he learns the truth. He's got you worked out pretty well, I reckon. To align your friends *and* your enemies so fortuitously—that takes *real* talent."

"But not you?" Cayal said. "Is that what you're implying? We'll all fall into line, but you're waiting to see what Arkady wants to do?" He laughed. "Tides, there's a word for men like you, spymaster, and it's not a very nice one."

"How can you assume to know what Brynden will do?" Kinta asked, a little miffed by the suggestion.

"I don't know," Declan said. "Not for certain. I'm basing my judgement on what I know *of* him, my lady. If Kentravyon is to be believed, Lukys is motivated—when you get down to it—by nothing more than undying love for Coryna. Didn't Brynden cause a Cataclysm over you for much the same reason?"

"Mindless rage driven by insane jealousy isn't undying love, Rodent. It isn't any sort of love," Cayal said, and then he shook his head. "Tides, it seems wrong now, calling you that. I'll have to think of something else."

"You could try, you know, my *name*."

Cayal flashed a grin at him. "Now where would be the fun in that?"

"Will you still help Lukys open the rift, Declan?" Kinta asked, ignoring Cayal. "Now you've heard what Kentravyon has to say?"

Declan shrugged. "One minute Kentravyon is telling us that opening this rift might destroy the world, the next minute he's offering up hope of a future free of immortal interference and the Cataclysms that go with it. Tides, he's even got *me* thinking that if we open a rift and even *some* of the immortals leave this world, Amyrantha will be a better place, and that may be worth risking its total destruction."

"If he's planning to leave Syrolee and her lot behind after the rest of us have gone, total destruction might be preferable," Cayal said with a sour laugh. Then his amusement faded and he added thoughtfully, "I wonder why he's so keen to bring Elyssa along, though?"

"If he perfects his method for transferring consciousness from one body to another, she would be a prime candidate for the procedure," Kinta said. "If Lukys offered her the chance of a new body, don't you, think she'd do absolutely anything he asked of her?"

"Are you sure of that?"

Kinta nodded. "You know as well as I do, Cayal, that Elyssa would trade her immortality for the chance to be rid of her curse."

"Which is what exactly?" Declan asked.

The two immortals hesitated for a moment before answering.

"Elyssa was a virgin when she was made immortal," Kinta told him, when it seemed Cayal wasn't planning to volunteer the information. "Which means every time she takes a lover, her hymen has to be re-broken, and then it begins to heal again, almost immediately."

Declan winced at the very thought of it. He'd experienced enough of immortality's agonising rapid healing to imagine how painful that must be.

"If she's not quick about it, it heals while she's still trying to do the deed," Cayal added with a grimace. "That's caused some problems in the past, let me tell you."

Kinta nodded in agreement. "She kills her lovers now, as soon as she's climaxed, I hear. That way she can get rid of them at her leisure and doesn't have to explain to the poor lad why—in his moment of ecstasy—her hymen has grown over his manly pride and joy and the only way out for him now is to be surgically removed from her."

The image that created in his head was one Declan could well have done without. "So what happens when she takes an immortal lover?"

"We heal up just as fast," Cayal said. "We can take the fun if we can take the pain. It's not something I've ever felt the need to try, however."

"Hence the reason for Elyssa's unrequited love for our poor Immoral Prince," Kinta said, smiling at Cayal. "She really has never gotten over her crush on you, you know."

"Well, at least you have a reason now to get her to cooperate," Declan said.

"I'm not sleeping with her," Cayal said. "I'd almost rather go on living."

"You don't have to," Declan pointed out, wondering why he was bothering to help Cayal with anything. It wasn't as if he cared about the fate of the Immortal Prince one way or another. And he certainly didn't want to do anything that might result in the destruction of Amyrantha. At least, he hoped that was the case. Perhaps Lukys knew his son better than he thought. Perhaps, for that one chance to be rid of Cayal, Declan *was* willing to aid his quest for immortal suicide, even at the risk of destroying Amyrantha.

He didn't have time to dwell on his motives now, however, and Cayal was looking at him, expecting an explanation. "All you need to do is tell her what Kentravyon told us. Tell Elyssa that Lukys has a way to transfer her consciousness into another body—one without the problems she has now. If Kinta's right, you won't have to coax the Chaos Crystal from her; she'll hand it over willingly and follow you all the way back to Jelidia like a little lost puppy."

Kinta nodded in agreement. "He's right, Cayal. She would."

Cayal thought on it for a moment as he walked, but Declan couldn't tell what he was thinking. The water, however, was starting to lap at his bare feet. "Tide's coming in."

"Well, thank you, Rodent. I don't think the rest of us noticed."

"I meant the water," Declan said, looking down as he took a step sideways to avoid the next wave. "There's Kentravyon."

The others looked in the direction he was pointing. Kentravyon was kneeling by a rock pool some way up the beach, poking around in it with great interest. He must have felt them approaching on the Tide. No sooner had Declan spoken than Kentravyon looked up and beckoned to them.

"Look!" he said, holding out his cupped hands. Declan reached him first and discovered Kentravyon holding a handful of molluscs, only they were like no molluscs he had ever seen before. The shells were rubbery and flaccid and bent to fit the form of Kentravyon's cupped hands.

"What is that?" Kinta asked as she peered at Kentravyon's offering.

"Proof there's a King Tide on the way."

"Ah, molluscs," Cayal said with a sage nod. "The famed universal indicator for Tide magic."

Kentravyon glared at Cayal, not appreciating his flippancy. "Look at their shells."

"They're not solid," Declan noted, puzzled by the phenomenon.

"This always happens when there's a King Tide coming. The sea is getting warmer. It changes the water; turns it into a weak sort of acid. The crustaceans are always the first to go."

"But the Tide hasn't peaked yet," Declan said, as the implications of something so apparently minor occurred to him. He was learning very quickly that nothing on Amyrantha happened in isolation, and, however obscure, there was always a connection to the Tide, even if it wasn't immediately obvious. But an ocean without crustaceans? Tides, that was almost inconceivable. What of the larger fish who relied on them for food . . . and the even larger fish who relied on *those* fish for survival?

"I should be getting back," Kinta said, frowning. Declan suspected she was thinking along the same lines as he was. "And after I think of a way to explain where I've been all night, I need to get back to Ramahn and talk to Brynden. He needs to know about Lukys's plans, as well as . . . this." She frowned at the flaccid mollusc in Kentravyon's hand then turned to Cayal. "Do I have your word you're heading for Glaeba, Cayal, and don't plan to stay around here looking for trouble?"

"Torlenia's not worth fighting over, Kinta," Cayal said. "Besides, the spymaster here won't be happy until he's found his girl again and begged her forgiveness for being such a prick. And Kentravyon's fixated on finding the Chaos Crystal. You can tell Brynden to save his posturing for someone who'll notice. We're not interested in Torlenia."

Kinta nodded and turned to Declan. "It was fascinating making your acquaintance, Declan Hawkes. Perhaps, at some time in the future, we will have a chance to talk again. I know Brynden will be very interested to meet you."

"Just don't let him catch you eyeing off his woman," Cayal advised.

Kinta glared at the Immortal Prince. "Tides, I don't know what I ever saw in you, Cayal."

"The same could be said for you, Kinta."

Kinta apparently thought answering that remark was beneath her dignity. With a farewell nod in Declan's direction—while pointedly ignoring Cayal—she turned and headed back along the beach to her chariot. Kentravyon was talking to the molluscs now, trying to engage them in a conversation in which they didn't seem inclined to take part.

Cayal sighed dramatically. "And so, the first meeting between the Rodent and the Charioteer ends without bloodshed. You know, I think that means she liked you."

"I thought you were going to think of a better name for me than Rodent?"

"I will . . . I will. Rodent just has a certain ring to it. Did you have a childhood nickname I could use?"

"None I'm ever going to tell you."

The Immortal Prince smiled. "I shall have to coax it out of Arkady then, when we find her. Assuming we find her alive, that is. I mean, Jaxyn may have had his evil way with her by now, then killed her and left her out for the crows. Or worse, she's decided one prick is as good as another, and they're now firm friends and she's bestowing her considerable charms on someone who appreciates her." He clapped Declan on the shoulder, smiling even wider. "Do you know, I think *you'd* rather she was left out for the crows."

"It truly is a miracle that nobody has found a way to do you in before now," Declan said, shaking Cayal's hand from his shoulder.

Over by the chariot, Kinta took the reins and climbed aboard. She turned the horses inland without looking back. Just then the sun set fire to the horizon, turning her into a dark, shrinking shadow outlined against the morning light.

Not getting any sense from the molluscs, Kentravyon tossed them aside, waved to Kinta once and then turned to the other Tide Lords, smiling. "I've always liked that girl."

"Is she yours?" Declan asked.

"Mine?"

"Well, you claim we're all descended from the five original immortals. I was just wondering, that's all, if the reason you're so fond of Kinta is because she's one of yours."

Kentravyon didn't answer immediately, content to stare at Declan thoughtfully for a moment. Then he shrugged, ignoring the question, and opened his arms wide. "Shall we move on, lads? The day is new, the Tide beckons, the Chaos Crystal awaits us and I've a hankering to do a bit more fishing. We can use my cloak to travel until we find something more suitable."

"I still think skinning the Rodent alive and using his hide is the preferred option," Cayal remarked, falling into step beside Kentravyon.

Declan thought of a score of responses to that, none of which would have achieved anything other than alert Cayal to the fact that his needling had hit the mark, so he said nothing. Instead, he followed the other immortals up the beach to continue their journey toward Glaeba, wondering if, when he got there, he should find a way to contact the Cabal.

And what their reaction would be to learning that not only was the ocean turning on them with the rising Tide, but that—for the Tide Lords—it wasn't about the Tide; it was all about a rat.

PART 2

"What is the reason," said I, "that the tide I see rises out of a thick mist at one end, and again loses itself in a thick mist at the other?"

"What thou seest," said he, "is that portion of eternity which is called time, measured out by the sun, and reaching from the beginning of the world to its consummation."

"The Vision of Mirza"
—Joseph Addison (1672–1719)

Chapter 21

"What is this place, your grace?"

Stellan pulled the bag from the back of his packhorse before answering Boots. Swaddled in furs against the fine snow that was falling, the canine Crasii was standing at the entrance to the ruins. She was clutching Missy to her chest, and looking up at the remains of a building so ancient and overgrown that the weathered caryatid supporting what was left of the stone roof struts were barely recognisable as female figures. The two male pups were tucked into a pannier that Boots had already unloaded and placed in the shelter of the ruins on the crumbling top step. Above them loomed a rocky outcropping—a useful feature as it was that landmark which made this place possible to find. Stellan had only been here once before, and that was years ago. He was a little surprised he'd been able to find it again.

"I suppose it was a temple or something like that, left over from an age before the last Cataclysm," he said. "That's what Arkady thought it might be."

"She's been here too?" Boots sounded surprised.

"We visited this place once, a long time ago," Stellan said, remembering how excited Arkady had been to see these unexplained ruins. "It wasn't long after we were married. Nyah's father brought us here, actually. We were visiting Cycrane on official business for the Glaeban crown. The Prince Consort knew of Arkady's interest in history and hoped she might have some idea of the ruins' original purpose."

"Whatever happened to the Duchess Arkady, your grace?" Boots asked, turning to look at him curiously.

"I wish I knew, Boots," Stellan said, dumping the pack on the step beside the pups. "I've not had word of her since I left Torlenia."

"Do you think she's all right?"

"I hope so. I sent someone to search for her who will look after my wife—if he can find her. Under the circumstances, that's the best I could do, I'm afraid."

Boots smiled at him encouragingly. "I'm sure she's safe. At least I hope she is. I liked your wife, your grace. We all did. She was always good to the Crasii."

Stellan nodded in agreement. With everything that had happened recently, it was easy to forget there was a time when Boots was his slave and Arkady the mistress of his estate, who had performed the duties of a duke's wife better than he could ever have hoped.

"I'm sure Arkady has found a way to survive, Boots. Now let's get you and the pups inside before you all freeze, eh?"

The Crasii nodded and moved toward the entrance. One of the pillars holding up the roof had crumbled under the weight of its age so they were required to step over the tumbled snow-covered stones to enter the main hall. It was dark inside but noticeably warmer, simply because they were out of the wind. Stellan lifted the pannier with the two sleeping male pups over the stones, putting them on the floor on the other side and then went back outside and pulled a torch from the pack. He lit it with his flint and held it high, lighting the hall as he walked back inside. A carpet of dead leaves covered the floor, the walls were draped with creepers and the surprisingly sound roof, further back inside the building, was criss-crossed with cobwebs.

"You weren't kidding when you said nobody comes here, were you?" Boots said, looking around with a frown.

"This is not ideal, Boots," he said, "but with the lake frozen solid and no boats available, this is the best I can do on short notice. I'm a guest in this country, you know. I don't exactly have the wherewithal to send you home."

She shrugged apologetically. "I'm sorry, your grace. I should be more grateful, I suppose. Is this all there is, or is there somewhere a bit less exposed around here where we can make camp?"

Stellan indicated further into the hall with the torch. "There are rooms off the main hall that should be sound and a staircase down to the lower levels, if I remember correctly. I'm not sure how safe it is down there, though."

Boots looked around the hall thoughtfully. "Might be safer than being up here; someone might spot the smoke from our fire and come to investigate."

"Fair point," Stellan agreed. "Although you'd be very unlucky to have anybody stumble over you here. The weather doesn't exactly lend itself to idle strolls along the lakeshore at the moment."

"Still, I think I'd feel safer if we were a little bit less vulnerable to a chance discovery," she said. "We're not *that* far from the city here."

Stellan thought her fears unfounded, but he also recognised the needs of a protective mother trying to keep her pups safe. If he didn't assuage her anxiety, Boots might well decide to bolt and make her own way home as soon as his back was turned, and that would, without question, prove fatal to her and her pups.

"Very well, Boots," he said, turning to pick up the two sleeping pups. "Let's look a little further inside and see what we can find."

Two hours later, Stellan was on his horse, riding back toward Cycrane, mentally rehearsing the story he'd invented to explain away the loss of Boots and her pups.

Admittedly, he had time to perfect his lies. The only soul in Cycrane who really cared about the fate of Boots and her pups was Elyssa, and she had left the palace several days ago with Warlock in tow to put into action his grand plans for defending Cycrane. He wasn't sure his idea would work, but the immortals seemed to like his suggestion, despite how strange it felt to him to be advising the leaders of a foreign country on the best way to protect themselves against his own people.

Elyssa had gone south of the city to where the largest of the Caelish tar seeps were located. If Tryan and the other immortals couldn't find a hot spring or some other orifice into the ground that they could manipulate with the Tide, Stellan's plan might be their only chance to protect themselves against invasion.

Of course, Tryan had appropriated the idea and made it his own when he realised it actually might work, but the immortals still hoped for a way to melt the ice now forming a land bridge between Caelum and Glaeba.

Although Stellan had originally voiced the idea of melting the ice by channelling some natural force into the lake to heat the water, in truth he thought the idea optimistic in the extreme. He had suggested the tar seeps as an alternative, thinking it a better option in the short term.

There was no way to prevent Jaxyn's army from marching on them. He knew nothing of the workings of the Tide, but suspected the sort of power required to melt the frozen Great Lakes was far more than a Tide Lord could muster, unless it was High Tide and they didn't mind causing another Cataclysm. Nobody wanted that. Destroying the kingdom that the Empress of the Five Realms and her kin had earmarked as their own before the Tide had even peaked was the last thing anybody—mortal or immortal—wanted.

No, even if it was possible, melting the ice was a last resort, not their first line of defence. For that, they had an army gathering all along the Caelish coastline, preparing to face the superior Glaeban numbers.

This war, Stellan feared, would be fought the hard way.

He had advised the Caelish against taking the fight onto the ice. The further Jaxyn's army—he never for a moment considered Mathu behind this invasion—had to march on the ice, the more exhausted and less ready to fight they would be when they arrived.

As for using magic—well, the ice needed to be shattered now, not slowly melted. Jaxyn and his army were already on their way.

But even if they couldn't turn back the Glaeban army, Elyssa would be gone long enough for him to save Boots and her pups, as he'd promised Warlock he'd do.

It was dark by the time he reached the edge of the city, and the tavern—named The Wounded Grasshopper for no logical reason Stellan could discern—where he'd dumped his guards earlier in the day. He had human guards now, which meant they were much more corruptible than felines. Fortunately, several days ago Ricard Li had replaced the felines ordered to guard Stellan on his arrival in Cycrane. The Caelish spymaster claimed they needed all their Crasii troops for the coming fight, and couldn't waste them guarding a man who clearly didn't need guarding. Tryan had agreed to the change with an absent wave of his arm, his attention focused on the news that the Glaeban army was finally on the move. The men were still in the taproom where he'd left them, although they were considerably drunker than when he'd ordered them to stay here this morning.

"Your graish!" the only one of his guards still conscious called out, when he spied the duke entering The Wounded Grasshopper's smoky taproom. "You're back!"

Stellan wove his way between the tables to where the men were sitting. The low-ceilinged room was warm, crowded, and full of men discussing the possibility of war. Of the three guards assigned to protect and watch over him, two were either asleep or passed out drunk. The third man was well on his way to being in the same condition. Stellan was a little afraid to find out what their bar tab might be, particularly as he had agreed to pay it.

"We got caught in the snow. I lost the bitch and her pups."

The man shrugged. "What's one less flanking canine and her litter, eh? Wanna drink?"

"No, thank you. If you're able to rouse your companions, I'd like to return to the palace. Losing Tabitha Belle and her pups has quite upset me, I fear."

The guard was too drunk to care about the tender sensibilities of the man he was guarding. He elbowed the guard next to him, whose face lay in a puddle of beer on the table. The other guard was slumped in the seat opposite, softly snoring. "Hey, wake up! His lordship's back. Time to go."

The man mumbled something incoherent but didn't seem inclined to move. "I'll settle up and meet you outside," Stellan said, and turned for the bar, hoping he had enough on him to pay the tab. Unless they were particularly cheap drunks, the guards must have drunk a heroic amount of ale to get into such a state in only a few hours.

Stellan shouldered his way to the bar and waved his hand to attract the attention of the barkeep. The man nodded when he saw Stellan, finished serving his most recent customer and then headed down the bar to speak with the duke.

"M'lord," the man said, wiping the bar in front of Stellan with a grubby cloth he kept tucked in his apron, as if it made any sort of difference to the general state of his establishment. "Those boys of yours have been puttin' a fair hole in my ale barrel."

"For which I'm more than happy to pay," Stellan assured him. "I hope they've not been too much trouble?"

"No more'n the rest of these reprobates," the barkeep assured him. "That'll be—"

"They're here!"

Stellan and the tavern owner both turned at the shout coming from the entrance of the taproom. A lad of about sixteen stood in the doorway, clutching his cap in his gloved hands, his face flushed with excitement. "They're here!" he repeated loudly, to make sure everyone heard him. "You can see them on the lake!"

"Who's here?" the barkeep demanded. "What are you prattling on about, Seth?"

"The Glaebans!" the boy answered impatiently. "You can see them coming!"

Stellan's tab was forgotten as everyone in the taproom clambered to their feet and headed for the door. Swept along with the crowd, Stellan soon found himself standing in a slight rise at the back of the tavern, looking out over the frozen waters of the Lower Ryrie. It was dark, the surface of the lake a grey, featureless sheet of ice stretching away into the distance. The air was bitterly cold, the recent snow coating everything in white.

"Where are they?" someone asked, as the rest of the tavern's patrons lined up to get a look at the invaders.

"There!" Seth called, pointing toward the ice.

Stellan spied them a few moments later. Not men, but torches; specks of distant golden light stretching in a line as far as the eye could see in either direction. They were a fair way from the shore yet. Stellan doubted the army would be here before morning, but the line of torches was disturbingly long, and moved slowly and relentlessly forward at a pace that spoke of an army on the march.

The crowd fell silent as the reality of impending war pierced their ale-fogged minds.

"Tides," somebody else remarked. "There must be thousands of them."

"I never thought they meant to actually *invade* us," someone else said. "Told my brother-in-law that the other day when he suggested we should join up and fight. That's what we got felines for, I told him."

"How many felines do you suppose the Glaebans have out there?" a rather worried-sounding voice a little further along the slope asked.

"All of them, by the look of it," somebody else replied.

Stellan stared at the invaders, feeling sick to his stomach. Those were his countrymen out there, and this war was—in no small part— because of him.

"Should we raise the alarm or something?" another man asked.

"They'll have lookouts at the palace," the barkeep said. "Don't need us to tell 'em the Glaebans are comin.'

"Bastards," somebody else muttered, which prompted a general murmur of agreement from the patrons of The Wounded Grasshopper regarding the dubious parentage of all Glaebans.

Stellan stayed watching the advancing line of torches for a long time, until his lone, almost-sober guard found him in the crowd and tugged on his sleeve.

"Your grace," he said in a low voice, so as not to attract the attention of the men around them. "We should be gettin' back to the palace."

Stellan looked back over his shoulder to find the other two guards conscious, if not exactly alert, standing with their horses, waiting for him.

"Yes, we should," he agreed. Stellan looked around for the barkeep and found him standing a few feet away, staring at the invaders. He made his way over to him, fished a silver piece out of his purse and pressed it into the man's hand. "This should cover everything."

The tavern owner glanced down at the silver coin glinting in the starlight and nodded. "Should cover it nicely, m'lord. Not a lot in this world can't be fixed with the application of the right number of silver pieces, I always say."

Stellan smiled at the man's simple philosophy and then turned and followed his guard back toward the tavern where the other guards and their horses were waiting, wishing the tavern owner was right about being able to buy his way out of anything.

It was going to take a lot more than the simple application of the right number of silver pieces to stop the Glaeban invasion of Caelum.

Chapter 22

"They're coming, my lady."

Elyssa looked up from the rice-paper map she was studying by the light of a lantern—a diagram of the map Stellan Desean had discovered on the back of the Lore Tarot dug up in a cave at the foot of Deadman's Bluff. The immortal had revised her opinion about the map in recent weeks, certain the landmarks on it—few that they were—were not in the south, as she'd first suspected, but located much closer to Lebec.

Warlock had no idea how she thought she could tell *what* it meant. The map was thousands of years old, after all. It wasn't hard to imagine the landscape had changed quite dramatically since the Cabal hid the Chaos Crystal to keep it out of the hands of the immortals—particularly as it was a map drawn before the formation of the Great Lakes.

"Damn." Elyssa rolled up the map and rose to her feet before walking down to the lakeshore to stand beside Warlock, who was hugging his arms around himself against the bitter cold. In the darkness, the glimmer of several thousand torches stretched out in a line as far as the eye could see across the ice. They had barely a day before the Glaeban army arrived, Warlock guessed. Hardly long enough to finish the job.

"He's not wasting any more time then."

"*He*, my lady?"

"Jaxyn." Elyssa was so used to Warlock's presence and his fawning Crasii manner that she rarely questioned anything he did or asked any longer, and often answered him with a frankness that shocked the canine Scard. Warlock was careful to keep his questions as banal and obsequious as possible, so as not to raise her suspicions. Still, it was sometimes hard to believe he had fooled her so completely that she never thought to doubt him.

Warlock wasn't sure how he should answer her this time, so he fell back on something suitably Crasii-like. "You will use the power of the Tide to defeat the invaders, my lady, and we will all be safe."

Elyssa glanced sideways at Warlock and smiled. "If only it were that simple, Cecil."

"The Tide rises, does it not, my lady? And you are a Tide Lord and therefore omnipotent?"

"Yes . . . and no. The problem is one of action and reaction, Cecil. If we fight Jaxyn using the Tide, he'll fight back using the Tide. A kingdom is no fun to rule if there's nobody left in it alive once the dust settles."

Warlock didn't have to feign surprise at her answer. He never expected restraint from any immortal, particularly not one of Syrolee's clan. "But are not you and Lord Tryan combined, stronger than Lord Jaxyn, my lady?"

"If we cooperate, yes, but that's not something I like doing, particularly with my brothers."

Warlock fell silent, fairly certain there was nothing a loyal Crasii could say to that. The conflict caused by siding with one Tide Lord over another should be enough to drive a normal Crasii crazy. Elyssa seemed to know that. She placed her hand on Warlock's arm and gripped it in a comforting manner. "Never fear, Cecil. You'll not be asked to choose between us. But we have work to do. For now, we must see what we can do about defeating those wretched Glaebans, eh?"

"To serve you is the reason I breathe, my lady," Warlock replied, which was always the safest way to respond to an immortal.

"And a much better world it would be," she replied, "if everybody thought the way you did, Cecil." She tucked the rolled-up map under her arm, and then, lifting her skirts out of the snow, turned back toward the camp where the rest of the workers were resting after the day's labours, in order to rouse them. There would be no rest tonight for the Crasii she had brought to the tar seeps south of Cycrane. There was war on the way and, by the look of it, it would be starting tomorrow. That meant they had only one night left to work on their defences.

Warlock hoped it was enough. He didn't know where Boots was, but what he did know was that if the Glaebans won this war, one of the first things victorious invaders did when taking over enemy territory was hunt down every enemy Crasii they could find and kill them. Even the pups. That might not happen now the Tide Lords were in charge . . . after all, a Crasii was compelled to serve any immortal they encountered. But Warlock wasn't prepared to take that chance. He was going to find his family and protect them. No matter what.

———

By morning, dawn had extinguished the pinpoints of light on the lake and the fifty or more canines responsible for digging the channels from the tar seeps to the lake were exhausted. The sticky black oil that bubbled out of the ground here—and in other sporadic locations along this side of the lake—was slowly working its way down into the channels Elyssa's workers had cut into the ice over the past couple of weeks. The past few days they had cut three shallow channels the width of a mattock blade about ten paces apart. The channels stretched north all the way along the ice past the city of Cycrane, where similar squads of Crasii had painstakingly dug connecting channels to allow the oil to flow along the ice.

The idea was Stellan Desean's, proving once again what a brilliant tactician the Glaeban duke was.

The Caelish could not hope to match the Glaebans' superior numbers, particularly when it came to fighting felines. But if felines had one weakness, it was their pathological fear of fire. Feline Crasii warriors might baulk at the stench of the oil channels, but Glaeban felines had probably never *seen* an oil seep, or the gooey—and highly flammable—black liquid that seeped from the earth and bubbled in small pools hidden in the foothills of Caelum, ready to trap any unwary animal or woodsman wandering by. The chances were good that even if they noticed the oil, they'd merely step over the shallow channels and continue on their way.

Warlock wasn't sure if the Glaebans had rested on the ice overnight or kept walking, but it seemed as if they hadn't moved as close as they might, had they marched through the night. In the daylight, there proved to be thousands and thousands of them in a long line stretching into the distance, their ranks too deep to make a guess at their numbers. Elyssa stood at the lakeshore by the head of the channel they'd cut leading from the oil seep, cursing the slow pace of the liquid, which seemed to progress at a snail's pace once it reached the ice.

"Will the channels fill in time, my lady?" Warlock asked, guessing the reason for her frown as she watched the sluggish oil flow.

"They'd better, Cecil," she said. "Or you'll be bowing to Lord Jaxyn by tomorrow evening. Tides, if only I could risk heating the oil a little. That would make it move."

Warlock guessed she didn't want to draw on the Tide with Jaxyn so close. They could just make out a large podium with a red valance out on the ice in front of the Glaeban troops. It was towed on a sled by a phalanx of canines, and on it stood a number of human figures, surrounded by the flags of Glaeba snapping proudly in the breeze. Jaxyn had brought his own stage with him, apparently. Or at least a platform from which to view and direct the battle. Besides the three men on the platform—whom Warlock assumed were Jaxyn and King Mathu, and perhaps a lackey—there were several women, only one of whom appeared rugged up against the cold. Warlock couldn't make out who they were from this distance. He supposed they were servants, or maybe Diala and Lyna—Jaxyn's immortal co-conspirators—here to watch the battle.

Perhaps the sight of so many Crasii dying in battle was their idea of entertainment.

"Can you not risk even a small amount of magic to speed the oil on its way, my lady?" Warlock asked, fearing he'd overstepped the mark by asking such a thing. It was important Stellan Desean's plan to scatter the Glaeban army worked. The truth was, Warlock found himself in the unenviable position of hoping his enemies would—if not win—then at least carry the day.

Maybe, if things get really chaotic, I can slip away. Elyssa will think me dead in the confusion of the battle.

Warlock consciously stopped his daydream before it could go any further. He wasn't close enough to the battle to have any such luck, and the chances of Elyssa allowing him out of her sight any time soon seemed remote.

"If Jaxyn feels me swimming the Tide, he'll retaliate with everything he has. That's what he did the last time we argued over a throne."

"*My lady?*" Warlock asked, hoping his question wouldn't make her suspicious.

"Fyrenne, Cecil. It was thousands of years ago, but Jaxyn hasn't changed much in the intervening years. It wasn't my fault, you know, although the others still blame me for it. Jaxyn just wouldn't let it be. The place was a burnt-out wasteland by the time we finished arguing about it."

"He shall not defeat you this time, my lady," Warlock assured her. "You will prevail."

Elyssa smiled at Warlock. "Ah, Cecil, if only you had the wit to say that because you knew it to be true, and not because you have no choice but to believe it."

Warlock was saved from having to answer her by the blare of a trumpet slicing through the chilly morning. Out on the ice, several heralds had stepped up beside the podium. They played their fanfare, which lasted a minute or two, and then a single sled broke away from the line upon line of feline warriors, most of whom were crouched down, rather than standing. It took a while for Warlock to work out the meaning of that, until he realised the felines were removing something from their feet. Whatever protection they'd worn crossing the ice, they did not intend to let it hamper their fighting. With their sharp retractable claws, a feline warrior needed no weapons at close range to gut her opponents, and their feet were as much weapons as their hands.

Whatever the outcome of the discussions with the envoy sent to meet the Caelish army, it was obvious Jaxyn intended his felines to fight this day.

"Perhaps if we widened the channel here, my lady?" Warlock suggested, looking at the thin black line stretching back toward the oil seep.

"Do you think it will help?"

"It can't hurt, my lady."

Elyssa nodded in agreement. "Have them start digging again, Cecil. We don't have long."

Warlock turned and hurried up the short slope to where the foreman waited with his canines. They were freezing, Elyssa having forbidden any fires that might give away their position or their intentions—not to mention the risk of fire so close to an open oil seep. The foreman glared at Warlock, clearly resenting the large Crasii's favoured position with Elyssa.

"My lady wants the channel widened," Warlock told him. "The oil isn't flowing fast enough."

The Crasii nodded with a frown, not pleased his orders were being relayed through a third party. But he turned to his workers, hefting his mattock. "Well, lads, seems we don't have to stand around here freezing our tails off after all. Let's do as my lady wants and make this channel wider. Get to it."

The canines quickly spread out along the channel and soon the thumping of mattocks pounding the frozen ground silenced any other noises coming from the surrounding forest. Warlock watched anxiously as they dug, willing the oil to flow faster, and after a time the canines' work seemed to be having an effect. As the volume in the channel increased, Warlock hurried back to where Elyssa was standing, watching the negotiations that preceded any war.

"Their envoy is heading back already," she remarked, as Warlock stopped beside her. There was no need to report on the improved oil flow; Elyssa could see it for herself. Across the ice, the smaller sled Jaxyn must have dispatched in Warlock's absence was heading back toward the portable podium where the King of Glaeba and his retinue waited. "The forms have been met, the offer for surrender rejected."

A figure leaned down from the podium to receive the report from his envoy. The two appeared to speak for a moment and then the figure on the podium straightened, turned and said something to the others standing with him. Then he signalled the heralds.

Another trumpet blast cut through the morning, this one different, more strident, more urgent, than the last.

"And so, Cecil," Elyssa said with a heavy sigh, as line upon line of Glaeban feline warriors rose to their feet and prepared to move forward, "the Tide has not even peaked yet and, once again, we are at war."

Chapter 23

Arkady pulled her fur coat a little tighter as the trumpets announced the order to advance. She stood at the back of the podium beside her father, behind the immortals, with Jaxyn's loyal Crasii bodyguard, Chikita, watching over them to prevent them trying to escape. The only other mortal standing on the war platform Jaxyn had commissioned for the invasion was Mathu Debree, the young King of Glaeba. To Arkady, he looked pinched and cold and uncertain. She could tell he was putting on a brave face to impress his wife.

Arkady had no sympathy for the young king. If he didn't want to be here, he could end this right now. He was the Glaeban king, after all, and if he ordered a withdrawal, Jaxyn would have to comply unless he was willing to completely blow his cover and reveal who he was.

But Mathu didn't have the spine to stand up to his wife, or the wit to know when he was being manipulated. So here they were, at war with their closest neighbour and ally for the most spurious of reasons, her husband leading the forces arrayed against his own countrymen—all for the entertainment of a handful of power-hungry immortals.

"Tides, I never thought I'd live to see this day."

Arkady was forced to agree with her father, but didn't answer his muttered comment. She wasn't sure what to say to him about anything any longer. Things had not been the same between them since she'd asked Jaxyn to heal him and saved him from certain death. Even worse, after their last failed attempt to escape and Clyden Bell's death, he had completely withdrawn from her. Arkady wasn't sure if that was because Clyden was dead, because she'd forced her father to live, or because he'd been forced to acknowledge that the Tide Lords were real.

Still, she understood what he meant. They were close enough to the shore to see the forces lining up against them. The Caelish army seemed pitifully few in number compared to the tens of thousands of felines Jaxyn had mustered and brought across the ice with them.

The delay frustrated Diala; Arkady could tell by the snide remarks she'd been making to Jaxyn on the way here. But the man couldn't be faulted for his tactics. He wasn't going to risk this invasion failing because he didn't have the numbers.

The felines rose to their feet and began pounding the ice with their spears, a rhythmic tattoo that reverberated through Arkady's bones. Felines were not fond of weapons as a rule, preferring to use their claws. The spears were for a series of single volleys designed to winnow the numbers of the advancing Caelish forces.

And to strike fear into the hearts of our enemies with that ungodly racket, Arkady decided.

She couldn't see Stellan from where she was standing on the platform beside her father, but she had no doubt he was out there somewhere, watching over the battle the same way Jaxyn was watching over it from this side. Arkady wished she'd had a chance to speak to her husband. There were so many questions she had for him. Questions about her father, questions about what had happened after he left her in Torlenia, questions about how Jaxyn had managed to frame him for the murder of the King and Queen of Glaeba, about how one of Glaeaba's favourite sons had found himself standing with the enemy. Her feelings for Stellan were so ambivalent. On one hand she despised him for what he'd done—imprisoning her father to silence him while letting her believe the old man was dead. On the other, Stellan had been her friend, mentor and confidant for more than seven years. She knew him to be a loyal Glaeban, devoted to protecting the king. To find himself facing Glaeba's army as an agent for their enemies must be tearing him up inside.

As the trumpets faded, Arkady wondered if Jaxyn's earlier message to the Caelish queen, which was—essentially—a demand for instant surrender, included a note that Stellan's wife and father-in-law were among the Glaeban forces and things would go much easier on them if the advice to surrender was heeded sooner rather than later.

Jaxyn would not have expected his threat to change the minds of the Caelish, but by delivering the warning Stellan would know she was out here.

Is Jaxyn hoping to distract Stellan by making him fear for my life?

He'd misjudged Stellan badly if he thought that would work. This was the man who'd let his own father-in-law rot for seven years in gaol to protect his secret. Threatening to harm the wife he'd taken for the sake of appearances, or the man he'd imprisoned to ensure his silence, wasn't likely to sway him from his purpose now. Not with a couple of Tide Lords at his back equally determined to secure themselves a kingdom. Stellan might wish his wife no harm—Arkady was certain of that—but he wouldn't risk the greater prize to save her.

Arkady glanced over her shoulder—as casually as she could manage—at the drop from the podium to the ice beneath them. The distance was about four feet. She'd have to be careful not to twist an ankle when she jumped, or she'd not get more than a few steps before they recaptured her. And then there was the problem of her father. He was healthier than he'd been in years—thanks to Jaxyn's magical intervention—but she doubted he was capable of making the jump without doing himself a serious injury.

Tides, who can think with that racket going on? She returned her attention to the lines of felines, wondering when the pounding would stop. Arkady glanced at Chikita surreptitiously, hoping the noise was distracting the Crasii too. It wasn't. Chikita smiled at Arkady when their eyes met, as if she knew exactly what Arkady was planning.

"The battle will be joined soon, my lady," the feline remarked, speaking up to be heard over the pounding.

"Won't that be fun," Arkady replied with a scowl. The feline seemed amused, and not very overawed to be standing in the company of so many immortals, which Arkady thought a little odd. Still, she was alert and had her wits about her. Arkady would have to find a way to distract Chikita before she and her father jumped, or she risked being shredded by those claws, which made the prospect of a twisted ankle academic.

A signal from the king this time—after consulting Jaxyn. Another blast on the trumpets so loud her father jumped in fright, and the felines began to move. Arkady had thought listening to them pound their spears was ominous, but when they marched, every third beat was of their spear butts on the ice, ringing off the ranges. The podium didn't move—Jaxyn had decided this was close enough—but the sea of feline warriors moved forward at a ground-eating, relentless pace that would cover the remaining distance between their army and the Caelish shore in very little time.

Step-step-bang . . . Step-step-bang . . . Step-step-bang . . .

"What are those black lines on the ice?" her father asked her in a whisper.

Arkady stood on her toes, straining to see past the immortals. The lines her father spoke of were narrow marks scoring the ice just in front of the first rank of felines. There seemed to be three of them—long parallel lines; the distance between them was hard to judge from here.

Step-step-bang . . . Step-step-bang . . . Step-step-bang . . .

"Range markers, probably," Jaxyn told him, glancing over his shoulder, just to make certain they knew he was aware of them, Arkady suspected. "Perhaps Stellan fears his Caelish marksmen aren't bright enough to work out when we'll be in range."

"Shouldn't our forces be carrying shields?" Lyna asked. "If they hit us with a volley of arrows, we'll lose our entire front rank."

Step-step-bang . . . Step-step-bang . . . Step-step-bang . . .

Jaxyn smiled, opening his arms to encompass their icy battlefield. "So what? There's plenty more where they came from." He looked back at Arkady and smiled even wider. "Lovely day for a battle, don't you think, Arkady?"

She didn't answer him. There was nothing to say, in any case. Arkady fixed her attention on the city in the distance with its ice-locked wharves and its useless ships trapped against the shore.

Step-step-bang . . . Step-step-bang . . . Step-step-bang . . .

Tides, I wish that noise would stop.

Amused by her rigid manner, Jaxyn turned his attention back to the battle. The Caelish forces hadn't moved yet. They were waiting for something, Arkady thought, and she doubted it was the Glaeban army. They would be foolish beyond words to allow the invaders to reach the shore, but then, perhaps that was their intention.

Was their plan to thin the Glaeban forces as much as possible with arrows and spears and then take the fight to the town? Cycrane was a hilly city with narrow winding streets and very few open places for a pitched battle to take place. Fighting in the streets would significantly reduce the advantage the Glaebans enjoyed because of their superior numbers.

Step-step-bang . . . Step-step-bang . . . Step-step-bang . . .

That would make it much harder for her to get away too, she realised. Arkady was counting on the battle coming to them. She was planning to grab her father and make a run for it in the confusion when the attention of Jaxyn, Diala and Lyna, and—more importantly—that wretched Crasii he'd set to watch over them, was fixed firmly elsewhere.

This time, it would be much harder for Jaxyn to find them. For one thing, he wouldn't have time. And for another, she had no friends in Caelum to hide her.

No friends he could randomly kill.

Arkady's grief for the kind and loyal Clyden Bell and her thoughts of escape were interrupted by a sudden whoosh as a wall of flame shot up in front of them. The felines' orderly march toward the city instantly transformed into a wild, screaming panic. Another two whooshes sounded, one after the other in rapid succession. Another two walls of flame shot up behind the front ranks, billowing black smoke as they burned, splitting the Glaeban forces and turning them from an organised army into four panicked squealing mobs separated by walls of fire. The felines' fear of the fire robbed them of any sense. The rhythmic *step-step-bang . . . step-step-bang . . . step-step-bang . . .* of their advance was gone, replaced with the panicked screams of thousands of trapped, frightened and injured Crasii. Her father gripped her arm in horror. The sound tore at Arkady's soul, making her feel ill.

Jaxyn's orders—even to those felines still within earshot—fell on deaf ears.

There was no time to wonder what had happened. The fires seemed to have leapt up out of the ice, but she didn't think it was magic that had caused the sudden conflagration. Jaxyn was screaming orders at the felines and generals, not turning his attention to the Tide. She was sure that would be his first reaction if one of the Tide Lords on the Caelish side had decided to stop the Glaebans by using magic.

Arkady glanced around, realising this was her chance—her only chance. Already the first wall of flame was burning lower. Acrid black smoke roiled across the ice toward them, making her eyes water. Although she was only a few feet away from Jaxyn and the others, she couldn't hear what they were saying over the screams of the wounded Crasii. Chikita, her feline guard, was staring at the flames, transfixed by the sight of them.

"Papa! You must come with me!"

Her father looked at her blankly for a moment and then nodded when he realised what she meant. "Are you sure?"

Arkady checked that everyone's attention was fixed on the chaos in front of them. "Yes, I'm sure!" she hissed. "Come on!" Without giving it another moment's thought, she ducked under the rope barrier circling the podium and jumped to the ice. She didn't twist an ankle; she slid and fell heavily on her behind. But she didn't have time to worry about it. Scrambling to her feet, Arkady turned to help her father down. He didn't try to jump, but clambered down awkwardly—and with heart-stopping slowness—to the ice.

As soon as he was standing, she grabbed his arm and turned to run. Her sudden movement caused him to fall heavily. Arkady hurried to help him up, which proved to be a struggle on the icy surface, but finally he regained his balance. However, he looked ashen and panic-stricken.

"Going somewhere, my lady?"

Arkady turned from her father to find Chikita on the ice behind her. The Crasii hadn't been *that* transfixed by the fires apparently.

"I . . . er . . ." Arkady began, with the sinking realisation that there was no hope now of getting a third chance at escape.

The feline stepped toward them, pulling a knife from her belt. The noise around them was horrendous; the air filled with screams and smoke and death and the stench of burning fur.

"Lord Jaxyn will not be pleased if you harm us!" Arkady shouted, wondering if she could bluff their way out of this.

Chikita stepped closer, near enough to grab Arkady by the arm. She pulled her close, making Arkady lean forward. "He'll be a lot less pleased if he thinks I let you escape," the feline said into her ear. "I can give you a few minutes' head start, my lady. After that, you're on your own."

The little warrior pressed the knife into her hand and stepped back, adding in a louder voice, "Tilly sends her love, by the way."

Tides, Arkady realised. *Chikita is a Scard. And working for the Cabal.*

Arkady didn't need to be told twice. She turned to grab her father's arm, but he shook her off. "You'll get further without me."

"No!" Arkady said. "I'm not leaving you behind! He'll kill you!"

"I'd already be dead but for you, Arkady," he said, his eyes misting with tears. "I don't fear death."

"My lady, you have to go!" Chikita urged behind her.

"Go!" Bary insisted. "I'll cover for you."

"I can't leave you again, Papa! Not when I can save you!"

"You can't save me, Arkady," he said, hugging her briefly. "Now go. For once, let me save you."

Although she was filled with doubts, this was not the time or the place to voice them. Her father seemed determined and he was right—she would travel much farther and faster without him.

But how could she leave him?

How could she stay?

"Go!" he ordered. "For once in your life, girl, do something I've told you to do without arguing about it."

Arkady wished she had more time to think about this. More time to feel something other than gratitude. Mouthing the words *thank you* to the feline and her father, she pocketed the knife and then turned and headed into the chaos. She had only moments before Chikita would have to raise the alarm and inform her immortal masters that Arkady and her father had tried to escape, or risk being found out as a spy herself.

So Arkady ran, not back toward Glaeba, but forward, through the smoke and the writhing burned bodies and the panicked felines. Taking a diagonal track across the ice, heading in what she hoped was a northerly direction, she deliberately forced herself not to think of what she'd left behind. She couldn't afford to head for the city. Even though Stellan was there and she could count on his protection, there was still a good chance Jaxyn would carry the day. Only the front ranks of his vast army had been affected by those walls of fire. There were still plenty more warriors in reserve, and once he got them under control, the battle would be well and truly on.

Slipping and sliding on the ice, she fought her way through the chaos, ignoring the burned Crasii's cries for help, and her guilt at leaving her father behind. She crossed the black lines scoured into the ice, which she realised, from the smell, must have been filled with tar or oil, until finally she stumbled onto the snow-covered shore and found herself clear of the battlefield.

Without stopping to look back, Arkady hardened her heart and turned north, heading inland, away from the city, away from the battle, away from her father and away from the screams of the burned and dying Crasii who'd been sacrificed this morning on the altar of immortal ambition.

Chapter 24

Warlock—like most canines—had no time for feline Crasii and, in the general course of events, cared little about their fate, one way or another. A day watching the felines caught in the fires on the ice had forced him to reassess his stance. Seeing them magically forced to climb to their feet to resume fighting, some of them bloodied and in agony, others with their fur burned away so badly there was nothing but raw flesh and muscle left behind, changed his opinion.

Once the fires were set, Elyssa had ordered the canine workers back to pack up their camp, and with Warlock at her heels to run errands for her, she had stepped out on to the ice to watch the battle. It was not long after they'd taken to the ice that Warlock discovered the immortals were resurrecting the felines.

The Glaeban felines were the first to resume the fight. They'd borne the full brunt of the oil fires, after all. To see them staggering to their feet, regardless of the injuries they'd sustained, was enough to make Warlock's flesh crawl. But it infuriated Elyssa. As soon as it became apparent Jaxyn was behind the magical resurrections, she began to swear savagely.

"My lady?" Warlock had inquired, wondering what had set her off.

"That cheating bastard is reviving the felines we killed with the oil fires."

"Is that how they're coming back to life, my lady?"

"Why do you think feline Crasii believe they have nine lives, Cecil?" the immortal asked as she studied the battlefield through a thin brass telescope. "I don't know where they got the number nine, though, because how many times you can bring a fighter back varies from feline to feline, and has more than a little to do with the severity of the injury that killed them and if their vital organs are still intact."

"And Lord Jaxyn is using the Tide to revive his warriors?" Warlock was astounded, wondering why he had never seen such a thing before. Of course, he knew of the feline belief in their own infallibility—that the Tide Lords had endowed them with nine lives because they were a cut above all other Crasii—but it was something he'd always put down to ordinary everyday, insufferable feline arrogance. He supposed that until now, it *had* been just that. But with the Tide on the rise, the Tide Lords could work their magic on the felines in a way that hadn't been possible for over a thousand years.

Elyssa was annoyed. She slammed the telescope shut so hard it was a wonder the lenses didn't shatter. "Fetch the horses, Cecil. We're going back to Cycrane. I don't know if Rance and Krydence have the wit or the power to respond in kind, and if they don't we'll be overrun before lunch."

"Surely my lord Tryan would not permit such a defeat," Warlock said, figuring a show of support for all immortals might be in order.

Elyssa didn't seem to care what Warlock's opinion on the matter was. "Tryan's going to be too busy pretending he's a general," she complained. "Tides, why is it always left to me to sort these things out? Go, Cecil. We need to get back before the situation is so desperate Engarhod and my mother decide to take a hand in things."

"To serve you is the reason I breathe, my lady," Warlock assured her, always amazed at the low opinion this immortal had of the rest of her family. Shivering a little in the icy breeze, he hurried from the ice and back onto the shore, past the sooty channel that still smouldered and smoked in places, toward the clearing where their horses were tethered, a little panicked by the thought of Elyssa returning to Cycrane.

Elyssa's plan, so she had informed Warlock, was to head off in search of the Bedlam Stone once the oil channels were dug, filled and fired. Warlock was counting on her absence from the city to give Boots plenty of time to get away. He could tell Elyssa wasn't enthusiastic about seeing out the next High Tide as the mere sister of a Caelish king. She had a far grander plan in mind, and it had something to do with this lost Bedlam Stone for which she'd spent so much time searching. The artefact—whatever it was—apparently endowed its immortal owner with unlimited power. Elyssa was playing along with her mother and her brothers, he suspected, doing just enough to further their plans so they'd not be suspicious of her ultimate goal.

Warlock was quite sure she had bigger ambitions than any of her siblings suspected and the reason she cared little about the outcome of this war was because once she had the stone, she planned to use it to take the whole continent for herself. Frankly, Warlock didn't care what she wanted to do to her family or the other immortals, provided his puppies were safe and out of her reach.

If that meant kowtowing to her now, he was willing to do it.

He reached the shore, pulling a face at the acrid stench of burned oil now smothering the fresh clean scent of the snow and the forest around him. He walked through the woods to the clearing where the horses were tethered. When he reached the clearing, he muttered soothing nothings to the horses, sensing their disquiet. Elyssa's palfrey was still waiting by the tree where Warlock had tied him earlier, away from the flames, but his own had slipped his reins and wandered off in the direction of the workers' camp.

Cursing, he headed after it, and then stopped as another smell reached his sensitive nose—a smell more foul and more disturbingly familiar than the stench of burned oil.

Warlock spun around, hearing the interlopers before he saw them. Instinctively he dived for cover, the reek of unfamiliar suzerain so strong that he knew there had to be more than one coming. He had no idea who they were. All the immortals in Caelum and Glaeba that Warlock knew about were north of here, involved with the battle. Elyssa was here with him, Krydence and Rance were directing the battle out on the ice, and Tryan was overseeing the fight from the city. Meanwhile Syrolee and Engarhod waited at the palace, keeping an eye on the drugged and almost blithely unaware Queen of Caelum, to make certain she didn't get any crazy ideas while they were otherwise engaged in a savage war with their closest neighbour. Like surrendering.

Warlock feared Jaxyn had more immortal help than they knew of. Was this the vanguard of a sneak attack? Had Jaxyn managed to gather other immortals to his cause in secret? Immortals who had crossed the ice under cover of darkness and advanced from the south to take them by surprise?

How long before Elyssa discovers she's not alone?

Perhaps she was so distracted by the battle and the feel of Jaxyn riding the Tide to revive his felines, she wouldn't notice even more immortals coming up behind her.

Warlock was torn with indecision, with no idea how a real Crasii would react in such a situation. A wrong move now and his cover was blown. He would never escape this place, never see Boots and his puppies again . . .

The decision was taken from him while he was still crouched behind the bushes, agonising over what to do. Three figures appeared on the other side of the burnt-out oil seep. They wore nondescript clothing that told him nothing about who they might be. All Warlock could smell was the overwhelming reek of suzerain.

"Tides," the immortal in the lead remarked, as he settled onto the ground. Warlock's vision was obscured somewhat by the bushes but it seemed to him as if the man had been hovering over the ground rather than walking on it. "What's that smell?"

"They've fired the oil seep," the second immortal remarked, the sound of his voice making Warlock's heart lurch. He knew that voice; he'd spent months incarcerated across the hall from its owner.

"Looks like they channelled the oil onto the ice to panic the felines," the third immortal said, pointing to the channel. At this point Warlock began to wonder if he'd fallen into a nightmare, because the third immortal was Declan Hawkes. Not only was he supposed to be dead, but the last time Warlock had seen him he *wasn't* immortal. Far from it—he was a pivotal member of the organisation actively working to rid Amyrantha of them.

"I wonder who thought of that?" Cayal asked, looking toward the ice. Warlock was certain the immortals had no idea they were being observed. They could sense each other on the Tide, but as a race, the Crasii meant nothing to them. They were slaves and beneath the notice of the suzerain. But Elyssa was still out there on the ice, almost within shouting distance. Even if she was distracted by the battle and didn't feel these other immortals on the Tide, if Warlock didn't return soon, she'd probably come looking for him.

"It's a tactic far too subtle for Tryan to have thought of it," the older immortal remarked.

Cayal looked up suddenly, and turned in the direction of the lake. "Someone's coming."

"Another immortal?" Declan Hawkes asked.

"Of course it's another one of us, you fool," the third immortal—the one Warlock couldn't identify—remarked impatiently. "Are we taking bets on which one of Syrolee and Engarhod's obnoxious offspring it is?"

"With my luck, it'll be . . ." the Immortal Prince began, hesitating at the sound of someone approaching from the lake. Warlock's mistress stepped into the clearing a moment later. "Elyssa!" he said, his cheerful exclamation at complete odds with his morose tone of a few moments ago.

Elyssa's eyes narrowed suspiciously as she studied the three Tide Lords. "*Cayal?*"

"In the flesh."

She looked around, as if she was expecting to see someone else "Where's Kinta?"

"Kinta?" Cayal asked, looking a little puzzled. "Oh! Kinta!" He smiled ingenuously. "Ah . . . about that. She and I aren't really . . . well . . . together much, these days."

Even Warlock, watching from behind the bushes, could feel Elyssa's pleasure at the news, but it was soon pushed aside by more immediate concerns. The Immortal Maiden's glare focused on the older of the new arrivals. "What's *he* doing here?"

"Who? Kentravyon?" The Immortal Prince turned to look at him. Shivering, Warlock studied the Tide Lord with interest too. Legend held that Kentravyon was frozen for eternity by his immortal brethren, trapped down in Jelidia somewhere.

So much for that myth.

"That's a very good question. What *are* you doing here exactly, old son?"

Before Kentravyon could answer, Elyssa pointed to Declan Hawkes. "And since when has *he* been one of us?"

"Since the fire that destroyed Herino Prison," Declan Hawkes told her, his voice betraying nothing.

Warlock remembered the fire of which he spoke. It was the fire during which Stellan Desean had escaped Glaeba and the fate of being hanged as a traitor. Hawkes was supposed to have died in the fire, too, while Tryan, Elyssa and Diala had watched the prison burn from the balcony of Herino Palace as if it was some sort of sick spectator sport. Although he couldn't begin to imagine how the fire had made Declan Hawkes immortal, Warlock gained a perverse sort of pleasure from the irony of it.

There they were, all those jaded immortals thinking they were watching men die, when quite the opposite was happening . . .

But an immortal Hawkes also raised another worrying thought—if the spymaster was now immortal, exactly whose side was he on these days?

"What are you doing here in Caelum, Cayal?" Elyssa asked, clearly mistrustful of the sudden, unexpected and uninvited arrival of three Tide Lords into her realm. What she thought of Hawkes's story, she kept to herself. That didn't surprise Warlock. Elyssa usually played her cards very close to her chest, a necessary skill when dealing with her mother and the rest of her family.

"I came to see you," Cayal said, smiling at her with all his considerable charm. Warlock knew that smile. He'd seen Cayal use it on the Duchess of Lebec. And it worried him a great deal. The whole time Cayal had been telling the tale of his long life to Arkady Desean while incarcerated in Lebec Prison, he'd spoken of nothing but his dislike and contempt for the Immortal Maiden. Yet here he was, acting as if his day was brightened simply because she'd stepped into his presence. "Want some help winning your war?"

Elyssa glanced over her shoulder toward the lake briefly and then shrugged. "I think we can manage."

"Are you sure?" Kentravyon asked. "Jaxyn's got you pretty comprehensively outnumbered."

Elyssa shrugged, as if the numerical superiority of her enemies was nothing to be concerned about. "Tide's up enough to revive the felines. We'll get by."

"Get by a lot quicker if that lake was a lake again," Kentravyon suggested with a wink that made Elyssa frown.

"You're offering to melt the ice?" she asked, as if she couldn't believe what she was hearing. "Why would you do that to help us? You hate Tryan, Cayal. And the Tide knows these other two owe us no favours."

"I happen to hate Jaxyn more at the moment," Cayal told her, taking a step closer to her. "As for the others . . . well, Hawkes here has a score to settle with Jaxyn over a woman, and you have something Kentravyon wants."

"And what about you, Cayal? Why do you care?"

"Well, I don't," he replied, more honestly than Warlock thought Elyssa was expecting. "At least, I don't care about your wretched little war with Jaxyn. But I need your help, Elyssa." He took another step closer; close enough to take her hand in his and raise it to his lips. "And I have something *you* want."

Warlock watched in amazement as Elyssa's anger melted under the intensity of Cayal's gaze. *Surely,* Warlock thought, *with the experience of thousands of years behind her, and her knowledge of how Cayal works, she isn't going to fall for such transparent flirting?*

But apparently she *was* going to fall for it.

"What do you mean?" Elyssa asked a little breathlessly. Behind Cayal, Declan Hawkes was looking on with an impatient expression, while Kentravyon was rolling his eyes.

Elyssa was too focused on Cayal to notice. Warlock was almost overcome by the irrational desire to leap out of the bushes and warn his mistress that no good could come of any deal she was about to do with the Immortal Prince and his highly suspect companions. He controlled the urge, however, realising he had another, much more pressing problem. Both Cayal and Declan Hawkes knew Warlock was a Scard. The moment they laid eyes on him, he would be exposed.

"If you help me, Elyssa," Cayal said, in a voice so velvet and seductive that even Warlock found himself enticed by it, "I can offer you a new life."

"I don't need a new life, Cayal," she said. "The one I have now will go on forever."

"What if the life you have now were to continue in a *different* body?" he asked softly; so softly, Warlock had to strain to hear him. "One that is young and beautiful and doesn't have your . . . current problems?"

Elyssa stared up at Cayal in astonishment for a moment while she absorbed what he had just told her. Warlock could tell she was sorely tempted by his unexpected offer. He had seen the dead men in her bed often enough to appreciate *how* tempted. *Tides, but can they do that? Take the mind from one immortal body and place it into another?*

The Immortal Maiden was apparently thinking the same thing. She looked past Cayal and asked Kentravyon, "Is he serious?"

Kentravyon nodded. "Lukys has just about perfected the technique. Of course, it takes a lot of power, and we'll have to do it when the Tide peaks. Oh, and Cayal is hoping it will kill him. Hence the reason he needs you. But yes, so far it looks very promising."

Elyssa's eyes were alight at the prospect. "I could choose a new body? Take any body I want?"

"Of course," Cayal said, which prompted Declan Hawkes to open his mouth to say something. However, he never got the chance because Kentravyon elbowed him in the ribs to shut him up. Hawkes fell silent, shaking his head.

Elyssa seemed entranced by the notion, and didn't notice the exchange between the other immortals. But then she frowned and took a step back from Cayal, shaking free of his hand. "Tides, you want the Bedlam Stone."

"That would help, my dear," Kentravyon agreed cheerfully. "Do you have it?"

She shook her head. "No. But I know where to find it."

"Then we have a deal!" the older man said, stepping forward as he rubbed his hands together gleefully. "Lead on, Elyssa. Where have you stashed it?"

Elyssa took another step back from them. "Not so fast, Kentravyon. I haven't agreed to anything. And if you think I'm going to hand over the source of ultimate power in the universe to you three on the strength of a vague promise from a liar, a madman and a . . ." She glanced at Hawkes and shrugged. ". . . a trained *killer*, then you have another think coming."

"It's not the source of ultimate power in the universe," Kentravyon scoffed. "It's a lump of polished crystal about the size of my head actually, and all it does is channel power. Tides, girl, if it was the source of ultimate power in the universe, no mere mortal would survive touching it, let alone stealing it from us."

"But you still need it, don't you?"

"Name your price, Elyssa," Cayal said, a little too impatiently.

"I don't know," she said in a tone that indicated she'd begun to realise she held the upper hand in this negotiation. "I'll have to think about it. And you'll have to convince me that what you say about changing bodies is possible, too, before I lift a finger to aid you. In the meantime, I suppose you *could* do something about Jaxyn. As a gesture of good faith."

"You said you didn't need our help," Hawkes reminded her.

"I've changed my mind."

"You want us to melt the ice?" Cayal asked.

She shook her head. "We've already thought of that. It would take too long."

"You could break the ice, couldn't you?" Hawkes suggested. Then he added with a frown, "Of course, when it shatters that would send every creature—human or Crasii—standing out there, into the water where they'll die within minutes if they can't get to shore before hypothermia sets in."

Cayal glanced at Kentravyon who shrugged, apparently unconcerned about the potential body count. "Jaxyn will know what we're up to as soon as we start drawing on the Tide."

"Not if we do it fast enough," Cayal said. "The four of us together."

"I'm not going to help you murder several thousand innocent souls as a 'gesture of good faith,'" Declan Hawkes announced.

"Why not?" Cayal asked. "They're out there murdering each other at the moment." He turned to Elyssa with a reassuring smile. "Pay no attention to him. He's still operating under the delusion that he's mortal."

She frowned at him. "He's right, though. If we break the ice without warning, a lot of creatures are going to die."

Cayal stared at her evenly. "When all is said and done, Lyssie, do you care?"

Elyssa barely hesitated. "No."

Warlock wasn't surprised by her answer, but it firmed his resolve. He was done with this; done with these immortals and the intrigues of the Cabal. The very man who stood in the clearing, not twenty feet from where he was hiding—who had now joined their ranks—had recruited him to spy on Jaxyn, and then Elyssa. He'd endangered his family, and done nothing to stop the rise of the suzerain. Somewhere north of the city Warlock's mate and his pups were alone and defenceless while he was here—not saving them from their enemies, but helping them along.

And if he walked out there and exposed himself to Cayal or Declan Hawkes, he wouldn't last more than a few minutes, because Elyssa would kill him where he stood the moment one of them let it slip—either by accident or deliberate intent—that her favourite Crasii was a Scard.

But with Cayal here, Warlock realised, for a short time at least Elyssa was probably preoccupied enough for him to get away.

It took little more thought than that. Without waiting to hear the rest of their plans, and with infinite care, Warlock turned and crept backwards through the snow-covered undergrowth, away from the clearing, away from the immortals who would no longer be allowed to rule his life. As he fled, he discovered a greater sense of freedom than when the Duchess of Lebec had handed him a pardon and he'd walked away from the grim walls of the prison in Lebec.

Chapter 25

Stellan couldn't bear to imagine how many felines—some of them he'd probably bred and raised himself—were burned in the initial conflagration that announced the start of hostilities between Caelum and Glaeba.

He'd watched the battle from the vantage of the balcony outside the Ladies Walk of Cycrane Palace before the fires went up, but the sound of so many felines dying had driven him down here eventually, away from Syrolee and her murderous glee, Engarhod's inebriated indifference, and Queen Jilna of Caelum's inexplicable apathy. Although she'd been posturing about how old she was now and how, as heir to the throne, she should be involved in defending her country, Nyah had watched for a short time and then fled to her room, unable to bear the carnage.

Amplifying his distress even more was the news that Arkady and her father were out there on the ice with Jaxyn. The Glaeban envoy who'd delivered the formal surrender demand earlier this morning had made a point of delivering *that* message for the former Duke of Lebec. He'd had little time to wonder what Arkady's reaction might have been when she discovered he'd lied to her about her father's death, all those years ago. It was another unforgivable sin, he supposed, in a lifetime littered with them. Stellan could imagine the glee, however, with which Jaxyn had composed the demand informing his former lover that if he didn't surrender Caelum immediately and unconditionally, Arkady would be put to death.

Tryan, of course, had laughed in the envoy's face and told him to tell Jaxyn to go ahead and murder whomever he wanted. Stellan Desean was a guest in this country and did not have the authority to surrender on Caelum's behalf, even if he was so inclined.

Fortunately, Stellan wasn't there for that particular exchange, and was relieved beyond measure that the decision had been taken from his hands. He knew that with the throne of Glaeba at stake, he couldn't let sentiment get in the way. With the decision to ignore Jaxyn's ultimatum one step removed from him, it somehow made the knowledge that he would have answered no differently, had he been given the chance, a little easier to live with.

They wouldn't let him take a direct hand in the fighting, of course—his position in Caelum was too ambiguous to allow that—but his plan to disrupt the Glaeban forces had worked devastatingly well. The oil channelled from the tar seeps onto the ice had gone undetected, as Stellan suspected it would. Jaxyn, had he been *leading* his forces rather than watching them from his decorative platform behind the front ranks with his immortal allies, Arkady and her father—assuming they hadn't been murdered on the spot when Tryan refused Jaxyn's ultimatum—might have realised the purpose of the oil-filled channels. But the Crasii who made up the bulk of his army weren't under orders to notice things like that. They'd been told to march and fight and because it was an immortal who told them to march and fight, they had no choice but to obey. No feline was going to stop along the way to wonder why there was oil on the ice.

The walls of fire that shot up when Elyssa ignited the oil-filled channels had panicked the Glaeban forces so comprehensively that it took hours to get them back under control.

And therein lay the problem. They were under *immortal* control. A human army, or even a Crasii army commanded by humans, had a degree of free will not available to these creatures who were magically compelled to obey their masters. In a thousand years, no war had been fought like this. No battle had been engaged in living memory where the combatants didn't have the option to withdraw in the face of unthinkable carnage.

Jaxyn had numerical superiority, to be sure, and he was using it like a sledgehammer. Despite the dead, despite the burned and wounded Crasii crying out for help as their compatriots stepped over them to claw their opponents to death, the magically-compelled army just kept on coming.

It sickened Stellan to watch the slaughter. His disgust was made even worse by the knowledge their own Crasii warriors were similarly compelled. Rance and Krydence were down there on the ice, sending rank after rank of felines into the fray—felines who had no choice but to do as their immortal masters commanded. The Caelish had human soldiers in reserve, but Stellan couldn't imagine that any mortal man with his wits about him would willingly advance into the bloodbath taking place out there on the ice, once the smoke cleared and the battle engaged.

It was easily the worst day of Stellan's life, and given some of the things he'd been through recently, that was really saying something. As the sun began to dip below the palace turrets, the battle raged on as it had relentlessly for the better part of a day, with little progress on either side. Jaxyn's forces kept coming; their own forces had somehow managed to hold them off. But they couldn't hold them off for much longer and their human reserves were already reduced by almost a third due to desertions by sensible men who could tell a lost cause when they saw one.

"How long does Lord Krydence estimate we have before we must use the rest of the human reserves?" Stellan asked the messenger sent from the front lines to the palace. Stellan had intercepted him on the way there, in the hope of getting some intelligence not filtered through Syrolee's optimistic faith in her son's ability to prosecute a war successfully. The poor creature looked ragged, but he was here under immortal orders and probably would have scaled the outside walls of the palace to deliver his message, had he been told to do so.

"Less than an hour, your grace," the canine informed him, shivering in the chilly wind, even though he was running to keep up with Stellan as the duke hurried through the twisting Cycrane streets toward the command post. "Lord Krydence says that unless the Glaebans intend to stop at sunset, by midnight Cycrane will be overrun."

"Tell Lord Krydence we understand his dilemma and will send reinforcements as soon as possible."

Maybe, he added silently to himself. *If I can convince Tryan to release the human reserves.*

Stellan couldn't understand why the immortal hadn't done that yet, which was much of the reason he was on his way to the command post.

The canine bowed and ran off in the direction of Krydence. Stellan, feeling utterly helpless, shouldered his way forward through the press of human troops and wounded felines until he reached the building Tryan had chosen for his vantage to command the battle. He couldn't understand how this fight had gone on as long as it had without calling up their reserves. Their forces should have been utterly decimated long before now.

He took the steps of the wooden building two at a time, surprised to find Tryan alone on the balcony of the wharfside brothel he'd selected as his headquarters.

"Ah, Desean, come to watch the fun?"

"It's a massacre out there, my lord. Can't you do something?"

The Tide Lord shrugged. "Do what, exactly?"

Stellan frowned; he gripped the balcony, feeling the cold seep through his leather gloves. It was even worse from here. He could smell the blood and the smoke and hear the screams of the dying. He could even make out Jaxyn's observation platform, but he was too far away to identify individuals, so he had no way of knowing if Arkady or her father were still alive. Glancing down, Stellan saw several wounded felines he'd noticed on the way here, heading back out onto the ice. "I don't know . . . *something*?"

Tryan looked at Stellan oddly for a moment and then shook his head in wonder. "Tides, you know!"

"I beg your pardon?"

"You sneaky little bastard," the immortal said, his eyes narrowing. "You know who we are, don't you? That's what you're asking. Not if I can think of some brilliant military tactic to save the day—you want to know if I can do something with the Tide."

Stellan debated denying the accusation, or pretending he didn't understand. Then he realised how futile that would be. He met Tryan's eye and said evenly, "Well, can you?"

"We *are* doing something with the Tide, Desean. Why is it, do you think, that we still have an army after almost a full day of this fighting?"

"You're helping them by using Tide magic?" Stellan asked.

The Prince Consort shook his head. "We're bringing them back to *life* using Tide magic. Only ever works with the felines, for some reason, and you can't go on doing it indefinitely. But I believe that's where the idea that felines have more than one life comes from."

Stellan stared at him in horror. "You mean you're resurrecting the Crasii to make them fight?"

Tryan nodded as if it was nothing in the least bit remarkable. "The problem, of course, is that Jaxyn's doing exactly the same thing with his felines. This could go on for days, you know, before one of us gets tired of it."

Stellan was speechless. *Tides, those poor creatures.*

"Oh, don't look at me like that," Tryan said. "They're only animals,

Desean. You'd not rather have me killing the good citizens of Caelum over this, would you?"

Stellan didn't know what to say. Nothing in his experience had prepared him for this. "Isn't there something else—something less *cruel*—you can do?"

"Of course there is, but Jaxyn would just retaliate in kind and we'd be no better off than we are now. How long have you known who we are?"

"Since before I left Glaeba."

"And you never said a word. I've underestimated you, Desean."

"People often do," Stellan replied with a helpless shrug. "Why *can't* you do anything to stop this butchery? There are a half-dozen of you here and only two or three immortals on Jaxyn's side. Surely you can overwhelm them?"

Tryan considered Stellan for a moment before answering. When he did speak, he was much more forthcoming than Stellan expected. "Of the half-dozen of us here, Desean, only my sister and I can wield the sort of power needed to put an abrupt end to this conflict, and we'd have to do it before Jaxyn realised what we were up to."

"Do you fear he has spies among us?" Stellan asked, wondering if Tryan knew about Scards like Warlock.

But apparently the Tide Lord didn't fear mere mortals. He shook his head. "He can feel us on the Tide, and I suspect the only reason he's limited himself to regenerating his felines up 'til now is because he can sense that Elyssa isn't close by, so he's in no danger of us teaming up against him."

Stellan was confused. "So you command the Tide and yet your powers cancel each other out? Where's the use in that?"

Tryan shrugged. "I share your frustration, your grace, but believe me, unless we can take Jaxyn by surprise there is nothing to be gained by calling down the full force of the rising Tide, unless you plan to be lord and master of a graveyard once the battle is won. Clearly, you know something of us, but you need to understand that our power is elemental. I can't magically increase the size of our army, or make better weapons appear, but I can easily call up a wind that would blow Jaxyn's army back to Glaeba. Such a wind would likely kill our people and flatten Cycrane in the process and cause a natural disaster in somewhere like

Stevania, on the other side of the world. But if you really want me to try . . ."

"So there's nothing you can do," Stellan concluded, turning back to watch the fight. *Tides, is there anything worse than the sound of a dying feline? Other than hearing her dying over and over again?*

"There's plenty I could do," Tryan said. "Just nothing that won't make things worse."

"So . . . what? You're just going to let him win?"

Tryan seemed unconcerned. "He hasn't won yet, Desean. We still have our human reserves to throw into the battle. Once we take the fight to the streets, Jaxyn may find the going a little tougher."

Tryan's casual disregard for the feline lives already repeatedly lost this day left Stellan filled with impotent rage, not to mention a sense of futility that had nothing to do with this battle. The sick notion of making dead creatures fight on and on notwithstanding—even if a miracle occurred and they managed to carry the day—Jaxyn had brought the fight to Caelum. Stellan's main concern was—and always had been—the security of the Glaeban throne.

If these Tide Lords opposing Jaxyn were unable to protect Caelum from him, how were they supposed to help Stellan take back Glaeba?

"You do realise that it was Jaxyn who caused the Great Lakes to freeze?" Stellan said to Tryan, deciding to try a different tack. "How is it he did that and you couldn't feel him using the Tide?"

"Because he was very very careful," Tryan said. "We'd have felt it if the lakes froze overnight, but they didn't. It took weeks. If Jaxyn was responsible for it, he was disturbing the Tide as little as possible in order to make it look natural."

Stellan wished now that he'd confessed sooner to knowing the truth about the immortals. Perhaps then he could have said something about it. He might have warned Tryan and Elyssa that his contacts in the Cabal knew Jaxyn was responsible. Maybe then they could have done something to halt the freeze. Or melt the ice. Stellan didn't know enough about Tide magic to speculate what they might have been able to do, only that he probably should have said *something*.

"Are you *sure* there's no way to melt the ice?" he asked.

"Not quickly," Tryan said. "And unless you took him by surprise, Jaxyn would find a way to retaliate."

"But if two of you working together are more powerful than—"

"Then he won't try to fight us head-on. He'll do something else, like make the brains of every man in Cycrane explode out of his ears or something equally harrowing—something we'd have to stop melting the ice to counter. Tides, do you think we're like magicians from some children's story who stand there hurling lightning bolts at each other?" Tryan laughed sourly. "If it were that simple, why would sorcerers need mortal armies to fight their battles for them?"

Stellan had been wondering the same thing. He gripped the balcony railing in frustration, a little surprised to feel it trembling through his gloves. *Tides, how much of this carnage is my fault?* he wondered.

Oh, Arkady, have I killed you too, with my ambition?

The trembling increased. Stellan registered that fact about the same time that Tryan suddenly looked up, his expression confused and more than a little worried. *"What the . . . ?"*

The immortal never got a chance to finish his question. Without warning, a crack boomed across the ice, so loud it sounded like the world had been sundered in two. For a moment, even the fighting stopped. And then Stellan saw what had caused the sound and gasped—a large fissure had appeared in the ice without warning or any logical explanation.

Down on the ice, Krydence and Rance had the wit to call their troops back as soon as they realised the ice was about to go, but Jaxyn, further from the action, couldn't see what those higher up could see. The cracks spread like a virus, spider-webbing across the ice sheet, which seemed to be growing more translucent by the second.

"What's happening?" Stellan called to Tryan over the shout of panic engendered by the sudden orders to withdraw. The felines that had—until a few moments ago—been trying to claw their opponents to death, were now slipping and sliding on the bloodstained ice, trying to reach the shore. "Is it Tide magic?"

"It's Tide magic, all right," Tryan agreed, yelling to be heard over the ruckus. "But it's not Jaxyn who's wielding it."

"Then *who?*"

Tryan must have known the answer, although he seemed disinclined to share it with Stellan. The immortal started cursing savagely.

And then the ice gave way.

For a time, even Tryan's curses were overwhelmed by the sound of breaking ice and the screams from thousands of drowning felines. Stellan stared at the lake in horror. The cracks were spreading faster now and opening up to reveal the icy black water beneath, no longer needing magic to sustain their progress.

"Arkady!" Stellan cried, but it was a useless, futile cry, lost amid the screams of dying Crasii.

With alarming speed, the splintering cracks reached Jaxyn's sledded podium. A few seconds later, it tipped into the freezing water, taking all its occupants—human and immortal—with it, into the dark icy depths of the Lower Oran.

Chapter 26

It was evening before Arkady was game enough to stop. She ran—or rather stumbled—over the rough terrain for most of the day.

Fear of pursuit shredded her nerves. Every snapped twig, every unexplained sound in the woods, had her jumping in fright. Even after almost a full day on the run, she still couldn't quite believe she'd managed to get away—or her good fortune that Jaxyn had appointed a Scard who happened to work for the Cabal to watch over her.

That wasn't the stroke of luck it had seemed at first, she decided on reflection, brushing the snow from a fallen log so she could take a seat on it to catch her breath and rest her weary legs. The Cabal made it their business to place Scard spies as close as possible to the immortals to keep an eye on them.

In all likelihood, Chikita's placement at Jaxyn's side had nothing to do with Arkady. The little feline was merely helping where she could, and only because at that moment in time, during the turmoil of battle, it wasn't likely to get her into trouble. She'd shown no inclination to help Arkady before the chaos of the invasion. In fact, nothing about the Scard's demeanour, right up until she let Arkady escape, gave any hint that she wasn't a perfectly well-behaved Crasii, as subject to immortal whim as any other feline.

Whatever motives drove Chikita, Arkady wasn't going to pass up the only opportunity she had to escape. She was quite sure that as soon as Jaxyn was no longer distracted by the battle, he would come looking for her. How she was going to stay out of his grasp when he did, was something she had no idea about just yet.

She tried hard not to think about leaving her father behind. She'd already grieved him as lost once, many years ago. The memory was just another invisible scar on a soul scored with more scars than she cared to count these days. Their abortive attempt to escape that had resulted in Clyden's death seemed to sap the last of his remaining spirit. By staying behind, she was free to do what she had to do in order to save herself. He'd known that. It was the reason he'd refused to escape.

One way or another Bary Morel was determined to sacrifice himself to save his daughter. Arkady had realised that when she found him in his room with a noose around his neck. Her attempts to prevent him from doing anything foolish hadn't stopped him, only made him more creative.

Of course, Papa, your grand plan to nobly sacrifice your own life to cover my escape will all turn out to be moot, because I'll probably freeze to death before sun-up, she decided, looking around to see where she was.

With the daylight fading, the temperature was dropping rapidly. The sun was already sinking behind the mountaintops in the west. Arkady was exhausted, hungry and chilled to the bone, despite the fur coat she was wearing. Her feet were frozen, her shoes soaked; she could no longer feel her toes and she was sure she wouldn't survive a night in the open without the means to make a fire.

Arkady didn't have long before her situation moved from dire to critical. Without shelter or a fire, for sure she would evade capture by going to the one place Jaxyn couldn't follow: into death.

She had been able to assuage her thirst with snow, but had nothing else to sustain her, nor did she know enough bush-craft to find her own food. The woods made her nervous. She'd grown up in the slums of Lebec and then spent the rest of her life in a palace. City streets held no surprises for Arkady Desean. Declan had taught her how to look out for herself as a child, which had stood her in good stead for her turn as a duchess. Negotiating the pitfalls of Glaeban high society proved surprisingly similar to facing the perils of the slums. But even as a slave in Senestra or in the stark deserts of Torlenia, she'd not been alone like she was now, in an unfamiliar environment where she didn't have the tools to survive.

Arkady knew there was a way to start a fire by rubbing sticks together, but making fire was not a skill she'd ever needed before. There was always someone around with a flint, or another fire from which one could borrow a hot coal. She wasn't so worried about eating. A person could go days without food if need be; she was prepared to sacrifice a full belly for freedom.

But freedom wasn't freedom if she was dead and with nightfall, that fate was a real possibility.

The overcast sky concealed the setting sun, leaving Arkady with no accurate notion of where she was, other than somewhere north of

Cycrane. She'd only been out of the Caelish capital once before, and that was years ago, on her honeymoon, when Stellan's role as the king's personal envoy had brought them to Cycrane on official business. Nyah's father, the late Prince Consort of Caelum, had taken them to visit some ruins north of the city to see if Arkady knew anything of their origins. They'd made quite a day of it, with a picnic lunch and much laughter, interesting conversation and overtures of friendship. It was hard to believe that in such a short time, the two countries were now at war.

Although she wasn't sure of their exact location, she figured she must be close to the ruins by now. They were a short way inland from the lake, she recalled, and probably the closest thing to shelter out here. Arkady glanced up at the sky, wondering how much daylight she had left. And what the chances were of finding shelter. She could see the rocky bluff that she recalled as being near the ruins, jutting out from the hillside just ahead of her. Perhaps, if she made her way toward it, she might have some hope of locating shelter. She didn't have long. In the short time since she'd stopped, it was already noticeably colder and she was no longer shivering, which she knew to be a bad sign.

Arkady forced herself to her feet and then froze at an unfamiliar noise. She strained to listen, certain she could hear a mewling cry that sounded nothing like the other forest noises she'd grown accustomed to this past day. She waited, wondering if she'd imagined it. For a time, she heard nothing. And then, just as she was on the brink of deciding she really *had* imagined the noise, she heard it again.

Curious, Arkady followed the noise. She moved inland a little way in pursuit of what sounded very much like the crying of a Crasii pup, although Arkady couldn't imagine what such a young creature would be doing out here alone. She pushed through the undergrowth as the crying grew louder, finding the source of the cries hiding between the roots of a gnarled and ancient tree in a small clearing. It wasn't a newborn, Arkady realised as she approached. It was probably a couple of months old. Certainly old enough to move under its own power, even if only at a crawl. The pup was covered in fine brown fur, its large brown eyes were fully open and alert—albeit filled with tears—and it was dressed in a loose smock, which meant it wasn't feral. Somebody owned this puppy.

"There, there, sweetie," Arkady said softly as she approached the pup. "Where did you come from?"

It looked up at the sound of her voice. The crying faltered for a moment, and then the pup began to wail even louder in that odd way Crasii pups had of mimicking both human babies and dogs simultaneously.

"Hey . . . it's all right," she said soothingly, crouching down to get a closer look at the puppy. "I'm not going to hurt you."

As Arkady reached out to the pup, she heard a low growl. She looked up in time to see a brown blur leaping at her. Before she had time to register what she was seeing, she was bowled over sideways, the wind knocked out of her. Bruising her ribs on another fallen branch, the weight of a full-grown adult canine on her, she struggled to free herself, fighting off the growling mother with all her strength. Exhausted as she was, she fought like a demon, aware there was nothing more savage than a canine bitch protecting her pups and this one seemed determined to tear out her throat. Finally, after it clawed her face and bit her arm a couple of times, Arkady managed to push the creature away long enough for her to plead her innocence.

"I wasn't going to hurt him! I was only trying to help!" she cried, speaking Glaeban without thinking about the consequences. Panicked, under attack, and trying to avoid having her throat ripped open, it never occurred to Arkady to speak in anything other than her native tongue.

Her plea gave the creature pause. Suddenly the Crasii broke off the attack and she sat back on her heels. Still astride Arkady, she looked down at her in surprise. "Your *grace?*"

Being addressed as "your grace" was almost more surprising than being attacked out of nowhere by a vicious Crasii dam, protecting her pup. She studied the creature in the fading light. "Do I know you?"

"It's me, your grace. Boots."

Arkady stared at the canine in confusion, trying to remember who Boots might be. And then it came to her. *It's the young female canine who ran away from Lebec the night Declan came to the palace and asked me to interview Cayal.*

"*Boots?* Tides, girl, what are you doing here? And with pups?"

"I should be asking what *you're* doing here, your grace," Boots said, climbing off her. The canine held out her hand to help Arkady up. She staggered to her feet and looked down at the puppy who had stopped crying when its mother had attacked this strange interloper. In fact, it was smiling. Apparently, the puppy found the prospect of its mother tearing a human into little pieces rather entertaining.

"It's a long story, Boots, and one I'm not sure you'd believe."

Boots reached down and picked up the pup. "My tale's pretty much the same, your grace. Are you out here alone?"

Arkady hesitated, wondering if she could trust this Crasii. For all she knew, Boots was part of a larger party belonging to an immortal waiting for them over the next ridge. And then she remembered the reason Boots had fled her home in Lebec. She had defied Jaxyn.

Only a Scard was capable of doing that.

"Alone, and on the run, I fear," she admitted. At this point Arkady couldn't see that telling the truth would make much difference. She would die out here in the open tonight if she didn't get help. "What about you?"

"Well, I'm not alone," Boots said, hefting the pup on to her hip. "This is Missy, by the way. She's always running off and finding trouble the moment my back is turned. And I'm not really on the run. Sort of waiting out the winter before I can run anywhere. Especially with three pups to feed."

Arkady's eyes widened in surprise. "You have *three* pups?"

Boots nodded. "And we'd best get back to the other two before they decide to wander off as well." She sighed with exasperation. "Tides, it was so much easier before they learned to crawl."

"You have a camp around here?"

"In some ruins back that way a bit," Boots told her, heading back the way she'd come, apparently assuming Arkady would follow. "You'd know them, probably. Lord Stellan said you've been here before."

"Stellan?" Arkady hurried after the canine. "You've spoken to Stellan?"

"He helped me get away from the suzerain," Boots told her, glancing over her shoulder. "He said he'd be back with some more supplies if he could, but I doubt that's going to happen. Not considering what happened on the lake today."

"You saw the battle?"

"Heard it mostly," Boots said, pushing through the branches to emerge into the clearing Arkady thought she remembered. Not that she could tell much in this light. "At least, I heard the screams. You can't really see much from here. We're too far north." She looked over her shoulder and smiled faintly. "Which is actually a good thing."

Wrapping her arms around her body against the cold, Arkady followed Boots for a short way through some more bushes on the other side of the clearing until they broke out of the undergrowth and came upon the ruins Arkady remembered from her honeymoon. Looking around with interest, she stepped over the rubble at the entrance, which seemed relatively undisturbed, and then followed the canine and her pup through the main hall and down a narrow stairwell at the back into the lower levels.

Here, not only was it much warmer, but Boots had built a cosy little nest for herself and her babies. There were furs on the floor, and a goodly stash of supplies in the corner. A small fire was burning in a fire-pit which was barricaded against curious little paws with a wall of stones that had obviously been retrieved from around the ruins. A door at the other end of the room, with presumably another dangerous staircase leading down to the levels even lower than this one, was blocked off in a similar fashion.

"It's not much," Boots said, when Arkady hesitated on the threshold. "But it's home."

Boots put Missy down on the floor, who immediately scampered on all fours over to the pile of furs where another two pups appeared to be sleeping peacefully—at least until their sister arrived and jumped on them. She dropped a wide strip of battered leather tied over the door lintel, cutting them off from the outside world, and the chill that had fallen with the darkness.

"I . . . it's wonderful," Arkady said, as she felt the cosy warmth of the room envelope her. Never had a place looked so warm or inviting. "I think it's the first time I've been warm in days."

And safe, she thought, afraid that if she voiced such an opinion aloud, she would jinx herself. *Tides, I don't believe it. I think—for the moment at least—I'm out of harm's way.*

Chapter 27

"Are you hungry, your grace?"

"I'm sorry; did you say something, Boots?"

"I only have dried meat," the canine told her. "But you're welcome to share it." She walked to the fireplace to stoke up the fire. The pups were all whimpering now that the little one had disturbed them. "Missy, leave your brothers alone and let them sleep!" The female pup sat on her haunches and stared at her mother with huge liquid eyes that seemed to shine in the firelight. "And there's no point giving me that look, either, young lady," Boots added in a stern voice, without even glancing at the pup. "I'm not falling for it."

Arkady smiled. "She really is quite gorgeous, Boots."

"You say that because you've only just met her, your grace. Give it a day or two, then you'll change your mind." Boots finished with the fire and walked to the furs. After a few moments, she had the other pups settled. She sat down beside them and allowed Missy to suckle, which the pup did with noisy enthusiasm.

Arkady glanced around the chamber, but there seemed no sign of any other adults. "Is their sire not here to help you?"

Boots frowned. "He's off being a hero. Tides, but I hate heroes."

"A hero wouldn't abandon his family."

"We'd have been a damn sight better off if this particular hero had done exactly that," Boots said, clearly unwilling to talk about who had fathered her litter. "It was a stroke of good fortune that we ran into Duke Stellan, your grace. And that he didn't hold killing one of his wretched felines against me."

Typical Stellan—even in the midst of all this, he was still looking after his Crasii, she thought. A pity he wasn't so fond of caring for the human charges in his care. *How can a man so thoughtful be so ruthless at the same time?* "Is he well?"

Boots nodded. "He seems well. He's certainly got the suzerain marching to the beat of *his* drum, and that's no mean feat." The Crasii turned to look at Arkady. "Do you know what a suzerain is, my lady?"

"All too well, Boots," Arkady said with a sigh, moving closer to the fire. "All too well."

"Then you know this war is about the suzerain and not really about whether or not somebody kidnapped poor little Princess Nyah?"

Arkady nodded and sat down, deciding she needed to remove her shoes before they dropped off with her feet inside them. "I know you're a Scard, too, Boots. And what that means. I've met quite a few immortals in the past year. I'm becoming quite expert on the subject."

Boots looked more than a little concerned by her admission. "Is that what you were doing wandering around the forest? Running from the immortals?"

"Running from the immortals and hoping to find Stellan," Arkady said. "I never thought it would be this easy."

"It's not," Boots said. "I don't want to give you false hope, your grace. I may never see the duke again. And I certainly don't plan to wait for him to come back. Soon as that lake thaws out, I'm finding a boat, taking my pups and heading home to Glaeba."

Arkady didn't blame Boots for her determination to be gone from here. She tugged off her soaking shoes and stockings and began to massage her frozen toes, a little surprised to find there was no sign of frostbite. "At least I know Stellan lives. Is there any way to get him a message?"

Boots shook her head. "Short of walking into Cycrane to deliver it yourself, none I can think of."

Arkady examined her pale, icy and blistered feet, frowning. "I'll not be walking anywhere for a day or two, I suspect." She looked up at Boots then, and smiled apologetically. "I'm so sorry, Boots. I'm assuming you'll allow me to stay without even asking. I'll move on tomorrow if you want. I have no wish to endanger you or your pups, and to be honest, that may happen if Jaxyn comes looking for me."

"You can stay until you're ready to travel again, your grace," Boots said, moving Missy to the other breast. The pup had started to fuss a little. "But if you've suzerain hunting you, I'd appreciate you not leading them here."

Arkady nodded, but before she could assure the Scard she would not willingly endanger her or her family, the ground shook so hard that some of Boots's carefully constructed barricade around the entrance to the lower levels, tumbled down the darkened stairwell. All the pups reacted to the tremor in terror, the two sleeping pups waking abruptly, before bursting into tears of fear and distress.

And then, after a moment or two, the tremor stopped as unexpectedly as it had started.

"Tides! What was that?" Arkady asked. "Do you think it had something to do with the battle?"

"That wasn't a part of the battle," Boots said, gathering her babies to her fearfully. "I think it was someone using the Tide."

"To do what?"

"I dunno," the Crasii said, nuzzling her puppies gently to soothe them. "But it was something big."

Arkady wasn't satisfied with such a vague answer.

"I'll go out and check if we can see anything from here." She reached for her soaking shoes, but the canine looked up and shook her head.

"Stay, my lady," she said. "Eat something first and be sure it's fully dark before you go back outside. Anyway, you'll never get those shoes back on until they dry a little."

Arkady couldn't fault the Crasii's logic. "Later then," she agreed. "When it's fully dark."

Once Missy settled in with the other pups and the two adults had eaten, Arkady had another go at putting on her shoes. The water bucket needed filling and she was still worried about the earlier tremor, wondering if there was any damage close by.

Arkady struggled to pull her still-damp shoes onto her aching feet and then pushed herself up, grabbed the water bucket Boots kept near the fire and, ignoring the pain, hobbled up the stone stairs, past the leather door hanging, through the darkened temple and out into the night.

Shivering in the cold, still night, she left the bucket on the steps, deciding to fill it with snow on her way back. It would melt quickly enough in the warmth of the underground cavern where Boots and her pups had made their home. The starlight reflecting off the snow gave Arkady enough light to see by so, following the unexpected sound of water, she hurried as best she could on feet that had no desire to go anywhere, through the underbrush to the shore of the lake.

When she reached it, Arkady came to a halt a few feet from the reeds that grew along the edge of the water and stared at the lake in shock. Only a few hours ago, there had been a solid sheet of ice stretching all the way to Glaeba. Now the ice was gone, broken into millions of smaller fragments which were already being consumed by the relatively warmer waters of the lake. Dark water stretched before her like a black sky dotted with stars made of ice, lapping at the reeds on the water's edge with a gentle *slap-slap* that seemed innocuous and strange so soon after the violence that must have caused the ice to shatter.

Arkady stood on the shore, trying to comprehend the forces that could have effected such a miracle. She'd seen Tide magic worked before. She'd watched Cayal and Declan use it to scare off the Senestran Trading Houses from the wetlands. She'd seen Crasii healed and limbs regenerated, and been brought back from the brink of death herself by Declan, when the chameleon Crasii of Watershed Falls had condemned her to death and tied her to the Justice Tree, so she could be eaten alive by gobie ants.

Until now, however, Arkady had never really understood what it was to have the power to break the world in half; the ability to affect things so directly.

She was still trying to take that in when she noticed other things bobbing beside the melting icebergs. Darker shapes dotted the water; hundreds, maybe even thousands of them. The regular *slap-slap* noise faltered for a moment. Arkady looked to her right and realised something had washed up a few feet away. She pushed through the reeds to investigate, horrified to discover that a waterlogged and long-dead feline had come to rest on the shore.

She squatted down beside her and turned the body over. Arkady didn't know the feline. She wasn't even certain if the creature was fighting for Glaeba or Caelum. Her fur was burnt off in places, but there were no other visible signs of injury. More than likely, she had drowned or frozen to death in the icy water, unable to swim to safety in time.

Her mind reeling, Arkady rose to her feet and looked out over the lake again. She knew now what those bobbing dark shapes in the water were.

They were Crasii. Tens of thousands of them. Dead because an immortal had waved his magical arm and decreed they should perish as a by-product of the wars they waged among themselves.

Tides . . . Papa was out on the ice with Jaxyn . . .

Arkady was too wrung out to cry; too weary to revisit the grief she'd lived over and over again, every time she'd thought she'd lost him. That her father was truly dead this time seemed more an inevitability than a shock; his insistence on staying behind, almost prophetic.

And Arkady hated herself for being relieved that her father was no longer a weapon that could be used to punish her.

I'm sorry, Papa, for everything I put you through.

It was the best Arkady could do. The closest thing to a prayer she could find within herself.

And the most fitting epithet she could think of.

Sickened at the shape the world was taking with the rise of the Tide Lords, Arkady turned and headed back to the ruins, leaving the dead feline where she was. She hoped her father's body washed up in some place where it might be treated with more respect than she could afford to spare the nameless Crasii she'd discovered. There was no point in trying to bury her and she was too waterlogged to be burned, even if Arkady has been willing to expose Boots's hideaway by lighting a fire.

Besides, by morning there would be more than one dead feline washed up along the shores of the Great Lakes.

It was only fitting they remain there long enough for the immortals to see what they had done.

Chapter 28

It took only a few minutes before they were gone—Jaxyn's army, Jaxyn and his endless ranks of felines who had been prepared to march to their death without question. Stellan stared at the lake in shock as an eerie silence descended over the city, pierced only by the occasional cry for help from a drowning feline.

"Tides . . . what happened?" Stellan breathed in awe.

Before Tryan could reply, a cheer rose up—mostly human—from the remainder of the Caelish army gathered on the shore who'd survived the disaster. They were clustered along the docks in front of the balcony, stunned by what had happened and glad to be alive. But the cheer was quickly replaced by the screams of the dying Crasii and the realisation that everyone who'd been out on the ice was in danger of drowning if they couldn't get to shore before the icy water robbed them of the ability and the will to save themselves.

"We have to organise rescue parties," Stellan said, overcoming his shock.

"Why?" Tryan asked, almost uninterestedly. He seemed preoccupied and worried about something, and it certainly wasn't the death cries of the thousands of felines in danger of drowning right before his very eyes. "They're only Crasii."

Stellan couldn't believe Tryan was so dismissive of their miraculous rescue. Given the cracking ice had likely saved Caelum from certain invasion, he would have expected a different reaction to Tryan's distracted irritation; it was almost as if his attention was elsewhere. But even if the Tide Lords cared nothing for the Crasii casualties, there were other souls out there on the ice—human souls—for whom Stellan expected Tryan to have some empathy.

"Your highness, Jaxyn's envoy said my wife was out there."

"He also said he was going to kill her if we didn't surrender. We didn't surrender. Chances are she was dead hours ago."

Tryan's logic was harsh but unassailable. Stellan wanted to scream at him, but knew it was futile. Besides, Tryan probably wouldn't notice his screams against the background of all the other tormented screams going on around them. "You can't just let them die, my lord."

"Yes," Tryan said. "I can."

"But isn't every Crasii you save, even those belonging to Glaeba, yours to command, once you order them to follow you?"

That gave the immortal pause. Tryan thought for a moment and then glanced at Stellan impatiently, waving his arm to embrace the chaos below them. "Tides, if you want to be a hero, Desean, go out there and rescue every wretched feline you can find. I'll be back at the palace if you happen to see my sister."

Without waiting for Stellan's acknowledgment, Tryan turned and took the stairs down to the street two at a time. He snatched the reins of the horse a canine had waiting for him, swung into the saddle and was gone before Stellan had a chance to respond.

What followed was the longest day of Stellan's life.

He hadn't meant to take charge of the rescue effort; it just seemed as if there was nobody else. Like Tryan, Rance and Krydence abandoned the battlefield as soon as they realised the battle was, if not won, then at least over for the time being, leaving a gaping maw in lieu of leadership for the vast Crasii army magically compelled to obey their orders.

They were not magically compelled to obey a word of Stellan's but he soon discovered that—traumatised as they were—issuing order after order in the name of the immortals was almost as effective. He organised work parties, arranged for the dead to be collected, prisoners to be billeted and the wounded to be housed and treated in a couple of empty warehouses along the wharf that he commandeered in the queen's name.

Few humans thought to question him either. Somebody needed to take charge, and even the regular Caelish officers were glad it wasn't their responsibility to sort out this mess.

So Stellan worked long into the night, seeing the survivors saved and confined, the dead piled up for later burial or cremation. While he worked he searched through the Glaeban casualties for a familiar face, of which there were far too many.

There was no sign of Arkady, however. Tryan might have been right about her fate. She may well have been killed earlier in the day or maybe her body was sucked down under the ice when it broke. Stellan had no way of knowing. However, sometime around midnight he was forced to give up worrying about his wife's fate because he received news that over-shadowed all the other bad news he'd received this day—news that had much greater ramifications for both Glaeba and Caelum.

Just after midnight, an exhausted messenger finally tracked him down while he was questioning the survivors in one of the makeshift hospitals. He interrupted Stellan to inform him that the body of King Mathu of Glaeba had been dragged ashore.

Somewhat to Stellan's surprise, and despite the chaos, the Crasii had had the good sense to separate Mathu's body from the countless other dead bodies, and had laid the young man out in the front room of the wharfside brothel Tryan had used as a command post earlier in the day. A small fire flickered fitfully in the fireplace of the main reception room, taking the chill off the air. The walls, painted in a tacky floral pattern meant to emulate the tasteful wallpaper used in the stately houses of Cycrane, only made the room look worse. It seemed almost disrespectful to lay a dead king in this place. The furniture was pushed aside to make room for a trestle table where the young man was laid out. Still dressed in the sopping, heavy winter clothing that would have relentlessly dragged him down once he hit the water, the flaccid corpse looked nothing like the boy Stellan had rescued, time and again, from places like this. Waterlogged, pale and wrinkled like an old man from the effects of the water, Mathu was barely recognisable as human, let alone the handsome, healthy, fit young man he'd been when he started on this quest.

Stellan ordered everyone from the tawdrily decorated, candle-lit room. He stared down at his cousin's body for a long time, wondering if the reason he felt nothing but relief that Mathu was dead was because of exhaustion or anger. It might well be the latter. This easily led young man had brought Glaeba to its knees with his blind ignorance, after all.

And I almost did the same, he admitted silently to himself. Stellan was the one who gave both Jaxyn and Diala their entrée into the Glaeban halls of power. He'd introduced Mathu to Kylia . . . or Diala, as she was better known among the immortals.

But the war, the invasion—all of that was Mathu's fault, if not his intention. He was their king. He had the power to veto anything the immortals proposed, from the notion of trumping up charges against his own cousin for murder he didn't commit, to marching an army across the ice to invade a country with whom Glaeba had enjoyed centuries of peaceful coexistence.

"Tides, Mat," he said softly, moving a little closer. "It shouldn't have ended like this."

The king's arms were folded across his chest, the royal signet sitting heavily on Mathu's shrivelled hand. Stellan stared at it for a moment and then reached forward to remove it. The ring slid off Mathu's finger with surprising ease, perhaps because it had been sized to suit his father's larger, meatier hands.

"Looting the dead?" a voice remarked behind him. "How very common-born of you, your grace."

Stellan spun around furiously, pocketing the ring as he turned. "I gave orders I was not to be disturbed!"

"You gave orders to the Crasii, Desean. My will outranks yours these days. At least when it comes to them."

Stellan stared at Declan Hawkes with open-mouthed shock. "*Hawkes?* Tides, man, what are you doing here in Caelum?"

"Long story," Declan said, shutting the door behind him. He crossed the room and stared at the dead king for a moment. "Always did think Mathu Debree would come to a sorry end."

The spymaster had not changed at all in the months since Stellan had seen him last. Not surprising, he supposed, given Hawkes was immortal now, but his presence was totally unexpected, and no doubt connected in some way to earlier events of the day.

Declan looked up and glanced around. "Guess this is the last brothel you'll ever have to drag him out of, at any rate."

"Declan, how did you get . . . why are you here?"

"Now Mathu's dead, I suppose that makes you Glaeba's king," the former spymaster said, ignoring Stellan's question.

"I suppose it does."

"Technically, that makes Arkady your queen. Unless you found time to have your marriage dissolved while I was off searching the world for her."

Stellan's heart sank at Declan's words. During the last conversation of substance they'd had, he had asked this man to find her. Hawkes's presence here and now meant he'd probably tracked her back to Glaeba.

"Declan . . . I'm sorry . . . Arkady was out on the ice . . ."

Declan shook his head. "No, she wasn't."

Stellan sighed, thinking he understood why Hawkes was in such adamant denial. Stellan was still having difficulty grasping the idea that Arkady was gone, and he didn't even love her the way Hawkes did. He took a step closer, trying to appear sympathetic. "I know you'd like to believe she's still alive, Declan, but I fear you're letting blind faith take precedence over the facts. I had a message from Jaxyn before the battle started. Arkady was his prisoner. She was out there watching the battle not three feet from where Mathu was standing when the platform collapsed and went into the water. There was no way . . ."

"She wasn't on the platform," Declan stated flatly.

"How do you know that?"

"Chikita told me."

"Chikita?"

"That feline you won in a bear-baiting when Mathu first came to Lebec," Declan said. "She was one of ours."

"Ours?" he asked, thoroughly confused.

"A Scard. Working for the Cabal."

Stellan stared at him blankly for a moment. He knew what the Cabal of the Tarot was, of course, but he had no idea they'd been watching him so closely, even long before he discovered the truth about the immortals.

Declan seemed unapologetic for sending spies into his household. "We needed to get her into your service to keep an eye on Jaxyn."

Stellan sighed heavily, shaking his head. "By we, I assume you mean the Cabal, and not agents of the king?"

Declan nodded, although his attention was still on Mathu's corpse.

Stellan remembered the incident well, but he was aghast to think he been so easily manipulated. "How could you possibly know I'd make an offer on her?"

"We didn't," Declan said, bending over the body as he studied it intently. "We had a plan which turned out to be unnecessary when you rather nobly—and very conveniently—made a wager for her. You don't . . . at least, you *didn't* . . . usually buy slaves on the open market; you tended to stick with the ones you bred yourself. And Jaxyn was your Kennel-Master by then, remember. We had to find a way to get her into your kennels. We figured he was rather fond of fighting felines, so he'd make an offer on her if she managed to defeat the bear."

"She could have been killed, Declan."

"But she wasn't." Declan poked Mathu's flaccid corpse with interest. "Do you think the water killed him, or did one of the immortals do him in beforehand?"

"What?" Stellan asked, the sudden change of subject confusing him.

"Mathu. What do you think killed him?"

"Either the cold water or he drowned," Stellan answered, a little bemused. "There don't seem to be any other wounds. I still don't see how Chikita could know that Arkady didn't drown when the ice broke, Declan. Or how she'd be in a position to tell you about it. Or, for that matter, what you're even doing here in Cycrane telling *me* about it."

"Been here most of the day," Declan replied, straightening up. He looked around the room curiously. "Nice trick with the oil, by the way. Do you reckon there's anything to drink around here?"

Stellan stared at the former spymaster, his mind swirling with possibilities of what his appearance meant.

"How did you even manage to find Chikita? It's chaos out there."

"It took me hours," Declan admitted. "But then I knew what I was looking for. That's how I found Mathu, too."

"*You* found him?"

Declan nodded. "I ordered the Crasii to put him in here, away from prying eyes, and have you summoned. I figured you'd want to be the first to know that he didn't make it."

"Well . . . yes . . . of course," Stellan said. "But why?"

"Why what?"

"Why did you want me to know before anybody else?"

"The king is dead," Declan Hawkes said pointing at Mathu's corpse, his expression unintentionally sinister in the candlelight. "Long live the king."

Stellan wasn't sure he was ready to deal with that just yet. And he was more than a little concerned—not to mention curious—about what had brought Declan to Cycrane in the first place. "Did *you* break the ice?"

Hawkes smiled, spying a decanter on the sideboard. "Hardly. No single immortal could have done that. Not with the Tide only two-thirds of the way up." He pulled out the stopper, sniffed the contents warily and then lined up two shot glasses on the grubby linen runner that— Stellan assumed—was supposed to add to the "classy" feeling of the establishment. "Care to join me?"

"How do you know the Tide is only two-thirds of the way up?"

"I don't. Not for certain. The others seem to think it is."

"The others? You've made contact with some of the other immortals then?"

Declan nodded and poured Stellan a drink, even though he'd not indicated he wanted one. "Hence the reason I am here in Cycrane." He handed Stellan a glass and raised his own. "Bottoms up."

Declan downed the contents of his glass in a gulp and then turned to fill it again. "Tides, do you have any idea how hard it is to get drunk when you're immortal?"

Stellan didn't know, or particularly care. "What happened out on the ice? Why did it break like that? Tryan said it was somebody using Tide magic."

"Some*bodies*," Declan corrected, downing the second glass. "Cayal, Kentravyon and Elyssa, to be exact. I declined to aid them in their en-deavours. Haven't been immortal long enough for tens of thousands of incidental casualties not to bother me just yet. But give me time; I'm sure I'll get there eventually."

"Cayal is here?" Stellan asked, concerned by Declan's bitterness. He didn't know what the spymaster had seen or done since leaving Maralyce's mine all those months ago in search of Arkady, but he clearly wasn't lik-ing what he had become.

"Oh, yes. Cayal is here."

"Who is Kentravyon?"

"Another Tide Lord. Interesting chap. Makes Cayal seem sane and well-adjusted."

"Have you any news of Jaxyn? Or Diala?"

"Well," Declan said. "I'm pretty sure they're not dead."

"That's not what I was asking, Declan."

The former spymaster shook his head and shrugged. "Truth is, I haven't heard a word on their fate. And we're not likely to, either. Even Chikita doesn't know what happened to them and she was right beside them when the ice gave way."

"They'll have felt the others breaking the ice, won't they?" Stellan asked, remembering how Tryan had known what was happening because he could feel it on the Tide.

"And they'll know they're outnumbered," Declan agreed. "The consensus seems to be that Jaxyn and his minions will slink away in the confusion and either regroup for a counterattack or find some other unsuspecting country—preferably on the other side of Amyrantha—to take over. One that's less work to take and hold and doesn't have the Empress of the Five Realms and her merry band of irritating offspring living next door."

Stellan stared at him with concern. "You sound just like one of them, Declan."

"Apparently I am *just one of them*," he said, putting the glass down on the sideboard. "Do you have the seal?"

"What?"

"The royal seal. Mathu's ring. Can't claim the throne of Glaeba without it, you know, and if you don't get back to the palace soon, your future majesty, it won't be yours to claim."

"Um . . . of course . . . yes . . . I have it. What are you talking about?"

Declan threw his hands up. "Tides, Desean, how dense can one man be? While you've been down here earning the undying gratitude of a vast number of Crasii who would gut you in a heartbeat, should an immortal command them to, Tryan is up at the palace, as we speak, doing a deal with Cayal and Kentravyon to enlist their help to secure Glaeba's throne. Something he's got a good chance of getting away with, what with their king dead and the bulk of their army floating face down in the Lower Oran. I suggest you get up there before the deal is done."

Declan's news seemed to make little sense. "Why would any other Tide Lords agree to help Elyssa take the throne of Glaeba?"

"She has something they want," Declan told him. "They're prepared to do quite a bit to aid her if it will enlist her cooperation."

"Then the throne is lost."

"Maybe it is. But as you're the rightful claimant at the moment, you won't know what they're planning unless you get back to the palace and invite yourself into the discussions, will you?"

"Of course," Stellan said, as Declan's warnings finally began to sink in. "I should go back. I think things are under control here now . . ."

"Go, Desean," Declan said. "I'll see to things down here."

"But you're a stranger. Nobody in Caelum is going to listen to a word you . . ." Stellan hesitated as he realised Declan had an advantage that outweighed his nationality. "Ah . . . you're immortal now. The Crasii will do whatever you command."

"So it seems."

"Are you not interested in their negotiations at the palace?"

"Only in so far as I think you ought to be there to represent Glaeba's interests." Hawkes folded his arms across his chest and stared at Stellan in a rather disconcerting way. "You're her king now, Desean. I'm just a former employee of the crown."

Hawkes was right. It was time to see this dangerous course of action he'd embarked upon when he brought Princess Nyah back to Caelum, through to its logical conclusion.

Stellan nodded. "Then I'll take your advice and return to the palace." He looked down at the body of his king; he was still numb, his mind already filling with the things he'd need to establish, concessions he would have to demand. *Tides, does it never end?* "Will you see Mathu remains . . . undisturbed?"

"If you really want me to."

"I do." Stellan took a deep breath and turned for the door, realising as he did so that Declan had warned him what was happening up at the palace, but had neatly avoided answering any other questions about how he came to be here.

He hesitated, his hand on the latch. "You say you spoke to Chikita. She's not a Crasii, she's a Scard. I believe they hate your kind. What was her reaction when she realised you were immortal?"

"She tried to lay me open with her claws."

"But you healed instantly?"

"One of the perks of immortality. Along with flying carpets."

That comment made no sense to Stellan but he wasn't sure he wanted an explanation. "Did Chikita give you any hint as to what direction Arkady was headed when she fled the battle?"

Declan shook his head. "She had no idea."

"If she headed back toward Glaeba . . ." Stellan began, almost afraid to give voice to the thought.

"Then she would still have been on the ice when it broke," Declan finished for him. "I know that."

"What do you think happened?"

"I think Arkady would be smart enough to head for the nearest shore."

"Then she might still be alive?"

"Maybe," Declan agreed with a non-committal shrug. "Maybe not."

"Will you keep looking for her?"

"What do you think I was doing when I found Chikita?"

Stellan should have known better than to ask. He nodded. "I should get back to the palace. Will I see you again, or are you leaving now the battle is done?"

Declan shrugged. "I'm not sure. Now I've spoken to Chikita, I doubt it'll take long for word to get back to the Cabal that I'm still alive. And one of the enemy."

"*Are* you the enemy now, Declan?"

He shrugged. "I guess that remains to be seen."

"What do you think the Cabal will do when they get word of your fate?"

"That also remains to be seen and is much of the reason," Declan said, "that I wish I was still capable of getting drunk."

Chapter 29

Warlock hadn't stayed to hear the rest of the conversation between Elyssa and the new Tide Lords. He slipped away into the woods, found his horse cropping a clump of tenacious dried grass that had somehow managed to push through the snow, and led him quietly away from the oil seep and back toward the workers' camp.

"My lady said you are to finish dismantling the camp and head back to Cycrane," he told the foreman without dismounting. "I have urgent and secret dispatches she has ordered me to deliver. You must return to the city immediately the camp is packed and tell no one you have seen me pass by."

The foreman, a motley canine with a grey muzzle, nodded and turned to give the orders without questioning Warlock's authority to deliver them. Although they resented his favoured position with their mistress, they were used to Warlock conveying orders on her behalf, and the orders made enough sense that nobody would think them odd.

Without waiting for the foreman to engage in any further conversation, Warlock urged his horse into a canter, found the road toward Cycrane and gave the horse its head. He had only one thought in mind—to find his family. Boots and the pups were hiding in a ruin north of the city, he knew that much, but he didn't know the exact location. All he knew was that the ruins were near the lake; rarely visited—particularly at this time of the year—but not that hard to locate if one knew where to look.

His first notion was to skirt the city, wending his way through the foothills until he emerged in the north, after which he could head back toward the lake where the ruins should be. His plan did little but highlight the fact he was still thinking like a Glaeban. Cycrane was built into the Caterpillar Ranges. There was no way to go around it, particularly not at this time of year when even the most navigable passes were blocked with snow. Even in the most clement weather, all the trade that took place up and down Caelum took place on the lake. If he wanted to go north, Warlock was going to have to go through the city or cross the ice—an idea he was forced to revise dramatically just on sunset when the ice shattered.

Warlock had no doubt about who was responsible for breaking the ice-sheet. Cayal, Kentravyon, Elyssa, and perhaps even Declan Hawkes had done it, conspiring together to wield more Tide magic than any one immortal could handle on their own.

And it had stopped the war in its tracks.

But the cost in lives was horrendous. Even if the bulk of the dead were felines, whom Warlock instinctively felt ambivalent about, they didn't deserve to die without warning like that. And the immortals *could* have warned the Glaebans they were going to break the ice. Confronted with such a coalition of Tide Lords, Jaxyn may have even backed down, had someone given him the opportunity to withdraw.

But the immortals didn't work like that. They didn't care about mortal lives.

However, the Tide Lords had inadvertently done Warlock a huge favour. Now the lake was flowing again, he should be able to find a boat, seek out the ruins, retrieve his family and sail them back to Glaeba without having to wait out the winter. When he realised that Warlock changed his plans and decided to risk going through the city after all, rather than trying to get around it.

The confusion of the battle's aftermath was such that nobody noticed a single canine wearing a tunic bearing the palace insignia. He left his horse to fend for itself on the city's southern outskirts and made his way toward the wharves, sickened at the consequences of the sudden disappearance of the ice, now he was close enough to see the damage for himself.

Someone had organised rescue parties who still worked by torchlight, even though it was well past midnight before Warlock deemed it safe to approach the water's edge, hoping to steal a boat.

There were no boats to be had, however. Anything that could float had been commandeered for the rescue effort. He stood there for a time, watching them drag the bodies ashore. There were only corpses to be found this late in the day. Anybody who'd survived the breaking ice had made their way onto dry land in the first few minutes or they'd managed to cling to something buoyant, like a wooden shield, until they were rescued. By now, anyone left in the water was long dead from hypothermia.

"You there!"

Warlock turned, wondering if the barked order was addressed to him. "Are you talking to me?"

The man who'd hailed him was human, wearing the insignia of a captain and the colours of the Caelish Palace Guard. "Don't just stand there gawking, Dog Boy," the officer said. "Get down there and help."

He was pointing along the wharf to where a barge heavily laden with bodies was tied up. Warlock had no desire to help, but it might be a good excuse to stay close to the water. He had no hope of finding a boat if he was sent on his way.

"I . . . er . . ."

His hesitation made the officer suspicious. The man stepped a little closer, noticing Warlock's tunic for the first time. He threw his hands up. "Tides, Dog Boy, why didn't you say you worked at the palace? What are you doing here, anyway, standing around like a lost puppy?"

"I . . . I have dispatches to deliver," Warlock said, falling back on the same story he'd been using all evening to get through the city. "I can't find the command post."

"Follow me," the captain said, turning away from the wharf. He stopped a few moments later when he realised Warlock wasn't following. "It's this way. Come on."

Warlock couldn't afford to refuse the offer of directions without raising suspicion, so he followed the captain along the wharf and out onto the main thoroughfare that ran along the waterfront. The officer said nothing as they walked, his breath frosting in the chilly night air, although he turned a few times to yell orders at other men or Crasii who didn't seem to be pulling their weight. All around them, cold, exhausted men and weary Crasii laboured to stack the dead in mind-numbingly large piles, awaiting the steady stream of wagons that were taking them—well, Warlock didn't know where they were being taken. A mass grave perhaps, somewhere on the edge of the city? Or maybe they'd just throw them in a ravine and cover them over, the way those bodies at the foot of Deadman's Bluff had been covered over and forgotten so many centuries ago.

Can one forget this many dead?

Finally they reached a building that Warlock thought looked more like a brothel than a military headquarters. Then the canine was forced to concentrate on more immediate concerns. The building had an over-hanging balcony and a wooden veranda at the front; Warlock could smell the suzerain inside before they even stepped onto it.

"He has dispatches from the palace," the captain informed the feline on guard. She nodded and opened the door for him. Warlock had no choice but to step through it.

The door closed behind Warlock, leaving him in a chilly, narrow, darkened hall. There was an immortal nearby—Warlock could smell the rank aroma of him—but there was no other sign of life. Which im-mortal it turned out to be was immaterial. Whoever it was would al-most certainly report his presence to Elyssa. She would know by now that he was a Scard because he'd run away. Unless he got out of this building in the next few minutes, he was dead and the only thing left to be determined would be the time, place and manner of his demise.

Warlock stared down the dark hall, wondering if there was a back door through which he could escape before the suzerain even realised he was here. He decided he had no choice but to assume there was an-other exit. There was nothing else he could do. Before he'd taken two steps in the direction of freedom, however, the door on his right opened and the suzerain stepped into the hall, colliding with Warlock, who barrelled backwards and dropped to his knees.

"I am so sorry, my lord," he gushed, his head lowered, his hands on the floor in the most submissive pose he could assume. "To serve you is the reason I breathe."

He was expecting a kick in the head, or something equally punitive, but nothing happened. After a moment, Warlock looked up, daring a quick look at the immortal he'd collided with.

"To serve me is the reason you breathe, eh?" Declan Hawkes remarked. "Didn't used to be."

Warlock's heart slowly relocated from his throat and back into his chest where it belonged. But even though he was relieved to find this immortal was someone he knew, he didn't know how to take Hawkes's comment. He didn't understand how Hawkes could be immortal, either. Or why, after devoting a lifetime to saving the world from the Tide

Lords, he had somehow found a way to join them. Still on his knees in the dark, freezing hall, Warlock studied the former spymaster warily. "You're one of them."

"So everybody keeps reminding me. Get up."

Warlock climbed to his feet cautiously, not taking his eyes from Hawkes. The spymaster stood back from the door and indicated that Warlock should step inside. Not sure what else to do, Warlock walked through the door—only to see by the light of some candles, Mathu Debree's body laid out on a trestle in the centre of what looked like the main reception parlour of a very tacky brothel.

Hawkes closed the door and leaned against it. "It was stupid of you to run, Cecil," the spymaster said. "Elyssa's figured out you're a Scard."

"Then let me go, and I'll not bother you or your kind ever again."

For some reason, Hawkes seemed to think that was amusing. "You know, I was impressed when I realised you were still with her. And she was quite taken with you, too. She was livid, actually, when she realised you'd bolted from the lake this morning. You've done remarkably well, not to be caught before now."

"I'm still not caught," Warlock said. "Unless you're planning to hand me over to her. Now you're on *their* side."

"I'm not on anybody's side," Hawkes said. "Can you get a message to the Cabal for me?"

"No," Warlock said flatly.

"You can't, or you won't?"

"Both," he said, forcing himself not to look at the dead king beside him. That was a human problem he wanted no part of. "I'm done with your intrigues, Hawkes. I'm going home."

"You'll never get near the wharf, let alone near a boat. And don't you have a mate around here somewhere? She'd have had her pups by now, too, I suppose."

Warlock didn't trust Hawkes enough to admit to any such thing. Actually, he didn't trust him at all. "It's of no matter to you where my family is. It's your fault they're in danger. So let me go or kill me. I'm not helping you or the Cabal any more, Hawkes. Or your immortal friends."

Hawkes studied him for a moment with an expression Warlock

found impossible to read in the candlelight, and then the former spy-master nodded, pushed himself off the door, and opened it for Warlock. "Come on, then."

"To where?"

"You've got no chance of getting out of Cycrane on your own, War-lock," Hawkes said, addressing him by his real name for a change, and not the hated moniker "Cecil" he'd been awarded by the Cabal. But just being called by his given name wasn't enough to make him trust this man . . . or immortal . . . or whatever he was these days. "Not tonight. And certainly not with Elyssa on the warpath now she's just realised how badly she's been had by a miserable Scard."

"*You're* going to help me get out of the city?" Warlock asked, deeply suspicious of the offer.

Hawkes nodded. "We'll go down to the wharves and commandeer a boat for you."

"How? You're a Glaeban—"

"Immortal," Hawkes finished for him. "I could commandeer the whole damned Caelish fleet if I wanted to, provided there's a Crasii in charge of it."

"Won't the other immortals have something to say about this?"

"I wasn't planning to tell them," Hawkes said. "Were you?"

This was too easy. "How do I know this isn't a trap?"

"Because you're not important enough in the general scheme of things to warrant a trap," Hawkes told him with brutal honesty. "Now, do you want my help or not? I do actually have other things to be getting on with, you know, rather than hanging around here offering my help to ungrateful Scards who are too stupid to recognise a flanking escape offer when they're hit over the head with it."

"You won't try to follow me?"

"I don't care enough about your fate to be bothered," Hawkes said.

That, Warlock thought, *has a ring of truth about it.*

"I'll need something big enough to make it back to Glaeba once I've collected Boots and the pups."

"You pick the boat, and I'll order them to hand it over. And to forget they've ever seen you."

"Why?"

"So they won't report you to Elyssa," Hawkes explained, as if Warlock was just a little bit dense.

"No—I meant why are you helping me?"

"Because I can," the former spymaster told him, and then he stepped into the hall, effectively putting an end to the discussion, and Warlock realised that was all the answer he was ever likely to get.

Chapter 30

Dawn gilded the Lower Oran, turning the millions of scattered icebergs dotting the lake's surface into golden nuggets gently bobbing in a sea of molten gold. Sickened by the slaughter, and yet oddly detached from it, Declan watched the sun rising over Glaeba in the distance, wondering if his apathy to the death he had witnessed yesterday was the first sign that he was losing his humanity.

When that thought proved too disturbing, he focused on something much more practical—wondering what he should do next.

The chaos left in the wake of Jaxyn's unsuccessful attempt to invade Caelum still went on behind him along the wharves, the job now that of lesser mortals who were charged with cleaning up the mess. Much of the work was done, or the workers had finally given in to fatigue and sought their beds. To his right, another exhausted work party was dragging the last of the bodies that had washed ashore overnight into a pile that a party of tired canines, wearing numb expressions and slumped shoulders, was loading onto a flatbed wagon to be taken away for disposal.

Declan understood why they were still working to clear the lake. It wasn't just aesthetics that made them devote so much effort to clearing the bodies out of the water. The Great Lakes were the lifeblood of both Caelum and Glaeba. Nothing but disease and even more death could follow if that many rotting bodies were left to pollute the main source of potable water on the continent.

Declan glanced over his shoulder toward the city for a moment, his breath frosting in the early-morning chill. The temperature seemed to have risen somewhat, now the ice was gone, but it was still cold. They were still in the depths of the coldest winter anybody in Caelum or Glaeba could remember.

Stellan Desean was up at the palace, Declan supposed, fighting for the crown that was rightfully his. He wondered how the negotiations were going. If Stellan played his cards right, Syrolee and her clan might even let him have the crown. For a time. They were immortal, after all, and Stellan wasn't likely to produce any heirs to muddy the waters of succession a few years from now, even if they left him on the throne until he died of old age.

Declan smiled. Perhaps they'd suggest that Elyssa marry Stellan and become his queen. That would suit everybody, he thought. Except Stellan, who was already married. And Arkady, who would likely have to die to facilitate such an arrangement. Assuming they could find her.

Declan's amusement faded as he realised it wasn't such an outrageous notion. The immortals had been around for a very long time. Whatever their individual character flaws, they understood how much easier it was to work within a country's existing infrastructure. Nations were made up of more than kings and queens and palaces. They were made up of people—farmers, merchants, blacksmiths, soldiers, tailors, felters, weavers, bakers, carpenters, fletchers, shopkeepers and beggars; even the prostitutes that plied their services on the corners of every street of every city Declan had ever visited. Nations were a complex tapestry of interwoven threads; of landlords and tenants, shopkeepers and their customers, craftsmen and their apprentices. Nations were economic as much as political entities.

War disrupted the flow of commerce and made things harder to govern. Coups by strangers the populace considered undeserving of power, or worse—those who helped themselves to a nation's wealth—tended to give rise to resistance movements that invariably enjoyed the support of the now-feeling-very-put-upon population, making the country all but ungovernable. The people needed to feel safe. Or—even if they didn't join the resistance—they tended to hoard their money rather than spend it. And for a nation to grow, people *needed* to spend their money, not flee with it or hide it under the mattress.

For that reason, Declan now realised, Syrolee's original plan to take control of Caelum had centred on Tryan marrying the heir to the throne. When that scheme was thwarted by Ricard Li—and Nyah, the young Caelish heir herself, it had to be said—the immortals modified their plans.

Tryan had married Nyah's mother, the queen, instead. He didn't have the crown, or even power in his own name, but he was effectively ruling the country in Queen Jilna's name. And in the end, that was all that mattered really.

Jaxyn and Diala had done the same thing in Glaeba. Jaxyn hadn't tried to take the crown by force. He'd disposed of King Enteny, certainly, but only because the old king would never have ceded any power to a man like Jaxyn Aranville. But his son—Prince Mathu—had been allowed to live. Easily led by his immortal wife, Declan had once feared Mat would be murdered in his bed as soon as the immortals had no further use for him. But then he realised Mathu *did* have a use. Upon his father's death, he was Glaeba's true king. Jaxyn and Diala could rule through him and nobody would raise an eyebrow over Mathu's right to sit the throne.

Had the ice not broken and Mathu drowned, he'd probably still be king.

There had been no sign of Jaxyn, or Diala, or even Lyna, who was apparently now posing as Jaxyn's fiancée. No reports of seeing them. No sign of what had happened to them. Declan wasn't surprised. Any order the immortals issued to the Crasii to conceal their presence would be slavishly adhered to.

They were not dead, that was certain, but they'd lost their front man. With Mathu gone, they had no claim on the throne and no way to regain it. Jaxyn had long ago burned his bridges with Stellan Desean, so if he wanted Glaeba he was going to have to take it by force. And that was something nigh impossible to achieve now his Crasii forces had been decimated by his unsuccessful invasion of Caelum.

For that reason also, Declan knew, Stellan Desean might well find himself Glaeba's king before the day was out. Not because of his persuasive arguments or any other pressure he might think he could bring to bear; it was just so much easier for the immortals here to bring Glaeba to heel with the help of the rightful heir to the throne at the helm. They may even give him enough freedom to maintain the illusion that Glaeba remained an independent sovereign state free of immortal domination.

But it *would* be an illusion. Glaeba and Caelum were both lost, in the control of the immortals. Declan knew that for a certainty. Whatever way he wanted to spin it, Stellan Desean, if he took the throne of Glaeba, would owe his crown to his new immortal masters.

To serve you is the reason I breathe.

Stellan might be human rather than Crasii, but—king or no king—he would learn the meaning of that phrase soon enough.

Cayal and Kentravyon were up at the palace too, doing their own deals with Elyssa, which was one of the many reasons Declan wasn't. That wasn't his fight either.

He wasn't even sure he knew exactly what his fight was any longer.

Declan had come here to find Arkady but he had no idea what had happened to her. She might already be dead—as Stellan feared—or she might have fled into the city when Chikita let her escape—which was the smart thing, and therefore the most likely thing Arkady would do. Or she might have been desperate to attempt a return home to Lebec and decided to risk crossing the ice on foot. If she'd done the latter, Arkady was dead as sure as the sun was rising over the lake this morning.

Somehow Declan couldn't bring himself to believe she would have been so foolish.

But her location remained a mystery and one it might not be wise to try to solve. He'd come to Caelum to rescue her from Jaxyn—something she'd managed without any help from him at all. Even if he found her, it might not be a good idea to reveal that fact. Not with Cayal here.

Right now, wherever Arkady was, she was probably better off without the added complication of immortals.

Besides, there were other things to take care of, Declan thought, as he stared across the water at the distant blur of mountains that marked his homeland. The Cabal would hear within days—perhaps even hours, if their spies in Cycrane had access to carrier birds—that Declan Hawkes lived. More than that, they would have heard Declan Hawkes was going to live forever.

He wasn't sure what the Cabal would do about that. He even allowed himself a small smile as he realised that the one thing he could guarantee they *wouldn't* do was hunt him down and kill him.

But the Cabal would want an explanation for what he was quite sure they were going to consider the ultimate betrayal.

And Declan felt the need to give them one. He wanted Tilly to know he hadn't asked for this; hadn't even imagined it could ever happen to him. And yet, here he was, the enemy. He had become everything he was raised to despise. He wanted the Cabal to know he hadn't sought this. He wanted them to know that given a choice between immortality and death, he'd have chosen death in a heartbeat.

Or would you? a traitorous voice in his head asked softly. *You say that now, but if you were given a choice, would you really have chosen death over eternal life?*

He had no answer to that question, but in the course of his idle musing, he discovered he had come to at least one conclusion. Whatever happened to Glaeba, whoever claimed its throne, the former king's spymaster had unfinished business there.

Declan glanced around the wharf on which he stood, hoping to find some method of transport across the lake. Theoretically, he supposed, he could have jumped on a broken slab of ice and ridden it across the water the same way he'd ridden Kentravyon's carpet and Cayal's section of roof-thatching across the ocean. But Declan was after a more traditional mode of transport. He wasn't ready to let a magic carpet ride across the lake announce his presence quite so publicly.

He glanced at the work party of canines. One of them had a small rowboat, a craft about the same size as the dinghy Stellan Desean had stolen when they escaped the prison fire in Herino that had immolated Declan and made him immortal. It would take him most of the day to row his way to Glaeba, but he could always fall back on the Tide, he supposed, if he tired of the physical effort.

Declan frowned. *Tides, I'm starting to think like one of them.*

"You there!" he called down to the canine in the dinghy. "Come here!"

The Crasii complied without question, turning from his task of poling the corpses toward the shore. He laid the pole across the bow, picked up the oars, and rowed over to the wharf where Declan was standing.

"I am taking your boat," Declan informed him, as it bumped gently into the pylon.

The canine didn't even think to question his right to commandeer the craft. "To serve you is the reason I breathe, my lord," he said with a bow before standing carefully to toss a line onto the wharf. Declan caught it and waited for the Crasii to climb up to the wharf.

"I am leaving now," he informed the canine. "If anybody asks where I am, you're to say you haven't seen me. Is that clear?"

"To serve you is the reason I breathe, my lord," the canine repeated, in complete awe of him.

Declan frowned. He was in no mood for fawning Crasii this morning.

"Go help the others with the bodies," he ordered, mostly to be rid of the creature.

The canine bowed again and hurried away to join his companions on the shore. Declan turned and made his way backwards down the narrow ladder to the water. He jumped into the dinghy, which rocked dangerously as he landed, and then took a seat and picked up the oars.

As the sun climbed over the edge of the Chevron Mountains on the Glaeban side of the lake, he dug deep into the water and turned the boat for home.

Chapter 31

Arkady woke to the sound of distant laughter. For a while she didn't realise what she was hearing. It seemed a strange sound, pleasant yet distant and somehow totally unconnected to anything in Arkady's world. It was a tinkling sound, full of joy and good humour; a sound contrasting so starkly with the dark nightmares that haunted her dreams, it didn't seem real.

She opened her eyes, blinking in the sudden light. Before she left, Boots had pulled back the leather door of their underground chamber to air the place out. Daylight streamed through the entrance at the top of the stone steps, making the lair uncharacteristically bright.

And it was empty. Arkady rubbed her eyes, wondering how long she'd been asleep. She hadn't meant to doze off. Boots had gone out to see if she could hunt up something to supplement their diet of jerky and hard cheese. She was feeding three pups, after all, and was starting to feel the strain. Boots needed meat. Fresh meat. And she'd left Arkady watching over her pups while she went hunting.

Arkady was still exhausted by her escape from the battle and her subsequent trek through the woods. Her feet hurt and she was emotionally wrung out from all that had happened to her these past weeks, since discovering her father still lived. Abandoning him to die was something she didn't want to think about, mostly because she simply didn't have room in her heart to deal with it. Arkady had walled off her grief and her guilt; putting it aside for a time when she could afford to indulge it. She heard the giggling again and sat up. The noise—and what it meant—began to register in her mind. It sounded like the pups. But they weren't anywhere she could see.

"Oh, Tides," Arkady swore, pushing herself to her feet. She winced as she put her weight on them, the stone floor icy against her blisters. "Ow, ow, ow!" she exclaimed with each step, as she headed toward the stairs, wondering how far the pups could have gone while she dozed off. She could hear them laughing, so she guessed it wasn't that far. They could only crawl, after all, and only shakily at that. But she knew Boots would be furious to learn she'd let the puppies out of her sight, just as she understood how important it was their hideout maintain its deserted appearance. Their safety lay in staying hidden. Their safety lay in no passersby—either hunters in the woods or fishermen on the lake—realising there was anybody living in these ruins.

She heard the giggles again, and Arkady realised the sound wasn't coming from upstairs in the main hall of the ruins, but from behind her. She turned and cocked her head. The odd acoustics of the place were confusing, making the sound appear to be coming from a different place every time she heard it. She began to worry, too. She remembered Shalimar, Declan's grandfather, telling her on countless occasions that the only time you truly had to worry about children was when they went unexpectedly quiet or when they were laughing out of sight when they should be otherwise engaged.

Arkady frowned and looked around the small hall with its countless shadow-filled nooks and crannies, trying to determine where the sound was coming from. Then she spied the barricade Boots had built around the stairwell which led even deeper into the ruins. It had crumbled last night when the tremor caused by the shattering ice had dislodged the stones. Wincing on her painful feet, Arkady hobbled a little closer to the dark maw and again heard the distinct sound of giggling.

Tides, how had they gotten down those stairs without breaking their necks?

She stared down the stairwell, but it was too dark to see anything. "Missy? Dezi? Tory?"

They didn't answer her of course, but they did fall silent for a moment. *For pity's sake, they're not even three months old! How can they fall into such a guilty silence at that age?*

There was nothing for it, she realised. They were too young to come when called, and whatever had them giggling down there in the darkness of the lower level was obviously far more enticing than any incentive this strange human—who'd suddenly appeared out of nowhere last night—could offer them. Arkady hobbled across to the fire-pit and lit one of Boots's precious torches from the coals. Once it was burning brightly, she limped back to the stairwell, stepped over the crumbled barricade, and began to descend the stairs.

Keeping her hand on the rough stone wall to help her balance, Arkady flinched at every icy step, wondering if she should have taken the time to put something on her raw and aching feet before venturing down here into the darkness.

But, pain aside, the historian in Arkady was fascinated by this place. She knew from her last visit here with Stellan—back when the world was a very different place—that it pre-dated history as the Glaebans or Caelish knew it. There was no long-lost culture they knew of that might have built it, and whatever decoration may have once adorned the building in its heyday had been painted onto plaster, rather than carved into the stone; plaster that had long ago disintegrated into dust, leaving only the masonry shell of the temple behind.

Arkady knew now that her incomplete view of history was the result of the many Cataclysms caused by the Tide Lords; that her world had a rich and varied history dating back thousands of years prior to the start of their limited knowledge. *I wonder,* she thought idly, as another giggle beckoned her forward into the darkness, *where would society be now, if our progress hadn't been constantly interrupted by the internecine battles of the immortals?*

Ironically, the mystery of this temple's very existence was one of the things—besides covering for her father—that had fuelled her interest in history, which had led her to studying the oral history of the Crasii, which led to Declan asking her to interview Cayal, which led her to becoming involved with the immortals. In many ways, she had come a full circle. However, in a million years Arkady could never have imagined the path her life would take from that moment on, or the cost her seemingly innocent interest in history would exact.

"Missy? Dezi? Tory?"

The giggling stopped again at her call.

"Come on! I know you're down here. Where are you, you little rascals?"

The torch provided only a small circle of light in the darkness. She figured they couldn't be that far away, given she'd been able to hear them upstairs. Arkady took a further step and let out a yelp as she stubbed her toe on another fall of rock that must have been dislodged during last night's tremor.

Her eyes watering with the sting of yet another scrape added to her litany of aches and pains, she squatted down to examine the small rock fall blocking her way. As she did, she spied three pairs of eyes shining in the darkness off to her left. The fall had exposed another chamber on the other side of the wall. Somehow, the three pups had managed to find their way down here and crawl inside.

"Tides, how long was I asleep?" she muttered to herself. Then she forced a smile, putting on her very best coaxing voice. "Come on, you three. Mama's waiting for you upstairs. Are you hungry?"

The pups giggled but made no move toward her. It was a foolish idea to think they would. They didn't know her. They couldn't speak. They couldn't understand a word she was saying. Arkady moved the torch a little closer. Although the chamber beyond gave the impression of being quite large, she doubted she could fit through the small hole the pups had found to enter it.

Arkady sat back on her heels to rethink the problem, moving the torch away from the entrance in case the pups were afraid of the fire. She jammed it between the stones off to her right, and turned to look at the pups again, surprised to discover the cavern where they were hiding wasn't completely dark at all, but lit by a soft blue light, although Arkady couldn't determine its source.

"Come on, sweetie," Arkady coaxed to the nearest pup, not sure which one it was in the odd blue light. "Come to Aunty Kady."

The pup giggled again and rolled something toward her. Arkady had no idea what it was, but it proved to be the source of the strange blue light. She reached through the opening and scooped it up, surprised by the weight of it. As soon as Arkady touched it, however, the strange glowing object went cold and dead. She moved it closer to the light of the torch and let out a yelp of disgust. About the size of a small melon, it seemed to be made of polished quartz. And it was shaped like a skull.

"Oh, that's just horrid," she muttered, but she turned back to the entrance to the cavern and held up the quartz skull. "Is this what you want?" she asked, holding it just out of reach. "Come on, then; come and get it."

The pups were too young to understand what Arkady was saying, but they wanted their shiny toy back. The nearest pup—Arkady still wasn't sure which one it was—reached for the skull, which began to glow blue again as the pup approached. When Arkady pulled it away, the glow disappeared. Fascinated, she moved it toward the pups once more, and sure enough, the closer it got to the Crasii the more it began to shine.

Arkady was entranced, but she was also acutely aware that Boots was due back at any moment and would not be pleased to discover her pups had been allowed to wander down here on their own while Arkady was— quite literally—asleep on the job. But she understood what had fascinated the pups so much. The skull—its purpose, its age, or who might have crafted it—were all questions begging for answers. But not now. Not until the pups were safe. Putting aside for the moment the mystery of this strange artefact, Arkady held it closer to the entrance, the blue glow filling the chamber beyond as it neared the puppies.

"Here you go," she called in a sing-song voice. "Come and get the pretty skull. Come on."

The pups probably weren't even listening to her, so spellbound were they by the shiny object beckoning them forward with its soft blue glow. They approached it warily, giggling a little in that odd way Crasii pups had of mimicking human children. "That's it—come to the shiny skull. Follow the pretty light . . ."

Dezi emerged first from the hole, so as a reward, Arkady let him hold the skull. The other two didn't seem to like that at all, and quickly followed their brother, scrabbling over the fallen stones to get to his prize.

"Ha! Gotcha!" Arkady exclaimed, grabbing Missy first, followed by Tory. The pups wriggled in her grasp, trying to free themselves, not so much to escape from her as to get to the shiny skull their brother was holding. With some difficulty, Arkady managed to secure both pups under her left arm. She scooped up Dezi, glowing skull and all, glancing at the torch with a frown as she discovered she didn't have a hand free with which to hold it. Then Arkady glanced down at the puppy in her arms and realised she wouldn't need the torch while one of the pups had the skull.

"You hold on to that now," she told Dezi, who was paying her absolutely no attention. "Because if you drop that thing and break it and the light goes away, we're going to be stuck down here until your mother gets home."

Dezi giggled in response, while the other two pups struggled in her arms, trying to get to the shiny skull. With the three of them balanced precariously in her arms, and their way lit by the eerie blue glow of the strange artefact, she headed back to the surface on her aching feet, wondering what was going to be harder—explaining to Boots what it was the pups had found, explaining *how* they'd found it, or trying to figure out exactly what it was.

Arkady took the time to rebuild the barricade once the pups were safely back upstairs in their furs. She left them playing with the glowing skull while she worked because it kept them amused, although she did have to intervene a couple of times when Missy became a little possessive of it and wouldn't share it with her brothers.

By the time Boots returned, the barricade was repaired, the pups asleep, and Arkady was sitting by the fire examining the skull, trying to glean some sense of its origin.

"Tides, you got them to sleep?" Boots said in a low voice as she descended the stairs. She was carrying two rabbits in one hand and a large knife in the other. From the look of her bloody mouth, Arkady guessed she'd already eaten her fill.

"I think they wore themselves out," Arkady said with a smile. "You had some luck, I see?"

Boots nodded. "Not a lot out there to find, but it should see us through the next few days. Can you cook?"

Arkady nodded. "I wasn't always a duchess, you know, Boots. Do you like cooked meat?"

"I used to," she said, tossing the rabbits onto the floor by the fire. "But ever since I got pregnant I seem to prefer it raw. I go by the name Tabitha Belle now, by the way, your grace. Not Boots."

"I beg your pardon?"

"Boots is a slave name. I'm free now. Tabitha Belle is my *free* name."

Arkady smiled at the canine's proud but slightly defensive demeanour as she declared her emancipation. "Technically you're an escaped slave, Boo . . . *Tabitha*. Being on the run and wanted for murder doesn't really qualify as freedom."

"So you say," Boots said a little huffily. "What's that you've got there?"

"I don't know," Arkady said, handing the skull to Boots, certain she was never going to be able to think of her as *Tabitha Belle*, a name much too pretty and, well, *girly*, for a creature as feisty as this canine. "The pups found it down in . . . Well, it doesn't matter where—but they found it. It seems to glow whenever a Crasii touches it."

Sure enough, as soon as Boots took the crystal from Arkady, it began to glow, but not quite the same shade of blue as it did when the pups touched it. When Boots held the skull, it had more of a greenish tinge.

"Do you know what it is?"

Boots shook her head. "Never seen anything like it. What happens when *you* touch it?"

"Absolutely nothing."

Boots frowned, turning the polished skull this way and that as she examined it. "It's kind of morbid, isn't it? Maybe it's something to do with Tide magic."

"How do you figure that?"

"Crasii can't swim the Tide, but we can sense it. At least we can sense the immortals on it. Even Scards can do that, although it reeks something awful to us. You're just a mortal human, so you wouldn't even know the Tide was out there if someone hadn't told you about it. Maybe it's just reacting to how much sensitivity you have to the Tide."

That was a plausible explanation, Arkady supposed, but it still didn't explain the *purpose* of the skull. "It glowed blue when the pups touched it. Not green."

Boots's frown deepened and she tossed the skull back to Arkady as if she was suddenly impatient with it. "It's probably because they're younger. I don't know. I don't really care, either. You gonna do something with those things or not? Rabbits don't skin themselves, you know."

"What should I do with the skull, do you think?"

"Give it to the pups to play with."

"But it might be valuable."

"Valuable to who? Let them play with it. It's not like they have much else—" Boots fell abruptly silent at the sound of someone calling out above them in the ruins.

"Hello?"

Boots looked at Arkady, her eyes panicked. "Did you let the pups out?" she hissed. "Did someone see you?"

Arkady shook her head. "We never went near the surface," she whispered back. "I swear."

"Hello! Is anybody here?" The distant voice was muffled and sounded male, but not especially threatening. It might just be a passing fisherman from the lake or a woodsman, who'd caught a whiff of smoke on the air and had come to investigate.

"Stay here," Boots ordered, turning for the door.

"No!" Arkady protested softly. "I'll go."

Boots looked at her askance. "You can barely walk."

"You have pups," Arkady replied.

The canine hesitated and then nodded. Tossing the skull onto the furs beside the pups, where it began to shine a soft blue, Arkady quickly pulled on her stockings and damp shoes, ignoring the pain in her feet, tied up the laces, and stood up. Boots handed her the knife she was holding. "Can you slit a man's throat if you have to?"

Arkady nodded. "If I have to."

"Then go. Get rid of him. Do whatever it takes."

Arkady hefted the knife, a little surprised at the weight of it, and then tucked it into the waistband at the back of her skirt. "I'll get rid of him if I have to promise to leave with him," she said. And then, before she could think better of it, with the knife pressing against her back, Arkady turned and climbed the stairs to the surface.

The interloper proved to be male, certainly, but he wasn't human. He was Crasii, wearing a hooded jacket against the bitter cold, which obscured his face. Arkady found him poking about the main part of the ruin upstairs, calling out periodically, and making no attempt at stealth. Although there was nothing overtly threatening about his behaviour, he was huge and acting as if he knew there was somebody hiding here. She watched him for a time from the shadows and then edged her way around the hall, trying to put as much distance as possible between herself and the hidden entrance to Boots's lair, more than a little worried by the sudden appearance of this canine Crasii.

Despite her attempt to be stealthy, however, Arkady was still limping. A scrape of shoe leather on stone betrayed her. The canine's sharp ears picked up the sound. He spun around to look in her direction but Arkady was able to draw back behind a column before he caught sight of her.

"Is someone there?" the Crasii demanded. Even more worryingly, he demanded it in Glaeban.

Arkady's heart hammered in her chest as she tried to work out what that meant. He was Crasii, so it was reasonable to assume he was here at the behest of an immortal master. With so many immortals abroad these days, all Crasii were suspect, except Scards like Boots whom Arkady had known since she was a pup, and whom she'd witnessed firsthand defying a Tide Lord.

Was this creature here at the behest of Jaxyn Aranville? Had he sent someone in pursuit of her? This wasn't likely to be a Crasii sent by Elyssa, she reasoned, hunting a lost dam and puppies. Any Crasii she sent in pursuit of Boots would be speaking Caelish. Unless, of course, it was a trap, and the canine was speaking Glaeban in order to deliberately lull Boots into thinking she was safe . . .

Tides, what should I do?

She could hear the canine coming to investigate the noise. Arkady had only seconds before she was discovered. If this Crasii—this creature magically compelled to obey the orders of his immortal masters—found her here, she could be back in the sadistic hands of Jaxyn Aranville before nightfall. There would be no reasoning with this beast. No chance of talking her way out of this one. No way to make him defy his orders . . .

Silently, Arkady withdrew the knife from the back of her skirt and held it in front of her. She knew what she had to do. Her freedom, the puppies' freedom, Boots's chance to reunite with her mate one day—all of them were dependent on not being discovered here and now.

Arkady thrust the knife forward as soon as the Crasii rounded the pillar, ramming the blade as deeply as she could into the belly of the enormous creature before he could react. The beast lashed out at her with a snarl, scraping the side of her face and her shoulder before he fell, gripping the hilt of the knife with a howl of agony.

Her face and shoulder stinging, her heart in her mouth, sweating as if it was high summer, Arkady jumped back as the canine crashed heavily to the leaf-strewn floor, blood seeping through the hooded jacket where he clutched at the knife.

"Help me . . ."

Arkady took another step backward. She wasn't stupid enough to get any closer. Even writhing in agony and obviously dying, the canine was still dangerous, and if he managed to get that knife out of his belly, he'd be armed as well.

"*Please . . .*"

Arkady hardened her heart to his pleas, figuring if she had the guts to kill this Crasii, she should have the courage to stand here and see it through. *And it isn't like you haven't killed countless Crasii before*, she reminded herself harshly.

"Tides, my lady, what happened?"

Arkady spun around to find Boots running toward them. "It's all right, Boots, go back. I've taken care of it."

The dying canine looked up as she spoke. "*Boots . . . ?*"

"I heard someone howling like the . . ." She stopped and stared down at the howling Crasii. "Tides, woman. What have you *done*?"

"Stay back, Boots," Arkady urged, trying to stop the young female from getting any closer. "He'll be dead soon."

"He'd better not be," Boots said, shaking off Arkady. She ran to the canine and fell to her knees beside him.

"Boots! Don't go near him! He's still dangerous!"

The canine ignored Arkady. Instead, she pushed the hood from the intruder's head and pulled him onto her lap, her eyes filled with tears, muttering soothing nothings to him as she rocked him back and forth, tears streaming down her face. It was then that Arkady got her first good look at the canine. He seemed familiar, but she couldn't recall where she'd seen him before.

It was Boots's distressed cries that finally revealed who her victim was. Arkady's heart lurched as Boots stared up at her accusingly.

"He's not dangerous," the Scard said with a tear-filled snarl. "This is Warlock. The father of my puppies." Boots leaned down and kissed his forehead before adding with a sob, "You stupid bitch. You've killed my mate."

Chapter 32

Cycrane seemed unnaturally peaceful. For a city that had been at war a couple of days ago, it was surprisingly quiet. Cayal leaned on the balcony of the Ladies Walking Room of the Cycrane Palace, barely noticing the bitter winter chill in the air. He looked out over the warm dots of light that marked the snow-shrouded city below him, and the dark stain behind the town, sucking in all the light, that marked the deep waters of the Lower Oran.

"Admiring the view?"

Cayal didn't bother to turn. He'd felt Elyssa approaching on the Tide and had time to brace himself. "I was trying to remember what this place looked like before the lake was here."

"Really?" she asked, coming to lean on the balcony beside him. "And here I was thinking you were just sick of listening to my mother."

Cayal allowed himself a small smile. "Well, there's that, too. Don't you ever get sick of her?"

"All the time."

He turned his back on the city, brushed the snow from the railing and perched on the edge of the balcony to study Elyssa in the starlight. She hadn't changed at all in the thousand or more years since he'd seen her last. She was still cursed with a receding chin, eyes set too far apart and a face that could most kindly be described as *unfortunate*. "Why do you stay around this insane family of yours, Lyssa? You have the power to do anything you want. You could beat Tryan into a bloody pulp if you wanted to, and the rest of them can't hold a candle to you."

"They love me."

"Is that what you call it?"

Elyssa turned from looking at the city to face him. "They love me, Cayal. And they've been there for me. Through ten thousand years of immortality, they've *always* been there for me. Everyone else leaves eventually. If they're mortal, they die. If they're immortal, they just let you down."

"You're very bitter."

"*I'm* bitter? Tides, Cayal, you're suicidal." She searched his face in the darkness, as if she was looking for answers he was certain she could never find in him. "Do you really think Lukys can help you die?"

"The question you should be asking yourself, Elyssa, is: *can he help you live?*"

"In another body? One that's beautiful? One that's not a virgin? One that doesn't devour every lover she takes as he tries to enter her?" She smiled sceptically. Kentravyon had told her the story about Coryna and Coron the Rat. Cayal didn't think she believed a word of it. "You do *know* Kentravyon is mad, don't you, Cayal?"

"Yes."

"And yet you still believe him?"

"It's not just Kentravyon. I've seen the lengths Lukys has gone to, to make this happen. Tides, he's built a palace in Jelidia for his one great love, Lyssa, to rival the one your mother built in Magreth."

"That's kind of romantic, when you think about it." After a moment, Elyssa's dubious smile faded and she shook her head. She wasn't convinced. "Kentravyon says Lukys has a new body selected for his lover."

"Bred for it, would be a more accurate description, I suspect," Cayal said. "Apparently, the only way to *ensure* someone will become immortal when you immolate them is to burn a mortal who's more than half immortal to begin with."

"Is that how Hawkes became immortal?" she asked. "Is it because he was more than half immortal to begin with?"

"Five-eighths, if you believe him. I assume Oritha has a similar pedigree."

"Where is he, anyway?" Elyssa asked. "I haven't seen our newly forged immortal spymaster since before we broke the ice."

Cayal shrugged. "Don't know. Don't care that much either, to be frank. He irritates the hell out of me. He'll be around somewhere. Looking for his girlfriend, I don't doubt. Or brooding about her. He broods about her a lot. And with good cause, I have to say. He messed up that particular love affair quite spectacularly, with only a very small amount of help from me."

"Is she pretty?"

"Who? Arkady?"

"Not Arkady," Elyssa said. She clearly wasn't interested in Hawkes's love life. Or indeed Cayal's, either. "I meant Lukys's wife. Oritha."

Cayal nodded. "I suppose she is. Bit short and dark for my taste, but Lukys seems quite taken with her."

"Does she know what he has in store for her?"

He shrugged. "I couldn't say."

"So her active cooperation is not required to effect the transfer of Coryna's mind into Oritha's body?"

"To be honest, I never thought to ask."

Elyssa contemplated that notion for a moment before she spoke again. Cayal found her questions encouraging. She was obviously considering their offer. At least he hoped she was. Without the location of the Chaos Crystal, there was nothing *on* offer. "What happens to her after the transfer?"

"She becomes immortal."

"No, I mean what happens to the mortal wife? To the entity known as Oritha? What becomes of her personality, her memories; her soul if you like? Does she simply fade away? Or does she stay in the body, constantly fighting for control of it?"

"I have no idea."

"I think I'd like an answer to that question before I commit to your cause, Cayal."

"I can't give you an answer, Lyssa. You'd have to ask Lukys."

"Then what *can* you give me?" she asked, ever the pragmatist. "I think I deserve some sort of compensation. You want me to surrender the key to ultimate power."

"The Chaos Crystal isn't the key to ultimate power," he scoffed.

"Oh? So Lukys wants it just because it's shiny, does he?"

"It *channels* power, Lyssa. It isn't powerful in or of itself."

"Really? And when did you become an expert on the Bedlam Stone? You don't even know what it looks like."

"Truth be told, neither do you," he said, crossing his arms impatiently. "According to my spies you have a Tarot that's falling apart, a map you can't read, a rough idea of where the crystal's hidden and not much else."

"That's more than you have, Cayal."

True enough. He sighed, sick of this verbal bantering that was getting them nowhere. "What is it you want, Lyssa? Name it."

"I want you."

"What else do you want?"

She smiled again, and it wasn't pleasant. "How badly do you want to die, Cayal?"

Not that badly, used to be Cayal's automatic response to that question, but now the opportunity to find the Chaos Crystal was almost within his grasp, he discovered his determination wavering. *So what if she's dangerous, cruel, vindictive, psychotic, and bordering on, well . . . ugly. If it means I'll be dead by the time the Tide peaks, why do I care?*

"Do you still kill your mortal lovers when you get frustrated with their screams?"

"What if I do? I can't actually kill you, Cayal, so you've nothing to fear."

Cayal smiled, cynical enough for her comment to amuse him. "There's not a lot of romance in your soul, is there, Elyssa?"

"Those are my terms, Cayal," she said with a glint in her eye that indicated she knew she had the upper hand. "You want the location of the Chaos Crystal? I'm your first port of call."

"Fine."

"I'm not interested in a one-night stand," she said, clearly mistrusting his ready capitulation. "I want something lasting."

"I'm planning to die, Elyssa, as soon as I possibly can. How lasting a promise do you expect me to make?"

"Till death us do part?" she suggested, with a sly smile that made Cayal's blood run cold. "In fact, now I think of it, a wedding is just what this situation calls for. You want to die so badly? Fine, then. You can marry me first."

"You can*not* be serious."

With a sour smile, she turned from the balcony railing and headed for the diamond-paned door leading back into the Ladies Walking Room. "Have a nice life, Cayal," she said with a wave. "I *know* it's going to be a long one."

"Elyssa, wait."

She turned with her hand on the latch. "Yes, Cayal?"

"Isn't there some way we can . . . ?"

"No. So, if we're done here, I'm going back to my family. The ones who always stick by me. Unless there's something you want to ask me?"

Tides, she's going to make me ask. Cayal studied her in the starlight, wondering if there was ever a time when he hated her more than he did right at this moment. "Will you marry me, Elyssa?"

She smiled triumphantly and Cayal discovered he *could* hate her more. Quite a lot more, actually. "Yes, Cayal, I will."

"And you'll give us the map? Now? Tonight?"

She shrugged, a little puzzled by his haste. "If you're in that much of a hurry you can have it now, I suppose. When do you think we should hold the wedding ceremony?"

"When we get to Jelidia."

She shook her head and moved toward him, stopping in front of him with her hands on her hips. "I'm not waiting that long."

Oh, yes you are, you obsessive little bitch. This situation was bad enough. He wasn't going to let her dictate *all* the rules. "I'll marry you when we get to Jelidia, Elyssa. *After* we've retrieved the crystal. *Before* we use it. That's when I'll do it and not a moment before."

Elyssa clearly didn't like that timetable. "Suppose I decide that's not good enough?"

He shrugged and turned his back on her. "Then go explain it to Kentravyon. I'm sure he'll be quite reasonable."

"Kentravyon doesn't care if you live or die, Cayal," she said, although there was a lack of confidence in her voice that betrayed her unwillingness to push the madman too far.

"Neither does Lukys, I'm sure," he agreed. He turned to look at her again. "But they've been planning this—near as I can tell—for several thousand years. And they can't attempt to restore Coryna for a few thousand or so after that, I believe, if they miss the King Tide this time around—thanks to you standing in their way. So dig your heels in, by all means. Try to broker a deal with Kentravyon that's any better than the one I'm offering you. Or better yet, explain yourself to Lukys. If I can't die, I can at least enjoy the pain he'll make you suffer for the next few millennia for screwing up his plans." He smiled coldly. "Tides, that may even give me something to live for."

Elyssa glared at him. "You're a first-class bastard, Cayal."

He raised a curious brow. "So the wedding's off then, dear?"

She raised her hand to slap him, but Cayal was expecting something like that. He caught her wrist before it connected with his face, twisting it painfully behind her back, forcing her against him. She glared up at him, struggling more for show than effect. He pushed her against the railing and kissed her, hard and savagely—not because he desired her, but because Cayal had been alive for a very long time and if there was one thing immortals were good at, it was manipulating people, even when those people were other immortals who should know better.

His kiss was rough and brutal, but Elyssa routinely murdered her lovers in the throes of passion, so it was doubtful she cared about anything so inconvenient as a few bruises that would heal almost as soon as they were acquired.

Cayal could feel the fight draining from Elyssa with his kiss. As soon as he felt she was no longer resisting, he let go his painful grip of her wrist and took her in his arms like a lover instead. Cayal didn't kid himself that she was melting in his arms just from his kiss. Several thousand years of anticipation probably did the work more than his lips, but within moments he sensed that Elyssa—provided he kept her wanting more—would be putty in his hands, ready to do anything he asked.

Except call off the wedding, maybe.

"Tides, Cayal," she breathed, when he finally came up for air. "Do you know how long I've waited for that?"

Yes, he wanted to tell her. *Which is why you're such a fool.* But he was too smart to ruin the moment with sarcasm. "How long?"

She looked up at him, her eyes shining. "Since the first time you walked into the palace in Magreth."

"That's a long time."

"Worth it, though," she said with a coy smile.

"Worth a look at your precious map?"

Elyssa pushed herself out of his arms, pouting. "Tides, I should know better than to think you care one jot about me." She didn't seem angry. Apparently being kissed by the object of an eight-thousand-year-long crush had a lasting effect.

"Why *should* I care?" he asked with a smile much more forced than Elyssa could imagine. "You only want me for my body."

That made her laugh softly. "Come to my room."

"We've discussed this already. You're going to have to wait until we're married."

"Not for that, you fool," she said, still smiling. "That's where the map is."

He nodded, more than a little relieved. "I'll fetch Kentravyon, then."

"Do you really think you need a chaperone?" she asked, rubbing her hands slowly up the front of his shirt, still trying—quite unsuccessfully—to look coy.

"He'll want to see the map."

Elyssa looked disappointed. Then a thought occurred to her that made her brighten considerably. She slid her arms around his neck and looked up at him with a disturbingly happy smile. "You know, Cayal, if this works, and I get a new body and a new face—a beautiful one, one that you find desirable—maybe I won't have to blackmail you into loving me."

He was tempted to point out that it wasn't possible to blackmail anybody into loving her, but things were going too well at the moment to rock the boat with a comment so callous. So he smiled, took her hands from around his neck and raised them to his lips. "Well, if I see something that takes my fancy in the way of beautiful bodies, Elyssa, I'll be sure to let you know."

Chapter 33

As a boy, Declan Hawkes had once tried to row across the lake from Glaeba to Caelum. He couldn't remember exactly why he'd attempted such a feat. It might have been a dare. He might have been running away. More likely, he was trying to impress Arkady.

Whatever the reason, after several hours of rowing he was still depressingly close to Lebec, his hands were raw and blistered to the point of bleeding, and every muscle in his back and shoulders had seized and refused to cooperate any further. A fishing boat had found him adrift late in the day in his stolen dinghy, sunburned, dehydrated and suffering badly from a combination of exposure and embarrassment. They had towed him back to shore where Arkady brought him to her father who treated his physical wounds (if not his wounded pride) and waited, to her credit, until he'd healed completely before she laughed at him for being such a fool.

Declan had no such concerns this trip. He kept up the steady pace of *dip, pull, dip, pull*, every stroke taking him closer to home.

It was dark by the time he reached the city, but that was fine by Declan. He didn't want to attract any attention, and a small dinghy would be ignored by any guards on the shore, who would assume—not unreasonably—that a lone man in a rowboat was unlikely to be a threat to national security.

Declan headed for Lebec, rather than Herino, where it was less likely there would be alert human guards on duty. Jaxyn would have replaced most of them with Crasii, and Declan had nothing to fear from them. Even so, it turned out he had nothing about which to worry. The sudden breaking of the ice-sheet had created just as many problems—and caused just as much shock—in Glaeba as it had in Caelum. They didn't have the bodies to clean up, and they'd had a lot more warning than those near Cycrane when it shattered, but the event had drawn out every citizen in the city, it seemed, to stare at the water, which was dotted with a flotilla of small craft attempting to clear the icebergs from the waterway.

He made his way on foot through the city to Tilly's townhouse with his collar up and his head down, glad Lady Ponting lived in the better part of town where he wasn't a familiar figure. Declan was far too well known in the slums of Lebec to risk passing through them if he intended to remain hidden.

When he reached Tilly's townhouse, he waited in the shadows across the street for a time, debating his next move. He could slip around the back, he supposed, and sneak in that way or he could walk up to the front door and knock.

In the end, he decided on the latter. After all, what could they do to him?

The canine who answered his knock dropped to one knee the moment he laid eyes on Declan. "To serve you is the reason I breathe, my lord," he said, before Declan could utter a word.

Declan found the Crasii's attitude a little unsettling. Tilly, being a high-ranking member of the Cabal and the Guardian of the Lore, firmly believed she had surrounded herself with Scards who would be immune to immortal manipulation.

"Tell your mistress I wish to see her."

"Of course, my lord, but she has retired for the evening."

"Tell her Declan Hawkes is waiting in her parlour. She'll get out of bed for me."

The Crasii bowed again and hurried off to fetch his mistress. Declan walked down the hall and opened the door to Tilly's morning room. It was an odd room, full of the paraphernalia of Tilly's public persona— her Tarot cards, her easel and her awful paintings; all the things that people associated with the eccentric old widow, Lady Tilly Ponting. Declan knew her as something quite different and this room had always seemed out of character for the sharp, ruthless Guardian of the Lore with whom he was familiar. The woman who ruled the Cabal of the Tarot with an iron grip and demanded a level of loyalty from her underlings of which the Patriarch and his criminal brotherhood in the underworld of Herino would have been envious.

"Tides! It really is you!"

Declan turned to find Tilly standing in the doorway clutching a tall lamp with a glass shroud. She was wrapped in a boldly-coloured floral robe over her nightgown, her hair (which seemed to be a rather dramatic shade of yellow this week) flowing down around her shoulders.

Tilly looked old, he thought. It wasn't because she'd aged, Declan suspected, so much as he was acutely feeling the fact that he hadn't.

"Hello, Tilly."

She moved a little closer and put the lantern on the circular table, never taking her eyes off him. "We hadn't heard from you for so long we feared you were dead."

"I should be so lucky."

There was a moment of awkward silence before Tilly responded to that. She studied him closely, as if trying to determine if there was anything physically different about him. "So, it's true then? The rumours we've been hearing?"

"Depends," he said, "on what the rumours are saying."

"Don't play games with me, Declan."

"Then don't try them on me," he said, a little impatiently. "You already know what I am, Tilly. You're not looking at me like that because I've suddenly turned blue. And even if your spies in Caelum haven't gotten a message to you by now, your Crasii just told you what I was, when he woke you up. And he *is* a Crasii, by the way, not a Scard. You'll need to be careful of things like that, now the Tide is back, if you plan to keep your affairs from the immortals."

Tilly sank into the nearest chair, her shoulders slumped. "How did it happen?"

He took the seat opposite, relieved she wasn't going to get hysterical on him. At least not yet. She'd probably ordered one of her Crasii off to round up all the other members of the Cabal in Lebec at the moment, while she kept him talking. They probably had plans to overwhelm him, tie him up and bury him alive out in her potting shed, or some such thing. "Turns out I had more than an immortal great-grandmother. My father was immortal too."

"Do you know which immortal?"

"Lukys claims he's the one responsible," Declan told her, watching her closely to see how she'd react to his next bombshell. "Although you know him better as Ryda Tarek."

Tilly was silent for a very long time. Finally she shook her head with a heavy sigh. "You know, I used to wonder about him. He always seemed to know so much more than he should. But my Scards always assured me he was human . . ."

"Your Scards aren't Scards, Tilly. They're just particularly fractious Crasii. He would have ordered them to tell you anything you needed to hear. For future reference, a genuine Scard all but gags on the stench of us."

"When did it happen?"

"During the fire that destroyed Herino Prison."

"That's why you disappeared for so long, then?"

He nodded. That question hardly needed an answer.

"So you were already . . . like *this* . . ." she said, apparently unable to bring herself to say the word *immortal,* "when you met with Aleki at Clyden's Inn and told him you were going to Torlenia to look for Arkady."

He nodded. That too seemed self-evident.

"Did you find her?"

"Eventually."

"You didn't see the need to save her from Jaxyn Aranville, I notice," Tilly said, obviously annoyed with him for more than just being immortal.

"Why do you think I came back, Tilly?"

"Well, if it was to save Arkady, you're a bit late, my lad. She was out on the ice yesterday as Jaxyn's prisoner when it . . . Tides, did you have anything to do with that?"

Declan shook his head. "It was Cayal. With some help from Kentravyon and Elyssa."

Tilly paled in the lamplight, the possibility of Arkady being dead apparently less important than the knowledge there was a mad Tide Lord on the loose. "Kentravyon is here?"

"Not here—he's in Caelum."

"And are you at liberty to discuss the intentions of your new immortal friends, or did you just drop by to gloat?"

"That's not fair, Tilly."

"Nothing in this life is, I've discovered," she said, rubbing at her temples. She closed her eyes for a moment. When she opened them again, Declan was stunned to see they were full of unshed tears. "Tides, Declan, I've known you since you were a boy. I've watched you grow up. I've nurtured you. I even had hopes that you'd become Guardian of the Lore someday. That maybe you'd be the one who would succeed where generations of us have failed in bringing about an end to the Tide Lords. And here you are, sitting across the table in my parlour—one of them. I don't know what to say."

"You think I did this on purpose?"

"No," she conceded, rising to her feet. She began to pace in front of the fire, her arms wrapped around her body against the cold night air, which the banked fire did little to warm. He waited in silence for her to digest the information, certain this was almost as hard for her to come to grips with as it had been for him.

After a while Tilly turned to look at him. "What does it feel like?"

He didn't need to ask what she meant by *it*. "I'm not sure I can describe the feeling, Tilly. I can sense the Tide all the time. And feel the others on it when they're near." He didn't really want to elaborate much more than that. The raging blood-rush he felt when he was wielding the Tide, the itching, the tormented need to relieve the tension any way he could afterward—that was something she didn't need to know about.

"Can you actually *wield* the Tide?"

Declan hesitated, not sure if he should answer that question. He'd betrayed the Cabal by simply becoming immortal. To admit he was a Tide Lord into the bargain might be more than Tilly could handle.

Tilly was a canny old bird, however, and took his hesitation for exactly what it was. "Tides, if you're Lukys's son and Maralyce's great-grandchild, I don't suppose there's a chance you could be anything *but* a Tide Lord."

He looked away, unable to meet her eye. "It's not like I asked for this, Tilly."

"And yet you have it," she said, turning to study him curiously. "Why did you come here tonight, Declan?"

He shrugged, not entirely sure of the answer to that question himself. "I thought you deserved to know the truth."

She shook her head, not accepting his answer. "Why bother? As you were so quick to point out when you arrived, the truth would have found its way to me, sooner or later. That's not why you're here."

Declan wondered why he'd ever thought he could get anything past this shrewd old woman. But if he couldn't fathom his own motives for coming here, he could, at least, tell her the truth. "Lukys claims he can kill a Tide Lord."

Tilly didn't seem surprised. "We discussed this the last time Ryda . . . *Lukys* was here. He said then that Cayal might have found a way to die."

"He also suggested we help him achieve it, if you recall, which makes a great deal more sense in hindsight."

Tilly shook her head unhappily. "Tides, he must have had some fun at our expense."

"He wasn't lying, though," Declan told her. "He really is planning to help Cayal die, only it's a sideshow to what he's really planning, not the main attraction."

"Killing an immortal is quite a sideshow, Declan."

"It's worse than you think," Declan told her. "According to Kentravyon, opening the rift that will kill an immortal is a dangerous business. It may well destroy Amyrantha in the process."

"Rift?" Tilly said with a puzzled look. "What rift?"

It was dawn by the time Declan had told Tilly everything he knew. He related the story about how Lukys's failed experiments to transfer an immortal from one body to another had resulted in Coryna's mind being transferred into a rat. He told her about the palace in Jelidia, the Chaos Crystal, their belief that Elyssa had found it—or at least knew where it was—Cayal's plans to die and Lukys's plans to restore Coryna using the body of his new wife, Oritha. He told her what he knew of his own origins; of how he would have been a likely vessel for Coryna's consciousness, but for the twist of fate that saw him born a male. He told her about Shalimar dying, and how he'd ridden a magic carpet over the ocean to return to Glaeba.

He told her everything he could recall, everything he'd learned about the immortals in the past few months. Once he started talking, he couldn't stop. It felt cathartic, almost penitent, as if by confessing everything somehow Tilly would forgive him for becoming immortal.

When he was done, Tilly said nothing for a time as she digested what he'd told her. When she finally spoke, her words shocked him. "You have to see this through, Declan."

"*Excuse* me?"

"Don't you remember me telling you last night that I'd hoped maybe you'd be the one who succeeded where generations of us have failed in bringing about an end to the Tide Lords? Maybe I was right. Maybe the way to finally take the immortals down *isn't* to fight them as we've been doing unsuccessfully for thousands of years, but to do it from the inside."

"If I help them kill an immortal, I'll be helping them find a way to kill me, too, Tilly."

She smiled tiredly. "You were prepared to die for the cause when you were mortal, Declan. Are you not prepared to do the same now you're *im*mortal?"

"Did you miss the bit about the risk to Amyrantha? Kentravyon says that opening this rift and channelling so much power through the Chaos Crystal could destroy the world."

"Isn't Kentravyon the madman nobody trusts and few believe?"

"That doesn't make him wrong, Tilly."

"Perhaps not," Tilly sighed. "Tides, I wish I had all the answers you seek."

He smiled wanly. "You mean you don't?"

She seemed to appreciate his poor attempt at levity. "That's just a carefully rehearsed façade I put on to keep you young 'uns in line. Truth is, Declan, I never expected to see the Tide turn in my lifetime. It's been a thousand years or more since the last High Tide. When I agreed to train as the Guardian of the Lore, my predecessor even went so far as to assure me it probably wouldn't happen for *another* thousand years. And yet here we are. The Tide is turning and already we've had a taste of what's in store for us."

She rubbed her eyes wearily. "Tides, how many died on the lake yesterday because only three Tide Lords joined forces to end a war that was—if you have the right of it—just getting in their way? And for no better reason, if what you're telling me about this magic crystal is true. How many more will be dead by the time the Tide peaks? And even if they don't find this crystal, how many more will die when the inevitable squabbles between your new friends result in some catastrophic disaster that will wipe out millions more souls? You worry about the eventual destruction of Amyrantha, Declan, and yet, if you look around, you'll see it's already happening, little by little."

She closed her eyes for a moment and massaged her temples again. Declan wondered if he should order her Crasii to bring her some tea.

They had been here most of the night, after all. "Perhaps when I wake up it will still be last spring and these last few months will prove nothing more than a particularly vivid nightmare."

Declan sympathised with her distress, but he hadn't come here to hear Tilly lament her own woes. "What do you want me to do?"

She opened her eyes and let out a sigh filled with resignation and regret. "I told you. See it through."

"You want me to risk every man, woman and child on Amyrantha on the off-chance I can find the way to kill an immortal?"

"Of course not," she said. "But it gets down to this, my dear. You say Arkady encouraged you to consort with the immortals to learn their plans. And she was right. You've told me more about the Tide Lords in the last few hours than we've been able to learn in the last thousand years, not because you're a brilliant spymaster, but because you're one of them now. We need you among them, Declan, to aid them in their quest for death if it will help us, or to stop them if they're going to endanger Amyrantha to the point of destruction."

"No pressure then."

She smiled. "You can do this, Declan. Anyway, what else have you got on your hectic schedule at the moment that's more important?"

"I want to find Arkady."

Tilly shook her head sadly. "She was out on the ice, Declan. She'll be long dead by now, dear."

"She got away."

"How do you know?"

"I spoke to the Scard who let her go."

The old lady remained unconvinced. She threw up her hands in a gesture of helplessness, leaving Declan with the uncomfortable realisation that he really *was* alone.

"I suppose, when it gets down to it," she said, "you're beyond my orders now. You need to find your own path, Declan, and decide what course of action you're going to be able to live with, because in that, at least, you no longer have an option."

Chapter 34

"We won the war!"

Stellan looked up and frowned at the little princess as she let herself into his room and bounded over to his bed where he was stuffing the few clothes he actually owned into a bag he'd borrowed from one of the queen's ladies-in-waiting.

It seemed odd, seeing Nyah back in petticoats and ribbons, after the time she'd spent in the mountains with Maralyce, dressed as a boy. In a futile attempt to make her look more like a young princess and less like a street urchin, this morning her ladies-in-waiting had dressed her entirely in pink. She wore pink ribbons in her hair, too, holding back two small pigtails that were too short to do much of anything but stick out directly from the side of her head, making her look faintly ridiculous.

Stellan gave no indication he thought that way of her, but he had a feeling she knew, because she pulled the ribbons from her hair impatiently as she spoke, and stuffed them into the cuff of her sleeve. Outside, it was snowing. Stellan wasn't looking forward to the trip across the iceberg-ridden lake in a storm, despite the fact it meant finally returning home.

"Thousands of Crasii died out there on the ice yesterday, Nyah. I'd hardly call that winning."

"But the Glaeban king is dead. Now you're their king. You should be happy."

"In theory, I'm their king," Stellan agreed, taking a seat on the bed beside the bag so that he was eye to eye with her. "But it remains to be seen what the people of Glaeba have to say about it."

"Lord Tyrone told Mama he's done a deal with you. That you're going to be Glaeba's king because you agreed to acknowledge Caelum as Glaeba's sovereign master."

"I'm aware of the conditions, Nyah," Stellan said with a heavy sigh at the concessions forced from him by Tryan and Syrolee. Word of the new agreement hadn't taken long to get around the palace if Nyah already knew about it. "I *was* there during the negotiations, you know."

Calling them negotiations was a bit of a misnomer. Stellan had listened while the immortals had told him how it was going to be. There had been neither need nor opportunity for any input from the new Glaeban king.

"Why did you agree to their demands if you don't like the terms?"

"Because enough people have died already, Nyah, and the alternative was very unpleasant."

"But the honourable thing to do—"

"Is to save lives," he cut in before she could finish. "I didn't think the people of Glaeba would appreciate me sacrificing their lives over an obscure point of honour."

That sage piece of advice delivered, he stood up and returned to his packing. Tryan had a barge at the ready and they were planning to be gone inside the hour. Hard as it was to believe, he would be home inside a day, returning as her king to the country he'd fled as a fugitive a few months ago—which made the fact that he was packing a few clothes into a borrowed bag more than a little ironic. Stellan could have ordered a Crasii to pack for him, he supposed, but he found them unsettling now, here in this palace full of immortals. They made him feel more than a little foolish for ever thinking the Crasii were his to command.

"I don't think they're going to appreciate the alternative to your *obscure point of honour*, Stellan, when it comes down to it," the little girl pointed out with insight far beyond her years. "Isn't surrendering your country to a foreign power, like, you know . . . treason?"

"Not if you've lost a war, have no forces left to fight and the alternative is to watch your nation razed to the ground."

That answer, although unpleasant, seemed to satisfy her. She sat on the bed, swinging her legs over the edge in the spot he'd so recently vacated, and smiled brightly. "Can I come to Herino with you?"

"I would have thought you'd seen enough of Glaeba."

"Please, Stellan, let me come. I won't get in the way. I promise."

"Why would you want to, Nyah?"

She shrugged. "There's nothing else to do here except watch Syrolee's husband drink our cellar dry, Mama mooning over Tryan while he does whatever he likes with the country, Krydence and Rance harassing the serving girls, and Syrolee marching around the palace bossing everybody about like she owns the place."

Stellan thought it interesting that Nyah was starting to refer to the immortals by their real names rather than the names they'd assumed as part of their mortal disguises. Before he could warn her to be more cautious, however, she added, "And with Elyssa going away, there'll be nobody around to care what I'm up to. Was she very angry when you told her you'd lost Tabitha Belle and the puppies?"

"I haven't told her yet," Stellan admitted, hoping to be gone before anybody noticed they were missing. "How do you know Elyssa's going away?"

"I heard her telling Tryan on my way here. She's going somewhere with the other two immortals who got here yesterday—you know, the one with the crazy eyes and the cute one she keeps drooling over."

Stellan couldn't quite hide his smile. "The *cute* one she keeps drooling over?"

"Well, he *is* cute. Sort of," she said. "And Elyssa's *sooo* in love with him."

"I assume you're speaking of Cayal? The Immortal Prince?"

"Is that who he is?" she asked, quite impressed. "Wow."

"How do you know Elyssa is in love with Cayal?"

"'Cause they're getting married."

That was news to Stellan. "They *are*?"

Nyah nodded. "She was just busting to tell someone. Made me promise not to tell anyone else, though, but I think she just meant the other immortals. I don't think she'd mind me telling you."

"Well, just in case, let's not mention that you've told me, eh?" Stellan was amazed by the news, and it drove home to him what he'd always suspected—the immortals took care of their own business first. Anything else—even when it involved the fate of nations—came a poor second to that. "Did she say where she was going?"

Nyah shook her head, but before she could add anything more, they were interrupted by raised voices in the hall. Stellan couldn't quite make out what the yelling was about, but it was Tryan and Elyssa doing the shouting. Of that, Stellan had no doubt.

Nyah hopped off the bed and ran to the door, opening it a crack to peer outside.

"Get away from there," Stellan scolded.

"Don't you want to know what they're fighting about?"

"No!" Stellan lied. "Of course not. Now come away from that door."

"Was a time you were prepared to wash the continent in blood for it!" Elyssa's voice screeched, close enough now for them to hear her clearly through the crack in the door.

"What do you think they're arguing about?" Nyah hissed in Stellan's direction.

"And you're willing to give it up for a good fuck!" Tryan's voice bellowed back, so loud that Stellan had no trouble hearing him through the tiny opening Nyah had created.

"Is he talking about the Bedlam Stone, perhaps?" Nyah asked, grinning in that guilty way all children did when they were exposed to words they'd not normally encounter in polite conversation.

"I have no idea," Stellan told her sternly, as he stuffed the rest of his shirts into the bag and turned to gather his shaving gear from the dresser. "Now close that door. No good is going to come from you eavesdropping."

"It's not eavesdropping if you can hear them on the other side of the Great Lakes," Nyah said with a grin, but she did as he bid. With a great deal of reluctance she closed the door, before turning to him with a smile that was all too knowing for one so young. "But you *do* want to know what they're fighting about, don't you?"

He really didn't want to admit to a smug twelve year old that he was almost as curious as she was to know about what the immortals were up to. "Perhaps . . . maybe."

"Cayal would know."

His heart skipped a beat. "You are not to go anywhere near the other immortals, Nyah. Do you hear me?"

"Why not?"

Stellan glared at her. "You are going to get yourself killed, young lady, if you insist on becoming involved in things that are no concern of yours."

"You *could* find out what's going on, though," she suggested with a sly grin. "I mean, they need *you*. You're the new Glaeban king."

It was unsettling, being manipulated so blatantly by a child. "You should return to your lessons, your highness, and leave well enough alone."

Nyah wasn't so easily deterred. "My lessons have been suspended. We're at war."

"The war is over," Stellan informed her. "Your lessons will no doubt resume any moment now. So go, and leave me to my packing."

Nyah's face fell at his unfriendly tone. She stared at him for a moment and when he seemed unlikely to relent, she turned back to the door, her shoulders slumped. There was no sign of anyone outside any longer when she opened it. The little princess glanced up and down the hall for a moment before turning to look at Stellan with eyes too old and weary for one so young. "I thought we were friends, Stellan."

"We are friends, Nyah," he assured her. "That's why I'm not going to let you get yourself killed over something that doesn't concern you."

"Everything that happens on this continent concerns me," she said, drawing herself up like a young queen. "I'll be Queen of Caelum someday."

"Then it's your duty to ensure you live long enough to help your people, Nyah," he advised. "And leave me to help mine as I see fit."

Nyah thought on that for a moment and then nodded. "Good luck, then, Stellan," she said with depressing finality. "Apparently, as I'll be at my lessons, I won't see you again before you leave. I hope one day we can meet again, when you are king and I am queen and we can decide things for our people because it's the *right* thing to do, and not because it's what the immortals want us to do."

Before Stellan could respond she slipped through the door and closed it softly behind her, leaving him with the uneasy feeling that the sharpest leader of her people he was ever likely to encounter had just left the room.

With his bag packed and a few moments to spare, Stellan found himself pacing his room impatiently, waiting on the appointed time to leave. The argument he'd caught so little of between Elyssa and Tryan still bothered him, as did Nyah's suggestion that the newly-arrived immortals might know what it was about.

He told himself it was none of his business for a good ten minutes before he let out a curse, shouldered his bag and stalked from his room in search of Elyssa.

She wasn't in her room, but Cayal was there, leaning over the precious map Elyssa had so painstakingly traced from the pattern on the back of the ancient Lore Tarot she'd found at the bottom of the cliff at Deadman's Bluff.

Stellan hesitated on the threshold. Although the immortal had been a prisoner in Stellan's gaol for months at one time, this was his first face-to-face encounter with the Immortal Prince. This was the man for whom Arkady was prepared to defy the king. The prisoner she had committed forgery and treason to save from torture at the hands of the man Stellan would have bet his whole duchy that she *was* in love with—Declan Hawkes. Stellan was never quite sure if Arkady loved Cayal or had just been smitten with him. Perhaps she was intrigued by him; perhaps he'd cast some mystical Tide spell on her to get her to cooperate. Whatever the reason, Stellan found himself unaccountably nervous when Cayal turned at the sound of the door opening.

"Yes?"

"I was looking for Lady Alyssa," he said, using the mortal name she was known by here in Caelum and not its immortal equivalent.

"She's not here," Cayal said, turning back to study the map.

He was younger than Stellan was expecting—at least he seemed younger. And he was every bit as good-looking as legend held him to be. No wonder Arkady had been attracted to him. And that Nyah called him the "cute one."

"Are you expecting her soon?" Stellan inquired.

Cayal looked up again, stared at Stellan for a moment and then straightened and turned to face him curiously. "You're the duke, aren't you? Arkady's husband?"

Stellan nodded and stepped into the room. "Yes."

The Immortal Prince smiled. "You know she was completely wasted on you, don't you?"

Well, Stellan thought silently, *that saves me a whole lot of wondering about how much Arkady told you about me and her life as my wife, doesn't it?* He shrugged. "Yes, I suppose she was."

"They tell me she was out on the ice when it broke," Cayal said, watching him closely. "Do you think she's dead?"

"I hope not."

"You seem to be taking it well."

"You've known me for under a minute, sir," Stellan said. "How can you tell *how* I'm taking it?"

Cayal smiled again. "Fair point. For myself, I think she's alive. That woman has a knack for survival that borders on magical."

"Well," Stellan replied evenly, "who'd know more about that than you?"

The Immortal Prince eyed him oddly for a moment. "So you know about us. Puts the deal you've done with Tryan in a whole new light."

"I am a pragmatist, sir."

"I worked that much out when I learned why you married Arkady," he said with a wry smile and then he glanced down at the map. Apparently the Immortal Prince had better things to do with his time than grieve for Arkady. "Elyssa tells me you're the genius who discovered the truth about the Lore Tarot map."

"It was an accident, I can assure you."

Cayal glanced sideways at Stellan. "Do you believe the map is genuine?"

"I have no idea."

"Do you have any idea what part of the continent the map indicates? Or, for that matter, *which* continent it is?"

"No."

"Would you tell me if you did?"

"If I thought there was something in it for Glaeba," Stellan answered quite honestly, "I'd tell you anything you wanted to know."

Cayal seemed to welcome his candour, but his appreciation was short-lived. He turned back to the map, shaking his head. "It's nonsense, you know. She said she had a map that gave the location of the Chaos Crystal. The Tide is on the rise and the flanking map turns out to be useless. There's no recognisable landmarks, no scale . . ."

And you agreed to marry her for it, Stellan thought silently, taking a certain degree of perverse pleasure in Cayal's pain.

Without warning, Cayal snatched up the map, crushed the rice-paper into a ball and tossed it across the room. When he realised Stellan was standing there watching him, he shrugged. "Sometimes the deals you make when you're desperate simply aren't worth what you get in return, Desean."

The Immortal Prince turned his back on Stellan and walked to the long glass doors that led to the balcony. He threw them open, letting in a blast of icy air and snow and simply stood there, as if he was enjoying the blizzard he'd invited into the room.

Stellan wasn't sure if he was expected to answer him. In the end, deciding he'd be safer not getting into any further conversation with the Immortal Prince, he bowed politely, just in case the man had some sort of magical ability to detect disrespect—or pity—and left the room, closing the door softly behind him.

Chapter 35

Dawn found Declan roaming the streets of Lebec, clad in a hooded cloak he'd stolen from a cloak stand in the foyer of a brothel in the Lebec slums while the patrons were too drunk to notice. For once he didn't fear being recognised. The wind-driven snow swirling around the streets kept most people indoors. Only the truly motivated and the truly desperate were out in a dawn like this.

Declan barely noticed the cold as he trudged through the snow with his shoulders hunched, his thoughts deep and dire, while he contemplated the end of the world.

If Kentravyon was to be believed, the annihilation of Amyrantha was the inevitable result of Lukys activating the Chaos Crystal to restore Coryna to human form. As he'd warned Tilly, Cayal's subsequent death (which Declan was more than a little dubious about, anyway) was a sideshow to the main event. The question of whether or not the world really might end when the crystal was activated was academic really. But when it came down to it, Declan was more inclined to believe a madman with no particular axe to grind over a suicidal manic-depressive immortal who'd lie about anything (up to and including the end of the world) if it meant he was finally going to be allowed to die.

Would Lukys—Declan still couldn't bring himself to think of the immortal as his father—really risk an entire world for one person? What happened to the noble sentiment that the good of the many outweighed the good of the few?

Is Lukys, for the sake of his one true love, prepared to break a world in half?

If he was, then the chances were excellent he would succeed. Lukys had Maralyce, Cayal, Kentravyon and possibly Elyssa on his side—and Pellys, if he was focused enough. But Lukys seemed doubtful about that. And Arryl and Taryx were there. Five Tide Lords and two lesser immortals channelling the power of the Tide at its peak.

Stopping them would be akin to trying to stop the Tide.

It would take more power than Declan could ever hope to command.

Unless . . .

Declan faltered for a moment as a dreadful thought occurred to him.

Lukys had gathered a half-dozen Tide Lords to channel the power he needed to restore Coryna.

How many Tide Lords would it take to stop him?

The idea was thrilling and terrifying at the same time, but with a sinking sensation that left him nauseous, Declan realised he may have hit on the only chance he had of preventing the end of the world.

Not all immortals were bent on destroying the world. There were other Tide Lords, other powerful immortals, who seemed quite content to stay here on Amyrantha—Tide Lords Lukys didn't like or trust enough to involve in his plans. Brynden might be a candidate. Kinta had certainly seemed unsettled by what Kentravyon had told her about his plans, and she was sure to have repeated his story to her lover by now. Then there was Tryan. He was busy trying to take over the whole continent, but would he side against his sister if she threw her lot in with Lukys . . . or, more specifically, with Cayal?

That left Jaxyn, the only other truly powerful Tide Lord Declan knew of. Including himself, that meant four Tide Lords. Probably not enough, but what if he could cajole the others into joining them? Would the combined power of the lesser immortals like Kinta, Diala, Lyna, Ambria, Medwen—even Syrolee and Engarhod, Krydence and Rance—be enough to counteract the power of Lukys's coterie and their Tide-focusing crystal? If Declan could gather enough opposition to what Lukys planned, could they stop Lukys from destroying the world?

And what would be the point? To save Amyrantha from destruction, just to ensure this endless cycle of destruction and rebuilding went on forever?

Declan agonised about that for another two blocks before a simple fact occurred to him. Enslaved but still in existence, Amyrantha had some hope—however slim—of eventually finding a way to free itself from the yoke of the Tide Lords.

Destroyed, there was no hope at all.

Tides, Declan thought, shaking his head as he realised what he must do. *I can't believe I'm even contemplating this . . .*

He stopped at the next corner to get his bearings. The streets here were achingly familiar. If he turned left at this intersection he'd eventually come to the neat little house with its surgery in the basement, jammed between a dingy apothecary and a delicious-smelling bakery, where

Arkady had lived with her father when they were children. To his right was the road that led to his grandfather's attic, and if he kept on walking south, eventually he'd come to the brothel where he'd lived with his mother until he was ten.

The Lebec slums were home, Declan realised, in a way no other place ever would be, no matter how long he lived. Draped in a clean blanket of snow that covered the grime and kept the beggars off the streets, the slums looked story-book pretty in the dawn's feeble light, the flaws hidden behind shadows and snowflakes.

For this, Declan realised, he had to fight. For every lord in this world with a majestic palace, like the one Arkady had acquired when she married into money, there were thousands of people like the citizens of the Lebec slums—Crasii and human alike—whose daily lives filled these cramped and tumbled-down houses, here and in cities all over Amyrantha. People with lives that had as much value as an immortal's life. Perhaps more. Mortals had a time limit, after all. They had reason not to waste what little time fate had awarded them.

Only an immortal could afford to waste his life on frivolous pursuits.

Only an immortal would consider the good of the one to outweigh the good of the many.

Declan threw back the hood of his cloak, and glanced around. He no longer cared about being recognised. Standing here, in these streets where he'd always belonged, he realised something else. While he remembered this place, while he fought for the people who were born here, who lived and died in these grubby streets, he would have some hope of retaining his humanity.

Regardless of the eventual fate of Amyrantha, if this place were destroyed, he would lose a part of himself which he couldn't afford to let go. Even if he fought to save the whole world, it would be because this place—his home—was a part of that world. To save one, he would have to save the other.

And to do that, Declan needed help. The worst kind of help.

He needed the Tide Lords that Lukys, in his wisdom, had deemed unfit for his brave new world. The Tide Lords he didn't intend to allow across the rift when he opened it to enable him to draw the power he needed from two worlds to restore Coryna.

To stop Lukys and Cayal, Declan needed the power of the most ma-

levolent and self-serving Tide Lords he could name. He needed the
only three immortals he could be sure would be prepared to do whatever it was going to take to stop Cayal trying to end his life and prevent
Lukys opening his rift—Brynden, the Lord of Reckoning, Tryan, the
immortal the Lore Tarot named The Devil, and perhaps the most
irksome of them all . . .

Declan needed Jaxyn Aranville, the badly misnamed Lord of Temperance.

He could feel the other immortals on the Tide.

They weren't close, but Declan was becoming more and more attuned
to the Tide, and getting better at identifying what each disturbance on
it meant. As he approached Lebec Palace, he knew his hunch had been
correct. With the battle lost and his Crasii army mostly floating face
down in the Lower Oran, Jaxyn had retreated to Lebec Palace with
Diala and Lyna to lick his wounds and plot his counter-attack.

Declan didn't waste time wondering if Jaxyn was planning to fight
for everything he'd gained thus far in Glaeba, or if he was willing to cut
his losses, cede the continent to the Empress of the Five Realms and
her family, and set himself up somewhere else. Brynden had already
staked out Torlenia, but Tenacia seemed free of immortals, and the
Commonwealth of Elenovia was always ripe for the picking.

For that matter, the Lord of Temperance would be better served
claiming Senestra. There were already cults in that country—powerful
cults—dedicated to his worship. A god could do worse than to settle
down among his already adoring congregation.

It was mid-morning by the time Declan reached the gates of Lebec
Palace. He arrived on foot, using the time it had taken him to walk from
the city to figure out how he was going to handle this. Declan was fed up
with explaining how he became immortal; it was one of the reasons he'd
not hung around Cycrane after the battle. He didn't particularly want to
go through the whole spiel again to every immortal he met, and there
was quite a gathering of them in Caelum.

Let Kentravyon and Cayal explain about the new Tide Lord. Declan
had better things to do.

Still, Jaxyn and his minions were the last remaining immortals to be informed of his admission to their ranks, and if he hoped to get a hearing from them, let alone their active cooperation in stopping Lukys, he was going to have to get their attention first. And he somehow had to explain the situation in a manner that didn't result in the total devastation of everything in a five-mile radius.

It was the Crasii standing guard on the main gate who gave him the solution. Despite orders to kill anything that walked up the road, the felines fell to their knees at his approach, assuring this immortal new arrival that to serve him was the reason they breathed.

Declan changed his original plan almost instantly, and once he was admitted to the estate, headed, not to the palace where Jaxyn and the others were holed up, but to the compound where the remainder of the estate workers were housed. Keeping far enough away from the palace so the immortals couldn't sense him in anything but the most general way—and working on the assumption that if he could barely feel them they'd only barely feel him—he made his way around to the village.

As expected, as soon as he arrived, Fletch, the old canine Stellan had allowed to govern the residents of the Crasii village, approached him and fell to his knees. Declan ordered him to stand and told him what he wanted, demanding complete silence from every Crasii in the compound. There were plenty of amphibians in the pools at the edge of the lake but there weren't many felines left. Most of those had been out on the ice when it broke. The males were still there, however, locked in their cages. Declan freed the two younger males, ordered them to behave themselves when they joined the others, and then headed across the yard to Taryx's enclosure.

With the rising sun, the weather had settled and the bitter wind of dawn had dropped to almost nothing. There was even a glimmer of sunlight breaking through the clouds in a few places, one of which was rather conveniently centred over Taryx's favourite sofa. The old male was sunning himself when Declan spied him across the yard. He watched the Tide Lord approach warily, not moving from the battered sofa where he reclined. Declan stopped outside the cage a moment and watched the magnificent male as he lay there, his genitalia exposed, his expression smug and disobedient. And then he smiled as he realised what Taryx's silent defiance meant.

"Tides, you wily old cat. You're a Scard."

The male stared at him for a moment and then lowered his head. "To serve you is the reason I breathe, my lord."

"Bullshit."

Taryx looked up, grinning faintly, and then he shrugged. "Jaxyn never picked it, you know, the whole time he's been here. You didn't used to be a suzerain, spymaster."

"You didn't used to be a Scard."

The male climbed to his feet and walked to the bars to study Declan more closely. "What do you want?"

Declan looked over at the other Crasii who were currently heading for the gate to stand with the canines gathering on the small village compound. "I need to talk to Jaxyn. I figured I'd show him how it is now, rather than try to explain it."

The old male thought on that for a moment, scratching himself behind the ear through his thick, silver-streaked mane. "I suppose that means if I don't go along with *you*, now you're one of them, Jaxyn will realise I've been playing *him* all this time."

Declan nodded. "On the bright side, I intend to give him other things to worry about this morning than his feline breeding program."

Taryx considered that for a moment longer and then he nodded. "You're probably right, spymaster. But I warn you. Let me out of here and I won't be going back."

Declan had known enough Scards in his time to understand how much slavery irked them. This majestic creature had the added complication of being a breeding male, which would have meant not just a lifetime of slavery, but a lifetime of confinement as well.

"Do this one thing for me," Declan said, "and you're free. Jaxyn will be none the wiser about you being a Scard and I'll see to it you're never confined again. In fact," he added, realising he had something truly valuable to this creature, "I'll go one better. I'll tell you how to find Hidden Valley."

"*You* know the location of Hidden Valley?" The feline male was clearly sceptical of his claim.

"I've been there."

"So it's likely everyone there is dead."

Declan shook his head. "I've known about Hidden Valley for a long time. Long before . . . this happened to me. I've no interest in harming the Scards who live there or of informing any other immortal of its location. Believe me or not, as you will, old man. But I can promise you this: if you don't agree to help me now, you're staying in the cage, and when Jaxyn asks me why you're not with the others, I'll tell him."

Taryx considered that for a time and then nodded. "Then let me out of here, suzerain. I want to die free."

It was less than an hour after he arrived at the Lebec estate that Declan figured it was time to move close enough to be sensed by the other immortals in the palace. By then, every Crasii on the estate had silently gathered on the lawn below the terrace where Arkady used to eat her breakfast. Every single Crasii, including the amphibian pearl divers, the field workers, the sick, the nursing females with their pups and kittens, and every house canine not actually on duty, was on their knees with their backs to the palace, facing their new master.

Declan commanded them to silence and waited.

It didn't take long for the other Tide Lords to sense his presence and come to investigate. Declan remembered Cayal's reaction when he'd first met him, how he'd immediately grabbed for the Tide when he sensed the threat from another Tide Lord. Declan was trying to avoid that happening here with Jaxyn.

He wanted to make a point, not get into a fight.

Not surprisingly, Jaxyn emerged onto the terrace bare moments after Declan sensed him, followed a moment later by two women whose gentle ripples were almost swamped by Jaxyn's powerful presence on the Tide. One looked no older than a seventeen-year-old girl. He knew who that was—Diala, the immortal who'd been posing as Stellan Desean's niece and managed to marry herself a king. The other woman he didn't know, but he figured it must be Lyna.

They stared at Declan, and at the scores of Crasii kneeling silently at his feet.

Declan didn't need to say anything. The ripples on the Tide he couldn't help but cause and the prostrate Crasii said it all. When Jaxyn didn't reach for the Tide and start tossing lightning bolts at him, Declan figured it was safe to move closer, the kneeling Crasii scurrying out of his path as he walked toward the terrace.

When he reached the steps he stopped and looked up at them. He said nothing. At this point, there wasn't much he could say.

"Tides," Diala said, after a long moment of tense silence. "It's the spymaster!"

Declan met Jaxyn's suspicious gaze evenly.

"If you want to stop Cayal killing himself and causing the end of the world," he said, "then we have to talk."

Chapter 36

Cayal was still standing on the balcony, letting the snow swirl around him. The conditions had calmed as the day warmed up a little, but it was still bitterly cold, the wind so sharp it cut through everything, even registering with Cayal who was all but immune to the vagaries of the weather.

He felt Elyssa approaching long before she burst into the room. He braced himself for it, reminding himself of what was at stake here. If anything, being with Elyssa was likely to strengthen his resolve. There was no chance he would change his mind in her company. No chance he would want to live a moment longer than he had to, trapped in a union that was going to be as brief as it was pointless.

Even in the throes of passion, there was nothing to be gained by an immortal getting married. No relationship was going to last for eternity . . . except maybe Lukys and Coryna's apparently eternal devotion. He wasn't sure how, but they seemed to have managed it.

Cayal smiled as the door slammed open and Elyssa stormed into the room. *I wonder if Lukys and Coryna vowed to love each other no matter what . . . even if one of them turns into a rat.*

"Are you laughing at me?" Elyssa demanded, when she saw him smile.

"I'd never dream of it."

"Then why are you smiling like that?"

"I was thinking of something else," he said. "Never fear, Elyssa, there is nothing about you that makes me laugh. Was that Tryan just now I heard yelling like a fishwife?"

She nodded, smiling triumphantly. "I told him we were getting married."

"He took the news well, then."

Elyssa pulled a face. "Pay no attention to him. He hates you just on principle. He says it's because he thinks you're going to break my heart."

"Really?"

She shrugged. "Well, no. Not really. Mostly he's mad at me because

I told him I wasn't going across the lake to Glaeba with him and Mother, and he'd just have to conquer Glaeba without me."

"You're not going with him?" Cayal asked in surprise. "I thought you'd jump at the chance to gloat over Jaxyn's defeat. Tides, I know I would."

She gave a short, cynical laugh. "They have to find him first. Nobody's laid eyes on him or felt a glimmer of him on the Tide since the ice broke. Anyway, you said we needed the crystal before the Tide peaks. Who knows how long that will be? Do you really think we can afford to waste the time on a side trip to Glaeba?"

"You could tell me where the crystal is and I could go on ahead," he suggested as casually as he could manage.

Elyssa's eyes narrowed, as she turned her gaze to the desk where the map had been resting before she left. "Where is it? What have you done with my map?" Before Cayal could answer, she spied the crumpled-up ball of paper on the floor where Cayal had tossed it. "What the . . . ?"

Elyssa hurried across the room, scooped the map up off the floor and began trying to straighten it out. "Why did you do that?"

"The map is useless, Elyssa. If you know the location of the crystal, just tell me where it is. There is nothing on that scrap of paper you're treating as if it contains the secret to the meaning of life to indicate *what* it's showing. There are no points of reference, no landmarks . . ."

"There are so," she objected, laying the map down on the desk. She tried to smooth it out with short, impatient strokes. When that proved insufficient, she turned it over and tried to straighten it from the other side. "I'm certain it's somewhere near Maralyce's mine. It makes sense that it is. She's been digging through those damn mountains for centuries, so she must know something. All we need to do is find this bluff here . . ."

"What bluff?" He turned from the window and crossed to the desk. Elyssa lifted the map to turn it over the right way, but Cayal stopped her, frowning, as the light caught the almost transparent rice paper she had used to trace the map.

"Hang on a minute. Put it down the other way."

"But it's backwards. I traced the map from the back of the Tarot cards this way."

"And the Tarot was drawn by mortals specifically trying to hide the location of the crystal from us, wasn't it? Trust me, Elyssa, turn the map over."

Elyssa shrugged and did as he asked, laying the map face down on the desk. The inked lines were much harder to see with the map this way up, but they were still visible. Cayal stared at the map for a time, and then turned it upside down and studied it for a little longer, his pulse quickening as he realised what he was looking at.

"I know where this is."

She shook her head doubtfully. "The map is upside down and back-to-front, Cayal. You can barely read the damn thing, let alone find anything on it."

"But that's the point. The mortals who stole the Chaos Crystal originally would have gone out of their way to make this map unreadable to the casual observer. They would have expected one of us to come after it, and didn't want us to find it, even if we managed to get hold of the map. That's why they broke it down into pieces on the back of the Tarot deck."

Elyssa looked thoughtful, warming to the idea. "I suppose once word got out the Tarot was the key to finding the crystal, they might have tried to take further precautions to confound us."

Cayal nodded in agreement. "Of course they would have. Tides, didn't you and Tryan terrorise the whole of Caelum and Glaeba a couple of thousand years ago, looking for it?"

She looked up sharply. "I didn't think you knew about that."

He shrugged, smiling at her. Now was not the time to give the impression he was passing judgment on his future bride. "I didn't know you were specifically looking for the Chaos Crystal, but I figured you and Tryan must be randomly killing Cabal members for *something* other than your own amusement."

Elyssa glared at him for a moment, annoyed by what he was implying, and then she shrugged. "We never found it, and Tryan lost interest in the end."

"Does he still feel that way?"

"He thinks I'm insane," she said. "He thinks you've learned of my interest in the Bedlam Stone and have come here for your own nefarious purposes—which have nothing to do with any lost magical crystal—and are using me and my interest in the stone to get whatever it is you want."

Which is pretty much right on the money, Cayal thought, although he was careful to give Elyssa no hint of what he was thinking. Time to distract her. He reached out and touched her face tenderly, smiling at her the same way he smiled at any woman he was trying to coerce into doing what he wanted. "Tryan has never appreciated you, Lyssa. Or your intelligence."

Elyssa visibly preened at his compliment. She turned her face slightly and kissed the palm of his hand. "You appreciate me, don't you, Cayal?"

"In ways I'll never be able to put into words," he told her honestly. He dropped his hand, resisting the temptation to wipe her kiss away on his trousers. "What happened with your search for the crystal back then?"

"We knew the Cabal had hidden it, so we were looking for a map . . . you know, a rolled-up bit of charred parchment with a big red X on it, marking the location of the Bedlam Stone. It wasn't until I heard, years later, that it wasn't a map as such, but the Tarot which held the secret to the location of the crystal that I decided to go back and try to find the last really ancient Tarot I remembered seeing." She stared down at the crumpled map traced off the back of the Lore Tarot. "Where is this, do you think?"

Cayal stabbed at the map with his finger, indicating the only recognisable landmark on the page. "The Temple of the Tide."

"It can't be. You destroyed that when you decapitated Pellys and annihilated Magreth."

He shook his head. "You're talking about the Temple of the *Way* of the Tide. This is the Temple of the Tide. The one Diala and Arryl set up here when you were in Tenacia playing god with the Crasii."

"The one where Fliss committed suicide?" she asked, watching him closely for his reaction.

"She didn't commit suicide," he corrected, a little surprised that even after all this time, he still felt the need to clarify how his daughter had died; still felt the need to stress it was an accident and not a deliberate act on her part. Or anything to do with him. "Fliss died accidentally, trying to become one of us."

Elyssa smiled nastily. "Perhaps she should have spoken to Lukys before she tried to set herself alight. He seems to have figured out how it's done."

Bitch. "It's ancient history now," he said with a shrug.

"And so is that temple."

Cayal shook his head again. "Maybe not. It was a substantial building. And it was quite high above the waterline when the valley flooded." He didn't bother to add that he was the one who had flooded the valley by dumping the entire inland sea from Torlenia in it. They both knew how the Great Lakes were created. "It's not that far from here, actually. Less than a day if we follow the shoreline by boat."

Elyssa's eyes widened in surprise. "Are you serious?"

"Do I look like I'm in a particularly jovial mood?"

If she noticed the edge in his voice, she chose to ignore it. "Then we could leave first thing in the morning."

"Why can't we just go now?"

"I have things to organise. I have some puppies I'm breeding to take care of. Some of us have responsibilities, you know."

Cayal look at her curiously. "You don't want to take a side trip to Glaeba because we haven't got the time, but you're prepared to wait a day so you can play with a litter of Crasii puppies?"

She smiled at him a little sheepishly. "It does sound a bit ridiculous when you put it like that. Did you really want to leave today?"

"Now," Cayal said. "You organise us a boat and I'll fetch Kentravyon."

Her face fell. "Do we *have* to include him?"

"Do you want to explain to him why he's *not* included?"

Elyssa shook her head. "Not particularly. Kiss me before I go, then. So I know you really love me."

Cayal didn't hesitate to give her what she wanted, aware that Elyssa was suspicious enough of his motives to be watching for the slightest hint he wasn't fully committed to her. So he pulled her to him and kissed her long and lingeringly and when she was breathless—more from happiness than impending suffocation—he let her go and smiled at her intimately. "Don't be long."

She stared up at him, her eyes shining. "I love you, Cayal."

"I love you too, Elyssa," he lied with absolute sincerity. And then he let her go, feigning reluctance. "I'll meet you at the docks in an hour. Don't leave without me."

"Don't worry, lover," she assured him. "I'll never leave you behind. Not ever."

She turned and headed for the door, stopping on the threshold long enough to offer him a smile and an intimate little wave of her fingers as she let herself out of the room.

Cayal kept the smile on his face until the door closed, and then sagged against the desk. *Don't worry, lover. I'll never leave you behind. Not ever,* she'd promised.

"Don't you threaten me," he muttered.

Chapter 37

Warlock was dying.

Arkady could see it in his eyes. Even if the stench from the wound in his belly didn't give it away—which was enough to make Boots gag every time she changed the bandages they'd fashioned from the hem of Arkady's petticoat—it was in his eyes.

Boots was beside herself and the pups were fretting in sympathy with her distress, although they didn't understand the reason for it. It was two days now since Arkady had stabbed Warlock as he searched the ruins for his family. Her poor aim meant she'd stabbed him in the gut—a slow and painful way to die, made all the worse by the knowledge that the woman who killed him was the same woman who had once set him free.

"Did you want me to fetch some more water?" Arkady asked softly, as Boots pulled the covers back up over Warlock. The fur on his forehead was damp with sweat, even though the fire-pit here in Boots's underground lair barely took the chill from the air, let alone making it warm enough to cause someone to perspire.

"No, I'll do it," Boots said, rising to her feet. "You can keep an eye on the pups. Assuming you can manage that without trying to kill them, too."

Boots had been like this ever since the stabbing. She was unrelenting in her censure. Arkady had struck without thinking, as far as she was concerned. Without thinking and without taking the time to establish if the intruder she was so anxious to destroy was *actually* an intruder and not the father of Boots's puppies.

Not that Arkady could really blame Boots for her anger. It *was* her fault. And if she'd waited a moment longer before striking, instead of being trapped here with three pups, on the wrong side of the lake, in a foreign country with no friends and no hope of rescue, nursing a dying Crasii, they'd be leaving in the small boat Warlock had tied at the edge of the lake.

That wasn't going to happen now. They were stuck here until Warlock died.

Boots snatched the bucket and headed up the stone steps to the surface. Arkady checked on the pups, who were across the room playing with that damned skull they'd found in the lower levels. They were rolling it across the floor to each other, giggling as the gentle blue glow waxed and waned when it left the clutches of one pup and neared another. Arkady thought the artefact too valuable to allow babies to be playing with it, as well as more than a little creepy, particularly the way it glowed around the pups and changed colour to a sickly green whenever Boots went near it.

Or maybe I'm just jealous, she thought. *Because when I touch the damned thing, nothing happens at all.*

Warlock muttered something incomprehensible, distracting her from the pups. She hurried over to him and knelt on the floor beside the pallet where he lay, picking up the rag soaked in snowmelt they'd been using to wet his lips. With his intestines laid open, there was no question of giving him food or water, but they could ease his thirst a little with the wet rag without him actually swallowing anything.

"Can I get you something, Warlock?"

His eyes opened slowly, fixing on her as if he had trouble focusing. "The pups . . . are they . . . ?"

"They're fine," she assured him. "Absolutely perfect."

"They are Crasii," he said, his eyes welling up with tears.

Arkady smiled down at him. "I know they are," she said soothingly. "The most beautiful little canines I've ever—"

"No!" he said, gripping her arm weakly. "You don't understand, my lady. You must help Boots . . . keep them out of the hands of the suzerain. They are *Crasii*."

It took a moment for her to grasp what he was telling her, but when she finally realised what he meant, she sat back on her heel, shocked. "But how can that be? Both you and Boots are Scards, aren't you?"

"Crasii throw Scard pups all the time," Warlock told her, struggling to speak. "Why is it odd to think the reverse can't happen to Scards?"

"So if you run into any immortals . . ."

"Then our babies will betray us," he said, his voice strained.

"I'm so sorry, Warlock," she said, leaning over to wipe his brow. "If I'd known it was you . . ."

"I would not have expected you to remember me, my lady," he assured her, every word an effort, his forgiveness all the more poignant for its generosity. "Our acquaintance was brief and more than a year ago."

"And what a busy year it's been," she said, smiling down at him. "You've found a mate, made a litter of beautiful babies . . ." *Got yourself killed by the foolish woman who thought she was doing you a favour by setting you free . . .*

The irony in knowing that had she not forged her husband's signature and given Warlock a pardon, he would be safe and well in his cell in Lebec Prison right now, did not escape Arkady. She wished she had more time with Warlock to find out what he'd been up to this past year. More time to discover how it was a freed criminal wound up spying for the Cabal. How he'd met the escaped slave from her own kennels who was now his mate.

Even as far apart as their worlds normally were, that they could still collide so profoundly left Arkady wondering if there really was such a thing as fate or destiny. It all seemed too coincidental to be mere random chance.

"Will you help protect my babies, your grace?" he begged, the strain of speaking so great his voice was little more than a whisper. "Boots acts tough, but she's very young and very frightened and three pups is a lot for any mother, let alone one on the run."

Arkady nodded, and wiped his damp brow again, the matted fur cold under her fingers. "I give you my word, Warlock. I'll do whatever I must to keep them safe."

Before Warlock could respond, Boots barrelled down the stairs in a panic with the empty bucket in her hand. "They're here!"

Arkady rose to her feet and looked at her oddly. "Who? Who is here?"

"The suzerain!" she said, her eyes wild. "Can't you feel them? No, of course you can't. You're only human." She hurried to the pups, snatching up Missy who was the closest. "Perhaps if we hide in the lower levels . . ." Then she turned to look at Warlock, her eyes filling with tears. "Tides . . . we can't leave him here!"

"Why don't you go and hide, and I'll go out there and talk to them."

"What for? To protect us?" Boots glanced pointedly at Warlock for a moment and then turned her baleful glare on Arkady. "Oh, yes. Let's. Because that worked out *so* well the last time."

"You have no choice, Boots," Arkady told her. "It nearly killed us getting Warlock down here, and we don't have the time to take him anywhere else. And you need to keep the puppies quiet. Let me go out there."

Boots was angry and frightened but she understood that Arkady was making sense. "What will you tell them?"

"The truth. That I am the wife of the Duke of Lebec and I managed to swim to safety when the ice broke. The Caelish have won the war and Stellan was fighting on their side. I'll probably be all right. You, Warlock, and the pups—you're the ones who can't risk being found."

"I don't know . . ."

"You have to trust me, Boots. Can you tell which suzerain they are?"

Boots shook her head. "I can only smell them. I can't tell them apart."

"Then let me go out there and lead them away from here." Arkady glanced at Warlock and added, "Under the circumstances, it's the least I can do."

Boots was still angry with her, but not so angry she couldn't see the sense in what Arkady was proposing. "You won't tell them we're here? Not even a hint?"

"I'll pretend to be grateful they've found me," she promised. "Tell them I haven't seen another living soul since the ice broke."

"What if it's Jaxyn?"

Arkady shrugged, a little surprised to discover that she really *didn't* care about her own fate if it meant saving Boots and her family from falling back into the clutches of the immortals. Or perhaps guilt was driving her, making her think she deserved to be recaptured. Freedom was a fine notion, but it was a hard pill to swallow when it felt as if it had come at the expense of her father's life. "I'll be fine, Boots. At the moment I have more value to these people alive than dead. You just find a way to keep the puppies quiet."

Boots nodded reluctantly. "All right. But don't let them come into the temple, because if it's Elyssa who's found us, I'll kill myself, my mate *and* my babies before I let that bitch get her hands on my family again." By the fierce look in her eyes and the proud way her tail was poised, Arkady could tell Boots wasn't making an idle threat.

"Then hide that damned skull while you're at it," Arkady suggested with a faint smile, trying to ease the tension a little. "You can hear them giggling all over the temple when they're playing with it." She gripped the young canine's shoulder reassuringly. "And don't worry, Boots. I'll do whatever I must to keep you and your family safe. I promise."

"That's what you said the last time," Boots said gruffly, shaking off Arkady's hand as she shifted Missy to a more comfortable position on her hip. "And you ended up trying to kill my mate." She quickly looked up the stairs. "The smell is getting stronger. You'd better go."

Arkady nodded, wishing she had time to say goodbye to Warlock or give the pups a hug, but if Boots could smell the suzerain from down here, then they were very close. She grabbed her coat from the floor, tugging her arms through the sleeves as she climbed the stairs. By the time she emerged into the main part of the temple, blinking in the bright daylight reflecting off the snow that surrounded the ruin, she could already hear their voices.

The immortals who were heading for the ruins weren't trying to conceal their approach. But then, why would they? They had no reason to suspect anybody was here. Arkady quickly swept some of the scattered leaves across the entrance to the lair in the hope it would pass idle scrutiny and then hurried to her right, away from the door, to stand near the pillar where she'd stabbed Warlock. Arkady could hear voices, male and female, but she still had no idea which of the immortals had found the temple. She truly feared it was Jaxyn, although the ice had broken days ago. Surely he would have stumbled ashore somewhere else along the lakeshore before now?

There was only one way to be certain; only one way to ensure the immortals came no closer to Warlock and Boots and their Crasii babies.

Arkady hurried forward, following the sound of voices. As she emerged from the ruins, she discovered it wasn't Jaxyn, with Diala and Lyna by his side, as she'd feared. These immortals were male and they had only one woman with them. Arkady hesitated on the top step, thrusting her hands deep into her pockets against the biting air.

Two men and a woman approached the temple. Arkady didn't know the woman, nor did she have any idea who the older man was, but the figure on the left she knew all too well.

I'll do whatever I must to keep you and your family safe, Boots. I promise, she'd foolishly told Boots.

Tides, Arkady thought. *I'll do anything but this. Please, I don't have the strength to deal with him again.*

Nobody was listening, however. The ground didn't open up and swallow her. No lightning bolt came out of the blue to strike her dead when the immortals stopped and stared up at her in astonishment.

The man on the left was the last person she wanted or expected to see here in Caelum.

It was Cayal, the Immortal Prince.

Chapter 38

"This is absolute nonsense, Jaxyn," Diala scoffed after Declan had finished explaining what Lukys and Cayal were planning. They'd retired to the elaborately decorated room that had once been Stellan Desean's study. It seemed strange to be standing here without Arkady gracing the room, looking every inch the duchess. Strange to be here and not have Stellan sitting at his desk staring at Declan with that odd look caught somewhere between fear and contempt that he always wore when Declan was in the palace. Declan used to take it to mean Stellan feared the spymaster knew the truth about him and was just waiting to expose his secret. Declan never did. He loved Arkady too much to expose her to that sort of trouble.

And he was protecting her now. In the past few hours, he'd told Jaxyn, Lyna and Diala as much as he could. He'd included almost everything in his tale—meeting up with Cayal in Senestra; Lukys's ice palace with its chamber designed specifically to channel the Tide; Coryna, Maralyce, Kentravyon's revival from his frozen prison—even the story of his own immortal transformation. He'd left out, however, anything to do with Arkady, particularly the bit about how the feline Crasii Jaxyn had employed as his personal bodyguard was a Scard in the employ of the Cabal of the Tarot and had actually let her escape.

Declan behaved and spoke as if he believed Arkady was dead, and held no hope for any other news about her fate.

In truth, Declan was sick over what might have happened to her. He felt even worse that instead of going after her—the very reason he was back here in Glaeba—he'd been forced to abandon his search for Arkady to concentrate on the much larger problem of, well, saving the world.

For his own sanity, he clung to the notion that Chikita had let Arkady escape in plenty of time for her to get clear of the ice. It was late in the day when Cayal, Kentravyon and Elyssa finally broke the ice-sheet with the Tide, after all. She could have been halfway to anywhere by then.

At least she was no longer being pursued; there was that to be thankful for. Jaxyn and his immortal conspirators had other things to worry about.

Jaxyn clearly considered breaking the ice nothing short of shameless cheating. At least that's how he referred to Elyssa teaming up with Cayal and Kentravyon to defeat him. That bothered Jaxyn a great deal more than the fate of any mortal human—even the wife of the man he was trying to browbeat into submission by threatening to kill his wife.

The immortals took the news, about the imminent end of the world well, all things considered. But then, Declan supposed, when you're immortal, after a while nothing must really surprise you any more.

"I don't know," Lyna said doubtfully. "His story has a ring of authenticity about it." She studied Declan thoughtfully for a moment and then turned to the others. "You can't deny he's telling the truth about being one of us now."

Jaxyn had remained silent while Declan spoke, offering no opinion or any hint as to what he thought about Declan's tale. He was leaning against the desk, his arms folded, and hadn't moved the whole time Declan was talking.

"I don't doubt for a moment that it's true," he said after a moment, surprising Declan by adding his weight to Lyna's argument.

"Why? Because he used to be your spymaster?" Diala asked, rolling her eyes.

"No," Jaxyn replied patiently. "I believe him because Cayal is a lunatic. Destroying the entire world just to end his own misery is exactly the sort of insane, selfish and entirely idiotic thing he'd do."

"I suppose you think Lukys is in love with that damned rat, too?"

Jaxyn smiled faintly. "Actually, I've always thought it was a little bit disturbing, how fond he was of that rat. I'm almost relieved to hear there's a good reason for his unnatural attachment to it."

"Then you'll help me?" Declan asked, not sure he believed he'd ever utter such words to an immortal like Jaxyn Aranville.

"No," Jaxyn said. "I won't help *you*. There aren't words to describe how little I care about the fate of you or your many boring mortal friends on Amyrantha, Hawkes. I might be willing, however, to do whatever it takes to stop that maniac, Cayal, from screwing it up for the rest of us by destroying a perfectly good world just because *he's* sick of living on it."

"What would be the point?" Diala asked, pacing behind the desk impatiently. She seemed much more interested in taking the fight back to Tryan and Elyssa to reclaim the throne of Glaeba. "If Hawkes is right, Lukys has a half-dozen Tide Lords lined up to help him open the rift. How would the two of you stop them?"

"We could stop them finding the Chaos Crystal," Declan suggested.

Jaxyn shook his head. "You don't know where it is and you don't know where the others are, or where they've gone to look for it. You could waste a human lifetime just trying to track them down. You'd be better off heading for where you know they have to go eventually, after they've found it."

"You mean the ice palace in Jelidia?" Lyna asked, sounding more than a little exasperated. She turned to Jaxyn, shaking her head. "Surely you're not thinking of doing this? Even if this fool were right, it'd still be only the two of you against three times as many Tide Lords. You'd not come close to the power the others can muster, let alone if they're amplifying all the power they can channel with this Chaos Crystal he claims they'll be using."

"We'd need help," Declan said, wondering why his grand plan had sounded so much more reasonable in his head. "Tryan and Brynden, specifically, and probably all the other immortals not aligned with Lukys if we're going to have a chance of stopping them."

"What an excellent plan!" Diala said, clapping her hands like a gleeful child. "Because we're so good at pitching in and working together for the good of all mankind. Maybe afterwards we could all get together and build a barn."

Ignoring Diala's sarcastic aside, Jaxyn pushed off the desk, his expression determined. "Well, let's get to it then."

Declan studied him suspiciously. "You're with me?"

Jaxyn shrugged. "It may be the only way to retrieve something from this rather awkward situation."

"*Retrieve* something?" Diala asked. "What are you talking about?"

Jaxyn turned to her impatiently. "We've lost the upper hand here, Diala. Don't you see that? They're on their way, as we speak, to claim Glaeba. The only way to stop Syrolee now is to give her something else to worry about. The spymaster's join-us-to-help-save-the-world idea is a corker."

Declan was amazed. Somehow, Jaxyn had found a way to make this all about his desire for conquest. "So you want to enlist Tryan and

Syrolee and the rest of them in your grand plan to save the world merely to distract them, while you figure out how you're going to steal Glaeba back from them?"

Jaxyn smiled at him with approval. "Got it in one, Hawkes. We'll make an immortal tyrant of you yet." Before Declan could respond to that, Jaxyn turned to Lyna. "You should be the one who goes to Senestra."

"Why me?"

"Because you get along with Ambria and Medwen better than anybody else in this room. It'll be up to you to convince them to join us."

Lyna didn't seem terribly enthused by the idea. "If Cayal couldn't convince them to help, why do you think I'll have any more luck?"

"Because this time they'll have a *reason* to help. Nobody cares if Cayal wants to die. Everybody cares if we don't have a world left to live on." He turned to Declan with a frown. "I'm a little hurt, actually, that Lukys doesn't want me in his brave new world. I imagine, if I put it to her the right way, Syrolee isn't going to be happy about that either."

"Do you think you can get them to join us?" Declan asked, wondering if this was what it felt like to sell one's soul. The idea of co-opting the likes of Jaxyn or the Empress of the Five Realms to his cause seemed so fundamentally wrong. But what other choice did he have? There was only one way to stop Cayal and Lukys. And only self-interest would motivate the other Tide Lords into doing something about it. *Jaxyn has just proved that in spades.*

But Declan was still full of doubt about whether he was doing the right thing. *Maybe I'm making things immeasurably worse. Maybe the world I save won't be worth living in.*

Is there really such a thing as "better off dead"?

"Trust me. I can deal with Syrolee," Jaxyn said. "And if you're right about Elyssa throwing in her lot with Cayal—which is no great surprise, I have to say—then I'm pretty sure Tryan will be with us all the way, too. He hates Cayal on principle. Having him court his sister will only serve to aggravate him further. That leaves you to deal with Brynden, spymaster."

That suggestion took Declan completely by surprise. He'd assumed that because they all knew each other so well, it would be left to Diala to deal with the Lord of Reckoning.

"Why me? I don't know him . . ." *And there aren't words to describe what I'd like to do to him for selling Arkady into slavery.* He kept the last part to himself, certain that voicing his opinion aloud would do nothing to help.

"You're all shiny and new and uncorrupted, Hawkes," Jaxyn said, slapping him on the shoulder. "Brynden has rather firm opinions about the rest of us, and they're not likely to get us a hearing with him. You've a much better chance of convincing that inflexible pain-in-the-backside of the worthiness of your cause without any of us around, believe me."

Even Diala nodded in agreement. "He's right, you know. Although you may not find him willing to help, even if you manage to get in to see him. I doubt he's going to lose any sleep over the thought of Cayal dying."

Lyna laughed sourly, apparently of the same opinion. "Knowing Brynden, he'll probably think Lukys is cooking up an apocalypse to cleanse the Tide or rid Amyrantha of all the impure mortals, or something equally idiotic."

Jaxyn eyed him curiously. "Are you prepared for that, spymaster? That you might present your noble cause to the Lord of Arrogant Self-righteousness, only to have him decide to throw in his lot with Lukys?"

"What's the alternative?" Declan asked. "Just let Lukys open his rift and crack Amyrantha in half because it was too much trouble to do anything to prevent it?"

Diala's pacing brought her close to Declan and Jaxyn. She stopped for a moment, eyeing him up and down with an approving smile. "You're so attractive when you're being absurdly noble, Declan. Why were you never like this when you were mortal? You were a rather ignoble and ruthless little prick back then, as I recall. Did the fires of immolation burn away your pitiless exterior to expose the noble champion of injustice underneath?"

Apparently it was a rhetorical question. She turned from him before he could respond, and strode across the rug to the sideboard where she poured herself a large glass of wine.

Jaxyn didn't seem interested in Diala's opinion. "Ignore her. You're right, I'm aggrieved to admit. I'd be monumentally peeved if I ended up helping to destroy this delightful world because we did nothing to stop a suicidal fool and a lovesick maniac from annihilating it."

"We'll have to move quickly," Declan warned. "Elyssa knows where the crystal is and the Tide is getting higher every day. We may not have long."

"Actually, you may have more time than you think," Lyna said. She was still saying "you" not "we," which Declan took to mean she still wasn't convinced she should join them.

"How do you figure that?" Jaxyn asked.

She put down her wineglass and turned to them with a thoughtful look on her face. "Well, I was just thinking . . . if this Chaos Crystal channels the Tide, then it's going to play havoc with anybody using the Tide around it, isn't it? I mean . . . it's just an inanimate object. It can't *choose* what it wants to do. All it can do is channel the Tide and if what you say is true, then only Lukys really has any idea how to use it properly."

"So?" Diala asked, turning to look at Lyna, drawn back into the discussion in spite of herself. "What difference does that make?"

"Well, I don't know that it *will* make a difference," Lyna said with a shrug. "I'm really just speculating. But if it was me, and I was lugging around something so potentially powerful, I'd be very careful about using the Tide around it until I knew what was likely to happen."

"Which means they may have to travel back to Jelidia by conventional means," Declan said, understanding immediately what Lyna was getting at, "rather than travel on the Tide."

"Then perhaps your desperately noble plan has a chance of working after all, Hawkes," Diala said, and then, without warning, she tossed her wineglass across the room, where it shattered against the fireplace. "Damn you, Lukys. I'm supposed to be the Queen of Glaeba."

"You have to have a world before you can have a throne," Lyna pointed out. Declan got the feeling there was little love lost between the two women, and that Lyna was taking a certain perverse satisfaction in seeing Diala so peeved about losing her throne.

"I put a lot of work into getting that throne, Lyna. Tides, I slept with that fool boy for a year. I don't want to leave Glaeba now."

"You're queen of nothing," Jaxyn told her with a dismissive wave of his hand. "Syrolee is on her way across the lake as we speak, looking to be rid of all of us. She's won the war and she's on her way with the blood heir to the throne of Glaeba trotting at her heels, at the end of a very short leash she happens to be holding. A crown is no good if you have nobody to rule, Diala."

Diala glared at Jaxyn for a moment and then shrugged. "All right. Have it your way. But if we do manage to stop this disaster from happening, if we manage to prevent Lukys and Cayal from doing something stupid, when it's over, I want my own kingdom to rule."

"Tell you what! You can have the Commonwealth of Elenovia," Jaxyn said, although Declan had no idea where he thought he got the authority to make such a promise. "When we've saved the world, and the mortals are throwing themselves at us in base gratitude, I'll make you Queen of Elenovia. You can have the whole damned country, Diala. Right down to the silly names they give their towns and that godawful brandy they drink that tastes like horse piss. Fair enough?"

Diala thought on that for a moment and then nodded reluctantly. Then she glanced at Declan and Lyna. "You're witnesses to that, right? Elenovia is mine."

Declan nodded, but his insides were churning. This insane, desperate plan to save Amyrantha might prove worse than the alternative. He couldn't have cared less about Diala's plans for Elenovia.

All he could think was: *Tides, what have I done?*

Chapter 39

"Arkady?"

It was hard for Cayal to decide who was more shocked when Arkady appeared on the steps of the ruined Temple of the Tide. The horrified look that flickered over her face in that first unguarded moment told Cayal more than he wanted to know. Arkady was shocked. She was also looking rather the worse for wear. Her face was scratched, her coat torn, her hair a mess . . . and she clearly wasn't pleased to see him.

"Hello, Cayal."

He stared up at her for a moment, drinking in the bedraggled sight of her, and then he realised what he was doing and forced his expression into a more cynical mien. "Well, well, well. Look what the cat left lying about."

"You know this woman?" Elyssa asked, glaring at Arkady.

Cayal smiled, hoping he looked amused rather than dumbstruck. "Oh yes, I know her. This, my dear, is—I suppose—the new Queen of Glaeba."

"What are you talking about?"

"This is Stellan Desean's wife."

Elyssa eyed Arkady for a moment and then a nasty smile spread across her face. "His *wife?* The one Jaxyn was threatening to kill the other day if Desean didn't immediately surrender all of Caelum?"

"The very same. Lady Elyssa, meet the former Duchess of Lebec, Arkady Desean."

"What are you doing here?" Elyssa demanded. "Why aren't you dead?"

"I escaped the battle before the ice broke, my lady," Arkady said. She seemed shocked, but had her wits about her enough to choose her words carefully. "I made my way ashore and was looking for shelter when I found this place. What a stroke of luck that you found me." She smiled. Cayal knew her well enough to know how insincere a smile it was. She was lying through her teeth.

"Luck?" Kentravyon said. He pushed past Elyssa and Cayal, stopped long enough on the steps to examine Arkady and then looked around with interest. "No such thing as luck. Can you feel it?"

"Feel what?" Elyssa asked, her suspicious gaze still fixed on Arkady.

"The Chaos Crystal. It's here. Can't you feel it?"

"I can't feel anything," Elyssa said, a little impatiently.

"That's my point," Kentravyon said. "I can barely feel *you* on the Tide and you're standing five feet from me. It's the crystal doing that. Only time you're ever going to be able to sneak up on another immortal is when you're in the vicinity of the Chaos Crystal." He fixed his gaze on Arkady again. "Where is it, my dear? If you tell the truth, I promise not to hurt you. Too much."

Arkady stared at Kentravyon in confusion. "I *beg* your pardon?"

Oh, Tides, Cayal thought, hurrying forward to put himself between them. "Don't mind Kentravyon, Arkady. He doesn't mean to frighten you."

"Yes, I *do*," Kentravyon said, trying to push Cayal out of the way.

Arkady stepped back from the Tide Lord in alarm. "*That's* Kentravyon? And you're Elyssa?" She turned to him, looking more than a little panicked. "What's happening, Cayal? What are you doing *here*?"

"How dare you question him," Elyssa retorted, still glaring at Arkady suspiciously. "Cayal, how do you know this woman? You never mentioned her before."

"I was in Glaeba for quite a while, remember? I met a lot of people." He pushed Arkady behind him as he spoke, alarmed at the jealous edge to Elyssa's question.

Kentravyon looked almost as anxious as Elyssa to get hold of Arkady. "You'll be pleased to know your husband lives, my lady."

Although she kept glancing over Cayal's shoulder nervously at Kentravyon, Arkady seemed genuinely pleased to hear the news that Stellan was alive and well. "Is he all right?"

"Sailing for Glaeba to take his rightful place on the throne, last I heard," Elyssa assured her. Cayal didn't like the brittle tone of the Immortal Maiden's voice. The problem was, of course, Elyssa knew about Stellan's sexual preferences and was fully aware his marriage had been in name only.

"I'm sure Lady Elyssa would be happy to arrange for you to join him in Herino, once our business here is concluded," he said over his shoulder to Arkady, hoping to take Elyssa's mind off *his* relationship with Arkady and fix it on her husband instead.

"That's very . . . thoughtful of you," she said, her voice trembling just enough for Cayal to tell there was something seriously amiss here. Arkady removed all doubt when she asked with forced nonchalance, "What business could you possibly have in this old ruin?"

"That is none of your concern," Elyssa said, looking past Arkady at Kentravyon, who seemed to have lost interest in the mortal woman and was poking around the ruins behind them. "Can you tell where it is?"

"Not specifically," the madman called over his shoulder. "The dampening effect makes it hard to pinpoint. But it's definitely here somewhere. Everything on the Tide feels dulled. Only the crystal could be doing that."

"Tell where *what* is?" Arkady asked. "What's he talking about?"

Elyssa didn't deign to answer her. She climbed the crumbling steps, her skirts trailing in the snow, sparing Arkady a disdainful sneer as she pushed between her and Cayal and followed Kentravyon into the ruins. Cayal took Arkady by the arm, wishing he could get her alone long enough to explain what was going on. And to kiss her.

Kissing Arkady might get the taste of Elyssa out of his mouth.

"Be patient," he told her softly. "I'll explain everything later."

She glanced back at Elyssa. "Cayal, you have to leave this place."

He looked at her oddly. "Why?"

"There's nothing here for you."

"Kentravyon seems to think there is."

"What could you possibly want from this place full of bad memories?"

So she's figured out this is the place where Fliss died. Cayal wasn't surprised. Arkady knew the story and she was nobody's fool. It would not have taken her long to put two and two together. "We're looking for the Chaos Crystal. Apparently the Cabal hid it here." Cupping his hands, he added with a smile, "I believe it's about so big . . . channels the Tide . . . probably glows in the dark. Haven't seen it lying about, have you?"

Arkady's eyes were wild. He'd never seen her in such a state. "Cayal, *please*," she hissed. "Get them away from here. Even if it's only for an hour."

He looked at her oddly. "What are you hiding, Arkady?"

"Nothing that concerns you."

"I can smell smoke," Elyssa remarked behind them, sniffing the breeze. "Does anybody else smell it?"

"I made a fire to keep warm," Arkady told her. She was speaking for Elyssa's benefit but her panicked gaze was locked on Cayal, silently pleading for his help. He didn't know what was going on here, but there was definitely *something* here she didn't want the others to find.

"Where?" Elyssa asked, stepping over one of the frost-covered fallen pillars as she looked around. "I see no fire here."

"Aren't there several more levels to this place?" Kentravyon called from somewhere inside. He was lost in the shadows, poking about, looking for the stairs that led down into the bowels of the temple. "I seem to remember something like that."

"They've probably collapsed by now," Cayal said. "Or been flooded. It's been a couple of thousand years at least since anybody's used this place. Let me go down and have a look." The relief on Arkady's face when he offered to investigate the lower levels rather than allow the others down there heightened his suspicion. "You'd better come with me, your future highness," he added to Arkady in a rough tone, mostly to ease Elyssa's mind. "I'm not letting you out of my sight until we decide what to do with you."

Arkady willingly complied, letting him lead her into the temple. He directed her unerringly toward the stairs that led to the lower floors, tugging her with more force than was absolutely necessary, when Elyssa glanced over at them.

When he reached what should have been a ruined doorway and discovered it covered by a makeshift leather curtain, his suspicion that there was something going on here solidified into absolute certainty. Arkady hadn't thrown a curtain up in the last few days after stumbling ashore during the battle.

Cayal pushed the leather curtain aside, bent a little to avoid banging his head on the lintel and stepped through onto the landing, pulling Arkady inside with him. It was dark inside, and the air smelled of canines, smoke and cooked meat. As soon as he let the leather fall back into place and they were out of sight of Elyssa and Kentravyon, he pushed Arkady against the wall in the darkness and kissed her.

For a moment, she kissed him back, almost as if she'd forgotten she was mad at him. And then she broke it off and pushed him away impatiently.

"Tides, Cayal, what are you doing here?" she demanded. "And with them?" Arkady brushed her mouth after she spoke, as if trying to wipe away the taste of him.

"I could ask you the same thing," he said, stroking the hair from her scratched and battered face. Her eyes were shining in the darkness and all he could think of was how he wanted her as much as he didn't want Elyssa.

Tides, the sooner I die, the sooner I'll stop getting myself into trouble like this.

"What are you hiding down there that you don't want the others to see?"

She stared at him for a moment, debating how far she could trust him, he didn't doubt. "You have to promise me you'll not say a word."

"About what?"

"I'm not telling you until you promise."

"All right then. I promise."

"You have to mean it."

"Tides, Arkady, what do you want from me?" he asked, wondering if he could get away with kissing her again. "Should we spit in our palms and seal the deal like real men?"

She pushed him away harder this time. "This is important, Cayal. If Elyssa discovers who else is here, she'll kill them."

Now Cayal was intrigued. "Who else *is* here?"

When she refused to answer him, he added impatiently, "I give you my word, Arkady. Your dire secret is safe with me."

Arkady studied him warily for a moment longer and then nodded. "Come with me. I'll show you."

Cayal followed her down the crumbling stairs to the room below which turned out to be quite well appointed for an abandoned ruin. There was a pallet made up in the corner, scattered with furs, a sizeable fireplace glowing red in the darkness and a pile of supplies stacked next to a makeshift barricade around the landing to the next level down. On his left were the "who elses" Arkady was so desperate to save from discovery. They turned out to be a family of canine Crasii. There was a young female with three pups cowering down next to another pallet with a prone figure, probably their sire. And a wounded sire at that. Cayal could smell the infection on him from across the room.

"All this subterfuge and secrecy for a family of flanking *gemang*?" he asked, wondering what was so special about these particular canines that had Arkady in such a panic.

"Oh, wonderful!" the female hissed at Arkady, pulling her pups to her as she glared at Cayal. "This is your idea of protecting us, is it?"

Significantly, the canine did not fall at his feet to assure her lord and master that to serve him was the reason she breathed. At the very least, the female must be a Scard. It hardly mattered what the injured male was, Cayal thought. He smelled as if he was only hours away from death.

"Cayal can help."

"I don't *want* his help. Just get rid of him."

"It's not me you have to fear, *gemang*," Cayal told her, walking closer to the prone male to get a better look at him. "I have friends upstairs who Arkady seems fairly certain you don't want to meet."

The female's eyes fixed on Arkady.

"Elyssa's out there," she said.

The young canine's big brown eyes filled with angry, fearful tears. "Tides, you've brought them down on us! I *knew* I shouldn't have let you stay! First you kill my mate, then you bring *them* here . . ."

"He's not actually dead yet," Cayal pointed out, squatting down beside the barely conscious male. The female pulled back in fear, but her cubs seemed to be struggling to be free of her so they could get closer to him. Cayal didn't stop to wonder what that meant. He pulled the covers back to get a look at her mate and then smiled at the delicious irony when he realised who it was that lay bleeding and dying at his feet.

He glanced up at Arkady. Nodding approvingly. "You did this?"

"It was an accident."

"You know who this is, don't you?"

"Of course I do."

Cayal sat back on his heels. "Tides, I warned the stupid *gemang* I'd be there to watch him die someday."

"You have to heal him."

Cayal rose to his feet, shaking his head. "The hell I do."

Arkady glanced up the stairs before pleading with him. "Elyssa thinks she owns these Crasii. If she finds them here she'll realise they're runaway Scards and kill them."

"And this is my problem . . . *how* exactly?"

The female growled low in her throat. Arkady glared at him. "Stop it, Cayal. I know you're only saying that to get a rise out of me."

"I'm not going to heal him, Arkady. This smug mongrel gloated over my pain every moment he spent on Recidivists' Row opposite me. Let him die. What do I care?"

"If you won't do it for him, then do it for me."

That wasn't fair. He threw up his hands. "What's the point? Elyssa's going to come down those stairs any minute. And even if I did as you asked, if I heal him with the Tide the others will feel it the moment I do anything and they'll come running."

Arkady shook her head. "No they won't. Kentravyon said something is deadening the Tide around here. They can't even feel *you* at the moment. You can heal him, let Warlock and his family get away, and the others need never know."

"What do I get in return?"

"What?"

"What's in it for me?"

"Tides, Cayal, we don't have time for this."

"Then you'd better make me an offer I can't refuse."

"What do you want?" the female canine asked. "If it's the human woman, you can have her, suzerain. We have no further use for her."

He smiled at the canine. "Nice loyal friends you've got there, Arkady."

"Heal him, Cayal," she insisted.

"Why?"

Arkady hesitated, as if she was debating something within herself, and then she shrugged fatalistically and said the last thing Cayal was expecting to hear.

"Because I know where your wretched crystal is."

Chapter 40

Arkady Desean figured she knew what it felt like to tumble off a cliff. She knew exactly what it must feel like to discover you were plummeting from a great and dizzy height toward your doom. That's exactly how she'd been feeling ever since they tied her to the Justice Tree in Watershed Falls back in Senestra. Back before Declan appeared out of nowhere to save her because he was now immortal and could wield the Tide. Before Lyna found her and brought her back to Glaeba. Before she'd discovered her father still lived. Before her father had tried to kill himself for reasons Arkady was still unsure about, but she suspected were mostly cowardice. Before Clyden Bell died. Before the battle. Before she'd turned her back on her father and proved she was a coward too, by abandoning him to die on the ice. Before she'd stumbled over Boots and the pups. Before she'd tried to kill Warlock.

It seemed as if there hadn't been a moment in the last few months when she wasn't in danger, putting someone else in danger, or making decisions that might have disastrous consequences for everyone she knew and cared about.

As for Cayal's appearance in this place, at this time—Arkady had given up trying to explain how or why her life seemed so intertwined with the fate of the Immortal Prince. She'd done nothing but what had, at the time, seemed the right thing to do. And yet, somehow, it always led back to Cayal. Somehow, no matter what she did, no matter how hard she tried to escape him, she wound up in the same place, time and time again.

Cayal was staring at her in disbelief. "You *know* where the Chaos Crystal is?"

"Help Warlock," she told him. "I'm not saying another word until you save him." Arkady didn't know if her threats meant anything. She was fairly certain they wouldn't have any impact at all if Cayal realised the Chaos Crystal lay barely ten feet from where he was standing, kicked carelessly under the furs to keep it out of sight of the canine puppies who'd been using it as a chew toy for the past few days.

At least, Arkady *assumed* the oddly glowing quartz skull the pups had found behind the crumbled wall on the lower level was the magical crystal Kentravyon was searching for.

I mean, how many glowing magical crystals could the Cabal have hidden in this place?

Cayal was staring at her suspiciously. "How do I know you'll keep your word?"

"Should we spit in our palms and seal the deal like *real* men?"

He debated the matter for a moment longer and then swore under his breath, before kneeling down beside Warlock. He placed his hand on the dying canine's belly, over the wound Arkady had inflicted in her haste. Boots backed away from them, pulling the pups to her. Cayal drew on the Tide. He seemed surprised at the effort it took, a fact Arkady attributed to the nearness of the crystal. A few moments later, Warlock howled in agony, his body spasming in torment and then he lay still, only the faint rise and fall of his chest giving any hint that he was still alive.

Cayal stood up, wiped his hands on his trousers and turned to Arkady. "There. It's done. Where is it? I know it's here somewhere."

Boots scrambled on her hands and knees to Warlock and pulled back the bandages. She looked up at Arkady in amazement. "The wound is gone. Completely."

"Of course it is," Cayal said over his shoulder, sounding a little hurt that Boots might doubt him. He fixed his unsettling gaze on Arkady. "Where's the crystal?"

"You have to help them get away first."

"The deal was that I heal him, Arkady, and then you give me the crystal."

"Heal him and help them get away. Those are my conditions. Can you distract Elyssa and Kentravyon for long enough?"

"I'm sure he could," a harsh female voice remarked from atop the landing. "The question that you should be asking yourself, my dear, is why he'd betray his own kind for a cheap little slut like you."

With a feeling of nauseating despair washing over her, Arkady closed her eyes for a moment and wondered why she had ever thought herself clever enough to save Warlock and his family from the immortals. Everything she'd done thus far in that direction had proved spectacularly unsuccessful.

She looked up in time to watch Elyssa descending the stairs slowly,

Kentravyon close on her heels, taking in the scene below—Boots, War-lock, the pups, and Cayal—with the air of a mother who'd just caught her children doing something very, very naughty. Kentravyon didn't seem interested in the Crasii. He was looking around, scanning the dark lair anxiously. In such proximity to the Chaos Crystal, he could feel its presence, and it seemed to be all he was interested in.

"Does this woman mean anything to you, Cayal?"

"Of course not," he said without so much as a flicker of hesitation.

"Then you won't mind if I kill her."

"Be my guest."

Arkady stared at Cayal in horror. *"What?"*

Elyssa smiled and turned on Arkady. "You sound so surprised, my dear. Did you think he cared for you?"

"Cayal?" Arkady couldn't believe he would just stand there while Elyssa murdered her, but that seemed to be what he was prepared to do. He refused to give her any hint of how she was supposed to respond.

"I think you know her better than you're letting on," Elyssa said, turn-ing to Cayal with a disapproving frown. "Is there something you want to tell me about her?"

"I find her very desirable," Cayal replied with a shrug. "Tides, any man with a pulse would. But I've no particular affection for her. Kill her if you want." He folded his arms across his body, a study in noncha-lant disinterest. "You might want to check with Kentravyon before you do it, though."

"Why?"

"She knows where the Chaos Crystal is."

"She could be telling you that just to save her neck."

"Well, you'd know best, my dear. Have you finished wasting time over there, Kentravyon?" he called over his shoulder. "Or should we just ask the person who's hiding the damn thing where it is?"

Kentravyon looked up at that, and turned from poking into the dark nooks and crannies of the underground chamber to stare at Arkady. "Hah! Didn't I say she knew?"

Behind Cayal, Warlock groaned as he regained consciousness. Arkady silently prayed he had the wit not to draw any further attention to him-self. Elyssa was focused on her at the moment, and had yet to remark on the unexplained presence of her slaves and their puppies in the ruin.

Inexplicably, in the presence of the immortals, the normally boisterous puppies had become remarkably subdued.

Kentravyon approached Arkady, his bulk blocking her view of Cayal, Elyssa and the Crasii. It took all her strength not to flinch. "You have to let them go!"

The mad Tide Lord stopped and stared at her oddly. "What?"

"I'll tell you where it is, but you have to let the others go."

"What others?"

"The Crasii. Let them leave and I'll tell you where it is."

"They're not going anywhere," Elyssa announced flatly. "They're mine and I'm going to strip their filthy Scard hides from their bones and then feed the meat to their own puppies."

So much for Elyssa not noticing the Scards.

"Charming," Arkady thought she heard Cayal mutter behind Kentravyon, although she couldn't see him because the looming presence of the Tide Lord blocked her line of sight.

"Tides, just kill her, Kentravyon," Elyssa said impatiently. She turned to the canines. "And then I'll kill the Scards, we'll find the stone and we can be gone from here."

"We can't kill them all," Kentravyon said, not taking his eyes from Arkady. She faced him gamely, but it took every ounce of courage she owned not to take a step backward. Cayal did nothing, seemingly content to let things unravel as they would, interested in saving neither her nor the Crasii.

"Why not?" Elyssa asked.

"We'll need one of them to carry the Chaos Crystal."

"We're not letting any filthy mortal touch it!" she objected.

"It's not about letting mortals touch it. The Chaos Crystal channels the Tide. It affects anybody *connected* to the Tide, and the more closely you're connected, the more trouble it'll give you. Unless you have enough solid gold handy to completely encase it, you won't be able to hold it for more than a few minutes without driving you insane, Elyssa. Believe me. I know."

Arkady wondered if that was the reason Kentravyon was mad, something the Tarot was quite vague about. Someone, after all, had taken the trouble to fashion it into the shape of a skull. If it was this Tide Lord who'd carved it, perhaps that explained his insanity.

"What does gold do to it?" Elyssa asked.

"It shields the dampening effect. Don't know why. Just does. Why do you think Maralyce was after so much of it?"

Cayal nodded in understanding. "Because she knew if she ever found the Bedlam Stone she'd not be able to carry it anywhere unless she could shield it."

Elyssa didn't seem very interested in Maralyce's motives for anything. "Tides, if it's such a problem, then one of the Scards can carry it."

"We'd rather die than lift a finger to help the suzerain," Warlock growled, taking with him any hope that the Scard and his family might survive this encounter.

Tides, Warlock, Arkady thought in despair, *couldn't you have pretended to be Crasii for a few moments longer?*

"One of you will carry it or I'll kill your puppies and make you eat them," Elyssa said in a chillingly uninterested voice. "Choose now."

"We are not taking a litter of flanking *gemang* all the way back to Jelidia with us," Cayal declared, sounding very annoyed.

Kentravyon turned to look at him, stepping back a little as he did so, which meant Arkady could now see everyone again. Warlock was on his feet, Boots and the pups behind him against the far wall near the fire-pit, the light from the flames casting demonic shadows on his features. He looked ready to die to protect his family, an eventuality that Arkady was afraid was all too likely if things didn't improve in the next few minutes.

Elyssa stepped in front of them, hands on her hips. Arkady's heart lodged somewhere in the back of her throat as she waited for the Immortal Maiden to strike them down. Before Elyssa could act, however, Cayal moved up beside her, cast his gaze over the Crasii for a moment and then fixed his attention on the Immortal Maiden. "The time for silly pets is done, Lyssa. Let them go. Arkady knows where the crystal is and she can carry it to Jelidia for us. If you promise to release these wretched creatures she's so fond of, out into the snow, I'll wager she'll even do it willingly."

The immortal woman glared at him impatiently. *Cayal's right*, Arkady decided. *She really is a thoroughly unattractive young woman.*

"They have betrayed me, Cayal. Why, in the name of the Tide, would I even consider letting them go?"

Cayal slipped his arm around her waist and pulled her to him, but right at the point Arkady feared he might kiss the Immortal Maiden, he gently turned her around until she was facing Arkady. With both arms around Elyssa's waist, his mouth nuzzling her ear from behind, he smiled. "Look at her. Look past the scratches and the dirt. Look at the new you, Lyssa," he said. "Men from one end of Amyrantha to the other have lusted after that body. Declan Hawkes would die for her, if he could. Even Jaxyn wants her, and you know how hard he is to impress. She's probably the most beautiful mortal woman alive on Amyrantha."

Despite Cayal's glowing compliments, Arkady got the feeling his praise wasn't meant to help her. She had no idea what was happening between Cayal and Elyssa. Cayal's words made no sense and she didn't like the way Elyssa was looking her up and down as if she was a particularly juicy side of beef.

"When the Tide peaks that could be *you*, Lyssa," Cayal added in a smiling, seductive voice, his lips next to her ear. "Tall, elegant, beautiful . . . free of pain . . ."

Elyssa seemed doubtful, but not completely unconvinced—although of what Cayal was trying to persuade her remained a complete mystery to Arkady.

"But she's not immortal. Or even close."

"Doesn't matter," Kentravyon said with a shrug. "I mean, it's *easier* to make the transfer with someone who's part immortal, I suppose, but not impossible. That flanking rat wasn't immortal, and it worked for Lukys and Coryna." He turned to give Arkady a considering look. "Cayal's right, you know. You could do a lot worse."

"Do you love her, Cayal?" Elyssa asked softly.

Arkady held her breath wishing she knew what Cayal's answer might be. And whether or not the answer would make things better or worse. Being loved by the Immortal Prince was not something likely to endear her to the Immortal Maiden, she realised, and since she'd last seen Cayal, clearly the relationship between him and Elyssa had undergone some radical changes.

"I want her," Cayal admitted after a long moment. His eyes met Arkady's but she couldn't tell if he was lying to save her, or telling the truth and just didn't care enough about her to pretend otherwise.

"Will you want me too?"

"I want you now, Lyssa."

"No, you don't. You *need* me now."

"And every moment we waste here debating the issue, the Tide is coming in."

Elyssa frowned at Arkady and then threw her hands up, pushing Cayal away. "Oh, Tides, what do I care about a pack of flanking *gemang*, anyway? Get them out of my sight."

The Scards didn't need to be told twice.

Warlock snatched two of the oddly quiescent pups from the floor, took Boots—who was still clutching Missy—by the arm and they all fled up the crumbling stairs. The pups started to cry for some reason.

Arkady wondered if it was because they were Crasii and didn't want to be taken from the presence of the immortal masters they were created to please.

Arkady watched them leave, her heart pounding. She didn't know what would become of the canines; she only hoped they had the sense to get away while they still could.

Once the leather flap fell back into place after the Scards' departure, Elyssa turned to Arkady. "All right. They're gone. Where is it?"

Arkady hesitated as long as she dared before pointing to the pile of furs the puppies had been using as a bed. "It's over there."

The three Tide Lords stared at the furs for a moment, a little stunned, Arkady thought, to realise their prize was so close.

"Fetch it," Elyssa ordered.

Arkady did as the immortal asked, seeing no point in fighting her just yet. Something was going on here that she didn't understand, but she'd been able to win Warlock and his family their escape. She was determined to give them as much time as she could before she made her own bid for freedom.

Squaring her shoulders, Arkady crossed the room to the pallet, threw back the furs and picked up the skull. She turned to the immortals and held it out in front of her. Although she could feel nothing unusual herself, the skull began to glow an angry, fiery red as she held it out toward the Tide Lords. Even Kentravyon took a step back.

"This is what you're after, isn't it?"

"Tides," Cayal said, staring at it in surprise. "It's a skull."

"That's not a skull, fool," Kentravyon said, sounding a little hurt. "It's me."

"You made the Chaos Crystal look like you?"

"How else were we supposed to tell it apart from all the other crystals?"

Cayal rolled his eyes. "You mean the bright red glow didn't give it away?"

"On the world where we found this crystal, they all glowed," Kentravyon informed him loftily, without offering any further information about the origins of the Chaos Crystal. "It's not a good idea to channel the Tide around it, by the way. Not until we get back to Jelidia."

"Why not?" Elyssa asked, staring at it as if it held the meaning of life.

"Because it's unpredictable. If you can't focus it properly, it'll end up causing more trouble than it's worth. Trust me."

"But that means travelling by conventional means," Cayal said, looking less than pleased. "That will take weeks. Maybe months."

"We've time yet, before the Tide peaks," Kentravyon assured them. "Provided we don't hang around here any longer than we have to."

"I should let Mother know where I am," Elyssa said.

"Why? Were you planning to invite Syrolee to join us in Jelidia?"

"Of course not."

"Then let's get out of here. Out of Caelum," Cayal said. "We have what we came for."

Elyssa considered the suggestion for a moment, then shrugged and pointed to Arkady. "What if she tries to escape?"

"Then we'll kill her and find another pretty girl for you," Kentravyon said. "Won't we, Cayal?"

Cayal nodded. "Absolutely."

Elyssa seemed satisfied with that. She turned on her heel and headed up the stairs. Kentravyon followed, leaving Cayal and Arkady alone. She lowered the skull, slipping it into the large pocket of her coat, the glow fading as the Tide Lords departed.

"Cayal, what's going on here?"

"I'll explain later." He reached out to her, almost as if he wanted to take her in his arms.

Arkady took a step back from him. "I want to know now."

"And if I take the time to explain, she'll kill you," he said, a flat statement of fact Arkady didn't doubt for a moment. "Just trust me, Arkady. I won't let anything happen to you."

It was a lot to ask, and before Arkady could answer, Elyssa appeared on the landing at the top of the steps. "Cayal? Are you coming?"

He sighed and gestured with his arm that Arkady should precede him up the stairs. With the crystal skull heavy in her pocket, she blinked in the bright daylight reflecting off the snow outside as she emerged from the ruined temple.

Without saying a word, Arkady followed Elyssa and Kentravyon toward the lake, with Cayal coming up behind her to ensure she didn't try to make a break for it.

A short time later, they stopped at the edge of the lake to discover Elyssa cursing like a sailor.

"What's the matter?" Cayal asked.

Elyssa was standing beside a battered, barely seaworthy rowboat that looked incapable of holding one person, let alone three or four of them. It was not, Arkady guessed, the same craft the Tide Lords had arrived in.

Her expression was thunderous as she stared down at the fragile dinghy. "Those flanking *gemang* stole our boat."

PART 3

The boundaries which divide Life from Death are at best shadowy and vague. Who shall say where the one ends and where the other begins?
                              "The Premature Burial"
                    —Edgar Allan Poe (1809–1849)

Chapter 41

If Tiji had learned anything in her time as a spy for the King of Glaeba's Spymaster, it was to smell when something was awry. She'd developed a sense for trouble, an ability to detect a web of lies, even when it
was invisible. She had that feeling now, here in the Palace of Impossible
Dreams, and for the life of her, she couldn't put her finger on the cause
of her disquiet.

Tiji's solution, naturally, was to snoop around until she discovered
the source of her suspicions, a course of action that had brought her
here this morning, far into the labyrinthine ice tunnels below the palace. She could feel the suzerain down here somewhere; smell their rank
aroma ahead of her. She had never been this far beyond the storerooms
below the palace before, and feared Azquil would be furious if he discovered she was down here now.

A strange winding ice staircase surrounded by walls glowing with an
eerie greenish light gave Tiji pause. Swallowing back the lump of fear
lodged in her throat, she crept ahead. She was able to hear people talking ahead of her, but unable to differentiate individual voices enough to
identify who was speaking to whom. She thought Maralyce might be
down here, along with Lukys and maybe even Pellys. She knew Lukys's
mortal wife, Oritha, had to be down here, because it was Oritha that
Tiji was following.

She took the steps silently, holding her breath, trying to avoid disturbing the moss that was providing the eerie green glow that lit the
staircase. The red-tinged light at the bottom of the stairs grew stronger,
the voices clearer. Flattening herself against the freezing wall once she
was past the moss, wishing it wasn't so cold she was required to wear
furs—which completely negated her camouflage abilities—Tiji stopped
when she reached the antechamber at the foot of the stairs and peered
cautiously around the corner.

The sight that greeted her made the little Crasii gasp. The small
outer chamber at the foot of the stairs opened into a vast circular hall
that stretched away into the distance. From what she could see, it was
almost perfectly round, the curved and ribbed walls lit by a ring of fire

that circled the chamber at the base of the walls, as if the very ice itself was on fire. At the centre of the room there was a raised circular platform made of solid ice beside which Lukys and Maralyce stood. There was no sign of Pellys but lying on the ice altar—Tiji could think of no better description for it—was someone wearing the same coat Oritha wore the last time Tiji saw her when she had been heading this way. It was hard to tell from where Tiji was standing, but the young woman lay still as death on the altar, which was remarkable, because Tiji was quite certain she'd only been a few paces behind Oritha on the way down here.

Tiji stared at the odd scene, which soon became even stranger when she caught sight of something small and furry moving on the altar beside Oritha. It took her a moment to realise it was some sort of rodent.

"Are you sure about this, Lukys?" Maralyce was asking her companion as Tiji strained to hear what they were saying.

The immortal woman stood looking down at Oritha, her arms crossed, oblivious to the rat scurrying around the young woman's body. The curved walls of the vast chamber amplified the voices to the point where it sounded as if Tiji was standing beside them, and not far away at the entrance to the cavern.

"Coryna is sure."

"You're guessing that, Lukys. You know as well as I do that she's hardly in a fit state to make a rational judgement about anything but her next meal." Maralyce seemed to notice the rat for the first time. "If you get this wrong . . ."

"I won't," Lukys said.

"And are you absolutely certain Oritha is suitable?"

"As certain as I can be."

Maralyce was silent for a moment and then nodded. "I suppose, if worse comes to worst, in an emergency you could use one of the Crasii."

Tiji shivered, and not because of the ice cavern. *What's going on here? What are they plotting, down here in this secret chamber?*

And what's that got to do with the Crasii?

Lukys shook his head. "We've considered that. Notwithstanding the unlikelihood of a Crasii surviving the surge, Coryna would be reluctant to take up residence in a body that might retain its compulsion to obey the wishes of another immortal."

"A valid concern," Maralyce conceded. "Still, there's Arryl's two Scards here at the moment. At a pinch, one of them might suffice."

Lukys seemed to find that amusing. "The idea is to *improve* her situation. I'm not sure Coryna would appreciate being made into a lizard until the next King Tide, Maralyce. Even a part-human one. Still, it may be worth keeping one in reserve when the time comes. Just in case."

Tiji frowned. *Who are they talking about? Who is Coryna?*

"I imagine my sister will have a few words to say about her current predicament, once she regains her voice," Maralyce agreed. "But shouldn't you wait until the others bring us the Chaos Crystal before starting this?"

Lukys shook his head. "They'd feel me working the Tide if they were here. I'd have far too many awkward questions to answer." He smiled down at his unconscious young wife. "She must be on the brink of death for this to succeed. I learned *that* the last time, too. Her heartbeat needs to be so slow it's barely moving, her consciousness so completely immersed there will be no resistance . . ."

"You don't think the others are going to ask what she's doing here, laid out like a human sacrifice, when you open the rift?"

"I suppose we'll have to tell them before we start," Lukys assured her. He smiled. "Learning I have my own agenda won't really surprise anybody."

"And if they object?"

"They mustn't," Lukys warned.

"But if they do?"

The white-haired Tide Lord shrugged. "By then, it shouldn't matter. They're all going to be here to help for their own reasons, after all. Kentravyon wants to know if we can do this. Cayal wants to die. Declan's still mortal enough to believe he'll be helping rid Amyrantha of immortals. And I suspect he's not averse to helping put an end to Cayal, either. Taryx believes opening the rift will make him stronger, and Arryl, well, she's a stickler for repaying debts. She'll help because she feels she must."

"Provided she doesn't realise the consequences."

"Well, I won't mention them if you don't," Lukys said, a little impatiently.

Maralyce glared at him, annoyed perhaps at his tone. "You haven't asked why *I've* agreed to help."

Lukys smiled, his impatience vanishing as if it had never been. "I don't need to ask you, Maralyce. I know why."

"Why?"

"Because you love her as much as I do."

Love who? Tiji was itching to know. *Tides, what*—who—*are they talking about?*

"Then know this, Lukys, that if you screw things up again, my wrath will be . . . dangerous."

"I know."

"How do you intend to proceed?"

"Carefully. Despite the inconvenience caused by having the damn thing stolen from us, this quest to find the Bedlam Stone has been an unexpected boon. It's certainly got the others out from underfoot while I lay the necessary groundwork." Lukys held out his hand. The rat scurried up his arm and took up residence on his shoulder. The Tide Lord idly scratched at the rat's chin and said, "You worry unnecessarily, Maralyce. We've been planning this for a very long time."

Maralyce didn't seem convinced by his reassurances. "That's what you said the last time, Lukys."

"I'll admit there were some . . . *unfortunate* consequences that time," he conceded. "But this time . . ." He stopped, reaching forward to stroke Oritha's hair. "I made her very beautiful, don't you think? A worthy vessel for my queen."

"She's very beautiful," Maralyce agreed. "And in the process of making your beautiful vessel, you've foisted another immortal upon us."

Lukys looked up. "You mean Declan?"

"You promised me you'd not make him immortal, Lukys."

"And I kept my promise. *I* didn't make him immortal. He did it all by himself. And I can't say I'm sorry. The only remaining doubt about this has always been exactly what mix it required to be certain the mortal body would survive immolation. Now we know."

Maralyce was silent for a time, staring at Oritha's unconscious form, and then she looked up. "Do you need my help?"

Lukys shook his head. "Not for this part."

Maralyce stepped back from the altar. "I'll leave you to it then." She glanced down at Oritha one last time. "When you invited her down here, I wonder if the poor girl had any idea she was going to die?"

Tiji stifled a gasp, even though she was far enough away for it not to be heard by the Tide Lords. But she'd seen enough, too much . . . and Maralyce was turning for the entrance.

Tides, they're killing Oritha . . .

Or were they? What had Lukys said? *She must be on the brink of death for this to succeed. I learned that the last time, too. Her heartbeat needs to be so slow it's barely moving, her consciousness so completely immersed there will be no resistance . . .*

Maralyce was getting closer. Her mind swirling with the possibilities, Tiji turned and fled up the ice stairs toward the levels above, wondering how she could prevent this travesty from taking place. For that matter, who would she even tell about it? The immortals didn't see life the same way mortal creatures did. Even Arryl would probably take the line that Oritha was Lukys's wife and if he wanted to freeze her so he could use her as a vessel for his queen—whatever that meant—he was quite within his rights to do so.

Tides, I wish Declan was here, Tiji thought as she slipped and slithered along the icy tunnels above the secret chamber. If she was caught down here, Tiji had no doubt about her fate. Lukys and Maralyce were in cahoots over something seriously nasty. And obviously important. So important, Oritha must die for it and all the other immortals prevented from learning the truth.

This was a secret too large for one small chameleon Crasii to bear.

Her heart pounding, Tiji raced up the glowing green stairs to the next level, slipping on the ice near the concealed entrance as she scurried ahead. She was back in the corridor where the palace stores were kept. Tiji could hear Maralyce coming, and here she was, shaking like a sapling in a high wind, without the breath to run any further without being caught.

Her training as Declan's spy kicked in without her consciously thinking about it. Tiji ducked into the nearest alcove to discover a dark ice cave filled with barrels of apples, pears, peaches, and various other exotic fruits from foreign places like the Chelae Islands. Although the immortals did not need to eat to maintain life, they liked their food and they had mortal servants to feed. She grabbed a small basket off the floor, stuffed a few pieces of fruit in it and turned, just as Maralyce emerged from the concealed steps that led to the lower level.

"My lady," Tiji said with a deep bow as the immortal passed her by.

"Good morning, Tiji."

"To serve you is the reason I breathe, my lady," she blurted out before she could stop herself.

The comment gave Maralyce pause. She stopped and looked over her shoulder with an odd expression. "You're a Scard, Tiji. You don't mean a word of that."

Tiji shrugged, smiling nervously. "It seems like the right thing to say around here."

Maralyce studied her in silence for a moment and then smiled. "What a strange little creature you are."

And with that, the Tide Lord went on her way, leaving Tiji clutching her basket of apples at the entrance to the storeroom, her palms sweating, her scales flickering and her heart beating so loudly in terror it was a wonder the sound wasn't echoing off the walls, alerting everyone in the palace to her fears.

Chapter 42

The arrival of a Tide Lord at Hidden Valley was perhaps the most traumatic thing that had ever happened to the Scards who lived there. And many of them had suffered unthinkable traumas at the hands of their human masters before finding their way to this one place on Amyrantha where they believed they were safe.

It was just on dusk when Declan arrived at the hidden settlement, approaching slowly on horseback rather than using faster, magical means. Although time was critical now, he did not wish to exacerbate a delicate situation by arriving at this den of immortal hatred, flaunting his newfound magical powers.

Lord Aleki Ponting was waiting for him, on foot, between the snow-covered walls of the narrow chasm that led into Hidden Valley. It was bitterly cold, an icy wind dancing around their ankles as Aleki stepped forward. He was holding a drawn sword and was flanked by a score of felines, claws bared, all ready to fight to protect their home. Tilly had warned her son that Declan was coming, of course, and that his former comrade-in-arms was now an immortal, but there was only so much information one could fit on a note small enough for a bird to carry.

Much of his tale, Declan knew, he was going to have to tell Aleki and the Scards of Hidden Valley himself.

Declan reined in his horse within earshot of his welcoming party. He waited for a moment, leaning on the pommel of his saddle, studying them warily. Aleki's cloak billowed out behind him, his expression impossible to read. The naked blade, however, gave Declan a pretty clear idea of where Aleki's sentiments lay.

"You know you can't kill me with that thing," Declan said after a time, pointing to the sword. The long blade glinted in the light of the setting sun, ominous but futile.

"Doesn't mean I wouldn't like to try," Aleki responded in an equally conversational tone. His breath frosted in the icy air but he didn't sound particularly cold or unfriendly. He'd come to greet Declan with a drawn sword and a phalanx of fighting felines at his back, however. He wasn't exactly rolling out the welcome mat.

"What's with the escort?" Declan asked, indicating the felines.

Aleki glanced at them and then shrugged. "They're here to remind you that not every Crasii on Amyrantha breathes merely to serve your kind."

"You think so?" Declan asked. He was a little annoyed at Aleki for implying he was no longer on their side. And he had a job to do here, as well as a point to prove. So he didn't answer Aleki directly. Instead, he turned to the felines and called, "Bow before your master!"

A good half of them did exactly that, dropping to their knees in the snow at his command. Aleki looked around in shock, and then raised the sword. "What are you doing?"

"Nothing more than proving a point," Declan said, dismounting slowly. He tossed the reins over the neck of his mount. "A Scard isn't a Scard because they've defied their human masters, Aleki. They're only genuine Scards if they're not compelled to obey the immortals. And they're a damn sight rarer than you think. Get up," he added to the kneeling felines, which had them scrambling to their feet.

Declan stepped up to Aleki's blade, not stopping until it was pressing against his chest. "Are you going to run me through to satisfy yourself this is real, or can we dispense with the formalities and get down to business? I'd prefer the latter, personally. For one, I'd rather not ruin this shirt, and for another, time is of the essence. But if you really feel you must . . ."

Aleki stared at Declan for a long moment, the blade poised over Declan's heart, while Tilly's son debated within himself the advisability of trying to kill an immortal he once called a friend. After a long, tense silence, he sighed heavily and lowered the blade.

"What did you just do to my Scards?"

"Nothing," Declan said. "Your mistake is *assuming* they're Scards. You'll find a lot of them are not. They're just recalcitrant Crasii, pissed off with their human masters whom they have the free will to obey or disobey as they please. Trust me, Aleki, the Crasii can't help it. They have no loyalty to you, even though they may think they do, and fully intend to follow you all the way to the gates of hell. Crasii must do the bidding of any immortal they meet. And until they meet a true immortal, you have no real notion of whether or not they're actually a Scard or a Crasii."

Aleki glanced around at the squad that he had—presumably—considered his most trustworthy Scards, at least half of which, it was now clear, would betray him in a heartbeat if an immortal commanded them to. "Can you tell the difference?"

Declan nodded. "It's not easy to tell a Scard who's pretending to be a Crasii, but there is no way a Crasii can pretend to be a Scard in the presence of an immortal. It's one of the reasons Tilly suggested I come here before I leave."

"So you can weed out your magically compelled minions and use them for your own nefarious purposes?" a young grey and white tabby standing behind Aleki spat contemptuously at Declan.

He turned to the feline, glaring at her. "On your knees, insolent cat!"

"Go to hell, suzerain!"

Declan smiled at Aleki and pointed to the tabby. "Now *she's* a Scard."

Aleki was frowning. It had probably never occurred to him that a good half of his secret Scard army weren't actually Scards. "What do you suggest we do?"

"Let me identify the true Scards for you," Declan suggested. "And then make sure the Crasii among you never leave this place, because the first thing they'll do if they run across an immortal—no matter how well intentioned you think they are—is tell them where Hidden Valley is."

Declan's announcement had an interesting effect on the felines. Those who had not knelt at Declan's command began to distance themselves subtly from those who had, as the danger their magically compelled sisters represented dawned on them. Even Aleki glanced at them thoughtfully for a moment and then, after giving the Crasii a long, considering look, he sheathed his sword and turned back to Declan.

"Some of them may not wish to be identified."

"You won't have a choice, Aleki. The Crasii will smell me and won't be able to stay away. The true Scards will be gagging on the stench of me."

"You're not welcome here now you're one of them, Declan. I hope you appreciate that."

He nodded. "And I understand why, Aleki, really I do. But I need your help."

"Tilly said as much in her note. What sort of help?"

"I need one of your Scards."

"For what, exactly?"

"For the very best of reasons," Declan told him. "We have to save the world."

It was much later that evening, by the cosy warmth of the longhouse fire—after Declan had related his tale and his request for help to Aleki and the Scards he knew to be *genuine* Scards—that Declan received a surprise visit from someone he was mildly amazed to find was still alive, let alone safe here in Hidden Valley.

He had retired so the others could rest and digest everything he'd told them. Declan didn't really need to sleep, although the oblivion of unconsciousness would have been a relief if he could relax long enough to find it. At the sound of a timid knock, he opened the door of the room Aleki had given him for the night, to find a female canine standing outside in the chilly hall.

"Do you remember me, Master Hawkes?"

He nodded, his eyes going to her flat belly. "Boots? No, you took another name. Tabitha Belle, wasn't it? You were pregnant the last I heard. Warlock was your mate."

"Still is," Boots said. "Can we talk?"

Curious, Declan nodded and stood back to let her enter. She looked around at the simple bed and the lantern on the side table, sniffed the air suspiciously for a moment and then screwed up her nose at him. "Tides, you smell foul."

"I'm not sure why that is," he said, closing the door behind her. "The Crasii think we give off quite the most wonderful aroma in the world."

"Then they're idiots," Boots said, turning to face him. "Last I heard, you were dead, Hawkes."

"Last I heard, you were in Cycrane, serving Elyssa."

"We escaped," Boots told him. There was quite a story behind that brief statement, Declan didn't doubt. He wasn't sure Boots was willing to share it with him, though.

"Is Warlock with you?"

"He's minding the pups."

Declan smiled. "Always the responsible one, our Warlock. How many did you have?"

"Three."

"That's quite a handful. How did you manage to escape Cycrane?"

Boots shrugged, but didn't seem inclined to elaborate. "We had some help. Only beat you here by a day, actually. Warlock nearly died trying to save us. And he rubbed all the skin off his paws rowing across the lake. Then we had to trek here on foot with three hungry pups in tow. It took us the better part of two weeks. I wasn't even sure we were going to make it until we actually got here."

"And yet, here you are."

"Here we are," Boots echoed, pacing the room nervously. She wanted something, of that Declan was certain, but she was hedging around the issue, making idle conversation as if she was afraid to mention what she'd really come here for.

"Warlock hates you, by the way."

"Understandable, I suppose."

"You're not exactly my favourite person in the world, either, spymaster. 'Specially not now you've gone and joined the other side."

"I haven't *joined* the other side," Declan said patiently, wondering why he was trying to explain himself to a Scard. "A freak accident made me immortal, that's all. Did you want something, Boots, or did you just come here to see if I smell as bad as the other Scards claim I do?"

She shrugged again and turned her back on him, looking around as if this bare room, normally used to house the occasional visitor to Hidden Valley, was the most fascinating place on Amyrantha. Something was obviously bothering her or she wouldn't have come here in the middle of the night to see him. Her expression in the lamplight was hard to read. Even her spectacular bushy tail remained in a neutral position.

"I think they're Crasii."

Declan waited for further explanation, not sure where she was going with this. When she didn't seem inclined to elaborate, he found himself asking, "You think *who* is Crasii?"

"Our puppies."

He smiled reassuringly. "I'm sure they'll do you both proud . . ."

"No!" Boots said impatiently. "You don't get it. I think they're *Crasii*, not Scard."

"Oh." Declan looked at her uncertainly, with no idea as to how he should respond to such a revelation.

Boots didn't appreciate the brevity of his reply. "Is that all you have to say?"

"I'm not sure what else I *can* say."

"Will you tell me for certain?"

Declan frowned, not sure what she meant. "How?"

"You're one of them now, aren't you? You must be able to tell. I mean, it's all over the camp that you exposed all the felines as being Crasii, not Scards, earlier this evening when you arrived. And that you're planning to test the rest of them before you leave."

"It wasn't all of them. It wasn't even half."

She shrugged. "Well, you know how these rumours go. Will you look at my babies? Will you tell me if they're Crasii or Scard?"

Declan wasn't sure how he was supposed to do that with creatures so young, but he felt he owed this poor female something. He'd endangered her and her mate, after all—and her pups—ultimately for very little gain. He shrugged. "I can try, I suppose, Tabitha, but they may be too young to tell."

"I know that. Will you come anyway?"

"To your cabin? Won't Warlock have something to say about that?"

"I don't care," Boots said. "I have to know."

Declan nodded. "Then I'll see what I can do."

It was pitch black outside, the night dark, cold and smelling of imminent snow. Jaxyn's unnatural winter still gripped the land. It had taken on a life of its own now and wasn't going to let go without a fight.

"Didn't Elyssa suspect anything?" Declan asked his canine companion after a time, as they trudged in single file along a narrow path through the snow toward the canine side of the valley.

Boots shrugged. "I don't know if she suspected the truth about Warlock and me. Well, she'd never guess the truth about *him*; he's too good at grovelling like a real *gemang* for her to become suspicious. But she used to look at me sometimes like she knew."

"You're lucky Elyssa didn't kill you, if she suspected the truth."

"Why would she?" Boots asked, glancing over her shoulder as they walked, her breath frosting in the moonlight. "When it would have been so much more fun to wait until they were older and have my own pups tear me to pieces to prove her point."

Declan suspected Boots had the right of it. Mere killing wasn't enough to entertain a jaded immortal. A murder tasted so much better, after all, when flavoured with the spice of delicious irony. He didn't bother to say so aloud, however. Boots had enough to deal with, fearing her babies were Crasii and might one day betray her to the immortals.

Warlock must have smelled him coming. The big canine was standing on the porch of the small cabin while they were still climbing the narrow path, his tail up, his chest puffed out in the typical stance of a dominant male protecting what was his. There was no need for Declan to explain who he was. Hidden Valley was a small community. Warlock would have known hours ago that an immortal had invaded their sanctuary and, more importantly, which immortal it was.

"Why did you bring *him* here?" Warlock demanded as they approached. Declan stopped at the foot of the steps, allowing Boots to approach on her own. "I want him to see the pups."

"No."

Boots stopped on the step below Warlock and looked up at him. "I have to know, Farm Dog."

Warlock had no answer to that. He looked over Boots's head at Declan, his gaze cold and unwelcoming. "My family will never be safe because of you."

Declan wasn't sure he could argue that point and win. He settled for an apology. "I'm sorry. I never meant to hurt you or your family, Warlock."

The canine smiled down at him humourlessly. "You know, I actually believe you, Hawkes. I don't think you spared us a thought. I don't think anywhere in your human arrogance you cared enough to even *wonder* what would happen to me and Boots, let alone worry that you might be endangering us."

Back when he was mortal, Declan might have feared this canine. He certainly admired the creature's unflinching condemnation. It was no mean feat for any canine, Crasii or Scard, to face down an immortal.

Declan turned to Boots apologetically. "I'm sorry. I'm clearly not welcome here. I'll go."

"No!" Boots said, grabbing him by the arm. "I need you to see the pups."

"They're asleep," Warlock said.

"We need to know for certain," she said, looking up at her mate.

"Then let him come back tomorrow when they're awake."

No sooner had Warlock finished speaking than a mournful wail came from inside the cabin. Boots pushed past Warlock and hurried inside. Declan didn't move. Warlock might not be able to kill him, but the canine could do some serious damage that would heal very painfully if he attacked.

A few moments later, the cabin door opened again and Boots stepped onto the porch, a two- or three-month-old pup in her arms. Although it wasn't easy to tell in the darkness, it seemed to be a rich chestnut colour, and was fussing hungrily at the opening of Boots's coat, trying to get to her milk. Warlock stepped between Declan and Boots.

"Leave, suzerain. You've caused enough problems. I'll not have you destroy my family on top of everything else you've done."

Declan nodded. "As you wish."

He turned to leave.

"Wait!" yelled Boots.

Declan turned back to her. Boots had placed the pup on the porch. "Call her."

Warlock was shaking his head. "Boots, please. Don't do this. Don't do it to our pups. Don't do it to *us*."

Boots ignored her mate, her gaze fixed on Declan. "Call her. Please."

Much as Declan didn't want to get involved in a domestic dispute between these two canines, the plaintive tone of Boots's request touched him. In her place, he supposed, he'd want to know the truth.

"What's her name?"

"Missy."

The pup was sitting on her haunches at her mother's feet. Declan took a step toward the cabin. The pup's tail immediately perked up and she looked around. After a moment her gaze fixed on Declan, her tail wagged happily.

"Missy, come here," he said. Not at all certain the pup would understand him, he gestured to her in a beckoning manner with his hand. Without hesitation, the pup crawled toward the steps, determined to reach her immortal master. Declan was hardly an expert on the Crasii, but he couldn't imagine any circumstance where a hungry pup only a few months old would prefer the company of a perfect stranger over that of her mother.

Warlock snatched Missy up before she could tumble down the steps, hugging the puppy to him, despite the fact she was struggling to reach out to Declan.

"I'm sorry, Warlock."

"Leave, suzerain," Warlock said, his eyes shining with unshed tears. "Leave and never come near this place again."

Declan didn't try to argue. Feeling the canines' pain, he turned on his heel and headed back toward the main hall, wondering how many more families in this once-safe enclave would be torn apart by the time he left tomorrow.

Chapter 43

Bundled in a heavy coat made from the skin of a Jelidian snow bear, a round white fur hat pulled down over her ears to protect them from the icy wind, Arkady cut a lonely figure standing in the bow of the boat, watching the black water speed past as the amphibians pulled them south toward Whitewater City. The Great Lakes were still dotted with myriad ice fragments left over from the shattering, the distant shore a blur of white on the horizon.

Although they were travelling at a good pace, the speed of their barge still irked Cayal. At this rate, it would still take them several more days to reach the coast, more than a month to reach Jelidia. Maybe even longer if the weather was unfavourable. Swimming in such conditions, the toll on the amphibians who were pulling their craft through the icy water was horrendous. Some of them barely lasted a day. But the Tide Lords could do nothing extraordinary to speed their journey. Even though the Tide was rising at a pace Cayal had never experienced before, with the Chaos Crystal in such close proximity there was no question of them trying to manipulate the elements with magic.

Cayal's feet slipped on the icy deck as he moved forward, wondering if Arkady was hiding up here in the cold to get away from the others or actually contemplating jumping overboard and putting an end to it all. Somehow he doubted it was the latter. Arkady was many things, but—unlike him—suicidal wasn't one of them.

"So, do you think watching the amphibians will make them go faster?"

She turned at his question, but didn't seem amused by it. "It's cruel, making them swim in such cold water, Cayal."

"To serve us is the reason they breathe," he said, realising his mistake almost as soon as he uttered the words. She was not smiling. But then, Arkady had always been a bit of a bleeding heart when it came to the Crasii. He sighed apologetically. "Tides, it's just a joke, Arkady. Don't look at me like that."

"It's not a joke at all, Cayal. That's what makes you people monsters."

He moved up beside her and leaned on the railing. "So I'm 'you people' now, am I?"

"How's your fiancée?" she shot back.

The edge in her voice left little room for doubt about her opinion regarding his arrangement with the Immortal Maiden. "My relationship with Elyssa is just a means to an end, Arkady. You have nothing to be jealous about."

Arkady smiled, shaking her head. "*Jealous*? Are you serious, Cayal? You think I'm jealous of Elyssa?"

"Well, you're mad about something," he said, a little wounded by her scorn. "And as all I've done recently is save that wretched *gemang* you're so fond of from certain death and allowed him and his filthy Scard family to escape, I figured it can't be anything I've done."

She actually seemed shocked by his words. "Cayal, you blithely killed several thousand people a couple of weeks ago, and then went and got engaged to a woman you despise to celebrate the event. Doesn't all that death you caused bother you in the slightest?"

He looked at her in confusion. "People? What people?"

"The people who died when you and Elyssa and Kentravyon broke the ice-sheet to end the war between Caelum and Glaeba."

"Oh . . . well, they weren't people, strictly speaking. Mostly, they were Crasii."

She turned away from him in exasperation. "I have nothing to say to you, Cayal."

"You're not reneging on our deal, are you?"

"No," she said, shaking her head. "I'll carry your wretched crystal to Jelidia for you, because you let Warlock and his family go, but then we're done. Do you understand?"

"Sure. We're done. I'll be sure to let all 'us people' know."

She didn't respond to that, which was a pity. Kentravyon had barely spoken to anyone since they boarded the barge so now Cayal's only alternative to standing here talking to Arkady was to go below and talk to Elyssa. Sticking hot pins in his eyeballs was preferable.

"You said, 'Look past the scratches and the dirt. Look at the new you,'" Arkady said suddenly, turning back to look at him. "What did you mean?"

"Sorry?" he said, hoping he sounded as if he had no idea what she was talking about.

"You said it to Elyssa back at the temple. 'Look past the scratches and the dirt. Look at the new you, Lyssa,'" she repeated. "What did you mean by that?"

"Nothing."

"Don't lie to me, Cayal. You were *selling* me to her."

"I was not."

"'Men from one end of Amyrantha to the other have lusted after that body,' you said. You told her I was the most beautiful mortal woman on Amyrantha."

"Then you'd think that by now you'd have learned to take a compliment, wouldn't you?"

She was not amused. Or easily deterred from this most unwelcome line of questioning. "'When the Tide peaks, that could be you, Lyssa. Tall, elegant, beautiful . . . free of pain . . .'" she repeated, demonstrating a disturbingly accurate memory. "What did you mean by that?"

"I just meant she could aspire to be like you," he said with a shrug. "What did you think I meant, Arkady? Tides, what else *could* it mean?" He met her distrustful gaze openly and innocently, as if he had absolutely nothing to hide.

"That's what I'm trying to figure out."

"Then stop worrying about it," he assured her, taking her gloved hand in his. He raised it to his lips and smiled. "You know I hate Elyssa. I was just trying to convince her I thought she was as beautiful as you."

"Why? Because you need her to help you die?"

"Tides, there's not another reason on Amyrantha I'd have anything to do with her otherwise."

"And she's just going along with it? This plan of yours to kill yourself using the Chaos Crystal?"

"Well, I did have to promise her my body first," he said with a faint grin, hoping to get a smile out of her that wasn't tinged with ridicule or contempt.

He achieved quite the opposite. Arkady scowled at him. "I'm starting to wonder if you've promised her *mine*."

He shrugged, deliberately misunderstanding her. "Elyssa's not that way inclined. So stop worrying about it. I'll deal with Her Royal Pain-in-the-Backside and do whatever I have to do to keep her happy until the Tide peaks. You just hold on to that crystal skull like your life depends on it. Which it does, I feel compelled to warn you. Where is it, by the way?"

"I tossed it overboard," she informed him with a perfectly straight face.

Cayal stared at her for a long moment. "That's not funny, you know."

"Or even remotely likely," Arkady pointed out, amused now that she'd been able to rattle him, even a little. "Don't you think you'd have noticed something by now if we were pulling away from the crystal?"

"Where is it?"

"Under the pillow on my bunk."

"Shouldn't you be keeping a better eye on it? Elyssa *will* kill you, Arkady—very slowly and painfully—if you lose it."

"Who's going to steal it, Cayal?" she asked. "We're on a boat staffed entirely by your magically compelled, tiresomely loyal Crasii, not to mention a trio of Tide Lords willing to go to any lengths to protect it. Who *exactly* am I supposed to be protecting your precious Chaos Crystal from?"

Cayal hated Arkady when she was in this mood—all cold logic and acerbic wit. He preferred the other Arkady. The one who was passionate and defiant. The one who made love to him like it was a voyage of discovery. The one who *wanted* to make love to him. This Arkady was much less fun. This was the Arkady who'd first walked into Recidivists' Row to prove he wasn't immortal; the Arkady who brought out the worst in him. Before he could stop himself, he said, "Your old boyfriend— the one who just happens to be immortal now—might be interested in getting his hands on it. And I'm not convinced you wouldn't betray me in a heartbeat, if *he* asked you to."

She looked at him oddly. "Do you mean Declan?"

Cayal nodded. "How many other old boyfriends who just happen to be immortal do you have?"

Arkady ignored the jibe, more intent on the information he'd let slip regarding the whereabouts of the former Glaeban spymaster. "Declan is here? In Glaeba?"

"I have no idea where he is," Cayal told her, honestly enough.

"You're lying, Cayal," she said, able to read him far too easily for comfort. "Is he here?"

Cayal looked around. "Not that I can see."

"Does anybody actually think you're funny, Cayal?"

He sighed. "All right, he *was* here. At least he travelled with Kentra-vyon and me from Jelidia. He bailed on us about the time we decided to break the ice. I haven't seen him since the night of the battle in Cycrane." And then he added, hand on his heart, "I swear that's the truth, Arkady. May the Tide strike me down if I'm lying."

The Tide, of course, did no such thing. Even then, despite such definite evidence of his honesty, Arkady still studied him with intense suspicion. "Why would Declan come back to Glaeba?"

He was amazed she had to ask. "Looking for you, of course. Why does that fool do anything?"

"And you didn't feel the need to mention this minor detail before now?"

He shrugged. "I wasn't hiding anything from you, Arkady. You, well . . . you didn't ask."

In typical Arkady fashion, she let that comment pass, worrying at the threads of the rest of his story like a dog chewing at a blanket until it unravelled. "Why did he leave?"

"Pardon?"

"You said he bailed on you. Why? Why would he travel all this way with you and then leave?"

"I don't know."

"Yes you do," she accused, hugging her arms against her body. Even through the furs she could feel the icy chill of the wind as they sped south on the water. "Declan wouldn't have anything to do with your plans to break the ice and kill all those Crasii, would he?"

Not much got past this woman, damn her. "He wasn't fond of the plan, no."

"So where did he go?"

Cayal was getting very tired of this conversation. He took her by the arms and turned her to face him, hoping to convince Arkady of his sincerity so they could move on. He was, by now, thoroughly fed up with all discussion relating to the noble intentions of one Declan Bloody Hawkes. "I swear, Arkady, I really don't know where Hawkes went. Maybe he's off contemplating the meaning of life in a cave somewhere. More likely he's off trying to explain how he wound up immortal to all his fanatical old pals in the Cabal."

Arkady's eyes widened in surprise. "What do you know about the Cabal?"

Cayal smiled at her question. "A damn sight more than the Cabal would like me to, I'd wager." He laughed then, at her shocked expression. "Tides, Arkady, do you think we're complete fools? Lukys has been a member of their inner council for years. That's one of the many ways he kept tabs on the progress of his son."

"I have to go to him." She pulled away, trying to shake free of him, but Cayal held her fast.

"Why?" he asked, drawing her even closer, his lips all but touching hers. "The last time you saw Hawkes, you promised to hate him for the rest of your life."

"He came looking for me, Cayal."

"So what? I'm the one who found you."

She wasn't impressed by his argument. "Purely by accident. You'd not lose a moment's sleep over my fate if I wasn't standing right in front of you."

Cayal loosened his grip on her arms and smiled, gently brushing away a windblown strand of hair that had escaped from under her fur hat and was whipping around her face. "He thinks you're dead, Arkady. He knows you were out on the ice at the start of the battle. One of the reasons he wouldn't have anything to do with destroying it was his *fear* of something happening to you. Wherever he is now, he's already grieving your loss. And you have no way of finding him. You will, however, be dead in a heartbeat if you give Elyssa the slightest reason to suspect you're thinking of reneging on our deal."

Arkady nodded reluctantly, seeing the logic of his explanation, although she was clearly unhappy with it. "But he came looking for me, Cayal. I can't just leave here, with Declan thinking I'm dead."

"You'll see him again in Jelidia," Cayal promised. "He's sworn to help me die, remember? Even if he's devastated by grief over your demise, he won't pass up an opportunity to see an end to me." *At least he'd better keep his word*, Cayal added silently to himself, *because that smug little bastard promised to help and even with Elyssa's power, I'm not sure we'll have enough to open the rift without him.*

Arkady didn't seem completely convinced, but it seemed she'd run out of arguments. Cayal took her in his arms again and held her comfortingly, wise enough not to try kissing her. She was still too conflicted for him to try that yet. He was immortal, after all, with the patience of an immortal. And it was a long way to Jelidia. There would be time.

Or perhaps not, he thought, when he glanced aft and spied Elyssa standing by the wheelhouse door, staring at Cayal and the mortal woman in his arms with a murderous gleam in her eye.

Tides, he told himself unhappily, pushing Arkady away in a futile attempt to make it look as if he'd merely been comforting her, not making a move on her. *Now I'm going to have to kiss Elyssa again.*

Chapter 44

Declan Hawkes called a meeting of all the Scards in Hidden Valley the night after he arrived. There proved to be depressingly few in number by the time he had spoken to most of the inhabitants of the valley and tested their status as either true Scards or just hopefuls. Genuine Scards—Scards who were not magically compelled to obey the immortals, as opposed to those who had simply defied their human masters—were a rare breed indeed. Warlock was surprised to see how many families in Hidden Valley were now fractured like his. He and Boots were far from being the only Scard parents in Hidden Valley to discover they had pure Crasii offspring.

The news did little to ease Boots's anger. And she *was* angry, more than anything else, about her pups being Crasii. It seemed so unfair to her that nature would punish them in such a cruel and arbitrary way. That others had been punished in a similar fashion did little to ease her pain.

They had gathered in the common room in order to hear Hawkes speak. The room was warm, with fires going in both stoves at either end of the wooden longhouse and the press of bodies adding to the heat. But there was a chill in the air and it had nothing to do with the weather. It had to do with fear—a fear every Scard in the room was trying to hide behind a façade of proud indifference.

Once Hawkes had finished explaining the situation, a heavy silence descended over the room as the Scards digested everything he'd told them. As far as Warlock could tell, the former spymaster hadn't held back or tried to soften the news about the rise of the Tide and the plans the immortals had for opening a portal to another world that was likely to destroy Amyrantha.

But then he delivered the killing blow. The reason he was here in Hidden Valley; the grand plan he had for stopping the immortals from destroying the world. He wanted some of the Scards to go with him, into the very heart of the Tide Lords' stronghold, and stop them opening the rift.

"You're placing an awful lot of faith in some of the most notorious immortals to ever curse Amyrantha with their presence," someone called out from the back of the hall. "How do you know this brilliant plan of yours will succeed, suzerain?"

"I don't," Hawkes told them. The immortal stench of him reached Warlock even several rows back from the table at the front of the hall where Hawkes sat with Lord Aleki Ponting. "All I can tell you is that Lukys and Cayal are planning to open a rift that will likely tear a hole in the very fabric of reality. None but an immortal is likely to survive it, and even then it may kill a few of them. We can do nothing, if you'd prefer, but that just means you should make plans to enjoy your last few weeks in this life, because it's all going to be over once the Tide peaks."

"But you said this rift will *kill* immortals," Boots called out.

"Boots! No!" Warlock hissed at her, a warning she ignored.

"That's what Cayal believes," Declan agreed, turning his gaze on Boots. "And what Lukys and Kentravyon have both confirmed."

"Then I don't get why you want to stop them," his mate said, ignoring Warlock's whispered urging to be quiet and not draw attention to themselves. "If the immortals want to die and they've found a way to kill themselves, then *let* them kill themselves, I say. I'm not going to miss them."

"Did you not hear the part about the rift destroying the whole planet, Tabitha Belle?" Aleki asked.

"But we don't know that for certain," she said, a comment that evoked a number of murmured agreements and nods from the other Scards in the longhouse. "For all you know, that's just a rumour the immortals have spread about to stop just this sort of discussion. Do you have any *proof* that opening this rift will destroy the world?"

"Not solid, documented proof, no," Hawkes was forced to concede.

"So, based on your suspicions, the ravings of a mad immortal, and not much else that I can see," Boots said, pushing her way to the front, despite Warlock's urging her to stay put and be quiet, "you're going to try to prevent the very thing we've all been praying for. You have the only chance in the last ten thousand years to rid us of even one or two flanking suzerain, and you're going to try to stop them because of a rumour."

"What if it's *not* a rumour?" Hawkes asked. "Will you be filled with quite so much righteous indignation, Tabitha Belle, when the world blows up in your face?"

"My world blew up in my face the day I discovered my pups were Crasii," she shot back, earning herself even more nods of agreement from the other mothers and fathers in the hall—feline and canine alike—suddenly faced with the same dilemma. "My babies were born with the ability, no—the very *will*—to betray me. One of your kind could order my children to eat me alive, and they'd do it gladly, and then ask what more they can do to please their immortal masters, with my blood still dripping from their jowls. My world is already destroyed, Declan Hawkes. Don't you dare sit there, smelling like a suzerain, and tell me you want to stop the people who destroyed it, from destroying themselves."

There was a smattering of applause for Boots when she finished speaking. It came mostly from the mothers in the room. Mothers suddenly faced with the prospect that their offspring—as soon as they were old enough—might want to leave their home, seek out an immortal, and then betray the families who raised them in order to please the masters they couldn't help but serve.

Warlock understood Boots's pain. He understood the principle for which she was fighting. He even agreed with it, up to a point. But he couldn't see the logic of allowing the immortals to tamper with such powerful forces of nature, if it meant they killed everyone else on Amyrantha along with themselves.

Principles were something you could really only afford if you were, well, alive.

"I realise the price, Tabitha," Hawkes said when the applause died down. "And if I thought for a moment that there was a way to kill the immortals and keep Amyrantha intact, I'd do it. As it is, I don't see how."

"It's not that you don't *see*," the feline standing next to Boots said. "It's that you don't *know*. Isn't it at least worth a try?"

Hawkes looked to Aleki for support as the Scards murmured their agreement, but Lord Ponting either didn't want to help or couldn't think of anything constructive to say.

"Why can't you do both?" Boots asked. "Why can't you let them open the portal, kill a few Tide Lords and then close it down again before they do any permanent damage to our world?"

Hawkes shook his head. "Even if I could do that, what guarantee do you have that the immortals who survive will make your life any easier than the immortals we manage to kill?"

"There are no *good* immortals, suzerain," someone behind Warlock called out. "It makes no difference which ones you kill, so long as you manage to thin out their numbers!"

The gathered Scards agreed with that comment so wholeheartedly they burst into applause again. Hawkes was looking frustrated. Warlock thought he understood the newly minted suzerain's problem. He'd come here for help, to find Scards who were willing to take on the Tide Lords—as they all believed they'd been trained to do—but here they were, when it came to the crunch, telling him, *so what? Let the bastards kill themselves. We don't care.*

"*Can* you stop them, though?" Warlock asked, his deep voice cutting through the general chatter that filled the room as they applauded the sentiments of the last speaker.

Hawkes looked straight at him, a silence descending on the hall as they all waited for him to answer. "I think so."

"How?"

"By countering them with equal force."

"But you say you've only got Jaxyn on your side, and that by the time you meet up with him in the Chelae Islands, hopefully he'll have brought Tryan along to help. Even assuming he can somehow manage to get Tryan and the Empress of the Five Realms onside after being at war with them so recently, including you, that's only three Tide Lords against—what?" Warlock did a quick count on his fingers. "Cayal, Lukys, Maralyce, Kentravyon, Elyssa and probably Pellys. Against six? And you say they'll be amplifying their power through the Bedlam Stone. You haven't a hope in hell of stopping them. You won't even get near them."

"Getting near them isn't the problem," Hawkes assured him. "I can get into the ice palace. I can get into the chamber. Tides, they're *expecting* me to help. And I seriously doubt Pellys will be taking part in the ceremony, because he has no control over the Tide. Once I'm in the chamber, I can destroy the crystal. That means, if we can get Brynden on board, we're down to four against five, and given we'll have all the lesser immortals on our side—with the exception of Arryl and Taryx—it should be close to an even fight at that point."

"It's the bit where you say *should* that worries me."

"It's not as impossible as it seems, Warlock," Aleki said. "I mean, they have to find the crystal before—"

"They have it," Warlock cut in.

"How do you know?" Hawkes asked.

Warlock realised his mistake as soon as Declan asked for further details. Admitting how he knew that they had the crystal meant admitting how he'd been healed by the Immortal Prince. It meant admitting they'd been prisoners of the Immortal Maiden and had been let go. Warlock couldn't risk that happening. When they arrived in Hidden Valley, they'd told Lord Aleki the truth about how they escaped Caelum, right up until the part about meeting up with Duchess Arkady.

Neither did they mention anything about how Warlock had nearly died, and how she'd bartered her own life for their freedom. He was certain the news they had been released by the immortals without any apparent harm, only to appear in Hidden Valley a few weeks later, would make them the object of mistrust and suspicion, perhaps even see them denied shelter here. Warlock and Boots had agreed there were some things that simply had to remain unsaid.

And they would have—if only he'd learn to keep his big mouth shut.

"Elyssa knows where the map is," he said, carefully editing the truth to fit the story they'd given everyone when they first arrived in Hidden Valley. "She has a map of its location. If not for being distracted by the war with Jaxyn, she'd have had it months ago. It's been what? Three, almost four weeks, since the battle on the ice? The chances are good that they'll have the crystal and be halfway back to Jelidia with it by now." It was the best Warlock could do; the safest way to deliver the warning about the crystal without actually letting on how he knew they had it.

"Even so," Aleki said, "you can't be sure . . ."

"Is it about this big?" Boots asked, holding up her hands to indicate the size. "Shaped like a skull? Glows in the dark?"

Aleki glanced at Hawkes, who shrugged. "I suppose. I haven't—"

"Then they have it already," Boots said, as Warlock looked at her in surprise. All their secrets, all their late-night discussions were apparently meaningless.

"How do you know?" Aleki asked.

"The Duchess of Lebec traded our escape from Cycrane for it."

Now she's done it. Hawkes seemed flabbergasted, but not because they'd seen the Chaos Crystal, which—because of his near-death delirium—Warlock only vaguely remembered. "Tides, you saw Arkady after the battle? *Alive?*"

Boots nodded and answered for them. "She found us hiding in some ruins north of Cycrane. That's where the pups found the crystal. A couple of days later, your precious duchess tried to kill my mate when he came looking for us, and then when the immortals arrived, she made Cayal heal Warlock and set us free in return for the crystal." Boots looked around at the silent, concerned faces of the other Scards, who were all staring at her with deep suspicion. "What? I told you all this when we arrived!"

"You told us you'd escaped the battle in a rowboat after the ice shattered, Tabitha," Aleki reminded her. "You left out the bit about the immortals and the Chaos Crystal."

"It didn't seem important," Boots said with a shrug. She pointedly didn't look at Warlock who'd warned her repeatedly—right up until he'd agreed to go along with it—that lying about their escape from Caelum would eventually bring them undone.

"Well, it's important now," Aleki said, and then he turned to Hawkes. "And I think you have your volunteer, Declan."

All eyes in the room turned to Warlock. It took him a moment to realise why. "Me? You want *me* to go? Tides, you are unbelievable! Absolutely not! I'm *not* going to leave my family unprotected again!"

"You know what the crystal looks like, Cecil," Aleki said in a reasonable tone.

"It's a flanking glowing skull," he shot back. "Trust me, you won't miss it."

"You can identify the other immortals—"

"Any Scard with a nose can do that."

"You've met them before, you've dealt with them," Aleki continued.

"And they know I'm a Scard," he added. "They'll kill me as soon as look at me."

"Brynden won't," Hawkes said. "And that's the main reason I need a Scard to help me. I have to contact Brynden and because of the magical barrier he's set around Torlenia, I can't do that without provoking a fight. But I can't send a Crasii in to deliver my request for a parley either, because a Crasii messenger can too easily be subverted by another immortal."

Warlock shook his head. "You can't ask me to do this."

"Given your previous dealings with the immortals," Aleki said, "and that you've brought three Crasii, pups into our stronghold, I'm not sure you're in a position to refuse, Warlock."

He was shocked at the suggestion. "Are you saying I'm *not* a Scard? That I can't be trusted?"

"There is no doubt you're a Scard, Warlock," Hawkes said. "No question you have free will. But that free will works both ways. Just because you're not magically compelled to obey an immortal doesn't mean you won't. Or that you haven't done some sort of deal with them to secure your family's escape."

"The Duchess Arkady helped us escape," he insisted, unable to believe that after everything he'd done for the Cabal, they were accusing him of being a traitor.

"And yet everyone else in Glaeba believes she perished during the battle."

"That's not actually my fault." He folded his arms across his chest defiantly. "I'm not going. I won't do it."

"Yes, he will," Boots piped up in the silence that followed his adamant declaration.

Warlock turned to her, horrified. "Boots!"

She didn't look at him. Instead, she turned to Hawkes and Lord Ponting. "He'll do it. You're leaving at first light, aren't you?"

Declan nodded, looking at Boots and then Warlock uncertainly. "Are you . . . ?"

"He'll be there!" Boots insisted, and then turned on her heel, grabbed Warlock by the arm as she passed and dragged him through the gathering into the chilly air outside.

As soon as the door closed behind him, he turned on her. "I can't believe you just did that to me! What happened to 'Don't you ever leave us again, Farm Dog? Don't you even think about haring off to be a hero, I need you here with me and the pups?'"

"Killing those bastards is more important," she said savagely.

"Hawkes wants to *stop* the immortals killing themselves, Boots. That's what this is all about. That's why he wants someone to go to Torlenia with him."

"Then he's wrong, Warlock," she said, her voice a low growl, her tail defiantly high under her coat. "Although he is right about one thing. We do have free will. We have the will to do whatever it takes to see as many immortals as possible perish in that rift when they open it."

"What if it really does destroy Amyrantha in the process?"

She looked up at him intensely, her eyes shining in the darkness. "Think of a future where your own children are destined to betray you to the suzerain, Warlock, and then tell me you *wouldn't* rather see an end to this world than wait for that to happen."

Chapter 45

"My lady, do you have a moment?"

Arryl looked up from the table where she was working. Not long after they'd arrived, Lukys had brought her a number of samples of moss—he'd used the Tide to encourage it to grow on the ice. Tiji recognised it as the same moss growing on the staircase leading down into the secret chamber beneath the palace. Arryl was fascinated by it, and had spent much of her time experimenting with the various strains in large trays filled with ice, to see what sort of light she could coax from it.

Lukys has that much right, Tiji realised with a sinking heart. *He knows what makes the others tick, what will pique their interest.* Since providing Arryl with the luminescent moss samples to play with just after Declan, Cayal and Kentravyon left, she'd barely emerged from her chamber to question what else might be going on inside the palace.

The immortal smiled, and indicated the stool next to the table. Arryl's chamber, like the rest of the palace, was built on a grand scale, with permafrost floors that looked like polished granite, and white ice walls decorated with colourful rugs and hangings to make it feel more homely. The bed, a raised platform made of ice, was against the far wall, softened by luscious white baby-seal furs.

"Certainly, Tiji, what's the matter?"

Tiji entered Arryl's chamber and took the seat she offered, not sure how she was going to broach the subject she'd come here to discuss.

"Have you seen Lady Oritha lately, my lady?"

"Lukys's wife?" Arryl shook her head, poking the moss about in the tray with a slender wooden skewer as she talked. She was prepared to listen to Tiji, but she was far from giving the Scard her undivided attention. "Not for a while, now you come to mention it. However, that's hardly surprising." She scooped a small amount of moss from another container and placed it in the tray, then began to gently pat it down flat. "This is a very large palace. One can go days without encountering another soul. Why do you ask? Are you afraid something has happened to her?"

"I think she's dead."

Arryl looked up from the moss-filled tray and stared at Tiji curiously. "What in the name of the Tide would make you think something like that?"

Here goes nothing. "I saw them. Lukys and Maralyce. They had Oritha laid out on an altar in this great big chamber they've built under this place. I think they froze her."

"You *saw* this?"

Tiji nodded.

"And there's no possibility you mistook it for something else?"

"I heard them talking, my lady," Tiji said, wishing she could gag on the stench of such close proximity to a suzerain, but knowing she wouldn't be listened to if she did. "Lord Lukys told Lady Maralyce that Oritha must be on the brink of death for this—whatever *this* is—to succeed."

Arryl studied her thoughtfully, placing the skewer down as she wiped her hands on her skirts. "Go on."

"He said he learned that much the last time. And then he said something about her heart beating so slowly it's barely moving. And something else about her consciousness that I don't understand, other than it had something to do with resistance . . ."

Tiji met Arryl's gaze evenly; at least the immortal wasn't dismissing her tale out of hand.

"Whatever they did, it's a secret, my lady. Maralyce was worried about what the rest of you might think when you discovered what had become of Oritha."

At that, the immortal smiled indulgently at her. "And don't you think we might have something to say about Oritha's fate, if what you claim is true?"

"Lukys said you all had your own reasons for helping, so you probably wouldn't object," Tiji said, annoyed by the immortal's patronising smile.

"It all sounds very dire, Tiji."

"You don't believe me."

Arryl straightened her skirts and turned to face her. "I believe you saw something, Tiji. But I also recall you spent your formative years apprenticed to a spymaster and are a suspicious creature by nature, with a tendency to see plots and conspiracies where there are none."

"I know what I saw, my lady. And there's no happy slant you can put on it."

Arryl smiled, but she squared her shoulders decisively. "Shall we investigate, then?"

Tiji looked up at her in surprise. "What?"

"Shall we go and investigate this dreadful accusation?" Arryl said. "You claim Lukys and Maralyce have done something to Oritha and that she's hidden beneath the palace in a secret chamber, on the brink of death, if not dead already. I can't confront Lukys with such an absurd accusation without proof. So take me there, Tiji. Lead me to your hidden chamber and I'll see the evidence for myself."

Tiji stared up at Arryl for a long moment. This was not at all the reaction she'd been expecting. She climbed warily to her feet. "Are you sure?"

"Take me to her," Arryl commanded.

Rather more reluctantly than she expected—now she'd found someone prepared to listen to her story—Tiji led Arryl through the Palace of Impossible Dreams. The immortal followed her down the stairs to the lower levels, past the ice-carved storerooms with their amazing bounty, down the long corridor that led to the glowing green stairs carved out of the very foundations of the palace, and into the chamber with its fire-lit walls and solid ice altar. Arryl stopped on the stairs. Tiji turned to find out why, only to discover the immortal staring closely at the luminescent moss.

"My lady?"

"I'm sorry, Tiji, I just didn't expect to see such a thriving colony down here. Do you think—"

"Oritha?" Tiji reminded her pointedly.

"Of course," Arryl said with an apologetic smile. "Lead on, dear."

A moment later, they stepped into the chamber. Arryl looked around in awe. The fires lighting the chamber burned around the walls as if fuelled by magic, but there was nobody here.

"What is this place, my lady?" Tiji asked, after Arryl had turned a full circle, her mouth agape with wonder.

"I have no idea," the immortal said. "I assume this is where Lukys intends to open his rift. The walls must be curved like this to contain the power amplified by the Chaos Crystal."

"What about that?" Tiji asked, pointing to the altar. There was no sign of Oritha in the chamber, or anybody else for that matter. She wondered where they'd hidden the body. And how she was going to prove to Arryl what she'd witnessed.

The immortal walked toward the altar with Tiji close behind. They crossed the cavernous hall in silence, the chill seeping into Tiji's bones. The altar, when they reached it, was taller than the little chameleon—a solid block of ice resting on a slight plinth at the base. Arryl circled the altar twice, her fingers trailing on the opaque surface, and then she stopped in front of Tiji.

"I see nothing odd here, Tiji. No dead bodies. No conspiracies. Nothing but an empty room and a chameleon with a very active imagination."

"I know what I saw, my lady," she insisted stubbornly.

"Did you tell Azquil about it?"

"Yes, my lady."

"And what did he say?"

"He said I should mind my own business."

"Then he is a very wise lizard."

Tiji frowned, certain of what she'd seen, and frustrated beyond words that nobody would believe her. "I didn't imagine this, my lady, and I'm not making anything up. Lukys and Maralyce were standing right here. 'I wonder if the poor girl had any idea she was going to die today?' That's what Maralyce said."

"Pity you didn't stay to hear the rest of it, Tiji," a voice called from the entrance. "Then you might not be as concerned."

Tiji spun around to see Lukys crossing the chamber from the entrance, with—to Tiji's astonishment—a perfectly healthy Oritha on his arm. She'd been so busy trying to convince Arryl that Oritha was dead, she'd not smelled the Tide Lord approaching. Oritha was smiling as they neared the altar, not in the least afraid or concerned.

And clearly not dead. Or anywhere near it.

Tiji, on the other hand, was starting to fear she was going mad.

"Tides, you poor little thing," Oritha said as they stopped by the altar. "How it must have looked to you, hiding back there in the shadows."

Arryl's eyes widened in surprise. "You mean she really did see something?"

"I imagine your little chameleon has told you exactly what she saw," Lukys agreed with a smile. "It must have seemed quite gruesome, I suppose."

"What are you talking about?" Tiji demanded. "You were killing her. Maralyce said so."

"I believe Maralyce was urging me not to make a mistake, Tiji," Lukys said. "Oritha is mortal, you see, and when we open the rift, she'll not survive if she's in this chamber and unprotected. I can, however, protect her by encasing her in ice, so that when the rift opens and we step through, she will be alive when we emerge on the other side. We wish to leave this world as we found it, Tiji. The only one who will perish is Cayal, who will be holding the crystal. And you may recall, he actually *wants* to die."

"But . . . she was dead . . ."

"No, I wasn't," Oritha said. Then she laughed, "*Clearly* I wasn't, if I am standing here now, assuring you of my wellbeing. Didn't you hear what Ryda said? In order for me to survive the rift, I need to be encased in ice, and in order for me to be able to survive *that*, my husband must be certain he can revive me. We've practised a number of times now, and each time I have emerged from the process completely unharmed." She took Lukys's arm and smiled up at him. "My Ryda would never allow any harm to come to me. Would you, darling?"

"Of course not," Lukys said, smiling down at her.

She must be on the brink of death for this to succeed, Tiji remembered Lukys telling Maralyce. *Her heartbeat needs to be so slow it's barely moving, her consciousness so completely immersed there will be no resistance . . .* Maybe Lukys was telling the truth. Maybe he really *was* just practising freezing Oritha and then reviving her, so she'd survive the rift and the journey to another world. After all, Oritha was standing here in front of her, alive and well . . .

Arryl turned to the little chameleon. "Tiji, I think you owe our host an apology."

Tiji glared at Lukys and Oritha. "But . . ."

"An apology, Tiji," Arryl insisted.

Tiji turned to Lukys and said through gritted teeth, "I'm sorry, my lord."

"For spying on you, and accusing you of murdering your wife," Arryl added with an expectant look.

"I'm sorry for spying on you, and accusing you of murdering your wife," Tiji echoed dutifully. She turned to Arryl when she was done. "May I go now?"

"I think you should," Lukys said. "And please, don't come down here again uninvited. As I'm sure Lady Arryl will tell you, the moss we're using to light the stairwell is very sensitive. I don't want it being harmed or contaminated inadvertently by strangers wandering in and out of here."

"Don't worry. I'm not coming back here," Tiji mumbled, and then she turned and fled toward the entrance, her silver skin flickering with embarrassment and anger.

Azquil was both furious and mortified when Tiji told him what had happened with Arryl, Lukys and Oritha. Although he claimed to be a Scard, he had an unhealthy attachment to these wretched immortals that left her wondering about him. His complaint this time, however, was more because he had told her to let the matter go, and she had defied him, than it was about accusing Lukys of murdering his wife.

"If you'd been there, you'd be on my side," Tiji insisted, as she realised this was the first real argument she'd had with Azquil.

"If I'd been there, I would have saved you from making a complete fool of yourself," he said, his skin a dull grey colour that indicated he was quite incensed with her. "Tides, Tiji, what were you thinking? Accusing a Tide Lord of *murder*?"

"Well, yes . . . because *that's* never happened before, has it?"

Azquil threw his hands up angrily and turned for the door of their small private chamber. Unlike the majestic rooms belonging to the immortals, there was only room in here for a bed and a narrow cupboard. Tiji didn't really mind, normally. It was so cold in the palace, the only safe way to sleep was snuggled up against another live body for warmth. "It's impossible to talk to you in this mood."

"Leave then!" she said, biting back tears that had more to do with Azquil's anger than defending her position. "Go wait on your precious immortals! You care more about them than me, anyway! I'm leaving this wretched place!"

Azquil refused to dignify her accusation with a reply, or acknowledge her threat to leave. Instead, he stalked out of the room, snatching his hooded jacket from the bed as he left, which meant he wasn't going to be back for a while.

Tiji paced the small, cold room angrily once he was gone, continuing the fight with him in her head as she rehearsed everything she intended to say to that wretched lizard when he came back to apologise.

Assuming she didn't carry out her threat to leave, which didn't seem like such a bad idea right now.

The candle had burned down quite a way before Azquil came back to Tiji's room. By then Tiji had exhausted herself by pacing and crying and was lying on the bed, curled into a ball, wishing sleep would take her and offer her some solace. There was a storm outside; it had been gathering all afternoon. Tiji didn't know if it was magically induced or a natural phenomenon, but she could hear the faint howling of the wind and ice throwing itself at the solid bulk of the palace. It seemed colder, too, but that might be her imagination working overtime, goaded by the blizzard.

She saw the flickering light of a lantern coming into the room, and feigned sleep so she wouldn't have to say anything to him until she was ready. A few moments later, she felt a gentle hand on her shoulder, but when she opened her eyes, it wasn't Azquil who'd come to wake her.

It was that wretched Crasii feline, Jojo.

"You must come with me," Jojo told her.

Tiji sat up, blinking in the candlelight. "Why?"

"Azquil is hurt. He slipped on the stairs. He has broken his leg."

Tiji jumped to her feet and reached for her jacket, which was lying across the end of the bed. "Has someone told Lady Arryl? She'll be able to heal him, won't she?"

"It was Lady Arryl who sent me to fetch you," the cat told her. "You must hurry."

Tiji didn't need any further encouragement. Her anger at Azquil forgotten, she followed Jojo closely. She wasn't surprised so much at the news that someone had slipped and broken something on these treacherous ice stairs, but that it hadn't happened sooner. She hoped Jojo was right about the broken leg. The immortals could heal a great deal, but if Azquil had broken his neck . . . well, she wasn't sure that even with the Tide nearly all the way up, immortals could cure death.

"When did it happen?" she demanded of the feline as she hurried to catch up.

"I don't know."

"How did it happen?"

"I don't know."

"You're a real big help, Jojo, you know that?"

Jojo didn't answer Tiji, but headed unerringly toward the stairs that led to the lower levels. The palace halls were silent and shrouded in darkness at this time of night. At least, it was as dark as it could be in a palace made of polished ice. The lamplight fractured as it hit the walls, sending back a spray of rainbow lights that were as pretty as they were useless when it came to lighting their way. Tiji hurried behind Jojo, wishing now that her last words to Azquil hadn't been uttered in anger.

They headed down the stairs, Tiji expecting to find Azquil every time they rounded another corner, but he was nowhere to be seen. In fact, they soon reached the bottom of the stairs that led to the storeroom level and kept on going along the lengthy corridor leading to Lukys's underground chamber.

"Jojo, where is Azquil?"

"We're nearly there," the feline assured her. A moment later Tiji caught a whiff of something rank, and then, before she had time to react, they rounded another corner and she discovered Lukys standing in the corridor waiting for her. Just as she realised she'd been tricked, she caught another whiff of suzerain and spun around to discover Taryx coming up behind them.

"You can go now," Lukys said to Jojo.

The feline bowed. "To serve you is the reason I breathe, my lord."

Treacherous flanking cat.

"Go, and say nothing of this," Lukys ordered the Crasii. "When you're asked if you have seen this lizard, you are to tell them you saw her leaving the palace during the night and have no knowledge of her whereabouts." The feline bowed again and then Lukys turned his attention to Tiji, as Jojo was swallowed by the darkness in the hall behind them.

Tiji's skin flickered wildly as she looked back and forth, trying to keep Lukys and Taryx in sight at the same time. "I'll scream!"

"If it'll make you feel better," Lukys said.

"What are you going to do to me? Kill me?"

"Probably," Lukys said in a frighteningly reasonable tone. "But for reasons far too complicated to go into now—reasons you cannot begin to understand—for the time being I want you alive, little Scard."

That was good news, Tiji supposed, but it still didn't account for this elaborate ruse to lure her down here into the bowels of the palace. "Why?"

"Didn't I just tell you I wasn't going to explain?" He turned to his left, which is when Tiji noticed the cavern sculpted into the wall behind him. "For the time being, this will be your new home. You'll stay here until I need you again. Or until I don't need you. At which point you'll be free to share the fate of your friends once we have departed Amyrantha."

Tiji peered into the ice cave. As far as she could tell, it was quite large and completely open to the corridor. She smiled. *Tides, do they think I'll stay put down here because they order me to?*

Ah, the arrogance of immortals, to think everyone, even a Scard, will do their bidding.

"To serve you is the reason I breathe," she said as she stepped into the cavern, her voice laden with scorn. She turned and smiled at the Tide Lord. "I'll just wait here until you get back then, shall I?"

"Why don't you do that?" Lukys said, his smile never wavering. "Taryx. When you're ready."

Tiji met the Tide Lord's eye defiantly, waiting for him to leave so she could escape this place. And by the Tides, she *was* going to escape. Who cared if it was in the middle of nowhere? Perishing in the snow outside in a blizzard while bravely searching for freedom was preferable to staying here among these monsters a moment longer than she had to.

Azquil could come with her or not. She was beyond caring about that.

Lukys stared back at her for a while, his smile never wavering, until he began to blur a little around the edges. It was only then that Tiji realised the opening between them was no longer an opening. There was a barrier there now—a thin sheet of ice that was growing thicker by the minute. She realised then why Taryx was here—the master manipulator of ice and water. Tiji threw herself at the wall as the ice barrier thickened and whitened before her eyes. She bounced off the solid sheet of ice so hard when she threw herself at it, she bruised her shoulder.

"No!" she screamed, pounding on the ice as the wall thickened so rapidly she could no longer even see the immortals standing on the other side. "Nobody will believe I've just up and left! They'll know you've done something to me!"

There was no response from the immortals. With a scream of frustration, Tiji sank to the floor as she realised the futility of her threat. Her very words echoed back at her in the sealed room, taunting her.

Nobody will believe I've just up and left.

Her last words to Azquil threatened exactly that.

Tiji looked around in despair. She was completely shut in and unless the Tide Lords chose to free her, suffocation, starvation or the cold would kill her long before anybody noticed she was missing.

Chapter 46

Stellan pulled the curtain aside and glanced out of the coach's window at the snow-draped city of Herino, glad of the darkness. Ice crunched beneath the wheels as they moved along the city streets, although this late, there were few people abroad to comment on their carriage. In fact, there was nothing marking his vehicle as belonging to a king, for which he was extremely grateful. Stellan had no desire to draw attention to this outing.

He let the dark curtain drop back into place and pulled his coat a little tighter. The more optimistic souls at court were starting to speak of the coming spring in hopeful terms. Stellan saw no sign of it yet.

Admittedly, the weather had improved since the massive ice-sheet had broken in the middle of the battle, abruptly putting an end to Glaeba's invasion of Caelum. However, it was still cold, foggy and thoroughly miserable, the day Stellan Desean brought Mathu Debree home.

The memory pained Stellan more than he could say. The Caelish had embalmed the young king's body and respectfully dressed it according to his rank for the journey across the lake, which was probably more than he deserved. And it didn't do anything to mitigate the tragedy of a life cut so short, so pointlessly.

Nevertheless, in his own strange way, Mathu had achieved a type of immortality, Stellan realised.

He'll never grow old. Never feel the ravages of time, he remembered thinking as he supervised the Crasii laying out the king's body in state, in preparation for the scores of mourners already lining up outside Herino Palace in the freezing wind.

Of course, he died making war on a country Glaeba once counted as an ally, Stellan added silently, leaning a little to the left to counteract the right turn the carriage was making. Perhaps, with the spectre of a world ruled by the Tide Lords looming on the horizon, Mathu's folly would eventually become a forgotten footnote in history.

A footnote that was fading all too fast, Stellan realised with despair. Since returning to Herino as Glaeba's king, Stellan had barely found the time to think, let alone wonder about Mathu's legacy. The coach rocked to a halt, forcing Stellan to turn his attention to more immediate concerns. The funeral was over and done with weeks ago, the country already moving on.

A moment later, the carriage door opened, and the canine coachman unfolded the step to enable the new King of Glaeba to disembark.

Stellan still hadn't got used to the idea he was King of Glaeba. The circumstances that had brought him to this pass were too tragic for him to take any pleasure from the title. It seemed like nothing more than an endless responsibility; a weight on his shoulders he didn't know if he was strong enough to bear.

If there was any joy to be had in kingship, Stellan had yet to find it.

Tilly's front door opened as he approached. Apparently, they'd been watching for him. Shivering in the brisk night air, he nodded to the doorman, wondering what had happened to the old canine who used to work for Tilly.

In fact, as the man led Stellan through the house to Tilly's main reception room, he saw little sign of any Crasii slaves, which was an odd state of affairs. Tilly liked her creature comforts—and the creatures who took care of her comforts for her.

The doorman stopped in the hall outside the parlour, knocked and then opened the door without waiting for an answer. He stood back to allow Stellan access and then closed the door behind him. Tilly was sitting in a large armchair by a roaring fire, wrapped in a warm knitted shawl with a chequered rug thrown over her legs. Her hair was a dull reddish colour and for the first time since Stellan had known her, she looked old.

"I wasn't sure you'd answer my summons," she said, holding her hand out to him.

Stellan crossed the room, took her hand and kissed it with a smile. "Who else in all the land would dare to so summarily send for their king, my lady?"

"You didn't have to come, you know," she said, pointing to the large armchair opposite. "You could have ordered me to attend you."

Stellan took the offered seat, still smiling. "How could I refuse your summons? You said it was important."

"Aye, and you'll have not heard that phrase a thousand times in the past few weeks, either, I suppose?"

Stellan shrugged, settling into the comfortable chair and relaxing a little for the first time in weeks. "Important is a relative sort of concept, these days. I deem you important, Tilly. So here I am."

The old lady's eyes narrowed. "You didn't used to deem me so important, your majesty. What changed your mind?"

Stellan hesitated before he shrugged and said, "An immortal named Declan Hawkes."

Tilly didn't look surprised. She studied him in the firelight for a time, as if debating something within herself. "How much do you know?"

"More than I ever wanted to," Stellan told her with heartfelt honesty.

Tilly spared him a thin smile. "Could you be a little more specific?"

"I know who the immortals are, if that's what you're asking. I know about the Cabal and your role in their governance. I don't pretend to understand what these immortals are up to, but I do know who they are. And I've seen enough of them to know that we should be very, very afraid of them."

"You do understand that both Caelum and Glaeba are lost to them, don't you?" Tilly asked, searching his face for his reaction.

Stellan nodded. "My hope is to mitigate the damage as much as I can. To be honest, I lie awake at night wondering if I'm a hero or a traitor."

"I suspect it will matter little in the long run. Chances are good there'll be nobody left to protect or betray if the Tide Lords follow their usual pattern."

Stellan sighed. "And to think, Arkady used to invite you to the palace to cheer us up."

"She's alive, you know," Tilly told him.

He was both amazed and relieved by the news. And puzzled as to how she might know of his wife's fate. "How could you possibly have news of Arkady?"

"Declan told me."

"You've seen him since the battle, then?" He was surprised Tilly was taking the news about Hawkes so calmly. Given her role as the Guardian of the Lore, learning one of her protégés had effectively joined the other side could not have been easy for her to digest.

Tilly appeared more than accepting of it; she seemed almost fatalistic about it. The old lady smiled wanly. "There's a certain poetic irony to it don't you think? Finding one's heir apparent is the scion of one's ene-mies."

"Poetic irony?" Stellan said, raising his brow curiously. "I could think of a few other, less-genteel ways of describing it."

"Life never turns out the way we think it will, Stellan," she said, look-ing older than he ever remembered. "This also happens—incidentally—to be the reason I requested an audience with you."

"To share your wisdom about fate?"

"To ask a favour of you."

He smiled, glad there was something useful he might do as king. "You only have to ask, Tilly. You know that."

Tilly's smile faded. "You don't know what the favour is."

"I'm sure, if it's for you, it will be a worthwhile cause."

The old woman nodded. "Worthwhile? Absolutely. But it's not for me, Stellan. It's for every living mortal on Amyrantha."

"A worthwhile cause indeed," he agreed. "What would you have me do? Declare the Tide Lords outlaw? Ban the use of Tide magic? Issue a decree telling them to behave themselves?"

"Actually, I'd like you to help us stop them destroying Amyrantha."

Stellan's smile widened. "So, it's only a small favour then?"

Tilly was not amused. "I'm glad you're finding some humour in the situation."

"I'm sorry," he said, forcing away his smile. "How can I help?"

"The Immortal Prince, Cayal—"

"Yes," Stellan interrupted. "I've met him."

"Then you probably know he's suicidal?"

"He told Arkady as much when she first went to interview him."

"Well, he's a little more determined than we thought and he has al-lies gathering to his cause. Specifically, the Tide Lord known as Lukys, a man who until recently was posing as a member of the Cabal." Tilly's expression didn't alter but he could hear the pain such an admission cost her in the slight tremor of her voice.

"I see . . ."

"I very much doubt that you do, Stellan. According to Declan, to kill an immortal one needs to open a rift, a portal to another world—he claims—that will allow the Tide Lords to access a vastly greater magical force than is available to them on the Tide in this world alone. They need this magic to restore one of their own to human form. As a result of this, the immortals—or at least some of them—intend to leave Amyrantha through that portal."

"Isn't that a good thing?"

"It would be," Tilly agreed, "if the process of closing the rift after they step through it isn't going to tear this world to pieces as it snaps shut."

Stellan had difficulty imagining such a force—a force so powerful it was capable of destroying a world. "Do you know this for a fact, Tilly, or are you just speculating?"

She shrugged, her face shadowed and grim in the firelight. "Declan seems reasonably certain. But even if he isn't, can we afford to ignore the possibility?"

"But how can we stop them? Even with Declan Hawkes on our side, that's still only one immortal against a score of them."

Tilly nodded. "And it takes a Tide Lord to stop a Tide Lord. That's where you come in."

"What do you expect *me* to do?" he asked, more than a little concerned by the notion that she believed him capable of doing anything to stop a Tide-wielding immortal from doing exactly as he pleased, let alone halt Amyrantha's destruction. "I'm no hero. Tides, when it gets down to it, all I am is a diplomat, Tilly. And a very reluctant king. I barely have the power to rule Glaeba. I haven't the power to order anybody else to do anything."

"No, but you have the ear of Tryan and the Empress of the Five Realms. Declan needs their help to stop Cayal, Lukys, Kentravyon, Elyssa and the other immortals they've gathered to their cause in Jelidia. Opening this rift requires a number of Tide Lords working in concert. It will take as many Tide Lords working in concert to stop them. You are going to have to arrange a meeting between the warring parties, Stellan. And somehow, you're going to have to make them hammer out an agreement that will stop the other Tide Lords and save Amyrantha."

Stellan stared at her, aghast. "You want me to hammer out an agreement between *who*? Declan and Tryan? Syrolee and her family? Who else?"

"The Imperator of Torlenia, for one."

Stellan looked at her blankly. "What's he got to do with this?"

"While you were hiding in the mountains, the young Imperator of Torlenia was taken ill. He emerged from his sick bed several weeks later, a changed man. So changed he now bears a striking resemblance to the immortal, Brynden."

Stellan shook his head in amazement. "Tides, is there *no* nation on Amyrantha they've not staked a claim on yet?"

"A few," Tilly said. "But that's probably because we have more nations than Tide Lords, rather than lack of ambition on their part."

Stellan could no longer sit still. He climbed to his feet and began to pace the small rug in front of the fire. "How am I supposed to do this, Tilly? Why would they even listen to me?"

"Because that's your unique talent, Stellan. You're a diplomat. You may well be the only man on Amyrantha capable of bringing these people to the negotiating table, working out an agreement between them and motivating them to take action before the Tide peaks and Amyrantha is destroyed."

He shook his head, but he wasn't sure if he was denying her compliment or simply dumbfounded by the dire nature of the problem. "I'm flattered by your faith in me, but it's sadly misplaced, I fear. I don't even have proof that this plan you say will destroy Amyrantha is real. I'm assuming Declan isn't here to back you up, otherwise he'd be sitting here with us now, and he could help explain it to his immortal brethren. Diplomacy is all about credibility, Tilly. One cannot negotiate from a position of strength when one can't prove they have the authority, moral or otherwise, to seal the deal."

Tilly nodded. "I know. I have someone who *will* help you. Declan is already on his way to Torlenia to speak to Brynden, but there is still one man in Glaeba who can vouch for this. One man capable of convincing Tryan and Syrolee of the urgency of your pact—provided you can get them to the table. With Declan talking to Brynden—assuming our newest immortal is successful in his attempt to secure the cooperation of the Lord of Reckoning and his consort—it should be a small matter to get the lesser immortals to join the cause."

"Who is there?" Stellan asked, still shaking his head. There was no man he could think of with the authority to make a Tide Lord listen to him about the dangers of opening this rift. "To bring Tryan to heel, you would need another Tide . . ."

His voice trailed off as the answer came to him before Tilly even had a chance to explain. "Tides . . . No. You cannot mean . . ."

By her sympathetic look, Tilly understood his pain, but she wasn't going to let it stop her doing what needed to be done. "You know yourself there is no other way, Stellan, otherwise you wouldn't be looking so pale right now."

He shook his head. "He declared *war* on them, Tilly. Tryan isn't going to listen to a word he has to say."

"Granted," the old lady conceded. "Not unless you intercede on his behalf and smooth the way for the discussion."

"I'd almost rather see Amyrantha destroyed," he said bitterly, "than face that lying, cheating little bastard again."

"That's a pity, Stellan, it really is," Tilly said with a sigh. "And it pains me to do this, but your tender feelings are not a consideration."

"It pains you to do what?"

Tilly reached for the small bell resting on the table beside her chair. It tinkled musically for a moment. Even before the chimes had faded, the door opened. It appeared the doorman had been waiting for his cue.

"My lady?"

"Would you ask our other guest to join us, Ceeby?" Tilly replied.

That was all the warning Stellan got; just a fraction of a second to control his anger. An eye-blink to compose his features and turn to face the man who stepped into the room looking exactly as he had several months ago when Stellan had last seen him, the day he came to torment him in Herino Prison.

He didn't even have the decency to look contrite.

But the new Duke of Lebec would never know how much his presence pained Stellan. The new King of Glaeba was a man expert in hiding his true feelings. So Stellan smiled urbanely, as if they were nothing more than acquaintances brought together by chance.

"Well, Jaxyn," he said, resuming his seat and leaning back in it with a casual air. "Tilly tells me you need my help to save the world."

Jaxyn put his hands on his hips, glancing at the old woman in annoyance. "That's not how I would have put it. But then the Cabal of the Tarot always have been prone to exaggeration."

Jaxyn's statement revealed so much. That he was here; that he knew the identity of Tilly and her role in the secret organisation dedicated to the destruction of his kind; that she not only tolerated his presence, but seemed to be aiding him—all this told Stellan a great deal about the state of the world and the dire trouble heading their way if he did nothing to help.

"I'm sure they are," Stellan replied, marvelling at the steadiness of his own voice. "How would *you* describe our situation?"

"Awkward," Jaxyn snapped. "But nothing we can't deal with if you can get me in to see Tryan. Given what's happened of late . . . well, I doubt he wants to speak to me, at the moment. The old girl and I agree," he added, glancing at Tilly who didn't seem pleased with his description of her, "—and there's not much we agree on—that you're the only one with the power and probably the brains to make it happen."

"Awkward? That's something of an understatement."

"So you'll do it?" Jaxyn asked, a little impatiently.

"On one condition," Stellan said, flicking a speck of imaginary dust from his trousers as he crossed one leg over the other.

"What condition?"

Stellan knew that there was no power he could exert over this immortal. There was nothing he could probably ever do to redress the ills done to him and his family by this man. Not the murder of his niece, the destruction of his country, the taking of everything he owned . . .

But for a fleeting moment, Stellan had all the power in the world. It may never happen again, he realised, but right now, in this instant, Stellan had something Jaxyn needed and that meant he held the upper hand.

The King of Glaeba met Jaxyn's eye and smiled poisonously. "You're going to have to say *please*."

Chapter 47

It was raining in Ramahn. Declan had never seen rain here before. It lent the city a melancholy air. Buildings normally bright, white and deceptively clean were now grey and mottled with moisture. The fine layer of sandy dust that lay over everything in this city, perched on the edge of a desert, turned to mud in the rain, streaking the sides of buildings, leaving the once colourful marketplace awnings hanging dull, limp and dripping, and driving even the beggars indoors.

Declan had sent Warlock to Torlenia to deliver his request for a meeting to Brynden. Given the magical trip-wire Brynden had set around the continent, Declan thought sending a third party to deliver the message—one who wouldn't set off the alarm and couldn't be corrupted by an immortal—the safest course.

He wasn't sure what Brynden's reaction would be to his request, and he wasn't prepared to risk innocent lives on a guess. It was one thing to trigger the magical barrier on the uninhabited west coast where only Kinta was nearby to respond. Quite another to set it off near one of the greatest population centres on Amyrantha.

But waiting for an answer had left his nerves frayed with anticipation. Two weeks was a long time to worry if Jaxyn was doing as he promised, to fret over whether or not Stellan Desean would be able to contain his own feelings well enough to deal with Jaxyn again, let alone bring the warring Tide Lords of Caelum and Glaeba to the table. And whether or not a rapprochement was even possible. The sheer inconvenience of the war between the two countries irked Declan. With the world on the very brink of destruction, who cared about a border dispute?

His worrying proved a wasted effort. Two weeks after he sent Warlock to Ramahn with a sealed note to be placed in the hands of the Imperator's Consort—on the very same day he decided that his offer had been refused, Warlock must be dead, and he was going to have to risk entering Torlenia himself—a message had arrived from Ramahn with news that Brynden would grant him an audience.

He turned from watching the city at the feel of someone approaching on the Tide. There were two of them, he decided. The powerful ripples of a Tide Lord and the lesser ripples of an immortal who lacked the same power, but who nonetheless was able to affect the Tide. Declan took a deep breath, his heart pounding as the Lord of Reckoning and his lover neared the audience chamber of Ramahn Palace. It was a large room, tiled in decorative mosaics depicting the many moral lessons the Lord of Reckoning had bestowed upon his people over the centuries. It was not clear yet, to the people of Torlenia, that their god now sat on the throne. They still believed him to be their beloved Imperator, changed by illness and a miracle into a man of wisdom and insight.

He wasn't sure how Brynden had managed to get away with such an elaborate deception. Having Crasii servants helped, he supposed. They were compelled to do and say anything he ordered. All the human staff Declan encountered on his way through the palace seemed to be priests, members of Brynden's own cult. Declan reasoned that with them in charge, there was nobody much around left to object.

Declan's skin tingled. Neither of the approaching immortals was using Tide magic, but the Tide was coming in fast. Even Declan could feel the difference. There was an urgency about it now; a feeling that before long, nothing would be able to hold it back. It was thrilling. It was terrifying. And it was all Declan could do to stop himself plunging into the magic at every meagre excuse he could find to wield it.

Given he was a legendary warrior, Declan was a little disappointed when the doors at the end of the cathedral-like audience chamber opened and Brynden entered wearing sandals, a loose white shirt and linen trousers of the sort you'd see any ordinary man in the street of Ramahn wearing. Well-built, clean-shaven, with close-cropped blond hair and the gait of a warrior, he seemed more mercenary than majesty.

Kinta, on the other hand, was dressed exactly as he'd seen her on the west coast of Torlenia a few weeks ago, after she'd removed her shroud—heavily armed and wearing a short leather skirt and a tooled leather breastplate. He wondered why she bothered. Armour was designed to protect vital organs from harm. There was no weapon on Amyrantha that could harm her. And no weapon that could harm him, either, if it came to it. Her mode of dress told him something else about this place, too. In a land where women must always remain shrouded in the company of men not of their own family, she was proudly dressed as a warrior. That meant she trusted every soul in the palace not to betray her.

It also meant there was nobody here, if things went badly, who would lift a finger to aid Declan.

Good to know these things ahead of time.

Declan stepped forward, all the speeches he'd been mentally rehearsing in his head vanishing as Brynden strode across the tiles with Kinta beside him, and stopped a few feet from him. He was prepared to hate the man who had sold Arkady into slavery, but couldn't afford his own prejudices to get in the way. He needed Brynden. There was an eternity waiting on the other side of this calamity for him to settle the score over Arkady, once Amyrantha was saved.

"Clever," Brynden said, speaking Glaeban, as he eyed Declan up and down. "Sending a Scard to deliver your message."

"I might not have been born ten thousand years ago, Lord Brynden," Declan replied, meeting his gaze as evenly as he could manage. There was no point in trying to pretend he wasn't nervous. Brynden would feel that on the Tide, just as Declan could feel Brynden's confidence. And his curiosity. "But I wasn't born yesterday, either. Where is Warlock?"

"Safe. For the time being."

"I'd like to see him."

Brynden studied him curiously. "Why do you care about the fate of one stupid *gemang*, Hawkes?"

"I gave him my word he'd be safe."

The Tide Lord smiled. "And then you sent him to me with a message demanding a parley? You have an interesting view of the word *safe*."

"I was led to believe you are a man of honour."

That gave Brynden pause. He was silent for a moment and then he turned to Kinta.

"I told you, Bryn—" she began, but he waved her to silence.

"Have the Scard brought here."

Kinta glanced at Declan uncertainly. "Are you sure?"

"I'm sure."

The warrior bowed to her lord and turned for the door. Declan couldn't hide his relief as Brynden walked past him through the arched opening and stepped out onto the rain-spattered balcony to stare at the city.

"It hasn't rained here for years."

Declan turned and followed him out into the rain. It was warm and not entirely unpleasant outside, and not the venue he expected for a meeting like this.

"Is the rain a consequence of what's happening in Glaeba?" Declan asked, recalling the numerous warnings he'd received about how using the Tide in one place often had a consequence in another.

Brynden shrugged. "You tell me, Hawkes. You've been there more recently than I have."

"They've never before had a winter as bad as this one."

The Tide Lord leaned on the marble balustrade, staring out over the rooftops. "Nor a summer as hot, a spring as dry . . . it's a common thing, when the Tide turns. There will be storms, violent storms, droughts, famines, floods—and that's without any of us lifting a finger. I used to think that was our purpose, you know; that we'd been put on this world to mitigate the effects of the Tide on others less fortunate."

Declan was surprised to hear Brynden admit such a thing. But then, maybe he shouldn't be. If any immortal had put thought into the meaning of their existence, it was this man. "Is that what you think now?"

"I don't know." He straightened and turned to face Declan. His expression was puzzled more than threatening, as if wrestling with the philosophical problems posed by Lukys's plans for Amyrantha was more exhausting than an actual battle. "The news Kinta brought me from her first meeting with you, has left me . . . unsettled. How certain are you of your intelligence, Hawkes?"

Although he suspected she would do so, it was a relief to discover he was right in his assumption that Kinta had passed on to Brynden what she'd learned in their meeting on the other side of the continent when Kentravyon had told them about Coryna. The detailed message Declan sent with Warlock would have done the rest, he supposed.

"I've seen the chamber Lukys has built in Jelidia to open the rift. Best we can tell, Cayal has the crystal and is on his way back to the ice palace with it. As for the risk to Amyrantha?" Declan shrugged, which allowed the water pooling in his collar to run down his back under his shirt. "To be honest, my lord, we only have Kentravyon's word on it.

On the balance of probability, given Lukys claims the forces released when the portal closes are enough to kill an immortal, I'm guessing the risk is substantial."

Brynden nodded and folded his arms across his chest. The rain had drenched his hair, and ran in rivulets down his face, but he seemed unaware of it, content to let it fall. Declan remembered riding in the rain with Jaxyn in Herino. He'd had no qualms about carelessly using the Tide to keep the elements at bay. Brynden was much more restrained, much more cautious of the power he wielded and the responsibility that went with it. "How do you intend to stop them?"

"I can't. Not on my own. That's why I need you."

Brynden frowned. "You'll need every Tide Lord on Amyrantha, I suspect, to counter the force Lukys can muster. That means involving *all* the immortals, including Jaxyn, who is a wastrel, and Tryan, who is a sadist. Neither can be trusted."

Declan nodded in agreement. "That's the main reason I need you and Lady Kinta along, my lord," he said, figuring a show of respect would go a long way with the Lord of Reckoning. "I need someone I can trust to watch my back." Declan was amazed to realise he spoke the truth. He probably could trust Brynden; more than he trusted any other Tide Lord, at any rate. That left him feeling more than a little disloyal toward Arkady.

But he couldn't worry about that now. There was a world at stake. It was alarming how quickly he was learning to put his own feelings aside to deal with that threat.

The Tide Lord studied Declan as if he understood Declan's moral dilemma, and then he smiled. "You believe you can trust me? How do I know I can trust you? You are Lukys's son. Prove to me this is more than an elaborate prank put together by one of my jaded brethren to amuse themselves on the rising Tide."

"How do you expect me to prove that?" Declan asked. The immortal had a point. Brynden really had little more than Declan's word and the second-hand story of a madman to go on.

Before Brynden could answer, however, Declan felt Kinta returning on the Tide. They heard the door opening and turned to find Warlock walking across the hall beside her, dressed in a plain linen slave's tunic, but otherwise unharmed.

Stepping back into the hall, Declan studied Warlock closely for a moment, looking for injuries, before asking, "Are you all right?"

"I'm in one piece, if that's what you're asking," the Scard replied with a scowl. He may not have been physically harmed, but he clearly wasn't happy with his treatment at the hands of these immortals.

The Lord of Reckoning followed Declan back into the hall, wiping the rain from his face with his hand, and then turned to Kinta. "Hawkes believes he can trust us."

"Can't he?" she asked, glancing at Declan. He could feel her uncertainty on the Tide, and wasn't sure what it meant.

"I'm more concerned whether we can trust him. Give me your sword."

Without asking why, Kinta unsheathed her sword and handed it to Brynden in an action that seemed suspiciously rehearsed. The immortal hefted the blade for a moment and then offered it, hilt first, to Declan.

"Kill the Scard," Brynden said.

"Excuse me?" Declan said, wondering if he'd misheard the order. Not that he seriously thought he had. The offered blade said it all, even without words.

"Kill the Scard," Brynden repeated, offering him the sword again. "You want to prove your noble intentions to me, then do as I ask. Kill the Scard."

Declan stared down at the sword for a moment in confusion and then looked at Brynden. "What purpose would that serve?"

"I will know you mean what you say."

Shaking his head, Declan looked at Kinta, who'd contributed nothing, thus far, to the conversation—other than her blade. "How will it prove that? Tides, it's not Kentravyon who's crazy. It's all of you!"

"You're not willing to do it then?" Kinta asked.

Tides, I was such a fool to think this man could be trusted. He sold Arkady into slavery. When did you stop listening to your instincts, you fool?

"No!" Declan said, taking a step forward to put himself between a rather worried-looking Warlock and the immortals. "Absolutely not. And the hell with you for asking. What are you people? Are you so far removed from your own humanity that mortal lives have become a tradable commodity?"

As he heard himself utter the words, Declan realised the irony. He sounded just like Arkady after she'd found out about the deal he did with Cayal over her future. That infuriated him almost as much as Brynden's absurd order to kill Warlock. And it forced a decision from him, one he found it surprisingly easy to make. He snatched the sword from Brynden and tossed it onto the tiles with a clatter. "You know what? The hell with all of you. I'll find another way to stop Lukys and Cayal destroying the world. Without your help. Or maybe I won't. Maybe, if it's the only way to put an end to monsters like you, I ought to go back to Jelidia and give Lukys a hand."

He turned his back on the Lord of Reckoning and his consort and looked at Warlock, making no attempt to hide his anger or his disappointment. "Let's get out of here, Warlock."

The Scard didn't need any further encouragement. He was probably fighting the urge not to retch on the stench of them, anyway. He fell in beside Declan without a murmur of protest.

They'd not taken more than two or three steps, however, before Kinta called them back. "Wait, Declan Hawkes."

Against his better judgement, Declan turned back to look at her. "What?"

She smiled, picking up her sword and checking the blade for nicks before she sheathed it again. "There is no need for you to leave," she said. "Brynden was merely testing you."

"And I failed the test miserably," he said. "I get that. See you around eternity, someplace."

He turned to leave again, but this time it was Brynden who stopped him. "Your refusal to kill the Scard means you passed the test, Hawkes, not failed it."

Declan turned back to stare at them in confusion. "I beg your pardon?"

"You are immortal, Hawkes, but you have a Scard by your side, willing to aid your cause. He must be gagging on the very stench of you, and yet you command his loyalty enough to send him here to Ramahn to deliver your message for you. That's a loyalty not bought cheaply. Scards are not easily fooled or coerced. You must have some good qualities if he will follow you. That you're not a wanton killer is apparently among them."

Declan stared at him in disgust. "But you were quite happy to take an innocent life to find out if I *was*?"

"When the good of many is at stake, the life of one becomes expendable," the Lord of Reckoning said with a shrug. "I have long believed my purpose in becoming immortal would one day be revealed, Declan Hawkes. Perhaps that time is come. There is no greater or nobler purpose, after all, than saving millions of innocent lives from the whim of a madman."

Declan was tempted to point out that Brynden's very own whim had caused the last Cataclysm, but decided that was a debate they didn't have the time for now. "You're with me, then?"

Brynden shook his head. "No, Declan Hawkes, you are with me."

Declan opened his mouth to object but Kinta never gave him the chance. "Brynden commands the respect of the other Tide Lords in a way you simply cannot, Declan Hawkes," she explained. "They have known you for less than an eye-blink. Brynden, on the other hand, has known them for thousands of years, and they know him."

"And from what I hear, they're not all that fond of him either, my lady," Declan reminded her.

"I don't need to command their affection, Hawkes," Brynden said. "But I do command their respect. Your note said the new King of Glaeba is capable of brokering peace between Jaxyn and Tryan. Is that true?"

Declan nodded. "The first meeting was due to take place the day I left Glaeba."

"Once Tryan and Jaxyn have settled their differences, they will listen to me. None of us wants to see Amyrantha destroyed, even if some of the immortals we must rely on to save our world have more venal motives than others."

Declan didn't like the idea of putting Brynden in charge, but he had a bad feeling there was no other way this would work. He'd never been sure how he was going to get the others to follow him, and had been lucky, so far, that he'd achieved even this much. And Brynden did have a point. The other Tide Lords may not like the Lord of Reckoning, but they respected him.

With a great deal of reluctance, he nodded. "Fine. But we don't have much time. I don't need to tell you how fast the Tide is rising, and for all we know, Cayal is already back in Jelidia."

Kinta shook her head. "Not yet. We still have time."

"How do you figure that?" Warlock asked. He'd wisely kept silent until now but apparently the Scard could no longer contain himself. Declan admired that about Warlock. Any other creature in his position would likely be a quivering furry ball of fear by now, in the presence of so many immortals.

Declan was surprised when Kinta answered him with no sign of irritation or impatience. "Immortals prefer to take over existing power structures for more than our love of pomp and ceremony," she said. "A functioning government is always easier to adapt than trying to establish order out of the chaos of utter devastation."

"And functioning governments usually come with established spy networks," Declan said, understanding immediately what she was trying to explain to Warlock. He looked at her curiously. "You have spies out there with news of Cayal, don't you?"

Kinta hesitated for a fraction of a second and then nodded. "He is on a ship heading south. It left the Chelae Islands about three weeks ago, and as far as my informants could tell, it was under sail, not propelled magically by the Tide. That could be because they have the crystal and can't work the Tide with it onboard. Kentravyon is with him and so is Elyssa."

"Was there a human woman with them?" Declan wasn't sure he wanted to know the answer to that question. His last word of Arkady was when she traded the Chaos Crystal for Warlock and his family's freedom. He still had no idea what had happened to her after that, but given Cayal's fascination for her, it wasn't hard to imagine he'd invited her along for the return to Jelidia. But would she go with him? Arkady had sworn to have nothing to do with either Cayal or Declan ever again. Would she change her mind? Had she been *forced* to change her mind?

"There may have been a woman with them, Hawkes. I didn't ask."

Brynden turned to look at her oddly. Putting his fears for Arkady aside, Declan wondered if this was also the first time Kinta had shared this news with him. "Do you know for certain that they've found the Chaos Crystal?"

"Would there be any point in returning to Jelidia without it?" Warlock asked.

Nobody answered what was, essentially, a rhetorical question.

There was a moment of tense silence and then Brynden turned to Declan. "In light of this information, if we are to do this, we don't have a moment to waste. Where have you arranged for everyone to meet?"

"In Denrah," Declan told them. "It's a deep-water anchorage port on the north coast of Chelae. Lyna left Glaeba for Senestra to speak with Medwen and Ambria some time ago, and will meet us back there if she can; otherwise she'll head straight for Jelidia. Desean will give Tryan, Syrolee and the others the exact location of the meeting once they've agreed to help."

Brynden nodded, satisfied, it seemed, with the arrangements. He looked at Warlock. "Are you coming with us, Scard?"

Warlock's hackles were up and his tail was high enough to betray his true feelings, but the Scard gritted his teeth and nodded. "Will I follow you to Jelidia for the chance to see an immortal do something useful for a change? Tides," the big canine growled, "I wouldn't miss that for the world."

Chapter 48

"Tell me you love me, Cayal."

The Immortal Prince sighed and dutifully responded, "I love you, Elyssa."

She turned to look at him in the darkness, her expression sceptical. They were sitting side by side on the steps leading up to the poop deck of the sailing ship they'd commandeered in the Chelae Islands. The night sky was clear and icy and sprinkled with stars, so bright here in the southern ocean one could read by them, even on a moonless night. The air was chilly but neither immortal really noticed it. If fact, were it not for the heavy coats worn by the crew—and the occasional iceberg they carefully sailed past—Cayal probably wouldn't have guessed they were approaching Jelidia at all.

Elyssa had found him here, looking for some peace, no mean feat on a ship barely large enough to contain the three masts whose sails billowed and snapped above them, let alone three powerful Tide Lords champing at their confinement. Not that being a Tide Lord was of much use to anyone on board at present. Cayal could sense hardly anything on the Tide.

The reason Elyssa had found him was a consequence of that. The dampening effect of the Chaos Crystal meant that for the first time in several thousand years—as Kentravyon had warned—another immortal was able to sneak up on him.

"I know you're lying, Cayal."

"Then why do you keep asking me?"

She shrugged and slipped her arm through his, snuggling up to him as if she was cold and needed his body warmth. "I keep hoping one day you'll mean it."

"Well, they say that where there's life, there's hope," he said, staring out at their silvery wake trailing behind them in the starlight, rather than looking at her and risk her seeing his true feelings reflected in his eyes. "Given you can't die, you must be fairly brimming with it."

As usual, she seemed to take his remark for an attempt at humour, not the snide comment he meant it to be. "You'll love me when I look like her," Elyssa predicted. Or perhaps it was just that she knew him well enough not to rise to his taunts. And he knew her well enough to know she was referring to Arkady.

"At the very least, I'll know how to tell if the transfer has worked," he told her.

"How?"

"She'll be talking to me again, if you're the one inhabiting her body."

Elyssa smiled. "Yes, I noticed your precious little Ice Duchess seems rather cool toward you at the moment. Why, Cayal? Did you break her heart?"

"You know, I honestly don't know the answer to that question. I'm not sure what I've done. Or that I'd even understand it if she told me. She's a complicated woman, is Arkady."

"I think she's an arrogant, stuck-up little bitch myself," Elyssa informed him with a smile. "And if it wasn't for the fact that I have a use for her, I would have tossed her over the side as soon as we left Glaeba and the Tide take her. I'm still not convinced we shouldn't. There must be another human woman around I can use. One that's less trouble."

"But we need her to carry the crystal," Cayal said, a little alarmed that Elyssa was entertaining such murderous thoughts.

"Not any longer," she said. "Now we're on our way to Jelidia . . ."

"And at the mercy of the elements because we can't use Tide magic," Cayal reminded her. "What happens if we run into a storm? If the ship is endangered, we're going to need someone to hang on to the crystal."

"Any mortal man in the crew could do that."

"If we're caught in a storm severe enough to endanger this ship," Cayal said, "I'd just as soon the crew was busy trying to keep us afloat, thank you very much."

She laughed. "Why? We can't drown, silly."

"No, but that wretched crystal would sink like a stone if we lost it overboard. Particularly as it's, well, you know . . . a *stone*." He smiled at her then, deciding it was time to get her mind off killing Arkady. "Besides, you want a beautiful body to inhabit, don't you? Even you have to concede they don't come much more beautiful than our regal Glaeban duchess."

Elyssa pouted at him for a moment, and then squeezed his arm while giving him a conspiratorial smile. "She's not *really* a duchess, you know. She's actually a slum-bred, common-born physician's daughter."

"And your mother was a whore, when it gets down to it." Cayal laughed suddenly, as it occurred to him why Elyssa so desperately wanted to get married, even though he had professed his clear intention of killing himself the first chance he got, leaving her a widow. "Tides, that's what this engagement is all about. You want me to legitimise your royalty."

"Don't be absurd."

"You do too!" he said, disentangling her arm from his so he could turn and look her in the eye. "You want to be a real princess and I'm the only prince you can extort a wedding out of, so you want to marry me and get a proper title. Tides, Elyssa, Kordana's been dead and gone for eight thousand years, so I don't know what you think my title is worth. And your mother was calling herself the Empress of the Five Realms for a couple of thousand years before that. Don't you think that title's stuck yet?"

"The key phrase in that statement is 'calling herself Empress,'" Elyssa pointed out grumpily. "Tides, but I hate it when you mock me."

He shook his head in amazement. "If it means so much to you, why not find some poor mortal prince to marry you and give you a crown?"

"I'm not beautiful enough. I'm always the one passed over for the pretty girl." Her tone was even more petulant than her words.

"You're an immortal Tide Lord, Elyssa. You can have anything you want at High Tide."

Elyssa shook her head. "Tide magic won't make someone want you, Cayal; you know that better than anybody. And I don't need to tell you how it works with Syrolee, either. The power *always* sits with her." Cayal listened to her with a growing sense of alarm. It was a little frightening that she still felt so bitter, even after all this time.

"Syrolee seems to be happy to let Tryan share the power in Caelum."

"Only because she couldn't figure out any other way to take the throne than have Tryan marry Princess Nyah. Or Nyah's mother, as it turns out, after the child disappeared."

"So why do you stay with them?"

"I told you why."

He rolled his eyes. "Ah, yes . . . Everyone else disappoints you eventually, don't they? How does your thinking go? 'If they're mortal, they die on me. If they're immortal, they just let me down.'" He shook his head. "Did it ever occur to you, Elyssa, that even the most beautiful woman in the world becomes excessively unattractive when she's wallowing in self-pity?"

She jumped up from the steps and turned to face him, her hands on her hips. "*Self-pity?* You're accusing *me* of wallowing in self-pity? The coward who wants to kill himself because he can't bear the thought of being bored? Tides, but you have a nerve!"

"At least I'm sure I'm doing the right thing."

"Only because you won't let yourself contemplate the future," she shot back. "You're such a flanking fool, Cayal."

"Maybe I am. But I've seen the future, Elyssa," he said. "And I'm not in it."

She was unimpressed. "Oh, so now you're prescient, are you? When did you acquire *that* talent?"

He shrugged. "Probably about the same time it occurred to me that we're *true* immortals," he said, feeling the sudden need to explain himself to someone who might have a slight chance of understanding. "Haven't you figured it out yet, Lyssa? We're not like the characters they put in children's stories who are immortal right up until they change their mind. Or until they're killed in single combat—a battle some noble hero is destined to win because his heart is true, or some such nonsense. The power to destroy one of us is the stuff that unmakes worlds. Short of lopping off my head and becoming a simpleton like Pellys, I don't see any other way out."

"What of this new world Lukys is leaving for? Doesn't *that* intrigue you?"

"It might have. Once. But we only get a King Tide every few hundred thousand years. No matter how intriguing this new world of his might be, I don't think I want to risk finding out I really couldn't care what the new one is like, when it's too late to do anything about it."

Elyssa couldn't think of an answer to that, so she swore at him in a very unladylike manner and headed below, leaving the Immortal Prince and his frustrating, infuriating logic behind her, which was exactly what Cayal had been hoping she'd do.

———

Even though he'd managed to drive her away, Cayal's discussion with Elyssa did nothing but unsettle him more. He could feel the Tide rising and with it, his uneasiness. And his uneasiness bothered him. He'd always imagined the closer he got to the end of his interminable existence, the more serene he would become, the more content with his path. He'd never felt this ill at ease before, even when waiting in Lebec Prison for the headsman to call his name. He couldn't fathom why, with eternal peace beckoning, he wasn't feeling calm, but jumpy and uncomfortable.

Elyssa had gone below, no doubt looking for Kentravyon to complain to. Perhaps the madman would sympathise with her. Even insanely obsessed with his own divinity as he was, Kentravyon was probably a better conversationalist right now. And the chilly night with its distant blanket of stars was no comfort either.

"Gonna be another cold one."

Cayal glanced up from where he was sitting on the steps to the sailor manning the helm. He stood behind the wheel, feet planted firmly apart, rolling almost imperceptibly with the movement of the deck as if he was bolted to the boards along with the wheel.

"Looks like it," Cayal agreed in a noncommittal tone. He was restless, unsure what he was looking for, but certain it wasn't a dialogue about the weather with some random sailor who happened to be stuck on the late watch. Climbing to his feet, Cayal headed below before the sailor could attempt to engage him in further conversation.

The passageway below the poop deck was narrow and dark, the door to the owner's cabin he shared with Kentravyon at the end of the companionway. The only two other cabins in the stern above the waterline were opposite each other; the cabin on the right allocated to Elyssa, the other to Arkady.

On impulse, he knocked on Arkady's door, hoping she wasn't yet asleep. Or if she wasn't, she'd not start asking questions about the identity of her late-night visitor through the door, forcing him to answer so loudly he'd alert Elyssa to the fact that he was seeking entry into Arkady's cabin in the middle of the night.

After a moment, the door opened. Although she'd not questioned who it was at this late hour, Arkady did not seem happy to see him. "What?"

"Can I come in?" he asked softly, glancing over his shoulder toward Elyssa's door.

Arkady didn't miss the direction of his gaze. She thought about it for a moment and then sighed and stood back to let him enter. She was still dressed, although the fur coat Jaxyn had given her to wear in Glaeba was draped over the narrow bunk, where clearly she intended to use it as an extra blanket.

"It's late, Cayal, and I'd like to get some sleep," she said as she closed the door behind him and then leaned on it. "What do you want?"

"I just wanted to talk."

"Go talk to your cabin mate." She pushed past him and walked over to the small cabinet beside the bunk where she splashed water on her face from the washbowl. Her voice sounded odd, but that could have been because she'd been trying to sleep and he'd disturbed her.

"Kentravyon's crazy."

"So you keep insisting." She dried her face off with a small towel and turned to look at him. "He seems perfectly rational to me."

"He murdered an entire town in Stevania, once. Killed every man, woman and child in a ten-mile radius because some careless farmer ran over his foot with a wagon and refused to apologise," Cayal told her. "He seemed perfectly rational then, too."

She shook her head in disgust. "Tides, you're all mad."

Cayal wasn't sure he could argue about that. He glanced around the cabin. There was a small candle, which barely lit the room, burning in the sconce by the door. He couldn't see the Chaos Crystal, although in here, so close to it, the Tide was barely perceptible. It was like one of his senses was muffled; as if a part of him had been hooded, bound, and thrown in the corner until the ransom was paid.

"Where is it?"

Arkady didn't need to ask what he meant. "Safe."

"I can feel it," he said. "Or rather I can't feel anything, which amounts to the same thing . . . Tides, Arkady, have you been crying?"

She wiped her eyes impatiently with the heel of her hand and shook her head in denial. "No."

"Don't lie to me."

"Then leave me alone so I don't have to."

He reached out, taking her by the shoulders, forcing her to look at him. There was nowhere she could go to avoid him in such a confined space, but she turned her head away so he couldn't see her tears or her puffy eyes.

"What's the matter?" he asked gently.

Swollen eyes forgotten, Arkady looked up and treated him to a baleful glare. "That's a joke, right?"

He smiled. "Let me rephrase the question then. What—out of all the calamities that have befallen you since I came into your life—has finally reduced you to tears?"

She tried to shake free of him. "You arrogant bastard. Why do you automatically assume that my being upset has anything to do with you?"

Cayal hadn't stopped to think about it, but she was right. He did assume her tears must somehow be related to him. "You mean it's *not* my fault?"

"As it happens, no."

"Then why are you crying?"

"I don't want to talk about it." Her bottom lip trembled as she spoke. She was one kind word away from losing her composure completely, he guessed.

"You look like you need to talk to someone." Gently, he pulled her to him and wrapped his arms around her. She resisted, rigid in his embrace. "Come on, Arkady. There's nobody you have to be strong for here."

"I'm not strong," she said, pulling away from him. "That's the problem. I'm weak. Spineless. A coward . . ."

"How do you figure that?"

"Because I left him behind."

Cayal looked at her with a puzzled frown. "You left who behind, where?"

"My father," she said, choking back a sob. "He was alive, Cayal, and I left him on the ice with Jaxyn. He told me to run and I did it with barely a second thought, and then you and the other immortals broke the ice, and now he's dead, and it's my fault, because if I'd *made* him come with me, he'd have been safe . . ."

The words fizzled out as the tears overtook her. Cayal gathered her into his arms again and this time she didn't resist. This time she put her arms around him and sobbed against his shoulder, as if everything had finally caught up with her. As if she no longer had the will to hold it back. Cayal said nothing for a time. He just held her and let her cry, partly because he wasn't sure what else he could do, and partly because he knew that her tears would ultimately be cathartic.

For a time, she sobbed like a broken-hearted child. Cayal held her, wishing he could ease her pain. And hoping that somewhere between here and Jelidia he could find a way to prevent Elyssa from killing her in a futile attempt to steal her body for her own—a process Cayal secretly believed was never going to work, even with the Tide magic of two worlds at their disposal to make it happen.

Chapter 49

Arkady woke in Cayal's arms. For a moment she couldn't imagine how she came to be there, and then she remembered breaking down last night and Cayal comforting her, which had led to Cayal kissing her, which had led to, well . . . this.

"You snore. Did you know that?"

She shifted on the narrow bunk. Cayal was awake. She wasn't sure how long he'd been lying there holding her, watching her. Long enough to realise that she was snoring, apparently.

"Well, aren't you the last of the true romantics."

He smiled. "I like to watch you sleep."

"Why? Particularly if I snore?"

"It's the only time you're ever truly relaxed, Arkady." He bent forward and kissed her gently on the lips. "It's past sun-up. I really should go . . ."

"Before your fiancée finds you in here?" she finished for him. *Tides, what have I done?* Last night's moment of weakness, Arkady realised, may end up costing her her life. She was under no illusions about the capacity of the Immortal Maiden for jealous retribution if she thought Arkady her rival for Cayal's affection.

"Don't worry about Elyssa," Cayal said, showing no inclination to get out of bed, despite his stated intention of leaving. "I'll take care of her."

"She looks at me strangely," Arkady said, making no move to escape the comfort of his unnaturally warm body beside hers on the bunk. The air in the cabin was freezing. She could feel it on her face. The rest of her, however, was snuggled beneath the fur coat she'd brought from Glaeba, pressed against Cayal's warm, hard-muscled length.

"That's just her way."

"If I was a horse and she looked at me the same way, I'd be certain I was destined for the knackery."

"Now you're exaggerating."

"No, I'm not," she insisted. "And I *will* be destined for the knackery if she finds out you spent the night in my cabin."

He nuzzled her ear. "Then we shan't tell her."

She shook her head and pushed him away as far as she could on the narrow bunk. "Tides, Cayal, do you any have conscience at all?"

"Not so's you'd notice," he said, in a better mood than Arkady had seen him for a very long time. "And before you start accusing me of being morally bankrupt, your holiness, might I remind you that you're lying here beside me, naked as the day you were born, a willing participant in my moral decline?"

"Your moral decline didn't need any help from me, Cayal," she said, a little miffed to think he was trying to make her equally culpable for the lapse in good judgement that had brought them to this pass, and this bed.

Why didn't I say no? Why didn't I tell him to leave when he started kissing me last night?

Arkady knew the reason. She'd been cold and guilt-ridden, frightened and lonely, and Cayal had a talent for offering her comfort when she was at her most vulnerable.

"And for your information, I'm lying here with you because you give off heat like a walking glass-furnace and I'm going to freeze to death the moment I get out from under these covers. Why couldn't you and your insane friends build your magical, crystal-powered, immortal-killing chamber somewhere warm?"

"It has something to do with being near the magnetic poles," he told her. "Are you going to keep complaining about the weather?"

"Every chance I get."

"Maybe I will let Elyssa kill you after all," he said with a smile.

Arkady eyed him curiously. "Is there a particular reason she *wants* to kill me, Cayal?"

"You know the reason," he said. "She thinks I fancy you. She's jealous."

"So why hasn't she killed me already?"

"Because I asked her not to."

"And the other reason?"

"What other reason?"

"The real reason Elyssa is allowing me to live." Arkady turned on her side, pushing herself up on her elbow so she could read Cayal's expression. "Elyssa is itching to be rid of me, Cayal. I can see it every time she looks at me. And yet she allows me to keep on breathing. Why?"

"You're carrying the Chaos Crystal for us."

"You could have *hired* someone in Glaeba to do that if you had to. You don't need me, just a cooperative human who can't touch the Tide."

Cayal looked away guiltily for a moment, and then he shrugged, as if he'd decided there was really no harm in her learning the truth. "Well . . . it might be because I . . . sort of promised her . . . your body."

Arkady wasn't sure what he meant. If Elyssa had a taste for taking pleasure with her own gender, Arkady had never seen any sign of it. "I thought you said she wasn't that way inclined?"

"I mean *literally*," he clarified, with some reluctance.

"I don't understand, Cayal."

He sighed, more than a little uncomfortable. "Ah . . . well, you see . . . Lukys's offer to help me die is, I recently discovered, only a sideshow to the main event, which is transferring Coron's consciousness back into a proper body. I may have . . . um . . . *implied* . . . during my discussions with Elyssa while I was trying to get her to help, that if she was willing to help me die, I'd ask him to do the same for her."

Arkady frowned, unable to grasp what he was telling her. "Let me get this straight. Lukys wants to transfer the consciousness of his pet rat into a human body—Tides, I don't even want to think about the story behind that—so *you* told Elyssa he could do the same for her, using *my* body?"

The Immortal Prince nodded and ventured a cautious smile. "It won't work. I mean, you're not even a little bit immortal. The process would most likely kill you anyway, so Lukys probably won't even agree to try it. You really have nothing to worry about . . ."

"Nothing to worry about? Are you insane? Well, yes, you are, aren't you?" she said, giving him no chance to answer. "What possessed you to promise her something like that, you fool?" No longer fearful of the cold in light of Elyssa's dire plans for her, Arkady threw back the covers, climbed out of the bunk and attempted to retrieve her clothes from the floor of the cabin while staying on her feet. She shivered in the icy air, trying to keep her balance. The deck was rising and falling with the roiling sea outside, something she'd not been quite so conscious of while lying in the bunk next to Cayal.

"I thought it would save your life," he protested, managing to sound both wounded and innocent at the same time. "Tides, I was only trying to help, Arkady."

"She wants to *possess* me, Cayal! How exactly is that saving my life?"

"You're still alive."

"I think I'd *rather* be dead!" She pulled her bodice on over her slip and began the laborious process of doing up the scores of tiny nacre buttons that held it closed. "I can't believe you brought me all this way just so Elyssa can kill me."

"I didn't bring you here so she can *kill* you . . ."

"No? Then how else do you think this is going to play out, Cayal? Do you imagine that when we get to Jelidia and arrive at this fabulous ice palace of yours, I'll hand over the crystal and then you'll say, 'Oops, my mistake. Sorry, Elyssa, Arkady has to leave now'?"

"Well, obviously we'll have to think of a plausible reason she shouldn't attempt the transfer," he said. "And find a way for you to return home. But I'm sure, if she hears it from Lukys, and he tells her it won't work, Elyssa won't try to force the issue."

"Assuming you ever have such a discussion," Arkady said, knowing Cayal better than he imagined. "She's here because you promised her my body. If she finds out she can't have it, she's going to tell you where you can shove your plans to die, refuse to help you at all and then you're screwed. So I seriously doubt you're going to tell her a damned thing."

With the buttons finally taken care of, Arkady turned and sat on the edge of the bunk so she could pull on her shoes.

"I won't let her hurt you, Arkady," Cayal assured her, reaching out to stroke her hair.

Arkady shook him off impatiently. "Of course you will. You've been trying to kill yourself for over a thousand years. You're not going to let the life of a mere mortal get in your way now. Not when your goal is so close."

"That's a cruel thing to suggest."

She glanced at him and then turned her gaze away. *Tides, he could look wounded, even when he's completely at fault.*

"Doesn't make it any less true, though," she said, tugging on her boots. Finally dressed, she stood up and turned to look at him, cursing herself for the weakness that left her so blind when it came to the true

nature of the Tide Lords—this man in particular. The icy cabin suddenly felt too stuffy and close. She couldn't breathe.

"You know what I think?" she said, reaching over to open the port-
hole to let in some fresh air. "I think—"

"Land ho!" came a distant cry from above.

Arkady closed her eyes. *Tides . . . we're here.*

"What do you think?" Cayal asked.

She had been going to say so much. And Arkady had a lot to say to
this man. She had been going to tell him how much she'd needed him
last night. But how much she loved Declan. And, despite his unique gift
for comforting her when she needed him most, how callous he was. How
uncaring of anything but his own pathetic, cowardly wish to die. But it
was pointless, she realised. Nothing she said would make a difference.
Nothing she could do would alter what was about to happen.

"I was just going to tell you to be careful," she said, taking the easy
way out. "If I leave first, and Elyssa doesn't see you coming out of here,
she need never know you didn't spend the night in your own bunk."

Before Cayal could say anything more, she turned, grabbed her fur
coat off the bed and then her fur hat from the dresser near the washbowl. Pushing her arms through the sleeves, she jammed the hat onto
her head, turned for the door and, without another word, Arkady
slipped out into the dim companionway, leaving the Immortal Prince
and everything she wanted to say to him behind her.

Pulling the fur tightly closed and the hat down over her ears, Arkady
made her way on deck to discover there was more than a distant smudge
of coast on the horizon. Icebergs littered the surrounding sea that dawn
gilded with a magical golden light. She'd heard that at the height of summer here, the sun never set, and last night had definitely seemed uncom-
monly short. That might have had more to do with how she'd been
occupied, she then realised, than the actual length of time that had
passed.

The crew were dashing about frantically, shouting at each other and
doing whatever it was that sailors do on ships sailing through waters
riddled with icebergs. Arkady had to stop and dodge and apologise
quite a bit as she carefully moved forward on the slippery deck, finding

the whole process of ocean sailing rather daunting and very fraught. Although she had grown up in a city near a lake, for her, sailing was something she'd come to later in life, after she married Stellan. Then it involved leisurely trips on calm water on a very large and well-provisioned barge, with lots of servants and even a small orchestra to entertain the guests. Her only ocean-going experiences, on the other hand, had been the short hop across the Sanorna Sea from Glaeba to Torlenia when they'd been exiled by the king, and across the ocean as a slave on the trip to Senestra—a journey she never wanted to relive, for any number of reasons, few of them related to sailing.

She spied Elyssa ahead, talking to the captain. Or rather, being talked *at* by the captain, who was gesticulating and pointing, making no bones about the fact that he was upset about something. Not far from them, some of the sailors were winching a longboat down to the water. The Immortal Maiden looked up and caught sight of her. She motioned Arkady forward with her arm as the captain fell silent.

"We can't take the ship in any further," she said, her breath frosting in the icy air. "Captain Spineless the Magnificent here is afraid of scraping his precious hull on an iceberg. We're going to have to go the rest of the way by longboat."

Arkady nodded, not sure if she was being asked her opinion, or being told what she must do. "Very well."

"You need to fetch your things," Elyssa informed her. "And make sure the crystal is safe."

"Of course."

"Have you seen Cayal?"

"Not since yesterday," Arkady lied, finding it interesting how unsettled the immortals were by not being able to feel each other's proximity on the Tide. The dampening effect of the Chaos Crystal was fascinating. The scientist in Arkady would have loved to have had the opportunity to study it—if studying a magical artefact could even be called *science*. "I could go look for him, if you want."

"You just get packed and make sure the Chaos Crystal is safe," Elyssa said. "I don't need your help to find Cayal."

"As you wish, your highness," she said with in inelegant curtsy, made even more difficult by the rise and fall of the deck. "Will we have to walk the rest of the way to the palace once we make land?"

"Hopefully there will be someone waiting for us with a sled."

"But how will they know to be waiting for us?" Arkady asked, looking over the side at the drop to the icy water below with concern. If she missed a single step climbing down to the longboat, that water down there would kill her in minutes.

"Lukys would have mounted a magical barrier around the continent," Elyssa said. "We probably sailed through it days ago, alerting him to our presence."

"Unless the Chaos Crystal killed it," Cayal suggested, coming up behind Arkady. She jumped at his sudden appearance. He'd obviously been back to his own cabin and changed out of the clothes he was wearing yesterday. Elyssa didn't seem suspicious. Perhaps the argument with the captain had distracted her. "Either way, they'll know we're coming."

"Does Kentravyon know we're leaving?"

"He's talking of swimming ashore."

"That's crazy."

"Well . . . yes."

Elyssa rolled her eyes, but made no further comment about Kentravyon. She turned back to Arkady. "Fetch the Chaos Crystal," she said. "It's time for us to leave."

Bowing respectfully to Elyssa again and not even glancing in Cayal's direction, Arkady did as she was ordered, figuring that, for now at least, doing as she was told—even if it meant suffering Elyssa doing the telling—was the safest course of action and probably the best way to stay alive.

Chapter 50

Located in a sheltered bay on the northern coast of Chelae, Denrah was a large village that enjoyed the unique advantage of being the northernmost deep-water anchorage of substance in Chelae. Strangers were not uncommon here and, as a rule, went unremarked. Declan could have set the rendezvous somewhere more remote, he supposed, but he didn't know the islands that well, and at least here in Denrah he could guarantee that all the immortals would know where he was.

"They're coming."

Declan squinted in the direction the Scard was pointing. Warlock was looking out to sea through the long brass tube of a Torlenian telescope he'd acquired on his visit to Ramahn. The telescope allowed the Scard to spot the approaching immortals even before Declan was able to feel them on the Tide.

The morning was bright, the sky a cloudless cobalt vault over the island. Declan had been tempted to leave Warlock behind for this initial meeting, figuring the inclusion of a Scard in their party was something he could broach later, once he found out how many Tide Lords he had on his side. But the big canine would have none of it.

"Are you sure it's them?"

The Scard nodded and returned the brass instrument to his eye. "It's them. And they seem to be riding . . . some sort of . . . I don't know . . . This will sound like I've lost my mind, but it looks like a magic carpet."

"Don't be ridiculous, Warlock," Declan couldn't help himself from responding. "There's no such thing as a magic carpet."

Warlock lowered the 'scope and glared at him, his teeth bared, a low growl rumbling in the back of his throat.

Declan still wasn't entirely certain what had made Warlock abandon his family, yet again, to follow him into danger. He was certain the Scard wasn't loyal to him personally, and there didn't seem any other reasonable explanation. It had something to do with Warlock's pups. Declan had worked out that much. But exactly how the Scard thought he was helping them—or, more to the point, how his mate, Boots, thought he could help them by following Declan—remained something of a mystery.

There was no time to start questioning Warlock now, however, about his motives. He had to content himself with the thought that Warlock had undertaken every task Declan had asked of him since they'd left Hidden Valley and the icy winter of Glaeba behind—the most important of which was delivering the message to Ramahn, which had resulted in his meeting with Brynden.

Declan hadn't wasted the intervening time. To keep himself occupied while he waited for the immortals from Glaeba and Caelum to join them, he'd drawn detailed plans of Lukys's palace—or what he could remember of it. He'd sketched out the location of the ice chamber, the size of it, the upper levels; any detail he could recall that might aid them in their quest. There was no way of knowing what magical defences Lukys would have put in place around the palace, or even if he'd bothered with them. There was a good chance he wasn't aware anybody was even thinking of trying to stop him from opening the rift.

"They're using the Tide to move it," Declan explained to placate his growling companion. "It's just a perfectly normal rug."

"As if you didn't smell bad enough, you even sound like one of them when you try to make jokes," the Scard said with an unhappy frown, turning back to watch the horizon.

"That's because apparently I *am* one of them," Declan said, raising his arm to shade his eyes from the bright sun. He could make out a number of black dots on the horizon that might be the approaching immortals. However, they were still too far away to see with the naked eye and certainly not close enough to affect the Tide sufficiently for Declan to guess at their numbers.

The specks on the horizon quickly grew larger, resolving into a group of people standing on a rug magically propelled by the Tide. Declan could feel them now, the lesser immortals' gentle ripples on the Tide almost swamped by Jaxyn and Tryan's more powerful presence.

"Nervous?"

Declan glanced at Warlock. "Of course not. I do this sort of thing all the time."

The Scard smiled—something he'd done rarely since leaving Hidden Valley—and collapsed the telescope in on itself. They were close enough now to see their visitors with the unaided eye. "For an immortal, you're a terrible liar," he said.

"I'm led to believe I'll get better with practice," Declan said.

"Good thing your life doesn't depend on it, then," the Scard remarked.

Declan chose not to respond to that. He had more immediate concerns than the caustic wit of his very reluctant canine companion.

It looked like Stellan had succeeded spectacularly. Using the Tide, the newcomers came in fast, settling on the sand near the clear water of the shallow lagoon where Declan waited for them. It was midday; the sun was high in the sky, burning the black sand and making them squint in the bright light. Although they were already making plans to meet as he was leaving Glaeba, he'd never really believed that Stellan Desean would manage to even get these warring Tide Lords in the same room together, let alone force them to agree to anything.

He felt another ripple on the Tide behind him. Kinta and Brynden would also have felt the arrival of the other immortals. Brynden had arrived yesterday, having made arrangements for his absence from Ramahn. He'd probably appointed some trusted monk from the religious order devoted to his worship, to mind things in his absence.

They were not alone on the beach. It was a favourite place for the local children, who had paddled large, flat polished planks rounded to a point on one end out into the water. There they would sit and wait for a wave to send them hurtling back to shore, squealing with delight. Declan had been intrigued by the game since the first time he had seen it several years ago on his initial visit to the Chelae Islands. Although to him, the game seemed a little pointless, given that as soon as they landed on the beach, the children turned around and paddled out to sea to await the next wave.

Jaxyn, Syrolee and Tryan stepped forward, followed by four other men. Declan supposed Engarhod, Rance and Krydence were three of the others. But he couldn't imagine who the fourth man might be, and they were still too far away for him to tell.

"So, this is our new Tide Lord," Syrolee said, when she reached him, staring him up and down with disdain.

Declan met her gaze unflinchingly. She was dressed in an elaborate, crimson and pearl Caelish-style hooped skirt with long flowing sleeves and a beaded velvet bodice. A lesser creature would be dead from heat exhaustion in such a gown in the tropics, if she were merely human.

Tryan, on the other hand, was dressed far more casually and proved to be every bit as handsome as legend held him to be. And just as charming.

He moved to offer Declan his hand as they approached. "Welcome to our very diverse and somewhat . . . fractious family."

Declan shook his hand cautiously, surprised by the warmth of his greeting. He was glad he'd been warned about him in advance, because there was nothing about Tryan that indicated that he was—of all the Tide Lords gathered here on this beach—the most callous and ruthless among them. Given he had arrived in the company of Jaxyn Aranville, that was really saying something.

"I have to say, I'm a little surprised you agreed to come."

"You won't be," Stellan Desean said, stepping up beside Tryan, "when you hear what he has to say." He was dressed for the Glaeban winter he must have so recently left behind, and already sweating in Denrah's tropical humidity.

Declan stared at the new King of Galeba in shock. "*Desean?*"

"Declan."

"What . . . what are you doing here? Shouldn't you be at home? Ruling your new kingdom?"

Stellan began unbuttoning his coat. "I'm doing nothing more than what you and Tilly asked of me." He shed the jacket and draped it over his arm, meeting Declan's gaze calmly.

"Who is Tilly?" Kinta asked from behind him. She knew Stellan, of course. She was still posing as the Imperator of Torlenia's wife when he was Glaeba's ambassador to her court. But she had no idea he was involved in this.

"The Guardian of the Lore," Jaxyn told them, throwing his hands up.

Tryan shook his head. "It's a sorry day, I have to say, when we're reduced to teaming up with the Cabal against our own kind."

Knowing Tilly as he did, Declan guessed he shouldn't be surprised she'd wanted the Cabal to have a hand in this, but he was stunned by her choice of envoy. "You're here on behalf of the Cabal?"

Jaxyn smiled at him. "Well, you can't really blame them, Hawkes. I mean, it's not like they're going to think they can count on you these days, is it?"

"What's this?" Brynden asked Declan, his expression filled with suspicion. "You were a member of the Cabal?"

Before Declan could answer, Jaxyn cut in. "Oh dear . . . Did you think he was one of the good guys?" He laughed at Brynden's scowl. "You never learn, do you, Bryn?"

Kinta scanned the others with a frown, ignoring Jaxyn. "Where's Diala?"

Syrolee answered her, pushing her way to the front of the small gathering. She didn't like the idea that she might be left out of something important. "Diala decided to follow Lyna to Senestra. Ambria's her sister, after all. She thought she might be more use there."

That made sense. Declan glanced over the others, able to tell more about them from their signature on the Tide than how they were dressed or their demeanour. Rance and Krydence were very alike and bore more than a passing resemblance to Engarhod, who had already found himself a palm tree to rest under a few feet away. He'd kicked off his boots, folded his arms and stretched out under the tree as if he was already asleep. He had little interest, apparently, in what the others were up to.

Fighting back the odd realisation that an hour ago he'd been lamenting how slowly things were progressing, Declan was now feeling like everything was moving too fast.

"You have information about this device Lukys plans to use to restore Coron to human form?" Brynden asked Desean. He didn't return Jaxyn's greeting or acknowledge Syrolee and Tryan at all. Small talk wasn't his forte.

"It's not a device," Jaxyn said. "It's just a lump of crystal, I gather."

"A lump of crystal that channels the Tide," Kinta reminded them.

"Ah, yes, well . . . there is that."

"Elyssa and I first learned about it not long after we became immortal," Tryan said, speaking to Brynden and Kinta more than Declan. "We overheard Maralyce and Lukys talking about it. We didn't even know what it was, back then, just that it was valuable and powerful."

"So, naturally you wanted it for yourself," Kinta said.

"Naturally," Tryan replied without a flicker of apology.

"But you never found it?" Brynden asked.

Tryan shook his head. "The best we did was track down some Cabal members who supposedly had a map of where it was hidden after it was stolen. All we found was a wretched Tarot on them, which—as it turns out—actually *was* the map, although we didn't realise it at the time."

"By 'we,' you mean you and Elyssa?" Declan asked.

Syrolee answered before her son could. "Which means, when we find it, the crystal belongs to my daughter. She's the one who found it, so it's only fair . . ."

"Naturally. Because if we can't trust Lukys with unlimited power, the obvious choice is your sexually frustrated daughter," Jaxyn suggested.

The older woman glared at him. "Don't push me, Jaxyn."

"Can you tell us anything specific about the crystal?" Declan asked, hoping to head off any unpleasantness.

Tryan answered him with a shrug. "Not much, truth be told, except for something Pellys said to me once, before Cayal lopped his head off and he forgot everything."

"What did he say?" Brynden asked.

"He was talking about regret," Tryan said. "About how hard it was to live with it. I thought he was talking about things he'd done since I'd known him, none of which seemed *that* bad, in hindsight. I told him to get over it. He was immortal now and if he couldn't deal with living with what he'd done, he'd go crazy."

"This was before you learned he was already immortal when the fire ripped through the brothel in Cuttlefish Bay?" Declan said.

Tryan nodded. "*That* little snippet I only just learned from Jaxyn, and it's much of the reason we're here now. You see, now we know Pellys wasn't made at the same time as the rest of us, what he told me back then begins to make sense."

"Well—what *did* he tell you?"

Declan understood Kinta's impatience. It seemed as if Tryan was drawing out the telling of his story for the dramatic effect.

"He told me he'd done things, *bad* things he couldn't live with. He said if he'd known what one small stone would do—and I'm guessing in light of what we know now, by 'one small stone' he meant the Chaos Crystal—he'd have offered to stay behind instead of Tameca, and he could have perished with all the millions of innocents they destroyed, instead of living forever among the guilty."

"Who is Tameca?" Brynden asked.

"The immortal they left behind when they came through the rift to Amyrantha," Kinta said before Declan could answer him. "I assume that's what he was referring to?"

Declan shook his head doubtfully. "I'm not sure it is. Kentravyon said only six of them had inhabited the last world they called home, and only five had come through the rift to this one. He didn't name the world although, I agree, he did say Tameca stayed behind when they left it."

Kinta nodded. "He said she was like Cayal. That she'd had enough. It was her time to die. But he didn't mention a massive loss of human life."

"You're assuming human life is more valuable than any other?" Stellan said, frowning at her. "Or that this other world they came from was even inhabited by humans."

The immortals seemed surprised to hear a mortal had an opinion on the subject. For a moment Desean's comment reduced all of them to a silence, which was finally broken by Jaxyn.

"I think it's safe to assume that if Pellys was carrying so much guilt he'd rather be turned into the village idiot than live with it," he said, finally able to get a word in. "We can also assume that his past is littered with some fairly impressive mistakes. I mean, he can't have spent eternity *just* killing ornamental fish now, can he?" Suddenly Jaxyn grinned at them. "Or maybe he has. Maybe *they're* the innocents he's lamenting."

Syrolee punched him in the shoulder impatiently. "Be serious, Jaxyn."

"I'll be serious when you lot start listening to yourselves. Tides!"

" 'She held the rift open for us, and the last one through almost never survives.' That's what Kentravyon said, Jaxyn," Kinta told him. "It was certainly enough to convince Cayal that Lukys's plan to open the rift will finally allow him to die."

Declan nodded. "Kentravyon only spoke of Tameca dying, though. He wasn't all that specific about the world they left."

"Pellys couldn't live with the idea he'd slaughtered millions of innocents," Syrolee reminded them. Given he'd fathered two children on her before she was made immortal, Declan supposed that gave her a certain amount of authority on the subject. "He let Cayal behead him, for the Tide's sake. Begged Cayal to do it, if you believe Cayal's version of events. I knew the old Pellys better than any of you. He was always feeling bad about something."

"And if they did destroy some world we've never heard of," Jaxyn asked again, "so what?"

Brynden turned to Jaxyn, his stern face filled with disapproval. "Then they are just as likely to do the same to this world. If you do not want to help us save Amyrantha, why are you here, Jaxyn?"

Tryan didn't give Jaxyn a chance to answer. "Look, whatever this fool's reasons for being here, the fact is, we have a problem. Under normal circumstances, I wouldn't spare even one of you the time of day, and I certainly wouldn't be doing anything the flanking Cabal of the Tarot approves of," he added, glancing at Stellan. "But Hawkes is right. This could be catastrophic for all of us."

"I agree," Brynden said, glancing at Kinta first before he spoke. "This is an extraordinary situation that calls for extraordinary measures."

Syrolee sniffed at them. "Well, just don't think this means I have altered my standards or that we now consider you or the stinking mortals of the Cabal our friends."

Declan watched in amazement as they forged their odd alliance by declaring their dislike for one another, but knew better than to interfere. So did Stellan, who wisely kept silent. These immortals knew each other better than he would ever know them. Trying to help their agreement along now would be counterproductive.

He stepped away from their discussion a short way, turning to watch the village children on their long polished boards riding the waves into shore.

A moment later, Stellan joined him.

"I recognise your hand in their arguments," Declan said softly.

"Really?"

Declan nodded. "Jaxyn and Tryan are both too self-centred to consider the wider ramifications of Lukys trying to restore Coryna. That they're arguing for it now means someone had planted the idea in their minds."

"I really don't think—"

"Don't be modest. Old King Enteny was right, you know—there is no better negotiator on Amyrantha than Stellan Desean."

Before Stellan could respond to that, Kinta announced behind them, "Then it is agreed. We will go to Jelidia, find out what they are doing down there, and put a stop to it."

"Agreed," Syrolee said. "That just leaves us with one rather burning question."

"What's that?" Brynden asked.

"How do we get there in time?"

"They have a substantial head start on us, you know," Jaxyn said. "That ship left Glaeba weeks ago."

"One could assume," Brynden said, with a perfectly straight face, "that given we're standing here discussing it, they probably haven't destroyed the world just yet."

"Tides, Bryn," Jaxyn said. "When did you acquire a sense of humour?"

Brynden stared at him blankly. "I wasn't trying to be funny, Jaxyn."

Declan heard the question about getting to Jelidia and turned back to the Tide Lords. "Is there any particular reason why we can't fly?"

They all looked at him for a moment before Jaxyn smiled at him condescendingly. "Leave the jokes to Brynden, spymaster. He's much better at them than you."

"And, like Brynden, I wasn't joking," Declan said, a bit peeved at the way they were staring at him like they'd just bestowed the title of Village Idiot on *him* instead of Pellys. "I travelled here from Jelidia on a carpet. Tides, for the last half of the trip, we rode a bit of broken roof. You just arrived in the same fashion. If we can move inanimate objects on the Tide, surely we can move ourselves in the same fashion?"

"You're the channel for the Tide magic," Kinta explained, the only one who seemed to appreciate his question was genuine and not his idea of being funny. "You can't push it out and pull it in simultaneously. It would be like trying to pour water back into the pitcher you're pouring it out of in the first place, at the same time."

"But if there's a barrier between you and Tide, then you can push against that," Declan said with a nod of understanding, Kinta's simple analogy making the problem immediately clear. "So we find a bigger rug and head on down to Jelidia. What's the problem?"

"Speed," Tryan said. "We can only move so fast before the friction of the Tide barrier propelling the rug—or whatever we're standing on—

against the air, starts to come into play. Go too fast and you'll burst into flames. It won't kill you, admittedly, but I can assure you, it's not a pleasant way to travel."

Declan thought about the problem, the laughter of the children further down the beach distracting him. He glanced over his shoulder at them, hoping they'd soon be called home to lunch, assuming they had parents who were willing to feed them. They looked skinny enough to have missed a few meals recently.

"What if . . . ?" Kinta began, but Warlock, who'd stood back from the discussion and not uttered a word before now, cut her off.

"Why can't you use *them*?"

The others turned to look at him. Warlock was pointing down the beach at the children and their polished boards slicing through the waves. "If you lay down on them, there'd be less of you to push against the air. You could go faster, couldn't you?"

Tryan was not impressed. "Idiot *gemang*. We'll never fit on one board."

Warlock stared down the Tide Lord without flinching. "I wasn't suggesting you share."

"Warlock would have to travel with me," Declan said, watching the children thoughtfully. "And Desean with one of you, assuming you're planning to come with us, your majesty?"

Stellan looked at the boards a little dubiously, but nodded. He'd already ridden a carpet to get here. Declan supposed riding a plank the rest of the way wasn't that much of a stretch.

Tryan glared at Warlock; he was unused to defiant Crasii he wasn't at liberty to annihilate as he pleased. Then he turned to the others. "It might work. What do you think?"

"I think," Jaxyn said, looking at Tryan as he rolled his eyes in disgust, "that even though we are destined to live forever, if we manage to save the world, we're never going to hear the end of the *gemang*'s one and only good idea."

Chapter 51

Even though Cayal couldn't feel the Tide well because of the dampening effect of the crystal, he could see it at work. The dancing lights of the aurora lit the night sky as they approached the ice palace, a dazzling show of vivid green light, beckoning them south.

As Elyssa had predicted, Taryx was waiting for them with a dog sled when they came ashore, which was a good thing because it was quite a long way across the ice to the palace. The distance meant little to the immortals but a great deal to Arkady, who was neither dressed nor equipped for a hike across this frozen landscape.

With their precious mortal messenger bundled into the sled, wrapped in furs against the bitter wind with the Chaos Crystal tucked safely in her keeping, they reached the palace just as the aurora began to bathe the southern skies in its mystical light.

The journey across the ice to the palace took less time than Cayal was expecting. A great deal more of the ice continent had given way in their absence. By the time the Tide peaked, the palace would be on the coast. He understood now why Lukys had constructed it so far inland. He must have known this would happen.

Lukys, Arryl and Maralyce came out to meet them. There was a repressed excitement about them Cayal had never seen before. Arryl seemed fidgety and a little distracted. The normally laconic Lukys could barely contain his excitement, and Maralyce seemed almost giddy as Taryx shook Arkady awake once they were inside. She pushed off the furs, blinking owlishly in the sudden light of the torchlit main chamber, and looked around in awe.

"You have it," Lukys said as Arkady climbed from the sled.

It was a statement not a question. The dampening on the Tide would have told Lukys where the crystal was long before they got here.

Arkady nodded, and reached inside her coat. Cayal held his breath as, a moment later, she pulled out a small bundle wrapped in hessian sacking. She opened it to reveal the crystal skull she'd so carefully carried from the shores of Caelum to the other side of the world in order to save Warlock and his family. The skull glowed a fierce shade of red, surrounded as it was by so many Tide Lords.

She thrust it forward toward Lukys who took a step away from it.

"You made a mortal carry it for you," Maralyce noted with approval. "We wondered how you were going to travel with it."

"Nice of you to let us know in advance that it sucks the very Tide out of everything it touches," Elyssa said.

"Kentravyon knew," Lukys said with a shrug. "Nice to see you again, Elyssa."

"I doubt it, Lukys. You need me to help you work your little magic trick, that's all. Don't pretend you and that old cow there want me here for any other reason."

"Charming as always," Lukys said with a smile and mocking bow. "Welcome back, Kentravyon. Cayal." He turned to Arkady with an urbane smile. "And who is this delightful creature who has cared so faithfully for our precious Chaos Crystal and carried it across the world for us?"

"This is Arkady Desean," Cayal told him. "Arkady, this is Lukys and, well, you already know Maralyce and Arryl."

"Welcome to my home," Lukys said, gallantly raising Arkady's gloved hand to his lips, while carefully avoiding the hand that was holding the Chaos Crystal. "And you've met these two already? Well, aren't you the dark horse? Are you one of Cayal's many lovers? I always imagined that if I grew bored enough, I could amuse myself by trying to find as many of them as possible."

"Leave her alone," Cayal said to Lukys, removing Arkady's hand from his. "We ran across Arkady in our travels and she offered to carry the crystal for us. Nothing more."

"What happened to Declan?" Arryl asked, with a brief nod of greeting to Arkady. She didn't seem any happier to see the mortal duchess than she was to see Elyssa.

"He was getting on my nerves, so I killed him," Cayal said.

Lukys smiled. "Very droll. What really happened to him?"

"He quit on us," Kentravyon said. "Some namby-pamby nonsense about the Crasii."

"Cayal said Declan didn't want any part of killing several thousand innocent felines," Arkady said, clearly taking umbrage at hearing the Rodent's name maligned, however justly. Cayal privately thought Kentravyon was right on the money. Hawkes *had* quit on them because of his squeamishness over killing Crasii. He wasn't going to let Arkady know he thought that way about her old lover, however. Things were looking very rosy between him and Arkady at the moment. In fact, they were getting along better than they'd been for a very long time. Hawkes was long gone, off saving the world in his own inimitable fashion, far from Jelidia. Amazing how much more smoothly events unfolded when there was no longer any competition.

Admittedly, Elyssa was still a thorn in Cayal's side. And Arkady still needed to move past that teensy little *I-offered-Elyssa-your-body-so-she-could-possess-you* problem she was having, but Cayal was confident she'd get over that. Eventually.

All things considered, things are looking quite rosy . . .

And then Cayal realised what he was doing and cursed his own stupidity. There was no point making plans for the future. He didn't have one. Didn't want one, either.

This is what Arkady did to him. This was the subtle danger of her. Arkady made him think of the future. She made him *want* a future, which was all well and good, except she was mortal so the future she offered was merely an illusion of happiness. It could never be the real thing.

Curse the woman. When she wasn't around, he had no need to make plans.

Maybe, if she was immortal, Cayal dared to imagine for a moment, there might have been *some* hope. Lukys and Coryna seemed to have found a way to make it work across endless lifetimes.

"Would you like to follow me?" Lukys said to Arkady, indicating the way with his arm. "I'm sure you're looking forward to being rid of your burden."

Arkady nodded warily and glanced at Cayal, who was still silently cursing his own foolishness for allowing his imagination, and his impossible dreams, to run away with him.

"I'll come with you," he offered. "What about you. Elyssa? Want to come down and admire Lukys and Taryx's handiwork?" His moment of weakness behind him, Cayal phrased the question that way deliberately, knowing it was the surest way to be rid of her temporarily. Nothing would irk Elyssa more than hearing Lukys and Taryx pat themselves on the back over their own cleverness in building the ice chamber.

"Thank you, but I think I'd rather be shown to my room. It was a quite a hike over the ice to this place and my clothes are soaking. I'd like a chance to change, at the very least."

"I'll show you the way," Arryl offered. Her tone seemed oddly flat, as if she had little interest in the new arrivals. There was no sign of her lizard Crasii, either.

Lukys watched them leave, smiling in a way that gave no hint of what he was really thinking. Taryx was busy with the sled and the dogs, and at some point Kentravyon had also slipped away.

Cayal looked around for a moment, as he realised someone else was missing. "Where's Pellys?"

"Up on the roof," Lukys told him.

"What's he doing up there?"

"Waiting for the Tide to peak."

"Really?"

Maralyce smiled at his expression. "Don't worry, Cayal. For once there's a sound reason behind something he's doing."

"I'm not sure if *sound* and *reason* are two words that actually apply to Pellys, Maralyce," Cayal said with a frown.

"We need to know when the Tide peaks," Lukys said. "We won't feel it inside the palace now the Chaos Crystal is here. He's up there watching for us. Shall we?" He stepped back to let Arkady precede him. A little warily, she headed in the direction he indicated.

"Elyssa was right, you know," Cayal said, falling in beside Lukys. "The damn thing sucks the Tide out of everything in the vicinity. Won't it do the same to us?"

Lukys nodded. "Initially, yes. But once you start forcing the Tide through it, it will actually start to amplify the Tide. With the power directed back at it by the chamber's walls, it'll suck that up too. Before long, we'll have gathered enough power to open the rift."

"And then you'll be able to transfer your rat's mind into your wife's body?" Arkady asked.

Lukys glanced at her oddly for an instant as they walked and then looked at Cayal. "You told her?"

"Only because Kentravyon told me," Cayal said. "When were you planning to share this minor but important detail with the rest of us, by the way?"

"When you needed to know," Lukys said with an unapologetic shrug. "Did he tell you about Coryna's little . . . accident . . . that necessitates this rather dire course of action to remedy the situation?"

Tides, Cayal thought as he listened to Lukys speak. *He's probably going to leave a pile of rubble the size of this planet in his wake trying to restore the rat's mind to a human body, and he's calling it "the remedy for a little accident?"*

And they say I'm *deluded.*

"Oh, he did better than that, my lord," Arkady said in a tone that made it clear she hadn't even begun to consider forgiving Cayal for his latest transgression. "He told Elyssa you would do the same for her. Using my body."

"Did he now?" Lukys said, looking at her thoughtfully.

"Of course, the attempt will apparently kill me, but he's not too bothered about that. Seems to think he'll be dead too, so he won't have to live with the consequences of what he's done."

"That sounds like our boy Cayal," Lukys agreed as they headed down the stairs to the lower levels. He'd taken a torch from the head of the stairs to light their way. The flames fractured into myriad colours that splattered against the ice-carved walls. "I take it you're not interested in taking part in such an exchange, my lady?"

"Of course not!"

Lukys sighed and glanced over his shoulder at Cayal. "You really should ask before you make these arrangements, Cayal. The lady clearly wants nothing to do with it."

"I needed to get Elyssa to cooperate."

"He did that by asking her to marry him," Arkady said, taking a perverse amount of pleasure in his discomfort. But her teeth were chattering as she spoke, the only one here who could feel the bone-chilling cold of the ice.

"Tides," Maralyce said from behind them with a sour laugh. "I think I finally understand how truly desperate you are, Cayal."

He stopped and glared at the three of them, feeling very misunderstood. He'd offered Arkady to Elyssa to *save* her life, not take it. "Tides,

I was just trying to help. And you *know* that, Arkady, so stop trying to paint me as the one at fault here. Yes, I promised you to Elyssa, but Lukys knows it won't work. I just need her to believe we're trying, that's all."

"So, when we come to open the rift, you want me to take time out from focusing the largest concentration of Tide ever gathered in one place, to pretend I'm helping Elyssa, so she'll help you?" Lukys asked.

"Well . . . yes."

Lukys shook his head without comment and resumed walking with Arkady at his side; Maralyce poked Cayal from behind to get him moving. "You're an idiot, Cayal."

"I'm an idiot?" he muttered under his breath, staring after the others as they began to descend the stairs into the ice chamber.

After a moment, he followed the circle of light that was Lukys and the torch he carried, more than a little peeved by the lack of sympathy he was getting from the man who professed to understand his pain so well he was willing to help him die.

A few moments later, Cayal heard rather than saw Arkady's reaction when she first spied the spectacular fire-lit ice chamber below the palace. Her gasp was audible even on the stairs.

"Tides . . ."

"Impressive, isn't it?" Lukys said with a smile in his voice. He really was inordinately proud of his wretched chamber.

"How are you fuelling the fires?"

"With methane trapped under the ice."

"It's . . . fantastic!"

By the time Cayal reached the bottom of the stairs, Arkady, Maralyce and Lukys were already halfway across the vast cavern floor on their way to the altar. Cayal followed them, no longer fascinated by the burning ice, although given the way Arkady's head was swivelling this way and that, he figured she was intrigued by it. He caught up with them as they reached the solid block of ice in the centre of the cavern.

It was then that Cayal realised Oritha was lying on the altar, hands crossed over her breast, apparently peacefully asleep.

"Put the crystal by her head," Lukys instructed Arkady. She was looking askance at the young woman laid out on the altar, but made no comment. Cayal wasn't sure if that was because she didn't care, or simply didn't want to know what had caused the woman's state.

Cayal wasn't nearly so confused about his feelings on the subject. "Isn't that your wife?"

Lukys nodded. "Beautiful, isn't she?"

"What's she doing here?" Cayal had quickly deduced she wasn't sleeping. Whatever Oritha was doing on that altar, he doubted she was doing it willingly. "Dead."

"She's not dead," Lukys scoffed.

"She's preparing for the transfer," Maralyce said, smoothing the young woman's hair with a gentle hand. "If there's any resistance at all, the transfer won't work. In this state, she's so deeply unconscious she won't feel a thing."

While they were speaking, Arkady carefully placed the glowing red skull near Oritha's head and stepped back, her task completed. She looked very relieved. "Now what?"

"Now we wait for the Tide to peak," Lukys said.

"How long will that take?"

"Not long, I hope," Maralyce said. "It pains Oritha greatly every time we're forced to bring her around again. She's not immortal yet, and the freezing process will eventually harm her if we don't move soon."

"What happens to me?" Arkady asked, looking around at the three of them.

"You should probably say your goodbyes, my dear," Lukys said with a benevolent smile.

"You're going to let me leave?" Arkady asked, looking a little surprised.

"In a manner of speaking," Lukys agreed, putting his arm around her shoulder. "Why don't we go back upstairs so we can discuss the arrangements?"

Lukys led Arkady away from the altar, his arm still around her shoulder like a generous uncle offering a favoured niece a special treat. Cayal watched them leave, watched them disappear into the eerie green-lit maw of the entrance to the stairs, a little puzzled by Lukys's words. He turned to Maralyce. "What's he talking about? Making arrangements?"

"He's just being nice to her, Cayal. You know how Lukys operates. Nobody ever knows what's about to happen to them."

"What's he going to do to Arkady?"

Maralyce rolled her eyes. "Tides, boy, do you have to ask?"

Cayal stared at her for a moment, and then he cursed under his breath as he realised what she was telling him. Cayal took off at a run, slipping on the icy polished permafrost floor as he bolted after Lukys and Arkady.

He was too late, of course. By the time he reached the top of the stairs, Arkady was already unconscious, barely breathing, laid out on the floor.

"Tides, what have you done?" he demanded of Lukys, sliding on his knees the last few feet to reach Arkady.

"What you asked," Lukys said. "I've done the same to her as I've done to Oritha."

"I never asked you to do that!"

"Elyssa will never believe you intend to keep your promise otherwise, Cayal," Lukys said with infuriating logic. "I'd have done it down in the chamber, but now the crystal's down there I didn't want to risk it."

"You could have warned her."

"What purpose would that have served?"

None, Cayal realised, but there was no point in saying so. He bent over her and kissed Arkady on the lips. They were already icy and faintly tinged with blue. Then he looked up at Lukys. "Will she be all right?"

"Of course she will," Lukys promised. "We'll lay your girl here out next to Oritha on the altar, and Elyssa will stand there and channel all the Tide you need to die, and she'll never be any the wiser."

"Until she wakes up on the new world and realises nothing has changed."

"Not my fault if it doesn't work," Lukys said with a shrug. "I'm not even sure it will restore Coryna."

"You won't really put Elyssa's mind into Arkady's body, will you?"

"I hardly think, given everything else that will be happening when we open the rift, that I'll have the time. Do you?"

That wasn't exactly a resounding denial, but Cayal figured it would have to do. He was sorry about only one thing, however. Lifting Arkady's unconscious body into his arms so he could carry her back down the stairs to the Tide chamber, he really wished he'd taken the time to tell her he was sorry.

Chapter 52

Tiji survived on ice-melt and anger for the first few days of her confinement. She paced her cell furiously, planning all manner of dire fates for Lukys and Taryx and all immortals in general, for sealing her up in here. When she tired of that, she started to wonder why they hadn't killed her outright.

For reasons far too complicated to go into now—reasons you cannot begin to understand—for the time being I want you alive, little Scard.

That's what he had said. *For the time being I want you alive.*

Tiji tried to figure out what Lukys meant by that, but she really had no idea. And why, if he wanted her alive, did he not just leave her in the palace, waiting on Lady Arryl? She was no threat to him there.

You'll stay here until I need you again. Or until I don't need you. *At which point you'll be free to share the fate of your friends once we have departed Amyrantha.*

Was Arryl planning to leave too?

Tiji knew they were intending to open a rift that would lead to another world. She'd heard them talking about it . . . well, *over*heard them, actually. And then, when she presented her case to Lady Arryl, Lukys had admitted it outright.

But there was something decidedly suspicious about the whole affair. Oritha's calm acceptance of the near-death state Lukys kept inducing in her so he could perfect his technique was downright creepy. Did he really mean to take her across a world-bridging rift to start a life with him on another world?

Admittedly, Lukys seemed fond of Oritha, but she was hardly worth this much effort.

No person was, human, Crasii *or* Scard.

Such were the troubled thoughts that occupied Tiji as she paced her icy cell, wondering why she hadn't suffocated yet. The cavern seemed to be sealed but there must be fresh air coming from somewhere. Or maybe Lukys had done something magical to the air in here, ensuring it never got stale. Fortunately, when they caught her, she'd been wearing the fur coat Arryl had given her—she never ventured from her chamber without it—so she hadn't frozen to death. Yet.

Nobody came to look for her. At first, it distressed her to think Azquil was so accepting of the Tide Lords' lies that he would believe their ridiculous story about her deciding to leave the palace and strike out on her own. Of course, her last words to Azquil: *Go wait on your precious immortals! You care more about them than me, anyway! I'm leaving this wretched place!* probably hadn't helped matters much.

But still . . . you'd think he'd have a cursory look around after I went missing, if nothing else.

Surely, despite her oft-stated intention of leaving this place, he didn't believe she would be foolish enough to pack up and go, without so much as a goodbye?

I mean, seriously, where does he think I'd go?

There was no ship waiting at anchor on the coast to spirit her home, assuming she could even make it that far without freezing to death. She wasn't even sure where *home* was, any longer. She didn't belong in Glaeba. She knew that now. But she wasn't sure she belonged in the Senestran Wetlands either, worshipping the wretched immortal Trinity.

Tides, it was so unfair. Ever since that moment, thousands of years ago, when the immortal Elyssa—driven by equal measures of anger and jealousy—had magically forced a piglet through a pregnant human woman's skin, into the woman's womb, and then finally into the child she was carrying, the Crasii had been torn between the opposing forces of self-preservation and the immortals. Tiji's race, like all the other magically blended species, had been bred to serve the Tide Lords, a compulsion impossible to defy by all but the rare few like Tiji—and Azquil, if you believed his assurances . . .

Right now, Tiji didn't believe a single word her mate had told her. Even with all the noises he made about following Arryl to Jelidia of his own free will, it seemed the immortal had more claim on Azquil than his mate. He'd not come looking for her. Even though he claimed to have a mind of his own, here she was, stuck in this icy prison with no hope of rescue, all because of Azquil.

Tiji's pacing brought her back to the translucent ice wall that separated her from freedom. Although she paced up and down it endlessly, she had given up trying to claw through it. It was too thick—although not so thick she couldn't make out shadows passing in the hall outside. But it was too dense to allow any sound to carry through the ice. Too thick for anybody to notice her and discover she was trapped.

I am such a fool. Azquil had the right of it. Toe the line. Give the Tide Lords what they want. Don't do anything to upset them. Tiji hated living like that.

And look what her defiance had gotten her—a frozen cell and a long slow death from starvation. Because nobody was coming to get her. Ever.

Tears of despair welled up in the little Crasii's eyes. The end was going to be long, slow and painful, because she had water here and could survive for weeks on that. But the hunger would get her in the end. The hunger and the loneliness.

There were other things that might bring her undone, just as slowly and painfully, but Tiji never got to wonder what they were, because right about the time she decided things probably couldn't get much worse anyway, a shadow appeared on the other side of the ice wall. A moment later, the wall of ice trapping her inside this frozen cell splintered with a deafening crack.

A few moments after that, several large chunks of ice separated from the wall and fell away to reveal a Tide Lord standing in the opening.

Tiji's heart lodged in her throat, but she stood her ground. If she was going to die, at least she was going to face death like a Scard, and not like a snivelling Crasii lackey, without the wit to know any better.

She braced herself as the Tide Lord leaned forward into the cell, studied her for a moment and then looked around curiously.

"Tides, little one," Pellys said with a concerned frown. "Aren't you Arryl's pet? How long have you been stuck in here, all on your own?"

Tiji stared at him in confusion. "A . . . a while, I think. I'm not sure."

"You should get back to her right now. She'll be wanting you to get back to work."

It was then that it dawned on Tiji that Pellys had no idea she was a prisoner. Apparently—except for Taryx who'd aided him—Lukys hadn't told anybody she was down here. Not even the other Tide Lords.

"Um . . . I should be getting back, I suppose," she agreed, afraid to do or say too much else in case it gave her away.

She had nothing to worry about, however. Pellys stared at her for a few moments longer, a little puzzled by the whole affair, and then he stood back from the splintered opening to let her out. Tiji hurriedly climbed through, relieved to find there was no sign of anybody else in the torchlit corridor outside.

"Where is everybody?"

"Down in the chamber," Pellys told her. "The Tide's peaking. I could feel it on the roof. I came down to tell them. Did you want to see?"

"Um . . . no thanks. How did you know I was stuck in the wall?"

"I saw your shadow moving behind the ice." He grinned. "You looked like a goldfish swimming in a bowl. How did you get in there?"

Tiji stepped back warily. Even she knew of Pellys and what he liked doing to goldfish. "I'm not sure," she lied. "Do you know where Lady Arryl is?"

"Down with the others getting ready to open the rift, I suppose. They're going to seal the chamber soon."

"Seal it? Why?"

"So the Tide doesn't leak out, of course, silly," he told her, looking at her as if she was a bit dim. "Why else?"

Tiji didn't have an answer to that. And she certainly didn't care enough about what the Tide Lords were up to, to ask for clarification.

She forced a smile. "Well, thanks for letting me out, my lord. To serve you is the reason I breathe and all that. But I need to be getting back to my . . . er . . . job . . . You know, serving the mighty Tide Lords."

Pellys nodded in agreement. "Arryl will be glad she found you again. She's been really sad since the little lizard died."

"I didn't die, Lord Pellys," she said. "See? I'm here! Alive and well because you found me."

"I don't mean *you*," the Tide Lord said. "The little *boy* lizard."

Tiji's scales suddenly felt like they were standing on end. "The boy lizard? You mean Azquil?"

"Was that his name? I suppose it was him, then. I mean, there's only the two of you here, isn't there?"

Tiji stared at Pellys in horror, almost too afraid to ask the next question. Shadows cast by the flickering light of the torches set in the walls around them made it hard to read his expression. "What . . . what happened to him?"

"I don't know," Pellys said with a shrug. "Took it into his head to walk back to the coast in a blizzard, near as I can tell. Got snippety about someone leaving. Arryl will know. She was quite upset when they brought him back. Frozen solid he was." The Tide Lord grinned. "Looked like a funny statue. You know, like those performers they have at carnivals, where a person pretends they're carved of marble and then changes position when you're not looking?"

Tiji couldn't speak, couldn't even think straight. *Tides, is that why Azquil never came looking for me? Because he really thought I'd left?*

Had he gone in search of her in the frozen wasteland surrounding the palace and perished in the attempt to stop her leaving?

She didn't wait for any more details. She turned and fled toward the stairs leading to the upper levels of the palace, determined to find Azquil, or somebody who could tell her what had happened to him.

Chapter 53

The coast of Jelidia came into view very quickly. After days channelling the rising Tide so constantly it set Declan's blood on fire, the icy cliffs of the continent appeared on the horizon, increasing in size with alarming speed as they raced toward the coast. The speed the immortals had achieved with the streamlined boards they'd commandeered from the children playing on the beaches near Denrah had proved to be spectacular. Even with a detour to collect Diala, Ambria, Lyna and Medwen in Senestra, they had raced across the world, taking days to complete a journey that would have otherwise taken them months, had they not been riding the Tide.

There was some heat from the friction, admittedly—enough that Warlock and Stellan complained about it every time they stopped—but they reached Jelidia in a matter of days. And nobody actually burst into flame.

It was still dark when they made landfall, the aurora illuminating the night sky in a spectacular dance of green and blue light, as if the lights were tuned in to the music of the universe, dancing to a celestial orchestra only the stars could hear.

And every one of the immortals was edgy, fractious and ready to explode at the slightest provocation by the time they arrived.

Warlock and Stellan had kept their distance, once they clambered off the boards they'd ridden to Jelidia. Warlock had ridden with Declan and Stellan had been perched behind Kinta. Although Descan seemed wary, the Scard seemed to be genuinely afraid of their collective mood. Declan didn't blame him. He could feel the rage, the lust, within himself, and knew that if he was feeling it, the others were too.

That was going to make working together almost impossible.

"Tides, let's not do that again for a while," Medwen said as she stumbled off the board she'd been riding with Jaxyn. He climbed off and collapsed into the snow, flat on his back. Beside them, the ground sizzled as the heat of their board melted the surrounding ice. In the background, the only other sound was the sea crashing against the cliffs as it threw itself at this continent-sized fortress of ice in an increasingly successful attempt to wear it down.

Exhausted, his whole body bristling like a lightning rod looking for somewhere to discharge, Declan fell to his knees, for the first time in his life in complete agreement with another immortal.

"I forgot what it feels like to do that at High Tide," Tryan agreed, looking as wobbly as Declan felt. He was taking deep, heaving breaths, as if he'd run all day and was on the brink of collapse.

And it was High Tide. Or if it wasn't, then the peak was awfully close. Even after he'd let the Tide go, it still hummed along Declan's skin, waiting for him, calling to him, seducing him, tempting him into diving back into its delicious embrace.

Tides, is it any wonder they can't help using magic when the Tide peaks. It seemed like a criminal waste not to do something with all this power.

Of all the immortals gathered on the icy shore, only Brynden seemed to be taking it in his stride. Even Tryan was looking a little green. Engarhod looked positively seasick, Syrolee was decidedly seedy, and Kinta seemed quite pale. Rance and Krydence were uncharacteristically quiet and Ambria and Lyna looked exhausted. Diala was still on her feet, but Declan could see her trembling with the effort to appear unaffected.

"You must all try to recover quickly," Brynden told them, as he abandoned his board and turned to look south. "I fear they have already started."

"I can't feel a thing," Tryan said. He sounded calm but although he had stopped gasping, he was visibly trembling.

"This is why I fear they may have started already."

"There was no barrier around the continent," Rance said, sinking to his knees.

"That could just mean they weren't expecting anybody," Ambria said, pushing herself up on her elbows. She had to move sideways a little to avoid her clothes being soaked by the melting snow around her rapidly cooling board. The other boards were doing the same, burning long steaming holes in the snow where the Tide Lords had abandoned them.

"Or it could mean that with the crystal here, they couldn't set one," Brynden suggested.

Tryan nodded thoughtfully, rubbing his chin. "You know, that could explain why we were never able to set a barrier around Caelum."

Jaxyn sighed. "And here I was, Try, thinking you hadn't done it just because you were incompetent."

"You never set one around Glaeba, either," Declan reminded him, for the first time wondering—if the Tide Lords could do such a thing—why Jaxyn had never tried to protect himself with one when he was trying to establish himself in Glaeba. "Maybe, if you had, Diala wouldn't have been able to sneak up on you the way she did, and end up married to Glaeba's king."

"He was always going to lose," Diala pointed out with a smug smile in Jaxyn's direction, looking rather pleased that everyone was being reminded of how easily she had outsmarted Jaxyn. "I made my move before the Tide came back. It wouldn't have made a difference what he did."

"And I'm sure it's something you'll happily gloat over for eons to come," Tryan said. "In the meantime, shouldn't we be getting a move on?"

Declan wondered if Tryan's impatience had to do with the fact that they were discussing Jaxyn's woes or simply because the discussion wasn't focused on him. Whatever the reason, it was an excellent suggestion. Declan felt as if his veins were on fire. He had to keep moving or he'd go insane. Maybe Tryan was feeling that way too.

Brynden also seemed anxious to keep moving. Perhaps his calm demeanour was more of an act than he was letting on.

"We should get going," he agreed, taking Kinta by the hand. "Because at the very least, if Lukys hasn't set a magical lookout, he will have set a physical one. It will be light soon. We need to reach the palace before dawn." He turned to the mortal and the Scard. "Are you two up for this?"

They both nodded, neither of them suffering the Tide-induced fatigue the immortals were suffering. They, after all, had merely ridden the Tide as passengers. "We'll be fine," Stellan said.

The rest of them nodded in agreement, perhaps too exhausted from swimming the Tide to argue the point. Declan studied the odd group—dressed in a variety of styles more suited to the climates they'd come from than the icy landscape in which they now stood—hoping that a dozen immortals who didn't particularly want to work together was going to be enough to save the world from a handful of immortals quite dedicated to destroying it.

Chapter 54

Curse that stupid lizard for being so foolish, Tiji thought as she ran.

She bolted up the carved ice stairs, running straight past the store-rooms, her aching hunger forgotten. When she reached the main part of the palace, she found it deserted. There was hardly a soul around.

A quick check of the common areas proved just as fruitless. Frantic now, she turned for the wing where Lady Arryl's room was located. Perhaps Azquil was in there. Pellys was a half-wit, after all, even if he was immortal. He was probably mistaken. Mixed up. Even playing a joke on her. He tormented and killed small creatures for amusement, didn't he?

Tiji never got as far as the guest wing, however. She heard noises on the upper level when she reached the foyer. Following the unexpected sound of laughter, she ran up the stairs to the dining hall from where the noise seemed to be coming. To her astonishment, she discovered every Crasii in the palace gathered there, partaking of a massive feast.

Tiji skidded to a halt at the entrance, wondering why, with such a feast laid out, it was the palace servants consuming it, not the immortals.

"What's going on?" she asked, looking at the table piled with food as she walked into the hall. To her it seemed as if all their supplies had been used up for this one spectacular banquet.

The canines ignored her, too busy demolishing the full oxen—shipped here some months ago and stored frozen in the ice below the palace for the servants to eat—which should have fed them all for months.

"We thought you were dead, Scard."

Tiji turned to find Jojo looking up at her from her place at the foot of the table. Her hands and mouth were bloody from the barely-cooked slab of ox-steak she was devouring.

A wave of hatred washed over the chameleon, which she forced under control. Much as she would like to have ripped holes in the fur of this wretched feline who'd helped trap her in the ice, Tiji's more urgent need was for information.

"What's going on here?"

"Lord Lukys arranged a feast for us. Told us we could eat everything. He is a truly wonderful master, Lord Lukys."

Her search for Azquil temporarily fogotten, Tiji looked around the room at the score of other Crasii busily tucking into their only food supplies like there was no tomorrow. "Why would he tell you to do that? We're in the middle of nowhere. What's happens when this is all gone? What will we eat then?"

The feline shrugged. "Our lords will provide for us."

"With what?"

"It is wrong to question your masters, Scard."

"They're *your* masters, Jojo, not mine. Have you seen Azquil?"

"Not since the day he ran away," the feline told her without any visible emotion. "That was your fault, you know. If you hadn't gone outside to sulk, he'd never have gone looking for you."

"I never went anywhere. You knew where I was, Jojo. You knew why, too. Why didn't you say something to Azquil?" She choked back the tears that were threatening to undo her. "Why didn't you stop him?"

"Lord Lukys told me not to." Jojo looked so puzzled as to why anybody would question such a thing, that Tiji—even while trying to contain her distress over the news about Azquil—actually felt an instant of pity for her. The feline had no free will when it came to the wishes of the immortals.

Worse, she didn't even understand what free will was. There was no point railing at her, no point in trying to apportion blame.

And no possible way anything Jojo said or did could be trusted.

"Do you know where Lady Arryl is?"

"She's down in the fire chamber with Lord Lukys and the others, I suppose." The feline frowned, and rose to her feet so that she was eye to eye with Tiji. "Shouldn't you be down there too?"

"No," Tiji said, backing away.

"Lord Lukys said he had plans for you," Jojo said, wiping her hands on her coat as if she was getting ready to unsheathe her claws. "Did you escape, little lizard? Is that it?"

"Lord Pellys let me out."

That made Jojo hesitate. Pellys was an immortal. Jojo was not equipped to question any action done by an immortal.

"He . . . he told me to come up here and check on everyone," Tiji added, trying to think of something plausible. Unless Jojo and the other Crasii believed Tiji was acting under immortal orders, they would try to stop her.

"Then you can report back to our lords that we are all here and doing exactly as they ordered."

"Well, yes . . ." Tiji said, nodding as she took another step backward toward the entrance. "That's exactly what I'll do. You eat up now . . ."

Tiji turned left as she reached the doorway, but Jojo wasn't so easily put off.

"The Tide chamber is the other way!" she called after Tiji.

"Silly me," Tiji said with a nervous laugh. She'd been planning to check the rooms further along the hall, in the opposite direction to the stairs that led to the lower levels. "This place is so big, I get all turned around in it sometimes."

"Then I shall escort you," the feline announced in a voice that brooked no argument. "If Lord Pellys wanted you to check on us, you must inform him we are doing exactly as he asked."

"It's fine, Jojo," Tiji assured her. "I can find my own way."

"No, I think I'll come with you."

There was no arguing with a feline when they used that tone. Jojo's ginger tail flicked back and forth impatiently as she stood there, betraying her true feelings. Tiji had two choices here. Let the cat have her way or end up bleeding on the floor, at which point the cat would still have her way.

"Wonderful," Tiji muttered as Jojo fell in beside her.

Filled with frustration, Tiji let Jojo lead the way. Together they headed down the stairs. The feline must have sensed something in Tiji's manner that wasn't quite right, because she stayed uncomfortably close to her all the way back through the palace to the stairs, past the now-empty storerooms, down the torchlit corridor and the green, moss-lit stairs to the secret fire chamber below the palace.

Not that it's much of a secret any longer. Every Crasii in the palace seems to know about it.

Tiji didn't have the will or the energy for small talk as they walked. She was still trying to deal with the news about Azquil and that was proving much harder than she'd ever imagined it could be.

She remembered the blizzard raging around the palace the night she'd been tricked into captivity.

Tides, did he really go out in that? Did he really perish in the snow, looking for me?

If he had, then this wretched cat had stood by and said nothing while he made his plans to follow Tiji out onto the ice, which made Jojo just as responsible for his death as the Tide Lords.

Her thoughts didn't waver from their dark path as she and Jojo followed the hall until they came to the stairs that led down into the Tide Lords' massive underground chamber—which, if Pellys was to be believed, they had built purely to contain the Tide.

Tiji had been hoping she might find a chance to slip away from Jojo's watchful custody, a hope she realised was utterly futile when they reached the bottom of the stairs, only to meet up with Lukys—complete with pet rat perched on his shoulder—and Maralyce emerging from the chamber.

"Ah!" Lukys said, apparently unsurprised to see either of them. "You brought the little Scard down. Thank you, Jojo. You can return to the party."

Jojo bowed, beaming under the benign smile of her master. "To serve you is the reason I breathe, my lord."

"Off you go, then."

Without sparing Tiji so much as a second glance, the feline turned and hurried back up the stairs toward the upper levels, and what—Tiji was starting to suspect—was the Crasii's final meal.

"Whatever you want me to do, you'll have to kill me first!" she declared gamely to the two Tide Lords.

"That can be arranged, you know," Maralyce informed her a little impatiently.

"But not necessary just yet, I think," Lukys said with a smile that made Tiji's blood run cold. "We just need you to hold something for us, my dear, in a little while. That's not too much to ask, is it?"

"Hold what?" she asked suspiciously. Lukys hadn't frozen her into a wall just to ensure she'd be on standby with the drinks tray.

"The Chaos Crystal, of course," Maralyce said, frowning at her question.

In response to Tiji's blank expression, Lukys added, "Under no circumstances must the crystal come in contact with the ice while we're channelling the Tide. Your job will be to ensure that if Lord Cayal collapses—as he may well do, given he's agreed to take part in the ceremony so he can die—you must take up the crystal so we can finish our work."

It sounded suspiciously easy. "What happens afterwards?

"You'll be free to go," he promised her.

That sounded far too easy.

"If this is such a straightforward job, why not get your pet pussycat to hold it for you?"

Maralyce shook her head. "We can't risk it with a Crasii. Cayal will be suffering intense pain during the . . . ceremony. If it gets too much for him, he could—conceivably—order a Crasii to take the crystal from him and let it go. He can't give the same order to a Scard."

"And that's all you want me to do?"

"Nothing more, nothing less."

Tiji glared at Lukys. "You didn't have to seal me up in an ice cavern to get me to agree to do that," she pointed out angrily. "Azquil is dead because of you."

"A regrettable accident," Lukys said. "But really, would you be here otherwise? Even if we asked nicely?"

"No."

"Well," Lukys said. "There we are, then." His conversation with her done, he continued up the stairs, on his way toward the storerooms that now contained nothing but tools, and empty barrels that had once held enough food to see all the slaves here through an arctic winter.

Before Tiji could object, Maralyce took her by the arm. "Come along, dear. Don't fret. There's nothing to be frightened about."

"I'm not frightened," Tiji lied, as Maralyce led the reluctant little chameleon Scard toward the chamber. Tiji glanced back over her shoulder at Lukys's retreating back, but the Tide Lord wasn't paying any attention to her. As he walked up the eerie green stairs, he was feeding titbits to the plump rat perched on his shoulder, whispering in a soothing voice . . .

"It won't be long now, my dear, be patient. It won't be long now."

Chapter 55

Due to the crumbling coastline, which was melting as the Tide warmed Amyrantha, it took a lot less time to reach the palace than it had the last time Declan made this journey. They arrived just on dawn. From the outside, Lukys's Palace of Impossible Dreams looked the same as it always had. There was nothing different about it, nothing sinister. It was simply impressive.

The palace drew gasps of wonder from everyone but Declan, who had the advantage of having seen it before. He stared it for a long moment from the top of the ridge, wondering if Arkady was in there. He still wasn't sure about that.

And if she was in there, was she alive? Was she frightened? Or had she reconsidered her options and decided Cayal wasn't such a bad prospect after all, and thrown her lot in with him? Was she in there now, asleep in his arms?

"Tides, why build something like that down here at the bottom of the world where nobody else can see it?" Medwen asked, breaking Declan's disturbing train of thought.

They had stopped on the rise overlooking the palace. It was less than a mile to walk from here, and everybody—with the exception of the fur-clad canine who walked beside Declan with a perpetual scowl on his face, and the mortal man here to represent the Cabal—was fully recovered from the magical journey across the ocean from Chelae. With the Tide up as high as it was, apparently their healing time was greatly accelerated too.

Does that mean, Declan wondered, *that we'll heal almost instantaneously when the Tide peaks?*

"It's made of ice, Medwen," Rance pointed out. "Where else was he going to build it? In the middle of Ramahn?"

"Wouldn't last more than a few hours in Torlenia's heat," Krydence agreed, joining his brother in a joke that nobody else found amusing. They seemed unlikely allies, but since agreeing to put aside their differences with Jaxyn and the other immortals to save Amyrantha from destruction, Rance and Krydence had been the least of Declan's problems. Even Syrolee was being civil. It was almost as if the war between Caelum and Glaeba had never happened. It irked him to realise how much Glaeban and Caelish blood these immortals had been prepared to spend on what had proved—in the face of a greater threat—little more than a distraction.

"You know what she means," Kinta said, as impatient with their childish humour as Declan was.

"As I understand it, Lukys never set out to build anything this impressive," Declan explained. "He brought Taryx down here to help him hollow out the ice chamber, and it was Taryx who decided they might as well do something with all the ice they'd removed."

"If they built that out of the waste from the chamber, it's some chamber," Diala said, studying the palace thoughtfully. She squinted, leaning forward a little and then pointed. "Is that someone on the roof?"

"Where?" Brynden asked, pulling a small telescope from the pouch at his belt, where he seemed to keep—along with more weapons than Declan could name—a number of other useful devices in various purpose-built pouches.

"On the left spire," Ambria said, pointing. "I see it too. There's something moving up there."

Brynden scanned the palace with his telescope until he found what the others were pointing at. "I think it's Pellys," he said after a moment.

"So we got here in time?" Syrolee said hopefully. "I mean, if they'd already started, they'd all be inside, wouldn't they?"

Declan shook his head. "I'm not sure Lukys wanted Pellys to help. He told me that focusing on the crystal would take more concentration than he thought Pellys could gather. It was half the reason he encouraged Cayal to get Elyssa involved in the first place."

"And the stupid, lovesick bitch took one look at those misery-laden, suicidal, big blue eyes and agreed to do anything he wanted, I suppose. Tides, I've never understood what women see in Cayal." Tryan turned to Kinta and Medwen. "You girls spread your legs for him the first time he looked your way, didn't you? What do you think his secret is?"

Brynden slammed the telescope shut with a growl and turned to Tryan before either woman could answer. Declan was quite sure Tryan had made that comment with the deliberate intention of baiting him.

"Does it matter?" he said, stepping between them. "The important thing is that Pellys is up there and he's waving, which means we've probably got a way in."

"He jumped," Warlock announced suddenly.

They all turned to look at him. The canine had his own telescope out, and had pushed back the hood of his fur-lined jacket so he could get a clearer view of the palace. "See? There. On the ground below the tower."

"Why would he jump?" Stellan asked, turning to see if he could spot the body Warlock spoke of, as Brynden opened his brass tube again and trained it on the palace.

Declan couldn't think of an answer. As far as he knew Pellys wasn't suicidal and even if he was, jumping from a tall building wasn't going to do anything to help him die. He squinted a little in order to focus. There was no longer a figure on the spire waving to them, but an unmoving figure splayed out on the hard-packed snow beneath the palace walls.

"Well," Jaxyn said, clapping Declan on the shoulder. "You wanted to know what happens when we try to fly."

"Do you think he's hurt?" Declan asked in concern.

"The snow would have broken his fall to a degree," Brynden said.

"Even if it didn't, knowing Pellys, he probably considered the pain of the healing was worth the shortcut," Tryan said in a tone so disgusted, Declan had to remind himself that Tryan was speaking of his own father.

Tides, do I sound like that when I speak of Lukys?

Sure enough, a few moments later the motionless figure at the bottom of the palace walls staggered to his feet. He swayed a little, as if trying to get his bearings, and then he waved at them again and began heading their way, arms and legs swinging vigorously as he fought his way through the snow.

"Let me talk to him," Declan said, as the Tide Lord approached.

"He barely knows you," Tryan objected.

"Which is why I should talk to him," Declan said. "He doesn't know me well enough to tell when I'm lying, and he's going to want an explanation about what we're all doing here."

"And as Brynden can't lie to save himself—or the world," Jaxyn added, surprising Declan with his support, "there's not much point in asking him to do it. Pellys won't listen to Kinta because she's with Brynden and he doesn't like Brynden much anyway."

"I should speak to him," Tryan said. "He's my father."

"And you and Pellys haven't exchanged a civil word in five thousand years, Tryan. I can't speak to him for the same reason. He'll assume I'm lying to him because, well, usually I am."

"He'll start sulking when he realises Syrolee's brought Engarhod to the party," Diala said.

Jaxyn nodded in agreement. "And none of you others has ever had any luck getting much sense out of him. Besides, he's expecting the spymaster anyway, so let him do the talking. It can't hurt."

Brynden nodded with some reluctance, seeing the logic in Jaxyn's argument.

Declan was stunned by it. He didn't think Jaxyn was either that insightful or that interested in the relationship between the other immortals to have worked it out.

"Fine," Brynden said putting the telescope away. He didn't need it now anyway. Waving at them excitedly, Pellys was close enough that they could just hear his shouts of welcome, carried to them on the icy wind. "You speak to him."

"Tell him whatever you have to," Tryan added to Declan unnecessarily. "Just get us inside to see Lukys so we can put an end to this nonsense before they start channelling the Tide and it's too late to do anything to stop them."

Chapter 56

In his mind's eye, Cayal imagined his death would be a sombre occasion, filled with long, meaningful silences, much pondering on the meaning of existence and a sense of awe about his impending demise. He imagined it would be a time of reflection. A time of fleeting regrets. A time filled with hope for a future devoid of all awareness.

A step into the abyss, from which nothing, not even the Tide, could save him.

What he got was Lukys checking things off a written list like a particularly fussy steward preparing for a royal banquet.

Send Pellys up the spire to tell us when the Tide peaks. Done.

Empty out the storerooms and let the Crasii eat whatever is left. There would be nothing here after the immortals were gone, according to Lukys. There was no point letting all that food go to waste. Done.

Make sure there's a Scard nearby to catch the crystal if it falls. Actually, Cayal wasn't sure *why* Lukys was insisting the Chaos Crystal mustn't touch the ice once they started channelling the Tide through it. He was adamant on this point, however, and the little lizard chameleon Arryl had brought with her to Jelidia proved the perfect solution. Providing she was standing close enough, she could catch the crystal if it fell. Even though the magical crystal reacted to her proximity, she would not—according to Lukys—affect its ability to amplify the Tide.

That seemed like a grand idea to Cayal. It would be beyond unbearable to find himself standing on the very brink of oblivion, only to be pulled back from the edge at the last instant because he'd inadvertently dropped the tool of his own destruction.

Cayal had his own theory about why Lukys was so anxious to have a Scard in the chamber—something he thought about every time he caught Lukys taking time out from yelling orders at everyone to whisper sweet nothings to his wretched pet rat. It was hard to imagine the creature contained the consciousness of another Tide Lord, even harder to imagine it being transferred into the body of the unconscious young woman lying on the altar in the centre of the chamber next to Arkady. Perhaps the Scard was here for more than her quick reflexes. Perhaps, if

Oritha didn't prove viable as a vessel for Coryna's consciousness, the little Scard, in an emergency, would suffice.

The chameleon Scard in question didn't seem too happy about her role in this historic event, whatever it turned out to be. Maralyce was all but dragging her by the arm toward the altar inside the ice chamber where Cayal was waiting with Arryl. Oritha and Arkady lay side by side on the solid slab of ice behind him, awaiting the imminent arrival of the King Tide.

Cayal consciously avoided looking at Arkady, afraid that even in her current state of suspended animation, she would be able to accuse him; that somehow she would know how badly he'd lied to her.

"Tiji!" Arryl exclaimed in surprise as Maralyce and the Scard drew near. "Tides, girl, we thought you were dead!"

"Lukys trapped me in an ice cave and kept me prisoner," the little Scard announced angrily.

Arryl smiled at her sadly. "I know. He told me. I'm so sorry about Azquil, my dear. I loved him too."

"You knew!" the Scard cried, throwing herself at Arryl. "You heartless bitch! How could you let him go outside looking for me when you knew what they'd done to me?" Her eyes streaming with tears, the little scard pounded on Arryl's arms and chest until Maralyce managed to pull her off.

"Tides, you stupid lizard! Control yourself!"

Cayal stared at the women, wondering at the reason for this amazing outburst.

"Am I missing something here?"

"Only the revelation, that Lady Sweetness-and-Light here is as heartless a killer as the rest of you," the chameleon spat at him, as Maralyce forcibly held her back. She managed to wriggle free and stepped away from them, her red-rimmed eyes blazing. Tears streaming down her silver scales, she sniffed loudly and wiped her eyes with the heels of her hands. "You know what? To hell with you and your stupid plans. I'm not lifting a finger to help a single one of you!"

She sounded a lot like the spymaster, but then that was hardly surprising. She'd been his pet for years before Arryl took her on. Cayal guessed something must have happened to her mate while they were gone, and that Arryl—even if she'd not actually been complicit in his demise—had done nothing to prevent it.

"Very well," he told the little Scard with a shrug. "If you think refusing to help us leave this world is the best way for you to get revenge for your mate, so be it. Off you go."

The lizard stared at him, full of grief, pain and rage—but not so angry that she'd lost all reason. In truth, he'd offered her a terrible choice. Stay and aid the immortals responsible for the death of her mate to be gone—one way or another—or leave, and risk the chance she would never be free of them. Cayal could almost see the war she waged within herself, but he was careful not to let her know it worried him.

Nothing must be allowed to go wrong. Not now.

Finally, the need for vengeance won out over pride. She threw her hands up. "Fine! If it means Amyrantha will be rid of you, then the least I can do is make sure you all kill yourselves . . . or . . . or whatever it is you're planning. I don't really care, just so long as you're *gone*."

Cayal breathed a sigh of relief that was as heartfelt as it was short-lived. Walking toward them across the chamber was Elyssa.

"Tides," Cayal muttered. "Here we go."

Maralyce glanced at him, looked past him and noticed that Elyssa was approaching, and then smiled. "Don't panic, Cayal. You're off the hook."

"Off the hook how?" he asked suspiciously.

"Lukys and Maralyce took us aside last night," Arryl said. "Me and Elyssa. They told us he'd been lying to you all along—that you weren't going to die today at all, and that Elyssa would be much better off waiting until after the transfer and we've arrived on the next world before we hold the wedding, so she can get married in her new body instead of the old one."

"And she believed him?"

"Drank up every word like it was the elixir of life," Maralyce assured him. "Lukys can be very convincing, you know."

Cayal couldn't argue with that, but still, it worried him a little. Suppose Lukys—just this once—had been telling the *truth*? He stared at Maralyce, trying to gauge if she knew what was really going on, but she was no more help than Arryl.

He hardly had the chance to worry about it, in any case, because Elyssa arrived at that moment, filled with an air of barely contained excitement.

"Pellys says the Tide is peaking. It's time to seal the chamber," Elyssa said, smiling adoringly at Cayal. He knew the reason for that look. She truly believed he wasn't going to die.

"Where's Pellys now?" Arryl asked. The little Scard had retreated behind her and was sulking in the background, her skin—what Cayal could see of it—taking on the coloured pattern of the lining of her fur coat.

"Lukys sent him back up the spire to watch for the Tide."

"Didn't you just say it had peaked?"

"Pellys said it would peak any moment now," Elyssa said. She rolled her eyes dismissively. "That could mean days, in his head."

"How will we know when it peaks down here?" Cayal asked. "I can't feel a damn thing with that crystal in the room."

"The Chaos Crystal will let us know," Maralyce assured them. "Trust me, you won't need to be told."

Cayal worried that it all seemed too calm, too easy. And why were they sealing the chamber with Pellys on the outside? For that matter, if the crystal was going to start reacting to the High Tide, why had Lukys sent him out there as a lookout in the first place? Surely he deserved a ticket to the new world, even if Lukys was happily planning to leave the others behind.

That thought made Cayal think of Declan. Was Lukys really going to leave without his son? Admittedly, there wasn't much love lost between the two men, and Lukys had taken the news about Declan Hawkes's defection remarkably well, all things considered. Now he was behaving as if Hawkes didn't exist, which worried Cayal even more, because he thought he knew Lukys pretty well, and yet nothing in Lukys's demeanour at this critical time was what he expected.

Is he hoping the Rodent will still turn up in time?

His unanswered questions left Cayal with a lingering uneasiness that refused to go away. Cayal glanced at the crystal skull sitting on the altar between the deathly pale bodies of Oritha and Arkady. It pulsed with a red light—with so many Tide Lords nearby—that flickered and surged, making the skull's dead eyes seem malevolently aware. Not being able to sense much on the Tide was disconcerting. For a moment, Cayal envied Pellys, sitting high above them, drinking in the rising Tide.

He, at least, would know what it was to be truly alive.

The irony of envying Pellys for being truly alive while awaiting the right moment to kill himself wasn't lost on Cayal, either.

"Lukys asked me to tell you he needs you," Elyssa said to Cayal, taking his arm possessively. "He's going to have to seal the chamber the hard way, he said, and he'd like your help."

Cayal nodded and turned for the entrance, but Elyssa refused to let him go quite so easily. She smiled up at him. "Kiss me before you leave me, lover."

Cayal didn't hesitate. Elyssa's cooperation in this venture was dependent on her believing she was doing this for selfish reasons. A new body. A chance to be rid of the curse of perpetual virginity. A chance to finally make him hers. She had to be convinced all her wishes would come true when they opened the rift. He couldn't risk her doubting for a moment that she wasn't going to get what she wanted. So he took her in his arms and kissed her until she was breathless, and then let her go. He turned away as if he couldn't bear the parting and strode across the ice chamber to the entrance, carefully keeping his back to Elyssa for fear that the look of revulsion on his face would betray him.

"Nice touch," Taryx said, as he approached. He was standing at the entrance with Kentravyon.

The madman was holding a pickaxe. He nodded in agreement. "Wouldn't kiss that mouth for a whole world of souls, myself, but then, you never were that picky, were you, son?"

"Shut up, Kentravyon."

Taryx grinned at Cayal's irritation. "Never understood what you see in her, myself."

"I don't see anything in her," Cayal said, snatching the axe from him. "Elyssa is a malicious, self-centred bitch. Wouldn't matter if she did look like Arkady. Wouldn't make her personality any more attractive."

"Hope you didn't let *that* little pearl of wisdom drop while you were whispering sweet nothings into her ear," Lukys said, walking down the stairs carrying a crowbar and another axe. Coron was sitting on his shoulder. Cayal was still a little peeved that Lukys had lied to him about that. The dead rat he'd shown him back in Torlenia was nothing more than a ruse to enlist his cooperation in Lukys's plan to restore Coryna. Why Lukys felt the need to engage in such an elaborate subterfuge was beyond Cayal.

Or maybe it wasn't. Cayal couldn't imagine being interested enough in Lukys's plans for anything, were it not for the promise of death at the end of it.

Lukys tossed the crowbar to Taryx, and then he squatted down, lifting the rat from his shoulder and holding it in front of him so he could address it directly. "Go to Maralyce. She'll look after you until I get there." He kissed the rat's forehead. "I won't be long now, my love. I promise." The rat scampered away as soon as Lukys let it go, heading inside the chamber and running straight toward Maralyce and the altar, as Lukys had ordered.

"You know, it's more than a little disturbing watching you talk with that rat," Kentravyon remarked. "Good thing I know who it really is in there, Lukys, or I'd be starting to worry about you."

"Well, I suppose if you have to lose sleep over something, Kentravyon, it might as well be me." He looked up and examined the ice over the entrance. "We'll need to bring down the ceiling to seal the break."

"Shouldn't be too difficult," Taryx said, tilting his head back to look up. "Be easier if we could use the Tide."

"Let's not," Lukys said, hefting his axe.

"Why are you leaving Pellys outside?"

Lukys lowered his axe and turned to Cayal. "Because he doesn't want to come with us," he said. "He likes it here."

"So Kentravyon was wrong?"

"About what?"

"About Amyrantha being destroyed when the rift closes?"

"I doubt there'll be anything left here in Jelidia," Lukys agreed, with a brief but meaningful glance in Kentravyon's direction. "But Pellys will survive. As for the rest of Amyrantha . . . well, I can't imagine it'll fare too well when the ice cap melts, but it's survived Cataclysms before. I'm sure it'll recover from this one. Eventually."

"Why do you even care, Cayal?" Taryx asked. "You're going to be dead pretty soon, remember?"

Cayal stared at them for a moment, with a sneaking suspicion he was being had, but then he shoved the feeling aside. The Tide was rising—here outside the chamber, even Cayal could sense the increase in power, muted though it was—and Taryx was right. In a very short time, he would be dead.

"You're right. I *don't* care," Cayal said, as much to remind himself as the others. And then he raised the pick, turned and slammed it into the ice above the entrance to the chamber, hoping the last of his lingering doubts would collapse with the ceiling, and he would finally be at peace.

Chapter 57

Pellys was thrilled to see Declan and the other immortals, assuming, Declan supposed, that they were here to help. He had no notion of the politics of immortality, it seemed or that the world was about to come to an end, and Lukys had left him out here to perish with it, instead of taking him inside.

"You came!" he cried, waving at them gleefully as they made their way down the ridge to meet him. He did a quick headcount and beamed at them. "You all came!"

"Tides, you'd think we'd been invited," Jaxyn muttered beside Declan.

They slipped and slid the last few feet until Pellys reached them. He was grinning broadly. "Look! Everyone is here! Did you come to help?"

"We certainly came to see what we could do," Declan agreed. "Where are Lukys and the others?"

"Inside already," he said.

"Did they have a mortal woman with them? Dark hair? Tall . . ."

"Arkady, you mean?" Pellys said. "She was very pretty. Did you know her?"

Declan's heart sank at Pellys's use of the past tense when referring to her. "Is she still in there?"

Pellys shrugged. "How would I know? Hello, Brynden, Kinta . . . Ambria . . . Tides, I can't believe you've all come! What brings you all the way down here?"

"We have come to view Lukys's remarkable chamber," Brynden said, in a tone that indicated he wasn't comfortable with subterfuge, even with a half-wit like Pellys. "Hawkes tell us it's quite impressive."

"You'll have to wait until later. They've sealed the chamber." Pellys spied Syrolee in the group and smiled at her coyly. "You came to visit me too."

"Not by choice, I can assure you," the Empress of the Five Realms grumbled. "Stop looking at me like that."

"She's right," Tryan said, stepping between his mother and Pellys. "What do you mean—they've sealed the chamber?"

"What I said," Pellys replied, trying to look past him. "They sealed it."

"Then we'll unseal it," Declan announced, fearing what that meant for Arkady, but before he could take a step in the direction of the palace, Jaxyn stopped him by grabbing his arm. "Wait a minute, spymaster."

"Why?"

"Can't you feel it?"

"Feel what?" Diala asked.

"*Feel* it," Jaxyn ordered.

Declan closed his eyes for a moment. Through his feet, he could feel a slight vibration. He opened his eyes and looked to Jaxyn for an explanation. "Am I the only one who thinks it odd that the Tide seems to have retreated in the past few minutes?"

"It hasn't retreated," Pellys said. "It's the crystal."

"Then they've started," Kinta said.

"Show us the way into this legendary underground lair, Pellys," Brynden commanded. "We have business with Lukys."

"Can't it wait until after he's finished?" Pellys asked. "I mean, if you're not here to help, he'd probably rather you waited."

Declan stared up at the palace while Pellys was talking, doing a quick calculation in his head. "We may not need a way inside," he said, stepping sideways a little. He wondered if it was his imagination, or he could feel a difference in the ground vibration?

"What do you mean?"

"I mean I think we're right over the chamber here."

"You mean we're standing on top of it?" Rance asked.

Declan nodded. "We might be able to break through from here. Probably easier, too, than trying to get through a barricade."

Tryan was staring at the ground now, too, trying to sense the edges of the chamber. "If we crack the ice, we might be able to get into the chamber from above."

"How big is it?" Ambria asked, staring at the ground. They were all examining the ground now, trying to feel out the chamber beneath them—even Warlock and Stellan and they probably couldn't feel a thing.

"Big," Declan said.

"Huge," Pellys confirmed with a grin. "Are we really standing over it out here?"

"We must be," Jaxyn said. "We're right on the edge of it, I reckon. There's a slight difference in the vibration here from back there where I was a moment ago."

"Then we should be able to feel the edges of it," Tryan said, moving a little further to the right, to see if he could find the outer limits of the chamber. "It's circular, you say?"

"Like standing inside a pumpkin," Pellys informed them cheerfully. "If you took the seeds out. And it was made of ice."

"But I can barely feel the Tide," Medwen said, looking very concerned. "Up on the ridge it felt close to peaking. Down here, it's dwindled away to nothing. How is he doing that?"

"The Chaos Crystal," Pellys said. "It makes everything feel soft."

That's not exactly how Declan would have expressed it, but it was an accurate enough description. Everything did feel soft around the edges, as if the crystal's power dulled the sharp edges of the Tide.

"You can feel it up there," Pellys told him, pointing to the palace's elegant spires. "That's why Lukys sent me up there to keep watch. To tell him when the Tide peaks."

Jaxyn stopped staring at the ground long enough to clap Pellys on the shoulder. "If he's sealed the chamber, how were you supposed to get back inside to tell him about it?"

Pellys frowned. He hadn't thought that far ahead, apparently. "I don't know . . . you should ask Lukys."

"We intend to," Brynden assured him ominously. "What is it, Hawkes?"

Declan was staring up at the spires thoughtfully. "Could we channel the Tide from up there and direct it at the chamber?"

"Provided we knew where the chamber was," Brynden said with a nod. "And provided some of us were prepared to climb those spires."

Kinta was considering the palace thoughtfully, "Do you think, if we marked out the edges, you'd be able to focus on it?"

Declan glanced up at the spires. "We'd see it better from up there, that's for certain. It would be easier to focus—"

"The fatal flaw in that plan," Tryan cut in, "being the words *we* and *focus*. You're not going anywhere, Hawkes. If you start trying to focus the Tide, who knows where it'll finish up. Jaxyn, Brynden and I will climb the spires. You can stay down here with the others and give us something to aim at."

Declan wanted to argue, but unfortunately Tryan was right. He knew in principle how to focus the Tide, but had no practical knowledge of how to do it.

He did, however, have some notion regarding the size of the underground chamber, which meant he had some chance of figuring out exactly where it was. And if he were down here, once they cracked open the chamber it would be easier to get in to find Arkady.

The others understood it immediately too. "How long will it take us to reach the top?" Brynden asked, shielding his eyes against the rising sun as he stared up at the palace towers. Declan was wondering the same thing, the sense of time slipping away from them becoming a very real feeling.

"You don't have to go all the way to the top," Pellys said cheerfully. "About two-thirds of the way up you can feel the Tide again."

Brynden nodded and turned to Declan. "That should give the rest of you time to find the centre of the chamber down here. If you mark the ice, we'll know where to focus the Tide, which should break us through the ice in no time at all."

Tides, we don't have time for this. "Then what?"

"Let's see what happens when the roof caves in," Jaxyn said. "The look on Lukys's face at that point will be something to behold. Cayal's too. Race you to the top, Bryn."

Without waiting for the others, Jaxyn turned and ran toward the palace. Tryan followed, as did Brynden a moment later. Pellys stared at the rest of the gathered immortals for a moment, and then he shrugged. "Better view from up there." He turned and bolted after the Tide Lords, waving his arms wildly, yelling, "Hey! wait for me!"

Kinta smiled as he left and then turned to Declan. "We've a little while before they're in position," she said. "What are we searching for exactly?"

"The centre of the chamber," Declan told them, her words doing nothing to ease his sense of urgency. "I think we're on the edge of it here." He turned to the Warlock and Stellan, who'd been hanging back and watching them talking, hugging their arms around their bodies against the cold. "Desean, can you stand here? Warlock, come with me. We'll try to pace out the rest of it. Can the rest of you feel anything?"

Ambria nodded, frowning. "Faintly. It's much stronger over there than near the canine."

"It's a circular chamber, remember, about fifty paces across. If Desean is standing on the edge of it, then it should go this way . . . and that."

Syrolee nodded at the direction he was indicating. "Let's do it then," she said a little impatiently. "Hopefully, before they reach the Tide, we'll have something for them to aim at and we can be done with this nonsense."

"Saving the world isn't nonsense, Syrolee," Medwen said as she began to pace out the edge of the chamber under them.

"It is when the wretched mortals you left behind start to think they have a say in their own future," Syrolee complained as she reluctantly began to do the same as the others and pace out the ground. "Tides, Engarhod . . . go that way!"

The immortals on the ground spent the better part of the next ten minutes marking out the edges of the chamber. Declan glanced up occasionally to check on the progress of the Tide Lords climbing the palace towers, wishing they'd thought to bring the boards with them they'd used to travel across the ocean. Then it would have been a simple matter to float to the top . . .

Or maybe, he decided on reflection, it wouldn't have worked at all. There was barely enough Tide down here to start a fire. Maybe, even if they'd had the wherewithal to fly, it wouldn't have been possible.

It might also account for why, earlier, when Pellys had first spotted them on the ridge, he'd fallen from the spire instead of floating down to the ground to greet them using the Tide.

"I think that's it!" Kinta called.

He turned to look at her. The others were spread out in a rough circle, a line trampled in the snow between them, marking the outer limit of the underground chamber. Declan guessed that from high on the palace spires, where the others were almost to the point where Pellys assured them they would be able to feel the Tide, it would be easily visible.

"We need to mark the centre point!" he called back. Kinta nodded in agreement and began to walk forward. Declan signalled for Warlock and Rance to do the same, the four of them heading toward the centre.

"Are we done now?" Warlock asked when they met in the middle. The canine looked rather agitated. Declan couldn't blame him. After being dragged across the world at a speed that made him dizzy, his entire contribution to saving the world since arriving in Jelidia had been pretty much standing around doing nothing at all.

Kinta glanced up at the spires and waved to the others. "I'd say so. Are you sure this will work, Hawkes? I mean, shouldn't we have at least made an effort to get in through the door?"

"Pellys said it was sealed," Rance pointed out.

"And something is going on," Desean added, "because even *I* can feel the vibration now."

Declan looked at him with concern. The trembling had increased markedly in the past few minutes, but in theory, if it was merely the other immortals channelling the Tide in the chamber beneath them, it shouldn't have affected a mortal human at all. That Desean could feel something did not augur well for any of them.

A distant shout caught Declan's attention. He turned to see one of the others waving from the spires. There were four of them up there now, two on either side of each spire, clinging like dark limpets to the icy surface about two-thirds of the way up. Although Declan wasn't particularly afraid of heights, he had not yet mentally adjusted to immortality well enough to let go his instinctive, very human—and not unreasonable—fear of plummeting from a great height to a crushing death on the hard ground below.

There would come a time, he supposed, when he'd be able to scale a tower made of ice and not care about the consequences, but he wasn't there yet.

And if Lukys succeeds in killing Cayal this day, I may never have to worry about it.

He pushed that thought away, deciding the implications of his own immortality were something he didn't need distracting him. What would happen would happen. The only thing Declan could do was act in accordance with his conscience.

Stopping Lukys and Cayal from destroying Amyrantha was his first priority. Finding Arkady came a very close second. And everything else came a poor third to those two goals.

Kinta waved back at the men on the towers and then the group on the ground moved out of the way. Not because they were in danger, so much as to give the Tide Lords a clear aim at the centre of the chamber. Beneath them, the trembling increased as they backed up.

Stellan looked at Declan worriedly as they took their places on the edge of the circle. "Are you sure you're going to be able to get into the chamber in time?"

"Yes."

"It might already be too late."

"I don't think so."

"How can you tell?" Kinta asked, looking almost as worried as Warlock.

"Because," Declan said, stepping back over the boundary line that marked the edge of where they thought the chamber might be, "as Brynden so rightly pointed out back in Chelae, my lady, one could assume that given we're standing here discussing it, they probably haven't destroyed the world just yet."

Warlock bared his teeth silently, shaking his head. He was not the slightest bit amused. "I'll bet you suzerain just crack each other up when you get together for a few drinks, don't you?"

Before Declan could answer, the trembling suddenly increased. The snow in the centre of their roughly trampled circle began to hiss and pop and steam as if the water trapped here in Jelidia was going straight from frozen to boiling without any liquid state in between. He glanced up at the spires.

The ground trembled even harder. The hissing increased as the snow and ice boiled away. A mist made of steam billowed out from the hole they were making in the ice. Declan still couldn't feel the Tide very well, If anything, he could feel it less than he did a few moments ago, which didn't make sense.

"I just had a thought," Stellan said.

"Do you think it's working?" Warlock asked.

Declan assumed he was talking to him and not asking Stellan his opinion. "It's hard to tell."

Kinta frowned. "They must be *pouring* the Tide into that hole."

"Maybe we should help," Rance suggested.

Rance wasn't the only immortal who was thinking that, apparently. All around him, Declan felt the others drawing on the Tide, something that proved incredibly difficult when he tried it. It felt like every drop of the Tide they were able to squeeze out was being sucked down into the vortex below, as if into a sinkhole.

"Tides, it's sucking the life out of me!" he heard Krydence complain.

"Which brings us to my thought," snapped Stellan a little impatiently.

"*What*, Desean?" Declan retorted, a little more harshly than he'd intended. It wasn't that he didn't care what Stellan had to say; it was just with four powerful Tide Lords channelling all the power they could muster at a hole in the ground at High Tide, there didn't seem to be much happening except some melting snow. And the Tide he was trying to channel felt like it was trying to drag him into an abyss. He couldn't imagine what a mortal would have to say at this particular moment that might merit more than his fleeting attention.

"The Chaos Crystal is meant to amplify power, isn't it?"

"Yes."

"And it sucks the Tide in, even when it's not doing anything."

"I suppose."

Warlock nodded in agreement. "It does, spymaster. I know that for a fact. It's how they found the crystal in Caelum. Because it sucks in the Tide and they could feel the dead spot."

"Is there a point to this?" Kinta asked impatiently. Her brow was actually beaded with sweat at the effort it was taking to channel the Tide.

Stellan was looking worried. "I just have a question for you, Declan, that's all."

"*What*, for pity's sake?"

"What happens when you pour a concentrated stream of the Tide into something that feeds off it? Something that sucks it up like a sponge?"

The immortals within hearing looked at the mortal man oddly for a moment. It was Declan who realised what Stellan was getting at first and the realisation made him ill. He swore savagely and turned to Kinta. "We have to stop!"

She looked at him in confusion. "What?"

"We have to make them stop! They're not helping to stop the rift from opening, they're making things worse!"

"The crystal *feeds* on the Tide, my lady," Warlock explained urgently, as he grasped what Stellan was saying, even if the immortals didn't get it. "All that power you're channelling into that chamber isn't interrupting Lukys's work; it's probably making it a sure thing."

Kinta swore then too, abandoned her efforts to summon the Tide and began to run toward the palace. As she passed the immortals she yelled at them to stop and waved her arms frantically at Brynden and the others up on the spires.

But it was too late to stop it now. They couldn't hear her—could barely see her through the cloud of steam—and wouldn't know the effect they were having. Quite the opposite—they were probably channelling more and more into the chamber out of a growing sense of frustration, not comprehending why their strategy wasn't working.

Desperately, Declan turned to Warlock. "There was only one entrance into the chamber. That's where they must have sealed it . . ."

"Which means it's probably the only part of the chamber wall that can be breached manually," Warlock finished for him with a nod of understanding, confirming Declan's suspicion that this canine was among the smartest creatures Declan had ever encountered. "Let's go."

Declan didn't stop to explain what he was going to try to Stellan or the other immortals. They were too busy, anyway, now they realised the danger, trying to catch the attention of the Tide Lords on the spires who, in their ignorance, were powering Lukys's plans, not defeating them.

Declan and Warlock took off for the palace at a run. Declan was terrified by what he might have unleashed, heartsick at the thought that far from saving his Amyrantha from destruction, he had brought the tools and enough immortals to finish the job.

If Declan couldn't stop this, and stop it soon, his noble attempt to save the world might be the very thing that destroyed it.

Chapter 58

Arkady felt nothing.

She was aware. She could hear. She could think. She could even panic. But she couldn't move a muscle. Not even her eyes.

Her world, therefore, was dark. Not black. Not completely. But it was dark and if she concentrated, she could focus on the inside of her eyelids and actually see the blood vessels there, sluggishly moving the blood around her body at a speed barely enough to keep her alive.

She didn't know how she got here. Her last clear memory was of placing the Chaos Crystal on the altar beside Oritha's head. She had a vague recollection of talking with Lukys after that. Of making plans to return to Glaeba . . . Of a sudden bolt of pain shooting through her body followed by a bone-chilling cold. But she wasn't sure about that.

All Arkady knew was that she was cold. And frightened.

And paralysed.

Arkady had listened to the Tide Lords making their plans; heard every word clearly. She figured she was back in the ice chamber, which meant Oritha lay beside her in a similar state, awaiting the new mind Lukys had bred her to accommodate. Her own purpose was to placate Elyssa. Lukys had told Cayal he didn't think the transfer would work. In fact, he said it would probably kill her, making a mockery of Cayal's attempts to save her. Arkady didn't want to die, any more than she wanted to vacate her body so some half-crazy immortal could inhabit it.

If anybody had thought to ask her, she would have chosen the former.

But nobody had asked her opinion. There was nothing she could do about it. She couldn't lift a finger. She couldn't blink, cough, nor produce any physical sign that might prove she was neither unconscious, nor a willing participant in this hideous experiment.

She heard them sealing the entrance to the cavern; heard the ice crashing down as they collapsed the ceiling over the doorway leading into the chamber, taking away any hope of a last-minute rescue from this place. She heard Cayal's shouted curses as he almost got caught on the wrong side, abandoning his tools as he dived through the collapsing entrance in the nick of time. She could even hear the chittering of a small rodent that occasionally stopped by her ear to sniff her hair.

Although she couldn't see the crystal on the altar beside her head, she sensed a change in it almost as soon as the cavern closed. The crystal's dull red glow was brighter now; so bright that even with her eyes shut, she—who couldn't even sense the Tide—knew the Tide was nearing its peak.

Arkady heard voices. The immortals talking. She'd heard Arryl telling Cayal he didn't have to marry Elyssa, because Lukys had lied to her about the transfer.

That meant a lot to Arkady. Not because she wanted Cayal for herself, but because Lukys apparently didn't mean to waste time trying to extract Elyssa's consciousness from her body and put it anywhere near Arkady's.

That's something, she decided, quite determined death was the only reasonable alternative if there was the slightest chance she would end up on another world, possessed by someone like the Immortal Maiden.

Her relief was short-lived, however, and disappeared when Lukys stepped up to the altar.

"See, the peak is almost here," he said. He sounded close . . . standing at her feet perhaps. "It's time to take our places."

"We have *places*?" Elyssa asked, her voice a little scornful. Arkady couldn't understand why. *You'd think, given she believes she is about to receive everything she's ever hoped for, she'd be a little more grateful.* "How very organised of you, Lukys."

"We need one of you in position at all four cardinal points," he said.

"But we're at the southern pole," she heard Cayal say. "Doesn't that make everything north?"

She heard Lukys sigh impatiently. "At equidistant points then, if you want to split hairs. Maralyce, why don't you go there and, Kentravyon, you take the opposite position? Arryl can take the left and, Taryx, I want you to take the right."

"What about me?" Cayal asked. He sounded very close. Near her head. *Look down, Cayal! Glance my way and realise I'm not unconscious. Discover I'm alive and screaming and want no part of this!*

"And me?" Elyssa added.

"I need Cayal holding the crystal. Elyssa, you need to be here too, but when I tell you to stop, you have to let go of the Tide. That was one of the mistakes we made last time with Coryna. I can't make the transfer if you're drawing on the Tide."

"That makes sense, I suppose." She sounded a little less snippy this time, a little less sure of herself.

"Where's the Scard?"

Scard? What Scard? What do they need a Scard for?

"I'm here."

The little voice that answered was belligerent and uncooperative. And frighteningly familiar.

Tides, that's Tiji. How does she come to be here?

"You must stand at Lord Cayal's side, little one. No matter what happens, you *must* not let that crystal touch the ice once we're channelling the Tide through it. If he falls before we're done, you must hang on to it for dear life. Do you understand?"

"Yes."

"Why can't I take it from him?" Elyssa asked. "We don't need a Scard for this, surely?"

"I can't effect the transfer of your mind into a new body if you're channelling the Tide, remember?" When Elyssa seemed to have no argument about that, Lukys addressed Tiji once more. "The crystal must not touch the ice, remember?"

"You keep saying that, Lukys," Arkady heard Arryl say. "Why?"

"Because allowing it to come into contact with anything inanimate while it's amplifying the Tide will stop the flow of energy," Maralyce explained. "And that much Tide magic backing up that quickly isn't just dangerous, my dear. It will be catastrophic."

"Just so long as I know . . ." Tiji sounded rebellious, but put up no further argument that Arkady could hear.

She wondered if Oritha was able to hear all of this too. If she was awake beneath the paralysis, was she frightened or excited? Fearing for what she might leave behind or looking forward to what lay ahead?

Had Oritha volunteered for this? Did she know what she was volunteering for? Did she truly comprehend it? Did she understand that if Lukys's plan succeeded, she would no longer be Oritha, but Coryna— Lukys's lover, Maralyce's sister . . . ?

"You'll need to get rid of your clothes," Lukys said, interrupting Arkady's thoughts. She wasn't sure who he was addressing until he added,

"Maralyce is right. We can't risk the crystal touching *anything* inanimate, not even cloth."

"Well, at least we'll have something pretty to look at," Elyssa said, confirming her suspicion that Lukys had been speaking to Cayal. And even though she sounded a little sarcastic, Elyssa was right about one thing: Cayal naked was something beautiful to behold.

Tides, listen to me. I think I've lost my mind along with all feeling in the rest of my body.

But then Elyssa asked doubtfully, "Are you sure this is going to work, Lukys? I mean . . . I can barely feel the Tide in here with that damned thing sucking it in, let alone tell if it's peaked or not."

"Wait until you start channelling," Kentravyon told her, his voice full of gleeful anticipation. "Then you'll feel it."

"So how does this work?"

That was Cayal's voice. Arkady found it amazing that he had let things progress to this point without getting any specific details from Lukys about how he was supposed to die. Maybe carelessness was a special flaw of immortality.

Who needed to be careful, when there was no consequence to be suffered at the end of the day?

That part of Arkady that couldn't abide not having some idea of what was happening to her—some semblance of control over her own destiny— was screaming silently in frustration. She was more helpless now than she had ever been in her life. Not as a slave, not as a duke's wife, not even as a frightened, timid little girl, tiptoeing through the streets of the Lebec slums, jumping at her own shadow—until she befriended Declan Hawkes, a boy who was as fearless as she was terrified—had she felt so alone and powerless. Declan had taught her how to be strong, and how to survive in the streets, but nothing had prepared her for this.

As Lukys explained the procedure to Cayal and the others— something about pulling the Tide in and focusing it on the crystal— Arkady had time to wonder what had happened to Declan.

Had the lure of immortality proved too much for him? Was he embracing it?

She suspected he'd returned to the Cabal. Tilly would want to know everything Declan had learned about the immortals. She'd want to know everything he could tell her.

Of course, in Arkady's opinion, he'd be better served doing something useful here. Like learning how to actually *kill* an immortal, perhaps. Or undoing the spell that held her paralysed and trapped on a block of ice like a human sacrifice awaiting execution, instead of having high tea and cucumber sandwiches with Tilly back in her townhouse in Lebec, while they discussed all the terrible things the immortals had done to Amyrantha.

It wasn't fair, Arkady knew, to think that of either Declan or Tilly. Fear was making her vindictive.

Tides, it's not Declan's fault. He never meant to become immortal.

"When will we know it's time to enter the rift?" Arkady heard Arryl asking. She hadn't been paying attention to Lukys's lecture. All those details about focus, and channelling, and the rift and the altar meant nothing to her.

"You won't need to worry about it," Lukys assured her. "Once you're close enough, the rift will pull you in."

"What if you don't want to go?" she heard Tiji ask unhappily.

"Then you need to hang on to something solid, little lizard, or you'll be coming with us to the new world, whether you want to or not."

Tiji had nothing more to say about it after that. Lukys issued a few more instructions and the group dispersed to their positions around the chamber. Arkady didn't know why she was certain they'd moved, only that they had. She was surprised they were so composed. Somehow she imagined this occasion would be much more fraught, the participants much more edgy and tense. But they seemed quite calm.

Is that because they've done this before? Or are they really so old, so inured to normal human emotion, that even the prospect of opening a rift to another world isn't enough to ruffle them?

Arkady wished she could open her eyes. She wished she could see what was happening. For a time, there was silence, and then she heard Lukys ask: "Are you ready?"

"Any time you are," Cayal replied.

And then, without warning, Arkady's world exploded into pain.

Arkady had no idea what was happening to her. She'd thought they hadn't begun yet. She believed she'd never be able to sense the Tide.

But she could feel it now.

The Chaos Crystal, which she assumed was somewhere nearby, was pulsing with a light Arkady could see, even through her paralysed eyes. It burned her retinas; her inability to open her eyes the only thing that saved her from instant blindness. She wanted to scream in agony, although she couldn't pinpoint exactly where the pain began and where it ended, any more than she could identify the cause.

It seemed as if every square inch of her body had decided to catch fire independently of every other square inch, and simultaneously send messages to her brain screaming at her that she was in flames.

She tried to cry out, but couldn't move her mouth. She wanted to writhe with agony, but couldn't move her body. She wanted to weep with terror, but couldn't shed a tear.

Someone else screamed, close by, yelling for Lukys. A woman's voice. One she didn't recognise. Then, through her own pain, Arkady heard Cayal shriek, a sound of such torment and pathos that it tore at her soul.

Just as abruptly, he fell silent.

Even through the agony, Arkady wondered if that meant Cayal had achieved his aim and if finally, this time, his cries were silenced forever . . .

She had no time to lament his passing, however.

No sooner had the sound of Cayal's torment faded than she heard Lukys shout something and a moment later, Arkady felt a strange pressure against her mind, as if an intruder was pushing on the door to her thoughts and she had to lean on it to stop them gaining a foothold.

Suddenly the pain, the prospect of impending death . . . all of those things became secondary to survival.

But not physical survival. Arkady found herself fighting for possession of herself.

Lukys had lied, Arkady realised, as she fought back with every ounce of strength she owned against the pressure in her mind. He'd lied to Cayal about not attempting to transfer Elyssa's mind.

Arkady didn't have the time to care if he'd lied about this being Cayal's only chance to die. She had other, more urgent concerns. Because whether or not Cayal lived or died, Arkady was engaged in a life-and-death battle for dominion over her very soul.

Chapter 59

Declan ran into the palace with Warlock on his heels and, much to Warlock's amazement, nobody tried to stop them. There were supposed to be Crasii in the palace—clearly they weren't guarding it—but he saw no sign of anybody, immortal, human, or Crasii, as he pounded after Hawkes.

There was no time to admire the immensity of the place, or marvel at its construction. Instead, he followed Hawkes along a confusing series of ice-carved corridors and down a treacherously slippery staircase to the lower levels. They kept on running, past a whole labyrinth of storerooms and then, when Warlock was convinced Hawkes had no idea where he was, they plunged down another set of stairs, lit with a sickly green light, where they ran into an anteroom blocked by a wall of crumbled ice.

Hawkes swore savagely for a moment, punching the wall with his fist.

"Can't you use the Tide to break it?" Warlock asked, examining the barrier closely. Unlike the finesse that had gone into creating the rest of the palace, this crude but effective wall seemed to have been created by bringing down a part of the ceiling. It wasn't done magically, Warlock surmised. The ice was jagged and rough and piled in a heap against the opening.

"I think the Tide will just make things worse," Declan said, frowning. "If all those immortals channelling the Tide above us can't crack it, this much closer to the crystal . . . I don't like our chances."

Tides, all that magical power they're so enamoured with, and they can't do a damned thing useful with it . . . "Then we're going to have to break it down the hard way."

"What do you mean?"

"This barrier wasn't magicked into existence using the Tide, Hawkes. They sealed the chamber the hard way, with pickaxes."

"How could you possibly know that?"

Warlock pointed to the tools lying on the floor near the foot of the stairs. There was a pickaxe and a crowbar, both partially buried under the ice, as if they'd been abandoned in a hurry. "Just a hunch."

Hawkes swore again and scooped up the pick handle, jerked it free and tossed it to Warlock, before turning his attention to the crowbar. "We don't have much time."

Warlock couldn't argue with that. Even he could feel the vibration down here, and not only because they were channelling the Tide. The ground was actually shaking.

Whatever they were doing inside that chamber, Hawkes was right about one thing—it wasn't looking good for anyone on the outside.

He slammed the pickaxe into the ice, pulling away chunks of it, as Hawkes worked the crowbar free and began to do the same. The wall resisted their attempts to dismantle it, however. Every inch of progress they made was hard fought, every inroad they made into the ice, seemingly not enough to do any good.

Warlock soon lost track of time. He had no idea how long they hacked away at the ice. His shoulders burned and his hands had begun to blister before the light changed a little on the other side and they were rewarded with some hint their efforts were not in vain.

The ice, where it was thinnest, had taken on a decidedly rosy hue.

Panting with exhaustion, Warlock lowered his pickaxe and bent over for a moment, trying to regain his breath. The ground was no longer trembling; it was fairly shuddering.

"We're nearly through!" Hawkes exclaimed, raising the crowbar for the final blow that would break through the wall.

"Wait!"

Mid-blow, the spymaster hesitated and turned to look at him. "What's the matter?"

"What's going to happen when you break through?"

"I don't know."

"Good plan!"

Hawkes lowered the crowbar and stared at him. "Got a better idea?"

Warlock nodded, drawing in deep breaths of the icy air. "*You* can probably withstand whatever we release when we break the wall, but I won't."

Hawkes thought about that for a moment and then nodded in agreement. "You're right. Get out of here. I'll break it down and go in."

"To do what?"

"Whatever it takes to end this," Hawkes said, a little impatiently. "Tides, Warlock, you're having doubts about this *now*?"

We have the will to do whatever it takes, Boots had said to him back in Hidden Valley, *to see as many immortals as possible perish in that rift when they open it.*

What if it really does destroy Amyrantha in the process?

He remembered her eyes shining in the darkness. *Think of a future where your own children are destined to betray you to the suzerain, Warlock, and then tell me you wouldn't rather see an end to this world than wait for that to happen.*

Warlock blinked away the memory and looked Hawkes in the eye. "I have no doubts, spymaster. I know exactly why I'm here. I'm coming with you."

"Then let's finish this thing," Hawkes said, raising the crowbar. "Get down."

Warlock did as Hawkes suggested, crouching down behind the rubble they'd hacked from the wall. Declan slammed the crowbar into the ice twice more, and the wall split open.

A wave of intense heat exploded out of the small opening, filling the outer chamber with a fierce red light, melting away much of the debris they'd dislodged. Hawkes was thrown back onto the stairs behind them with the force of the heatwave, landing with a crack that sounded horribly like the noise of his backbone breaking.

The ground was shaking even harder. Hawkes screamed out in agony. If his back was broken, it was also healing again, and it was exceedingly painful.

Ignoring Hawkes—he was immortal, after all, and would recover—Warlock staggered to his feet and managed to climb up the slick ice to the opening and look into the chamber. A moment later Hawkes joined him. Unharmed.

Together they gazed through the opening into the swirling, hellish nightmare that was the ice cavern. It seemed as if the very air in the cavern was a spinning red hurricane, like blood swirling down a drain.

It was hard to make out anything precisely. There seemed to be figures evenly spaced around the chamber. Near the altar in the centre there were several more people Warlock couldn't immediately identify.

One of them—a naked male—lay at the foot of the altar and appeared to be either unconscious or dead. There was a woman curled on the floor beside him, and behind the altar, standing with his arms held wide, a white-haired man Warlock guessed must the legendary Lukys.

Then he spied another creature cowering in the shadow of the altar. Warlock would have sworn it was a chameleon Scard if he didn't know better.

For a moment, both Tide Lord and canine were too overwhelmed by the sight before them to react to it, but then something moved on the blocky altar in the centre of the room. There was a woman lying on it, her back arched so fiercely they could see her face from here, screaming in such torment it made Warlock's soul bleed to hear her cries.

Beside him, Hawkes went rigid.

"Tides," he said, "that's Arkady."

Chapter 60

Hawkes was clambering down the ice and running across the chamber before Warlock could stop him. He cursed under his breath and scrambled after him, certain no good could come of charging into such a maelstrom without any forethought, and trying to interrupt the proceedings.

Warlock couldn't feel the Tide—not the magic of it, at least. But he could see it, or this hellish manifestation of it, filling the circular chamber with its sinister, swirling red light. And it terrified him.

Declan Hawkes reached the altar ahead of Warlock and pulled Arkady from it. That's when Warlock realised Elyssa was there too, lying on the floor, staring blankly at the ceiling as if she had no notion of what was going on around her.

At Lukys's feet lay another unconscious woman, next to the body of a rat. The Immortal Prince lay on his side on the floor by the altar, naked and apparently dead, but still holding on to the glowing red skull, which pulsed with a deep, crimson, malevolent light. Crouched in the shelter of the altar was Tiji, Hawkes's little pet chameleon, wearing a thick fur coat and a look of abject terror.

Lukys tried to stop Declan from rescuing Arkady. Warlock ignored that scuffle to concentrate on the source of the trouble—the Chaos Crystal.

He turned to Tiji, wondering what she was doing here; hoping she knew what was going on.

"How do I stop it?" he shouted, hoping she could hear him over the howling wind that tore around and around the chamber.

"I don't know!" she shouted back. "Just don't drop it! If you drop it, you'll kill everybody!"

That was good enough for Warlock. That's why he was here, after all. If Cayal was dead, then the others could die too. He glanced across at Hawkes, but he was too busy struggling with Arkady and Lukys to notice what Warlock was up to.

We have the will to do whatever it takes, Boots's voice echoed in his mind, *to see as many immortals as possible perish in that rift when they open it.*

What if it really does destroy Amyrantha in the process?

Warlock stared at the crystal skull, its red eyes glaring at him. *Tides, can one creature make such a decision on behalf of an entire world?*

The answer was there already, waiting for him to ask the question. *Think of a future where your own children are destined to betray you to the suzerain, Warlock, and then tell me you wouldn't rather see an end to this world than wait for that to happen.*

He needed no further urging. Determined and filled with a sense of complete *rightness*, Warlock snatched the crystal from Cayal's unresisting fingers and rose to his feet. The movement caught Lukys's eye.

He shoved Declan away and lunged for Warlock, screaming: *"Noooo!"*

Warlock stepped back, out of his reach, and raised the burning crystal skull over his head and then, with every ounce of force he could muster, smashed it into the floor.

For a moment, nothing happened. The skull didn't shatter. It simply bounced a few times and then rolled to a stop at the base of the altar where it wedged under the lip of the plinth.

Warlock stared at it, more than a little disappointed. He glanced at Tiji, who seemed just as puzzled.

And then, above them, the swirling red vortex began to narrow, contracting to a point above the altar. Warlock stared at it in fear.

Was this the rift to another world the immortals had been talking of?

Tides, have I opened it by mistake?

As if in answer to his silent question, the wind picked up, the sound of it howling through the chamber. Cracks appeared in the roof and on the polished permafrost beneath Warlock's feet. Warlock grabbed Tiji by the arm and dragged her away from the black maw that was growing in the centre of the red vortex, sucking everything to it.

Those nearest the vortex weren't so lucky; it swallowed them like a hungry monster. Lukys, Cayal's inert body, the woman lying at the base of the altar near where Lukys had been standing a moment ago. Then Hawkes lost his grip on Arkady and he vanished as well. Warlock shielded his eyes, turning away from the gluttonous whirlpool that was indiscriminately devouring everything in its path.

Averting their faces from the maelstrom, Warlock and Tiji tried to flee the sucking power of the rift, but the shaking ground was starting to split. Above them, the ceiling cracked even wider, exposing the chamber to daylight.

Breaking the chamber open did nothing to stop the vortex; nothing to halt the relentless forces dragging Amyrantha into ruin. Some of the immortals in the chamber ran toward it, some seemed frozen in place. But whichever direction Warlock looked, the world seemed to be breaking apart.

"Tides, you stupid dog," Tiji shouted at him as the floor began to give way. "What have you done?"

He never had a chance to answer her. The floor cracked open beside him and, without warning, the little lizard Scard was gone, swallowed by the yawning chasm that had opened beneath her.

Warlock stared after her in shock, the dawning realisation that this really *might* be the end of everything, suddenly settling on his shoulders like the weight of the world, as if it had decided to rest there for a moment on its way to complete annihilation.

Panic filled Warlock, temporarily paralysing him. He needed to close the rift, he realised, but had no idea how. He needed to put an end to that vortex; the sucking whirlpool was tearing Amyrantha apart.

He glanced at the pulsating Chaos Crystal, the engine driving the vortex. On his hands and knees, Warlock crawled back toward the altar, back toward the crystal skull that lay jammed beneath it, spewing out the rage of the universe and venting it on his world.

It took every bit of strength Warlock owned to reach the altar; more strength than he thought he possessed to free the crystal while resisting the pull of the rapidly expanding vortex that swirled overhead, swallowing everything within its reach.

Finally jerking the crystal skull free, Warlock held it up. With a final silent apology to Boots, he closed his eyes, certain that if he'd achieved nothing else here today, he was going to create the future Boots wanted from him—a future where no child of his would ever be subject to the whim or the orders of an immortal.

Then he opened his hand and let it go.

The vortex swallowed the Chaos Crystal whole.

Warlock felt nothing after that.

Chapter 61

Stellan felt the cavern go and staggered back across the ice to escape the collapsing ceiling of the underground chamber. He had no notion of what might be happening down there, only that it involved forces he couldn't begin to imagine.

With the ice shuddering beneath him, Stellan ran for the slight rise overlooking the palace, hoping it was far enough away to escape the worst of the damage. He wasn't sure if Declan and Warlock had succeeded in their attempt to stop Lukys opening the rift, but he was certain they'd done something dire. The palace itself seemed to be moving now, and for some reason, heavy dark clouds were gathering overhead, bellowing with thunder and streaked with jagged lightning.

Kinta managed to scramble free beside him and together they made a run for it. It was hard to tell, with the thunder above them and the screaming wind emanating from the underground chamber, if any of the others had managed to get clear.

"What's happening?" he shouted, doubting that even though he was screaming at the top of his lungs, Kinta would hear a word he said.

"They've opened the rift!" Kinta yelled back, her mouth as close to his ear as she could get it.

"Can they close it again?"

"I hope so!"

She grabbed Stellan's arm and pulled him further away as something cracked and shattered with the same deafening boom the ice had made when the Great Lakes were broken up by the immortals during the war between Caelum and Glaeba. A moment later, in the distance, Stellan saw the first of the fabulous ice palace's spires toppling to the ground. There was a Tide Lord clinging to it, but he was too far away to tell which one it was.

"I have to go back!" Kinta shouted in his ear when they finally reached the relative safety of the rise overlooking the palace.

Before he could answer, another spire cracked and tumbled to the ice, taking another Tide Lord with it.

"But my lady!" Stellan objected. "You'll be . . ." He stopped himself, realising how pointless his warning would be.

Kinta spared him a brief smile, as if she knew he was about to warn her she'd be killed if she returned to the palace. "Don't worry about me, your majesty. Go home. Be a good king."

Stellan nodded and watched her leave, not sure how he was supposed to fulfil such an order, given he'd been brought to Jelidia magically and the world appeared to be disintegrating around him.

"Stay safe, my lady," he called after her, for want of anything more profound to say. It was unlikely Kinta heard him. She ran back down the slope, heading into the melee.

Standing on the rise, Stellan watched the palace collapse as one spire after another broke off and shattered on the ice. There were large cracks in the ground now, spreading out from the underground chamber. A thick red swirling cloud of mist hovered around the black maw that had once been a fabulous fire-lit chamber of ice. Stellan briefly regretted never seeing the chamber, only having it described to him by Declan Hawkes.

It had sounded like a true marvel, with its fabulous high-ribbed walls carved from the ice and its methane fires casting a hellish light . . .

Stellan frowned, staring at the cracks in the ice as a terrible thought occurred to him. They were still spreading. The palace was collapsing before his very eyes. Six of the eight spires were gone now, and he could no longer see any of the Tide Lords who had been clinging to them, high above the dampening effect of the Chaos Crystal, in order to wield the Tide.

The underground chamber, according to Declan, had been lit by perpetual fires, fuelled by gas trapped under the ice. With the ice breaking apart so rapidly, would the gas escape? Would it explode? Would it leak into the air and suffocate any mortals in the vicinity? And if it did, how far would the effects of it extend?

Stellan found himself paralysed by uncertainty and fear. He'd faced down any number of catastrophes in his life, probably saved whole nations from the ravages of war with his skills as a diplomat. But this was too big to comprehend. It was too much for one mortal to deal with. Stellan found himself staring at a Cataclysm on an unimaginable scale and there was nothing he could do to prevent it.

The cracks in the ground were widening. Flames billowed out of the collapsed cavern. The snow steamed and spat and the sky darkened even more. The lightning was unnaturally frequent, as if something in the chamber was calling it down; the thunder so loud he could barely hear his own thoughts.

Stellan could see nobody alive down there, but given a score of them were immortal, that didn't mean much.

Of Warlock's fate, he had no doubt. No mortal could survive the fiery hurricane swirling over the remains of the underground chamber. Behind it, the Palace of Impossible Dreams was all but gone. Stellan never managed to see the inside of that, either.

Another explosion boomed across the ice, another crack rent the ground in a cloud of steaming mist. It began to rain, but the rain was falling sideways. Stellan wasn't sure if it was real rain or snowmelt driven outward from the fiery vortex at the centre of the storm.

And then, without warning, the vortex vanished.

A sudden and eerie silence descended over the scene. With the disappearance of the swirling red storm, the rain stopped and even the lightning held its breath for a moment.

Oblivious to the elements, Stellan pushed back the hood of his fur-lined jacket and wondered if it was over.

Is it done? Had Declan and Warlock succeeded? Had they closed the rift? Had they prevented the Tide Lords from drawing so much power through the rift, it would endanger Amyrantha?

For a long moment, it seemed as if they *had* succeeded. Stellan peered into the distance, half expecting to see Hawkes climbing out of the deep hole that was the remains of the shattered chamber, leading Arkady and Warlock with him, and any other survivors he'd managed to save.

Hawkes was like that. He was the sort who always came through . . .

But nobody emerged from the ice and just as Stellan was on the verge of risking a return to the chasm to see what had happened down there, the ground shuddered again.

A moment later, a massive column of fire shot up from the chasm, so hot that Stellan could feel the heat of it scalding his face even from this distance. He looked at it in awe, expecting it to subside, but it seemed to be growing rather than shrinking.

Stellan stared at the fire in wonder for a moment and then realised what it meant. He swore savagely under his breath and turned, running as fast as he could manage on the rapidly melting ice, knowing it was futile, but too mortal, too afraid of death, to do anything else.

The cracks multiplied apace as he tried to outrun the inevitable, many of the fissures exploding open in front of him.

Stellan lasted longer than he thought he would. He made quite a distance before the fire overtook him. His last thoughts were of Arkady, wondering if, instead of being consumed in the destruction caused by the immortals and their power-hungry rift, she'd managed to reach safety on the other side.

PART 4

I killed them, but they would not die.
Yea! all the day and all the night
For them I could not rest or sleep,
Nor guard from them nor hide in flight.

Then in my agony I turned
And made my hands red in their gore.
In vain—for faster than I slew
They rose more cruel than before.

"The Immortals"
—Isaac Rosenberg (1890–1918)

Chapter 62

The river sparkled in the morning light; the clear skies a mixed blessing, exposing both the cheery optimism of the couples walking along the south bank of the river and the grubby nature of the refugee camps that crowded the northern side.

Declan spied the man he had arranged to meet sitting on a bench overlooking the river. He was wearing a suit, of all things, leaning back against the wrought-iron bench, legs stretched out in front of him and crossed at the ankles. He didn't look up as Declan approached, or visibly react when he took a seat beside him.

"You got the message, then?" he said.

"So did you, obviously," the man replied. "Any idea what it's about?"

"Tide's on the way up," Declan suggested, quite unnecessarily.

"It's been coming and going for sixty-five million years, Rodent, give or take. Seems a bit odd to call us in, just for that now."

"We'll find out when we get there, I suppose."

"Is it time yet?"

Declan glanced at his antique Rolex. "The note said eleven. We've some time to kill yet."

Cayal looked up at him. Declan was surprised to see the Immortal Prince looking a little older than he remembered.

Or maybe he was imagining it. Maybe Cayal only seemed older because there was a world-weariness about him now, something that came with living not for thousands of years, but for millions of them.

"So, how shall we kill the time, Rodent?" the Immortal Prince asked. "Shall I tell you what I've been up to since I saw you last?"

"If you feel you must."

Cayal grinned. "Actually, I'd rather hear what *you've* been up to. Who did you roll for that watch and the suit?"

"The watch is a fake," Declan said with a shrug. It was easier to let Cayal think that than explain how he could afford the real thing. Then he compounded the lie by adding, "The suit's a cheap knock-off. But at least I bought it new. Do you shop at the Salvation Army often, or just for special occasions like this?"

"I see you haven't learned any more creative insults since the last time we met."

"Don't worry, Cayal. I'll keep trying."

"I'm sure you will, Rodent. Good thing you have until the end of time. Got a feeling you're going to need it."

The Immortal Prince seemed in a rare good mood today. It might be because the Tide was on the turn again, or it might be the prospect of catching up with the others. Cayal pushed himself to his feet and stretched, glancing around the riverbank. "Shall we start walking? It's a bit of a hike."

Declan rose to his feet beside Cayal, put on his sunglasses and fell into step as they headed along the river, toward the bridge. They walked in silence for a time, before Declan thought to ask something that he'd been wondering about since before he fell through the rift and landed on this world.

"You never finished telling me," he said, as they strolled along the road, "what happened in Kordana." The last time they'd run into one another was during World War II in London. They'd found themselves in the same bomb shelter during the Blitz. Cayal was bored and feeling garrulous and had begun to relate the tale of Kordana's destruction, but the "all-clear" siren had sounded before he got to the end of the story.

"Didn't I?"

Declan shook his head. "You got as far as being stabbed at Thraxis's hearth and surviving the experience. And there was a girl involved, as I recall. Serena? Selena?"

"Sirella," Cayal told him, smiling faintly. "You know, that little bitch was nothing but trouble from the moment I met her. She's the reason—indirectly—Kordana was destroyed."

"I thought you said it was Tryan's fault?" As Declan spoke, they turned right, away from the river, and headed onto the Avenue de Suffren, toward the hotel. Both of them knew the city well enough not to need directions.

"Well, it was, but she was the catalyst. Never try to convince one woman you love her, Rodent, when you've got another waiting for you back in your room, thinking the same thing about you."

"Doesn't say much for your intellect, Cayal, that you seem to have only just discovered such a self-evident truth."

The Immortal Prince eyed him curiously for a moment. "You go out in public dressed in *that* suit and have the nerve to question *my* intellect?"

Cayal thrust his hands into his pockets, and made no other attempt to needle him. Time appeared to have mellowed the Immortal Prince somewhat—not the few thousand years he'd already been alive when Declan first met him on Amyrantha, but the eons it had taken them to reach this point. Although it lasted several thousand years even after they'd fallen to this world, Cayal's determination to kill himself had eventually proved to be exactly what Lukys always insisted it was—a phase he was going through that he would eventually outgrow.

Declan had experienced a similar phase, too. Fortunately, he'd recognised his melancholy for what it was and not tried to end his own life by taking everyone on the planet with him, as Cayal had on Amyrantha.

"So what happened, since you finally seem in the mood to tell me?"

"The girl I took as a mistress to console me in my grief over losing the love of my life decided the price of keeping her as a mistress was the throne of Kordana."

That wasn't the answer Declan was expecting and he found himself intrigued. But old habits were hard to break. "So your preference for women you can't afford is something you've always suffered from, even back then?"

Remarkably, Cayal didn't rise to the bait. Instead, he smiled faintly. "Tides, but she was sharp, was Sirella. Sharp, cunning and fiercely possessive. She was a Tide Lord's mistress and she wasn't going to let *anybody* get in the way of her ambition once she realised what that meant."

"What did she do?"

"She started acting like my queen," Cayal said. "I mean, it was a novelty at first, I suppose. She seemed so happy to be with me. What I didn't know—or learn until it was too late—was that she had quite an agenda going in that nasty little head of hers. In Sirella's world, my sister was going to die and I—an immortal—would naturally take the throne, because at the very least I could kill all my siblings and nobody would be able to kill me."

"Last man standing," Declan said as they crossed the street. "There's a degree of megalomaniacal logic to that. No wonder you found her attractive." There was no need to stop and check for traffic. Even in this relatively affluent part of Paris, the cars lining the streets weren't waiting for their stately owners to emerge from their stately homes to go for a stately drive in the country. For the most part, the cars were now home to the families of the refugees who'd managed to find employment as servants and menial labourers in the houses of the wealthy minority, who still soldiered on as if the world's problems were something that would eventually sort themselves out, provided one kept a stiff upper lip.

"I don't know why I even speak to you, Rodent."

"I'm sorry. Did you end up killing the rest of the family?"

He shook his head. "I never *intended* to kill any of them. Quite the opposite. I was charged with bringing the Tide to Kordana, remember—and specifically the worship of Syrolee and her family as gods and goddesses—to have my exile revoked. You do that by performing miracles, Rodent. Not by knocking off the incumbent queen and taking her throne."

"So what happened?"

"When we got to Lakesh and Sirella realised I intended to *save* my sister from dying by healing her with my shiny new magical powers, rather than killing her and taking her throne the way she thought I would, she was rather pissed off. A few days later, when she caught me begging Gabriella to break off the wedding with my brother and marry me instead because I still loved her, she really lost it."

Declan smiled. Not at the notion of Sirella "losing it," but at how different the story must sound now to how Cayal might have told it back on Amyrantha. It was a necessary skill for immortals—the ability to blend into their surroundings, to adopt the language, idioms and vocabulary of the locals. It was something Declan rarely thought about any longer, so automatic had it become. But it sounded odd, hearing a story so ancient—a story that had, until now, probably only ever been spoken of in languages not even known to this world—uttered in a fairly good approximation of a North London accent.

Declan's own English had a decidedly American influence, mostly because experience had taught him it was easier to talk to computers in an accent they understood, rather than waste time training them to understand a new one.

"What did Sirella do?"

"She went to Tryan and told him I was planning to kill my sister and take the throne with Gabriella as my queen, and then outlaw any mention of the Tide, or any other gods, besides me." Cayal's voice remained even, which was hardly surprising, Declan supposed. These events had occurred a very, *very* long time ago.

"Tryan didn't receive the news well?"

"He tortured and killed Gabriella as a warning to me about the consequences of not toeing the line."

"Ah," Declan said.

He didn't need any further explanation. He knew Kordana's destruction had been the result of a falling-out between Tryan and Cayal, but not the details of what had caused it. Cayal's homeland, after all, was not—Declan had always assumed—something the Immortal Prince would annihilate on a whim. But destruction in response to the torture and killing of the one woman he had truly loved? That was something completely understandable.

At least, Declan *thought* Gabriella was the only woman the Immortal Prince ever truly loved. By unspoken agreement, not since falling through the rift and landing here on Earth, had they ever spoken of any other possibility.

"Ah, indeed, Rodent," Cayal agreed, stopping on the kerb. "Is this the place?"

Declan looked across the street at the reinforced entrance with its razor wire and armed guards on the street—as most five-star hotels were wont to have these days. He looked up. The building was at least ten storeys high and the power-hungry neon sign on the top floor proudly announced it was the "ilto." Even major hotel chains, it seemed, thought twice before forking out for frivolous things like replacing broken signage.

"This is it. How are we doing for time?"

"We've ten minutes or so, yet."

He frowned at Cayal. "It'll take us that long to get through the security cordon."

"That's the cost of living these days," Cayal said with a shrug, heading across the street.

Declan hurried after him. "Who's responsible, do you think?"

Cayal glanced at him oddly for a moment. "What makes you think one of us has done this?"

"Hmmm, let's see. The climate's a mess, the planet has almost run out of resources, there's barely a functioning economy left anywhere in the world. Gee, why would I think one of us is responsible? That's not what we do at all. What could I be thinking?"

"Well," Cayal said, fishing his invitation out of his coat pocket and offering it to the guard who blocked their way into the hotel. "I can tell you this much, Rodent; it wasn't me. It's far too subtle."

"Subtle? Is that what you call it?"

"Not my sort of Cataclysm at all," Cayal informed him, getting an odd look from the guard who was passing a hand-held metal detector over his body. "I prefer the direct approach."

Declan couldn't argue with that. This gentle decline of civilisation wasn't Cayal's style, at all. In fact, if Declan remembered correctly, the last time the Immortal Prince got pissed enough to cause a Cataclysm on Earth—which was just after they arrived and he realised Lukys's promise of certain death was a lie—he'd grabbed a remnant of Amyrantha out of the heavens, slammed it into the Yucatán Peninsula and wiped out the dinosaurs.

Chapter 63

The hotel where they'd been invited to meet the others had an LED noticeboard near the elevator, discreetly announcing the *Annual General Meeting of the International Flat Earth Society* was being held in Conference Room 2 on the mezzanine level. As Declan predicted, it took a while to get through security, particularly as they weren't registered guests here. Cayal glanced around the lobby with its fabulous marble floor and serene air of business-as-usual as they waited for the elevator, amazed at how everyone just kept on going about their daily grind as if nothing was awry.

The elevator dinged softly a few moments later and he stepped inside with Hawkes to take the one-floor ride up to the mezzanine level. The Rodent said nothing. Cayal wasn't sure if that was because he was still mulling over the story he'd told him about the destruction of Kordana, the reminder of what he did to the dinosaurs, or if there was something else on his mind.

The door to the conference room was open, a waiter arranging crystal water jugs beaded with condensation on the long polished granite-topped table. Maralyce was already seated near the head, sipping coffee as she chatted softly to Coryna and Arryl, who were sitting on the edge of the table facing her. He could feel the others around here somewhere on the rising Tide, but they hadn't yet arrived in the conference room.

Maralyce was dressed in a business suit. With her hair drawn back into a tight chignon, she looked like an accountant. Arryl still managed to look like a priestess, no matter what era she was in or world she was on, and her current colourful, floaty, caftan-like outfit only heightened the illusion.

Beside her, groomed to perfection, Coryna looked as if she'd just stepped off the cover of a fashion magazine. Or she would have, if there had been such a thing as paper magazines any longer and they had still had covers.

The women looked up as the two Tide Lords entered the conference room. Arryl waved when she caught sight of them. Maralyce frowned.

"Tides, you two look like a couple of insurance salesmen." She spoke Glaeban, a language no Earthborn waiter had a hope of understanding.

"Lukys's message said to be inconspicuous," Cayal said, answering her in English, a little wounded that all his care in dressing the part seemed to be wasted on her. And Hawkes didn't look *that* bad. "What's with ancient tongues?"

"I'm afraid we might have begun to attract some unwanted attention," Lukys said in Glaeban, entering the room behind them. "And as they're so fond of saying on this world, the walls have ears. Or, to be more specific, highly sensitive, electronic listening devices. Has anybody heard from Kentravyon?"

"Haven't seen him in years," Cayal said, as Lukys walked around the table and took his place at the head. He studied the older immortal closely as he took his seat. Lukys had aged a little. Or perhaps Cayal was just imagining it. His white hair always made it hard to judge.

Cayal still had no notion of how old Lukys and the other original Tide Lords were. He doubted they even knew themselves, given years were measured on a planetary scale and these immortals could stride across worlds at will. Like Amyrantha, Earth was just another world for them, and there had been many more before this one and would probably be many more after.

That made their age not just impressive, but almost incomprehensible.

"It's been over a century since I saw him last."

He might be imagining it, but Coryna's voice always struck Cayal as being a little bit squeaky, almost as if she'd brought some of the rat through with her, back into human form.

Coryna settled in beside Lukys—where she always sat in their meetings—briefly touching his hand and smiling at him intimately, before getting down to the business at hand. Nothing, it seemed—certainly not time—had lessened the affection or the bond between them. She had aged very little since coming through the portal. In fact, Cayal could still clearly remember meeting Coryna back on Amyrantha when she was Oritha, the Torlenian merchant's daughter who thought her husband was Ryda Tarek, a gem dealer from Stevania.

In all the time they'd been here on Earth, he'd never seen a hint of Oritha's personality in Coryna's demeanour.

Is Oritha dead? Cayal wondered. *Or trapped inside a body she's been forced to share with another consciousness for all this time?*

And what of the others? There had never been a trace of Pellys on this world, or Tryan, Jaxyn, Brynden or Kinta, Ambria or Medwen, Rance or Krydence, Syrolee or Engarhod or Lyna. He supposed they might have fallen through, but it seemed inconceivable for one of the others to have survived and the people in this room not know about it. Even Taryx, who was there in the Tide chamber with them right at the very end, hadn't made it through.

They were all gone now. Diala with her come-ravish-me eyes and her devious mind. Lyna and her desire for nothing more than somewhere comfortable to wait out the low Tides. Ambria and her no-nonsense manner. Rance and Krydence—not that Cayal thought those two were a great loss to anyone. Medwen—the perpetual bleeding heart when it came to lesser creatures. All of them were just memories now. They had gone the way of Amyrantha—finding the death Cayal sought and had never been able to achieve.

He envied them a little for that.

"It's been even longer since I saw him," Hawkes said. "Some time in the fourteenth century, I think."

Cayal remembered a time when the Rodent was so new to this, that he couldn't bear to think of himself as immortal. Time had helped him adjust. And they had been here on Earth a *very* long time.

Cayal shook his head as he took a seat at the table beside Arryl. "Are we sure he's not responsible for the current state of affairs? I mean, this *is* the man who thought up the black plague, remember, when somebody foolishly made a passing comment at a meeting like this sometime in the early Middle Ages that the human population was getting a little thick on the ground."

"That was unfortunate," Maralyce said, "but not necessarily a bad thing in hindsight. What have you been up to, Cayal?"

"Trying to keep my head down. I mean . . . what else is there? We're not allowed to do anything useful. That would be *interfering*, and Lukys made us all promise we wouldn't." He turned his gaze on Lukys, who had ordered the waiter to be gone while Cayal was talking. "Isn't that what you made us promise, Lukys? When your wretched rift spat us out here on this shiny new world, just waiting for us to remake it? The rift that apparently killed everybody *but* me? What was it you said? Amyrantha was ruined because we couldn't help but interfere? This is a new world. The worst of our kind are gone. Now we have a chance to do things properly? No Cataclysms. No abominations like the Crasii. No trying to take over the world every time the Tide peaks. This time we'll do it right. We'll just tweak things here and there, you said. Let nature take its course and nobody will suspect a thing."

Cayal sounded a lot more bitter than he meant to. He rarely entertained the notion of death these days. This world they had made was new and intriguing enough that he found himself much less anxious to find a way to end it all.

Suicide for an immortal was a fleeting obsession that time, if nothing else, eventually wore down to nothing.

"And nobody *does* suspect anything," Arryl said, looking around the table for some agreement. "Do they?"

"I have two words for you," Maralyce said, looking mightily peeved. "Intelligent Design."

"Between that and Darwin's theories," Lukys added, "they've pretty much got the whole thing worked out, except for who's responsible."

"It's like Harlie Palmerston's *Theory of Human Advancement* all over again." The Rodent seemed to find that several-million-year-old memory amusing. "Should we tell them the truth, do you think?"

"It wouldn't matter if you did," Coryna said. "They wouldn't believe you. Besides, our problem is much more immediate. And the reason Lukys thought it important we meet."

Cayal sat a little straighter in his chair. They had met like this no more than once or twice a generation since coming to Earth; even less since technology had improved to a point where they might be inadvertently photographed as a group. It would only take one dedicated conspiracy theorist with the resources to check a little too closely into the backgrounds of the people gathered around this table for some rather inconvenient alarm bells to go off in all the wrong places.

"What's the problem?"

"Well, it's mostly your fault, son," Lukys said, fixing his gaze on Declan.

The Rodent looked shocked. "My fault? What's *my* fault?"

"Your misguided attempts to save the world."

Cayal smiled and turned to look at Hawkes. "You know, you should probably stop doing that, Rodent. It never seems to work out too well for you, does it?"

Declan never got the chance to answer. The Tide surged around them. As if he'd been waiting for the chance to make a dramatic entrance, the doors at the end of the conference room suddenly banged opened, and Kentravyon strode into the room, declaring, "The world wouldn't *need* saving, you know, if you'd let me do things my way."

"Good morning, Kentravyon," Lukys said, not reacting visibly to the new arrival's decidedly theatrical entrance.

The doors closed gently behind Kentravyon of their own accord, with a slight push on the Tide. One of the others in the room must have done it. Kentravyon would have slammed the doors shut if it was left to him.

"Nice of you to join us."

"Your message sounded as if you were worried," Kentravyon said. He was dressed in a long black bishop's cassock, a jewelled crucifix around his neck. He stopped by the side table where the coffee was laid out and looked around in disappointment. "What? None of those little pastries?"

"What do you mean?" Declan asked.

Nobody commented on the way the madman was dressed. Every time they saw him, he was dabbling in one religion or another. Cayal had seen him preaching in a mosque, heard he'd bathed in the Ganges with a million followers at his back calling him Kartikay and was quite sure that if Kentravyon could have figured out a way to swing it, he would have done a stint as the Dalai Lama.

"I mean those little croissants they make with the cheese—"

"I mean about doing things your way," Declan cut in impatiently.

"Ah, that," Kentravyon said, taking the empty seat next to Cayal. "It's common sense really. Things never got out of hand on Amyrantha, or any other world we've been on, because we made sure society never developed much in the way of technology. Every time they looked like discovering the sort of know-how that has screwed this planet up so comprehensively, the Tide came back, we started squabbling with each other, and tah-dah! The end of civilisation as we know it. Back to the drawing board and discovering everything all over again."

"Which gets back to why it's your fault," Coryna said, looking pointedly at Declan. "You're the one who founded AEVITAS Inc."

"What's AEVITAS?" Arryl asked.

"Isn't that Latin for immortal?" Kentravyon said.

Declan shrugged, and shifted in his seat uncomfortably. "Actually, it's closer to eternal."

"Very droll," Maralyce said, rolling her eyes.

"Declan wasn't being funny, Maralyce," Lukys said. "It's an acronym, isn't it, Declan?"

The Rodent nodded. "It stands for Allied Exploration Ventures for Industrial Technology And Science, actually."

"*You're* responsible for that?" Arryl asked, somewhat awed by the news. "God, AEVITAS is one of the biggest privately owned companies on the planet."

Cayal wasn't nearly so impressed. "I thought some reclusive, nut-job trillionaire . . ." He stopped and turned to Hawkes as the pieces fell into place. "Ah, I get it. Declan Hawkes . . . Deke Hawkins. *You're* the nut-job trillionaire."

Declan seemed a little embarrassed to be unmasked, but he was unapologetic. "Lukys said to keep a low profile. He didn't say anything about starving."

"You can't starve, idiot. You're immortal."

From the smile on his face, Lukys wasn't exactly angry about it either. Cayal wondered if there was a bit of paternal pride involved. Hawkes was his flesh and blood, after all. What father wouldn't be proud of a son who'd made himself the wealthiest man on the planet—even if it had taken him a couple of million years to do it?

"I'm not blaming Declan for being wealthy," Lukys said. "We've all made and lost fortunes over the years. And made our share of mistakes."

"Not on the scale of this one," Cayal said.

"Really?" Lukys remarked with a raised brow. "I recall us having a discussion in a room, not dissimilar to this one—well, minus the data projector—some time ago, about the inadvisability of performing miracles when the Tide is at its peak."

"Wasn't my fault they saw me after I was supposed to have died," Cayal muttered, deciding it was probably better if they didn't bring up that particular past miscalculation.

Arryl's eyes widened. "That was *you*, Cayal?"

He refused to answer. Some things were better forgotten. "You said this was about the Rodent, Lukys. Let's hear what he's done this time."

Lukys nodded. "Declan's sin, if I can call it that . . ."

"You may," Kentravyon said, making the sign of the cross.

"Declan's sin," Lukys continued, as if Kentravyon hadn't spoken, "was his plan to mine the asteroid belt."

"How can that be a mistake? This planet is rapidly running out of resources," Declan reminded them, looking a little hurt that his altruism was being questioned. "One asteroid contains enough—"

"One chunk of Amyrantha, you mean," Arryl said.

Declan turned to look at her. "Pardon?"

"Well, let's call a spade a spade," she said. "That asteroid belt used to be Amyrantha. They're not asteroids floating around up there. They're gravestones. They're all that's left of a whole world *we* destroyed. You can dress it up however you like, but if you've started mining the asteroid belt, Declan Hawkes, you're basically robbing the graveyard of several million innocent people who died millions of years ago, so you could sit here on Earth and play god . . . or tycoon, or whatever it is you're doing these days."

"I didn't open the rift that destroyed Amyrantha," Declan reminded them tightly. "I was pulled through against my will trying to stop Lukys from opening it."

"Clearly the experience has left you emotionally scarred beyond redemption," Maralyce noted wryly.

"The point is," Lukys said, trying to get the meeting back on track, "the exploration of the asteroid belt is about to cause us some serious problems."

"What problems?" Declan asked. "I've had no reports of problems."

"That's because you're the boss, Declan, and underlings tend to be reluctant to report problems to bosses, particularly when they have a reputation for being—"

"Nut jobs," Cayal offered helpfully.

"What is the problem, then?" Arryl asked, sparing Cayal the briefest of smiles. She, at least, hadn't lost her sense of humour.

"The problem is that Declan sent out a mining exploration vessel and, as exploration vessels are wont to do, they went exploring."

"I'm guessing they found something other than enough iron ore to keep the planet going for the next two hundred years."

Cayal was a little surprised it was Kentravyon who came to that conclusion first, but then, Cayal reminded himself silently, Kentravyon was mad, not stupid.

"Oh, yes," Lukys said. "They found something."

He dimmed the lights with the remote lying on the table beside his left hand and then swivelled his chair around to face the screen behind him, at the back of the room.

"This is a recording of the live feed that's been coming in from the AEVITAS ship, *Cape Canaveral*," Coryna explained, as the picture resolved into a sharp 2D image on the screen. "As you can see by the date stamp, this happened about two weeks ago. Lukys called this meeting about five minutes after we realised what they'd found."

"Where did you get this?" Declan asked, his eyes fixed on the screen. "More to the point, *how* did you get it?"

The Rodent sounded surprised and more than a little displeased that Lukys and Coryna had video from his exploration vessel, even before he'd seen it.

"According to our sources," Coryna continued, "the crew of the *Cape Canaveral* feared if *they* didn't release this information, it would be buried along with their discovery."

"You really should vet your staff more carefully, Declan," Lukys added with a slightly disapproving frown. "Idealism can be very awkward when there are practical business decisions to be made."

Lukys sped the feed up a little as he spoke. They were watching a scan of an asteroid, the craft manoeuvring closer to a large, cigar-shaped lump of rock.

"How did you get this, Lukys?" Hawkes demanded.

"It was sent to a young woman working in the AEVITAS command centre, I believe. Apparently, she's engaged to the ship's medic, who prevailed upon his girlfriend to do the world a favour by releasing it before anybody could stop the news getting out. It'll hit most of the world's media outlets within a day, I'd say."

News of what? Cayal couldn't think of anything more boring than a live broadcast of a ship slowly scanning the surface of a dead lump of rock. He was about to say so when the image jerked a little. There was no sound with the feed, but something had obviously caught the eye of whoever was operating the camera. The focus moved. A speck on the horizon soon resolved into something larger. The camera zoomed in.

Across the table, Declan rose to his feet, leaning forward to examine the object more closely.

"Oh, my God," he breathed almost inaudibly.

Cayal stared at the screen as the image resolved, as he realised what had made Hawkes utter such a curse.

"Tides," Kentravyon said, squinting a little in the dim light of the conference room. "Is that . . . ?"

"Yes," Lukys said. "It is."

"Dear God . . . it can't be!" Arryl gasped. Like the others, she was transfixed by the image on the screen. She sounded almost as gobsmacked as Hawkes.

Cayal didn't know what to think. He didn't know what to feel. The pressure in his chest was mostly in his mind, he told himself, not destiny catching up with him and slamming his heart with a sledgehammer.

He glanced at Hawkes, seeing his own confusion, shock and disbelief reflected in the spymaster's face.

"What are we going to do now?" Arryl asked as the image silently resolved into clarity on the screen.

"Retrieve the Chaos Crystal," Lukys said, freezing the image.

"Do we know where it is?" Cayal asked, hoping he sounded as if that was all he cared about.

"Isn't it here in Paris?" Maralyce said. "In a museum?"

Coryna shook her head. "Our skull is in Chicago. It's part of a private collection. With the Tide up, it should be a simple matter to retrieve it from the owners." She smiled at Hawkes. "Tides, you're the richest man on Earth, Declan. You could probably buy it for us."

"And then what?" Hawkes asked with a worried expression.

"We start making preparations for the next King Tide, son," Lukys announced, turning from the screen to face the others, "because as soon as the people of Earth see these pictures coming in from space and realise what it means, it will be time for us to move on."

"Use the Chaos Crystal? That will destroy Earth," Hawkes reminded them, quite unnecessarily, Cayal thought.

"Shame about that," Lukys said with a shrug.

Chapter 64

The Med-Lab of the AEVITAS Deep Space Explorer *Cape Canaveral* was stark and white and carefully temperature controlled. And had been strictly sealed against all outside contamination ever since they'd found their prize floating in space. Randy checked the seal gauge on his suit one last time, making certain it was green all the way, before he opened the inner door. When he was satisfied it was safe, he palmed the lock with his gloved hand and waited as the clear glass door slid open with a faint hiss. He floated through, palmed the lock on the other side and went to check on his patient.

Dr. Randy Marks was more than a little taken with his patient. Even unconscious, she was beautiful, and he'd spent hours in here, checking her over, wondering who she was.

Physically, she was flawless. Almost too flawless. He couldn't find a single fault with her physiology—except for her continued coma. He couldn't pinpoint her ethnicity, either. She was like one of those exotic creatures who cropped up in late-night ads for virtual sex who claimed—with a seductive giggle—to be of Irish/Chinese/African/Spanish extraction.

Nothing about her DNA gave any hint of her origins, either.

Randy checked the monitors again, knowing that as usual, there would be nothing new, and then he turned to study her again. He dreamed about her sometimes. In fact, it was such a dream that had brought him here tonight—although night was a relative term aboard ship—to check on her progress.

The mystery of the Asteroid Girl—as the media networks had dubbed her back on Earth when word got out about her existence—defied all logic. Randy had not been able to explain how she lived, how she had survived the incomprehensible cold of deep space, how she'd not imploded from exposure to a vacuum—or, indeed, how she had managed to get here at all.

They were checking, of course. But the *Cape Canaveral* was the first Earth ship to make it out this far into the asteroid belt. Supposedly.

The scenario with the shortest odds was that she was the last survivor of a Russian ship sent out during the 1960s. Perhaps she was a cosmonaut. Perhaps her capsule overshot the moon and she ended up here in the asteroid belt.

Of course, for that to be the case there had to be a Russian capsule somewhere out there, too. And she'd been naked when they found her. Even assuming that was the case, any collision with an asteroid violent enough to destroy a space capsule and burn the clothes from a cosmonaut's body wasn't going to leave the cosmonaut whole, unharmed and with not a mark on her.

And still alive over a century later, after breathing nothing but vacuum for all that time.

Although he knew it was pointless, Randy checked the monitors again. As they had shown since they found her, everything was perfect. Her heart beat like a metronome. Her breathing was deep and even. Her brain activity was slow but more than enough to indicate there was an awareness hiding somewhere, waiting for a chance to return.

Because the Asteroid Girl was so physically flawless, a few of the crewmen were speculating that she was really an android. Randy had scoffed at the suggestion. If you cut her, she bled like any other human (as he'd discovered when he took blood for testing when they'd first brought her in), although she'd healed with unnatural speed.

Like everything else about this enigmatic woman, her blood work showed nothing but perfectly normal levels of everything that ought to be there and nothing that shouldn't.

That in itself was worrying. There wasn't the slightest trace of anything that might have chemically preserved this woman and stopped her from dying in space.

Randy looked up as the door hissed open and discovered another suited figure floating into the Med-Lab. The glare of the overhead lighting made the occupant's features invisible behind the plexiglass faceplate. The name on the suit's left breast, however, gave the newcomer's identity away.

"You're up late, Captain."

"So are you, Randy. Any change?"

He looked down at his patient and shook his head. "Nothing. What brings you down here?"

"The company wants another series of photos sent through. Something a little less necrophiliac-ish than the last shots you sent, is how the publicity people put it."

"Jeezus, can't they leave her in peace?"

"A beautiful woman found inexplicably alive and floating naked in space? The poor girl is never going to know another moment's peace as long as she lives." The captain reached down and stroked her dark hair gently. "Poor thing. She's square in the middle of a political storm she doesn't even know she's causing."

"How bad is it?"

The captain shrugged. "I've just been watching the news from Earth. Deke Hawkins has been on every channel who'll give him airtime, crowing about the value of exploration. Apparently, finding our girl here has made him a real hero, even though we all know the bastard would have said nothing about this if we hadn't blown the whistle on him before he got a chance to quash the news."

Randy nodded, glad now that he'd asked his fiancée, Sally, to risk her job by releasing the video onto the net.

"Of course," the captain added, "every nation on Earth with a space program is accusing the others of sending ships up here in secret to steal the resources of the Belt, now. Kinda glad we're up here with a transmit delay, so they can't drag us into the argument."

"They're assuming she's a survivor of a failed mission?"

The captain nodded. "That's the money bet. I hear there's several religious cults started up, too, who are already worshipping her image. One of them believes she's the Virgin Mary."

"She's not."

"Well, yes, Randy, I did sort of work that out for myself."

He smiled. "Actually, ma'am, I meant she's not a virgin."

"How do you know?"

"I checked."

He couldn't see her face clearly because of the reflection of the lights on the plexiglass, but he could imagine the look the captain was giving him. "I see."

"You ordered a thorough physical exam when we found her, ma'am," he explained, before she could jump to the wrong conclusion. "I took thorough to mean an external *and* internal examination."

That seemed to satisfy the captain. "How old is she, do you think?"

"Hard to say. There's no deterioration in her cells. She has all her adult teeth, so she's not a child, but as for her actual age—anywhere between fifteen and fifty. Take your pick."

"I'm fifty," the captain reminded him with a small groan. "And trust me, son, I'm in nothing like the shape this girl is in. Still, the trashy gossip sites will love her. She's pretty enough to pique their interest."

"Because God knows, the scientific miracle of her survival is only a mild curiosity," Randy said, shaking his head. "It's so much more important that she's pretty. God, can't they let her alone? At least until she wakes up?"

"Is she *going* to wake up?" the captain asked. "She's been like this for a while now, you know. Maybe she's doomed to spend the rest of her life in a coma? That sort of thing has happened before, you know."

Randy shrugged. "To be honest, there's no medical reason why she's *not* awake. Other than, you know . . . the whole we-found-her-floating-naked-in-space thing."

"Well, I don't suppose I have to tell you to call me if anything changes?"

"Not really, ma'am," Randy said. "No."

The captain pushed off the side of the bed and floated toward the door, saying something Randy didn't catch, which was odd, because the suits were radio-miked and they'd all learned the hard way that even the most inaudible comment was recorded for posterity by the ultra-sensitive pickup.

"Pardon?"

The captain turned back to him. "I didn't say anything. I—Oh, my God!"

She was looking at the bed. Randy followed the direction of her gaze and found himself looking into two dark eyes, blinking in the sudden light.

"Dim!" he ordered the computer after a moment of stunned inaction, as he realised the lights were causing her pain.

The woman stared up at him, her face resolving into a mask of abject terror.

"Take your helmet off!" the captain ordered softly but urgently, as she began to release the seals on her own suit.

"But the risk of infection . . ."

"The woman survived a vacuum, Randy. And we're scaring the shit out of her. Take it off."

The captain's orders made sense. The Asteroid Girl looked terrified. She was struggling to sit up, but the restraints meant to hold her on the bed in this zero-gee environment were preventing her from moving.

The captain got her helmet off first, let it float away and then gently pushed the girl back onto the bed, talking in a soothing voice. "There . . . there . . . it's OK, everything is going to be fine . . ."

Randy's helmet floated toward the autoclave, bumping into it with a clatter. A glance at the monitors told him her pulse and breath were a little elevated, but nothing about which he should be concerned.

"It's OK," Randy repeated, as she tried to push the captain away. "You're on a space ship. The mining explorer *Cape Canaveral*. In the Med-Lab. You've been in some sort of accident, but you're safe now. What's your name?"

The woman answered him in a language Randy had never heard before. Her voice was panicked, frightened and trembling. Maybe the Russian cosmonaut scenario wasn't far off the mark.

"What's she saying?" the captain asked.

Randy shrugged. "I don't know."

He glanced over at the main computer console. "Identify language spoken by patient Jane Doe."

He didn't need to face the console. Like the suits, the lab was miked with ultra-sensitive equipment and could pick up the sound of a dropped needle (assuming there'd been gravity enough to make it fall). But for some reason everyone, ship-wide, turned to look at the nearest console when they wanted to ask the computer something.

"Patient Jane Doe is speaking no language this database can identify," the computer's very English and irritatingly smug voice replied after a few moments.

"Excellent. She speaks fluent gibberish," the captain said, still trying to hold the struggling woman down. "Come on, sweetie, settle down. We're not going to hurt you."

Something in the captain's tone, if not her words, must have struck a chord with the Asteroid Girl, finally penetrating the panic she must have felt on waking to find herself in this strange place. She slowly relaxed against the pillow, but her gaze still darted nervously from one to the other, like a terrified animal on the brink of flight.

"Can you tell us your name?" Randy asked, as gently as he could. In truth, his heart was hammering excitedly the way hers should have been.

The woman looked at him blankly, not understanding a word he said.

"Randy," the captain said, pointing to the doctor. And then she pointed to herself. "Emma."

She pointed to Arkady with a questioning look. "You?"

When she got no response, the captain tried a second time. "Randy. Emma. You?"

The young woman finally seemed to understand. She pointed to Randy and repeated his name. And then she pointed at the captain and said, "Emma."

The captain smiled, nodding and then pointed to her again. "You? What's your name?"

The young woman hesitated for a moment, almost as if she had to stop and think about it. For an instant, Randy had a horrible thought that this beautiful woman might be a complete amnesiac, and they would never discover the truth of how she got here. But then she pushed herself up onto her elbows, almost as if she'd made a decision about something.

She looked around at the lab and then fixed her eyes on Randy. He bent closer to hear her husky voice. She said something inaudible, followed by several words he didn't understand.

And then she repeated the first word.

"I think she's telling me her name," he said, looking at the captain in wonder.

"And?"

"It sounds like . . . I'm not certain . . . I thought she said . . . Issa?"

The Asteroid Girl shook her head violently at his suggestion. He leaned into her again, straining to make out her words and then looked at the captain. "No, it's something else . . ."

He waited until she repeated the name to make certain he had it right and then he smiled at her.

"Arkady," he said. "I think she's saying *Arkady*."

Epilogue

"Your guest is here, Mr. Hawkins."

Declan flicked off his screen and its stockmarket report and rose to his feet. He hadn't needed the warning. He could feel the presence of another immortal on the Tide. He glanced out over the city through the hotel window. The view from the penthouse suite was spectacular. Or it should have been. In truth, all he could make out were the tops of the buildings poking up out of the smog haze that shrouded Tokyo and made it such an eye-watering place to live. Declan wasn't fond of Tokyo, but it was the most convenient place from which to embark on his upcoming journey, so he didn't have much choice about being here.

The young man who'd delivered the news was a bright young thing, straight out of the London School of Economics. Declan had hired him about six months ago to replace his previous assistant. He never kept any assistant longer than a year or two, and always made sure their next position in AEVITAS (or one of its many subsidiaries) was good enough—and well paid enough—that their lasting feeling towards Deke Hawkins was one of gratitude rather than resentment. It made them less likely to question him about the irregularities in his life.

This latest young man was of Pacific Islander descent, one of the millions of refugees left homeless by the rising sea level. He'd come to Declan's attention after winning a scholarship from one of Deke Hawkins's many charitable foundations—set up to ease his corporate tax burden and not from any innate nobility of spirit, according to the popular media.

"Show him in, Taine," Declan ordered. "And let me know when the jet is ready to take off again."

"Yes, sir."

Taine turned for the door and disappeared into the outer room of the suite. A moment later the door opened again and his guest entered, carrying a large, yet unremarkable, square wooden box with an ivory handle set into the top.

The newcomer was dressed in a well-cut suit, with an expensive silk tie. He was wearing a new gold watch that probably cost more than

Taine earned each year and genuine leather shoes, which only the most affluent of Earth's citizens could afford these days. His attire was in complete contrast to the last time they'd met . . . *and no doubt paid for by me*, Declan reflected.

That's what I get for putting the Immortal Prince on the payroll.

Cayal crossed the room without a word and placed the box on the glass-topped desk before he turned to Declan, looking a trifle smug.

"Have any trouble?"

Cayal shook his head. "Not really. Customs got a bit funny when we landed, but Arryl fluttered her eyelashes at them. That helped."

"Really?" Declan asked, a little sceptically. In his experience, customs officials—regardless of the country or port—weren't so easily diverted.

"Oh . . . and I think you're now putting at least five children with parents in the Japanese Customs Service through private school and probably college, too."

Declan nodded. A bribe like that seemed much more likely. "Where's Arryl now?"

"She took a commercial flight to meet Lukys and Coryna in Paris with the legendary 'Skull of Doom,'" he said. Cayal liked calling it the "Skull of Doom." Every time he uttered the phrase, he grinned.

Declan nodded but didn't return his smile. Cayal might be having fun with the idea of wreaking some long overdue vengeance on Lukys for the destruction of Amyrantha, but they didn't have time to relish the prospect just yet. "We don't have long before Lukys discovers it's a fake."

Cayal nodded in agreement. "I'm ready when you are, Rodent."

Declan glanced at the box. "Did you check—?"

"That this one is the genuine Chaos Crystal? No, of course I didn't check. I thought we'd waste all this effort for a bit of a lark."

Declan wasn't amused. He glared at Cayal, letting his silence speak for him.

The Immortal Prince grinned, and punched Declan lightly on the shoulder. "Lighten up, Rodent. If you don't believe me, open the box. It'll suck the Tide right out of you."

Declan wanted to open the box. Desperately. But he suspected that if he did, the tenuous trust he'd developed with Cayal since Paris would be destroyed. Besides, there was no way Arryl was currently on her way to Lukys with the real thing. Like Declan and Cayal, she still mourned the loss of Amyrantha and was quite determined not to let the same fate befall their new home on Earth. A second, secret meeting between the three of them, a few days after Lukys's announcement that it was time to leave Earth, had brought them to this moment and this dangerous subterfuge.

There might come a time, Declan knew, when he could look back at the trail of dead worlds he'd left in his wake, but that time hadn't come yet. Not for him, nor Arryl, nor—somewhat to his surprise—for Cayal, either.

"Tides. Just open the damn thing," Cayal said, shaking his head. "I won't be offended."

Declan needed no further encouragement. He opened the catches on the front of the antique box and lifted the lid. Although the box was deliberately plain on the outside, the inside was lined with pure gold. In it sat the Chaos Crystal. Much to his relief, the skull looked exactly as it had when Declan found it in the 1880s in the collection of a French antiquities dealer named Eugéne Boban. Declan had bought the Chaos Crystal from him for a few hundred francs, and then commissioned the less-than-reputable Frenchman to make several other copies in the hope of confusing anybody looking for the real thing—something quite easy to fake when the Tide was out. He'd then hidden the real one and all but forgotten about it . . . until the Tide had turned.

The Tides here on Earth were different to Amyrantha, their rise and fall much slower, and yet much more devastating. The King Tide that had allowed them to leave—and destroy—Amyrantha, had risen in a matter of months, which oddly enough, limited the damage it could do (providing the Chaos Crystal remained dormant). This King Tide, the one now consuming Earth, had been building slowly for more than a hundred years. No place on Earth was immune to its effects any longer, although nobody but a handful of immortals knew the truth about what was happening.

As he opened the box, it filled with an angry red light. Declan could feel the Tide draining from him as if the air was being sucked out of the room. The world, brought into sharper focus by the rising power of the Tide, was suddenly muted and dull.

There was no question that this was the Chaos Crystal.

"Satisfied?"

Declan nodded, and closed the lid. As soon as the gold shielding encased it once more, the Crystal's Tide-deadening effect vanished and the Tide came rushing back, a thrill Declan was hard-pressed to contain.

"We'll take the jet from here," he said, locking the box again. "I have a chopper standing by on Guam to take us the rest of the way." He studied Cayal for a moment, still wondering if his willingness to help in this enterprise was genuine. "Are you sure about this, Cayal?"

"Yes."

"Lukys is going to be very angry with us."

Cayal shrugged, unconcerned. "Only if we tell him what we did."

That was actually a fair point. Declan nodded and reached for the box.

"It's okay," Cayal said. "I've got it."

Declan shrugged. "If you want."

Cayal lifted the box from the desk and turned to Declan. "Let's do this, Rodent," he said, "before I change my mind."

The helicopter took off from Guam as the sun was rising. The island fell away behind them quickly as they headed south, the weather clear, the sky a cobalt blue—a shade rarely seen anywhere other than the tropics. Declan piloted the craft himself, having learned long ago that it was easier, sometimes, to do things for oneself, rather than rely on other people. Besides, as an eccentric trillionaire known to have a preference for flying himself from place to place, it was a convenient way to disappear when the time came to kill off "Deke Hawkins," something he would have to do eventually. Perhaps sooner, rather than later, now the other immortals had discovered who he was.

"How far is it?" Cayal asked, the precious box on the floor between his feet.

"A couple of hundred miles."

"And it's the deepest place on Earth, right?"

"So they claim."

Cayal fell silent after that and they flew on, heading for the Mariana

Trench and the Challenger Deep. As the sun rose, the shadow of their craft on the ocean's heaving surface shifted imperceptibly, until it was almost directly beneath them. Declan was checking his location against the GPS when out of the blue, Cayal spoke up again.

"Have you spoken to her yet?"

Declan looked at him, shaking his head. "No."

"Are you going to?"

"As soon as I figure out what to say. And *how* to say it." He made a minute course correction before adding, "Every word, every communication with the *Cape Canaveral* is recorded and monitored, Cayal. I can hardly sit down at the main console in Mission Control, have them put Arkady on for a chat and start explaining things to her in Glaeban, now, can I?"

"You could send someone up there. Don't you have resupply ships that visit the exploration vessels?"

"They're drones. They don't have life support."

"Well, that's not really a problem if you send the right person. Some expert in aliens floating in space that you've managed to dig up with your vast resources. Someone who won't mind the inconvenience of not having, you know, air, food, heat . . . that sort thing, on the trip."

Declan smiled. "Someone like you, for instance?"

"Well, you can hardly go yourself, can you . . . you being a nut-job trillionaire and all? And I'm not doing anything of consequence at the moment."

Declan gave a non-committal shrug. "Why don't we just wait until the *Cape Canaveral* returns to Earth?"

"That's two years away, Rodent, even if you'd ordered them to turn around the day they found her. I checked."

That was a little concerning. Clearly, Cayal had given this some thought. *Perhaps that's why he's here*, Declan wondered. *He's not trying to save Earth. He's hoping to impress Arkady.*

Declan didn't let on what he was thinking, however. He kept his tone deliberately neutral. "How do I explain putting a human in a drone without life support?"

"Lie about it."

Declan didn't answer him right away, realising Cayal's suggestion had genuine merit. He was equally certain Cayal was offering his help so he could get to Arkady first.

Fortunately, Declan was saved from having to agree to anything for the moment by a subtle beeping coming from the flight console. He glanced at the screen and moved the collective control forward. The chopper began to descend toward the ocean.

"We're here."

Cayal looked around at the endless expanse of the featureless Pacific Ocean and nodded doubtfully. "I'll take your word for it, Rodent."

Declan checked their altitude once more and then let go of the collective control stick as he plunged into the Tide. Then he reached forward and shut down the engines. The helicopter stayed in the air, its rotor blades motionless, held there by the Tide.

Cayal grinned in the abrupt silence as the engines cut out. He wasn't worried. He would have felt Declan drawing on the Tide. The Immortal Prince glanced over his shoulder at the empty seats behind them. "There's a trick I bet you've never pulled when you have a busload of your mortal minions on board."

"I don't trust the GPS any longer," Declan explained. "They don't maintain it like they used to."

"We're going to have feel for the deepest point using the Tide?"

Declan nodded and then warned, "Just don't open that box, or we'll be swimming back to Guam."

Cayal grabbed at the catch to open the sliding door. He leaned out over the side looking down at the heaving waves and then pointed a little to the west. "Over there."

Declan used the Tide to manoeuvre the chopper to the point Cayal indicated. He could feel it too, but not as well as Cayal could, as much of his attention was concentrated on keeping the chopper in the air.

They hovered silently in the air for a moment before Cayal turned to Declan. "This is the deepest place on Earth, right?"

"The Mariana Trench is close to seven miles deep, pressure down there is about eight tons per square inch and it's roughly fifteen hundred miles long by forty miles wide. Even if Arryl is telling Lukys right this minute what we've done with the Chaos Crystal, by the time he finds it again, and figures out how to retrieve it, the King Tide will have retreated."

Cayal nodded, satisfied that if they couldn't destroy the Chaos Crystal, the very least they could do was hide it in a place nobody—not even a Tide Lord—was ever likely to find it. He lifted the wooden box onto his lap and turned to Declan with a questioning look.

"Are you sure about this?"

Declan nodded without hesitation. One destroyed world was enough for his immortal conscience to bear. "Positive."

"We'll be stuck here."

"I know."

"I'm just saying—"

"Do it, Cayal!" he cut in impatiently.

The Immortal Prince nodded, took a deep breath and tossed the box out of the helicopter. It landed in the water a few seconds later, bobbing on the surface for a moment before proceeding to sink beneath the waves.

They sat in silence, watching the Chaos Crystal disappear, and then Cayal turned to Declan. "This moment may well go down in history as the most noble or the most stupid thing either of us has ever done, Rodent."

"Only time will tell," Declan agreed, reaching forward to restart the engines.

"And you do realise we are going to have to retrieve it eventually, don't you? We will want to leave this world someday. I mean, nothing lasts forever."

"Except us," Declan said as the engines roared to life. He pulled back on the stick as Cayal slid the door shut, not letting go of the Tide until he was sure they had sufficient altitude to avoid the waves. He turned the helicopter north, back toward Guam, back to the new future they had just created.

And back to figuring out what he was going to say to Arkady.